ESCAPE FROM ZARAHEMLA

ESCAPE FROM ZARAHEMLA

THE THRILLING SEQUEL OF
PASSAGE TO ZARAHEMLA

CHRIS HEIMERDINGER

Covenant Communications, Inc.

Cover images: *Palm Leaves* © Mypokcik, *Forested Hills* © KonradKaminski, *Jaguar Attack* © Ammit, courtesy iStockphoto.com. Images of people from the *Passage to Zarahemla* movie.

Cover design copyright © 2011 by Covenant Communications, Inc.

Published by Covenant Communications, Inc.
American Fork, Utah

Printed in the United States of America
First Printing: September 2011

17 16 15 14 13 12 11   10 9 8 7 6 5 4 3 2 1

ISBN-13: 978-1-60861-539-1

To Dave Ruff, who, more than anyone, made the prequel to this novel (and, therefore, this novel) possible.

Also great appreciation to my wife, Emily, who even while seven months with child gave me a detailed edit; Gordon Jones, whose edits keep me constantly on my toes and who continually insists that I properly use the words *imply* and *infer*; John Weeks, my ever kind and gracious computer guru; and Dustin Randall, who seems to know my books better than me and who did an edit just to keep this novel as congruous as possible with my other novels.

CHAPTER 1

THE LAMANITE REEXAMINED THE WOUNDS along his ribcage, a trio of diagonal slashes starting at his hip and traversing high up the abdomen on the right side. One of the cuts was alarmingly deep. Over several hours he'd lost a lot of blood.

When the injury was first inflicted he'd felt very little pain. This had seemed odd to him. It was the sort of wound that would have incapacitated most warriors. At the instant when he was struck, his body was pulsing, surging with vigor—a desperation to survive. Now, four hours later, the pain was at last starting to overwhelm him. It had been steadily increasing, like water slowly coming to a boil on a hearthstone. Soon, he realized, it would become unbearable. Anguish swept through his mind as he staggered beneath the forest canopy. He perceived that his life force was seeping out, drip by drip, emptying from his muscles, abandoning his senses, withdrawing from his body and mind. Tiny blackouts were becoming more frequent, forcing him to grab on to the nearest mossy trunk to steady himself, catch his breath, and reinforce his resolve.

He had to reach the sacred place, the *glowing* place, the place where the air became like vapors of steam. Not steam from heat, but vapors created by . . . something else. Something that he couldn't explain. It was a place where colors turned slowly in a circle, like the oily surface of a whirlpool, shimmering with rainbows. This whirling surface was vertical, like a wall. It smelled of lightning after it strikes the earth, sucking away the element that enters the lungs and sustains life. It was a place where darkness was sometimes daylight and sunset was often sunrise. It was the place where his father, his grandfather, and his great-grandfather had resorted in generations past to commune with God, contemplate the future, and witness secret visions.

It was the Place of the Whistlers.

He was almost there. These were the very woods where his friend had first appeared: the Hunter with the orange-colored vest. Or was it a kind of shield? Thirteen years. He realized it had been more than a decade since he'd first laid eyes on his friend. It seemed astonishing that so much time had elapsed, so much had happened. The Hunter, whose name had two parts—Chris McConnell—had first entered the ancient world in the midst of a violent skirmish with robbers of Gadianton. Chris, or Mi´con as he became known among his tribesmen, was suffering from an arrow wound to the shoulder. It had been fired from a Gadianton's bow. His puffy orange "armor" (as it was described by other Lamanites) had on that occasion utterly failed him. The Lamanite and his comrades had rescued him from certain death.

Mi´con may have been the most unique soul that the Lamanite had ever encountered. The pale-skinned, bearded hunter with unusual garb claimed to have emerged from the glowing place, the wall of miracles. In the beginning, Mi´con's only desire was to go back, return to his home. But the "passage" had faded; the miracle had disappeared. Since that time, Mi´con the Hunter had become an integral part of their lives and, moreover, an integral part of the life of the Lamanite's *sister*.

But a couple years ago everything had changed. One morning, near the time of the first harvest, the Lamanite's village was attacked. Most of the villagers were slain by a band of Gadianton robbers more bold and numerous than anyone had ever seen. The villagers' crops and homes were burned. Some of the men were enslaved, including him and Mi´con. The younger women were also taken hostage. But not Paísha. Paísha had escaped. At least . . . for a time.

That's why the Lamanite had come. His name was Ishlom. He desperately needed to find the blurry whirlpool that glowed beneath the archway of the dead-yet-*living* trunk of a mighty ceiba tree. He needed to find Mi´con. He needed to tell him all that had transpired—all that he had seen. Ishlom had risked everything: his own life, the life of his sister, the safety of his young nephew——to escape and find him. With each passing moment it appeared that all his efforts might prove futile. Vigor was fading fast from his limbs. His thoughts were becoming scattered and hazy. He had risked everything . . . and perhaps he had lost.

He wasn't even certain if Mi´con was still alive. Mi´con the Hunter—the strange, ashen-faced man who had joined his kinship— hadn't been seen for over six months. He'd escaped the clutches of his captors and presumably returned to the land of Zarahemla. A few of the most ruthless members of Giddianhi's band had gone in pursuit of him, including Kush, the dreaded assassin. But after a great and terrible battle in Zarahemla, near this very spot at the edge of the wilderness of Hermounts, only one member of the unit of renegades who'd enslaved them had returned, and he was *not* one of the warriors sent to pursue Mi´con. This Gadianton claimed that Mi´con was dead. He'd also claimed that Giddianhi—the king and commander of the Gadianton army—was dead. He'd warned that the Nephite army was marching toward their hiding place in the mountains, determined to root out and exterminate any other leaders, as well as their sons, kinships, and any remnants of the robber bands who did not surrender.

Ishlom had believed all of the stories told by this single surviving robber—except one. He did not believe that Mi´con the Hunter was dead. He felt certain that his friend still lived. And if Mi´con was still alive, he would certainly have returned *here*, to this sacred, mysterious place in the forest.

Ishlom had carefully planned his escape from the robbers' encampment. He'd managed to recruit several young Gadianton acolytes who wished to surrender to the Nephites rather than continue a dreary existence of hunger and squalor in the mountains. Five days ago, shortly after sunset, they'd executed their plan and fled into the forest. As should have been expected, the Demon Balám of Lord Akuhuun were unleashed. The Demon Balám had tirelessly pursued them for three days. In the end, his companions had not escaped their merciless clutches. He himself had survived only by leaping into the river gorge. But had he really escaped? His wounds continued to rack his body with agony. It seemed that Akuhuun and his Demon Balám might succeed in their murderous mission, after all.

Ishlom felt sure that he had nearly reached the place of miracles, the archway of the dead-but-living tree. Pain blurred his vision. Still, he was sure that he would recognize it. His father and grandfather had brought him here more than once. Ishlom would recognize the landmarks, the stones, as well as the trickling waters of the tiny creek. Of course, during all the other visits of his lifetime, the miracle had not been present. At least not in the way that Mi´con or his elders had described. There was no outward evidence to prove the existence of a magical "passageway." But what other explanation was there for the Hunter's arrival? A man with so many strange customs? So many unusual gifts?

Besides, Ishlom had felt the *spirit* of the place. He'd felt the cool and warm sensations against his skin as he stood beneath the archway of the ceiba's massive trunk. He could also hear the faint song on the wind. No, it wasn't "whistling" or "whispering," as Mi´con and his fathers had described. But it was audible nonetheless. Heard not by the ears, but by the spirit. By the heart. And it rang inside him like the immensity of time.

Ishlom pushed forward. He felt sure the archway would fall into view at any moment. He wasn't certain what he expected to see, how it might be different. He knew only that Mi´con had come here. The same inner "voice" that convinced him Mi´con had traveled here after his escape and had found the passageway open also whispered that a similar miracle might be awaiting *him*. Perhaps the same shimmer of rainbows. The same vapors of lightning.

A thunderclap resounded above the trees. The rain, as on many days during this particular season, was unleashed from the sky. Within minutes it became a downpour. If his eyesight wasn't foggy enough because of blood loss, the sheets of rain made familiar landmarks nearly impossible to distinguish. He felt a shudder of anxiety. He could not afford to crouch against a tree trunk and wait for the rain to subside. If he paused at all, he might not have the strength to go on. He had to fight the rain, find the archway, if it was the last thing he did. Ishlom brushed the wet hair from his eyes and staggered on. Blood from his wounds washed onto the forest floor in pink rivulets.

And then, there it was!—the mysterious archway. The majestic fallen ceiba loomed just ahead, its horizontal trunk festooned with another season of lush, verdant leaves despite its roots being torn from the earth and pointing skyward. The archway stood only a little higher than the height of a man, but if everything Mi'con and his fathers had told him was true, the miracles that took place beneath its curved shadow were as lofty as the stars of heaven.

His ears filled with a terrible ringing. He shook his head briskly. Not right. This was not the sound that Mi'con had described. It was neither a whistle nor a whisper. More like a chorus of shrill and angry voices, mingled with the rain's frenetic percussion. As Ishlom drew closer to the archway, he paused and squinted. In his present bleariness of mind, he didn't trust what his eyes beheld. It seemed that, indeed, something *was* happening beneath the arch—something perplexing and abnormal—but Ishlom couldn't fathom what it was. Moreover, he wasn't sure what it *meant*. For an instant the swirling colors seemed to coalesce into a face-like visage—the elderly, grizzled, and snarling face of a Lightning Deity—one of the unholy Bacab, the insatiable gods whom his ancestors placated with blood sacrifices in the decades before they united with the religion of Christ. The image frightened him. The shrill cacophony increased in volume, as if in warning. Despite this, he took several steps closer, trying again to focus and concentrate.

The window continued to shimmer, but the image changed. It was no longer a dreadful visage. The whirlpool of colors revealed a landscape, very different from the surrounding jungle. The foliage beyond the window was . . . desert-like. Arid. Prickly. But not "drier." Rain still spattered Ishlom's face. It was also raining on the *other side*. Not merely rain. The place beyond the window was experiencing a roiling torrent. The rich greens and mahogany browns of the surrounding jungle seemingly "flowed" into a place of muted yellows and pallid grays where water surged, as if some muddy river had changed course. A current rushed through the space beneath the archway, as though the window itself was the source of the torrent, or perhaps something *behind* the window. The water roared through a forest of scrubby-looking trees, uprooting and washing away thorny brambles. Was this the source of shrill, gnashing voices? The current was clogged with debris—branches, weeds, bark, and . . . Was that a lizard? Yes, he saw a lizard swimming helplessly against the current, swept into the distant terrain.

A flood? Ishlom wondered if he was witnessing a flash flood. It was a curious thing. Mi´con had once speculated that the "miracle" was influenced by nature's forces—the temblor of an earthquake or some other cataclysm. Could such delicate miracles be set in motion by a flash flood?

Ishlom joggled his head. Such questions didn't matter. The window was open. The miracle was taking place before him. It might close at any second. He had to act quickly. But what would happen to him? If he leapt into the archway, would he be engulfed by waters? Would he trade a slow death by loss of blood for a swifter demise by drowning? He was a strong swimmer. Such skills had saved his life when he'd leaped into the gorge. But that was hours ago, before the gashes in his ribs ignited so much pain and delirium. Still, the idea of swimming in floodwaters did not frighten him. And if he died—if he drowned—there was comfort in knowing that he would die in the midst of a divine miracle. He would drown in the waters of another world, the world of Mi´con the Hunter.

For a fleeting instant the illusion of the snarling Bacab reappeared. Ishlom squeezed his eyes to snuff the vision. He clenched his teeth and tightened his fists. The chorus of discordant voices amplified to a screaming pitch. Eyes still shut, he thrust himself forward, literally diving into the archway.

There was a flash of heat, a sudden shock to his skin, but the sensation ended quickly. When his eyes reopened, a wave of water rushed over his head. His mouth and throat were choked as his body was carried as helplessly as the lizard he'd seen a moment before. He reached toward the sky, but the torrent dragged him forward, as if the energy window really *was* a kind of whirlpool sucking its victims into the airless precincts of *Xibalba*, the underworld of the Great Maw. He seized the branches of a desiccated bush and coughed water from his throat. Just as fresh air reached his lungs, the current again pulled him under. He was carried downriver. But was it a river? A brief glimpse of the terrain again convinced him this was a flood. He was swept down a ravine filled with twisted, thirsty trees. The water was mixed with detritus: leaves and branches and even the carcass of a dead animal. A dog? A coyote? He kicked his legs; Ishlom realized the current was not deep, just strong. It carried him another twenty yards before his torso struck a stone. Wincing from the impact, his limbs became wedged between a boulder and another fallen trunk. Water splashed and sprayed around him, but his nose and mouth were clear.

After hoisting himself further out of the current, he lay on his back and searched the sky for any kind of sun. He found the jaundiced globe in a murky gray sky. Daylight had been obscured by storm clouds. The pale sun was poised at the lip of a steep ridge overlooking a forested valley. The sun was setting. Darkness would soon overtake this new and peculiar world. This realization brought on a fresh stab of pain from his ribs. With tear-filled eyes, Ishlom understood that his journey was near an end. Even assuming that the floodwaters would eventually subside, he still couldn't travel at night—not even if his legs gathered sufficient strength.

"Just let him find me," he whispered. "If Mi´con finds my corpse, it may be enough."

Enough, he thought, *to deliver my message. To warn Mi´con that he must return. Enough to let him know what I have seen. That his loved ones—his flesh and blood—require his help.* Enough, he hoped, for Mi´con the Hunter to conclude that he was their last and only hope.

Ishlom let his eyelids fall shut. Sleep settled around him like the wings of a thousand celestial butterflies. The same butterflies, he imagined, that would carry his soul back to the eternal realms of his Maker.

His Lord and Savior, Jesus Christ.

CHAPTER 2

MOM AND DAD WOULDN'T HAVE approved. But that only made this new adventure for the three young Whitman children all the more intriguing.

It was *so cool*! All of yesterday and throughout most of the night a flash flood had gushed through the "hollow"—that is, the narrow stretch of woods and wilderness that meandered along the valley floor west of their house. If the water level had been a mere two feet higher, it could have washed away their home's foundation! Or so Mom had said. As it was, Dad confirmed that it had washed away a sizable chunk of the road leading down to their property. Grandpa Lee speculated that it'd been more than ten years since a flood like this had visited the hollow. And what a *whopper*! No one had seen so much water before. It had flowed like a river through the foliage on the opposite side of their driveway. All evening and morning the Whitmans' phone rang repeatedly—concerned neighbors and friends verifying that everyone was okay.

Now that the sun was up, eleven-year-old Colter, eight-year-old Tessa, and five-year-old Sariah stood at the lip of the ravine, gazing downward. They could hardly believe their eyes. Virtually *everything* had been transformed. Every blade of grass, every patch of yerba mansa, every cluster of weeds had been washed flat or buried in sludge. Familiar logs and other deadfall had been twisted to face in a new direction or carried off into oblivion. It was like waking up to discover that someone had rearranged your entire backyard.

The water was gone now. All that remained was an ugly layer of reddish mud, streaked with black, white, and gray.

"Let's check it out," said Colter, grinning like a pirate with visions of hidden treasure.

Tessa nodded with equal enthusiasm.

Little Sariah, however, shook her head adamantly. "I'm staying here."

"Staying *here?*" mocked Colter. "What for?"

Sariah looked at her brother, then at her sister, studying them both carefully. "Didn't you hear it?" she asked.

"Hear what?" said Tessa.

Sariah didn't answer right away. Whatever the five-year-old had heard, she'd heard it as they walked out the front door. No, she couldn't hear it now. But a few moments ago, when she *did* hear it, she'd have described it as a whistling sound: a kind of musical echo that trilled and swooped as if from the throat of an exotic bird—surely a bird that didn't live anywhere near Leeds, Utah. In fact, she was sure it was a whole *flock* of birds. It reminded her of sounds made by the enormous pipe organ they'd heard while touring the LDS Conference Center in Salt Lake City. As they walked up the driveway, the sound had steadily faded in Sariah's ears until it disappeared completely. Sariah had felt certain that her siblings were hearing it, too. She realized, with some alarm, that Colter and Tessa had no inkling of what she was talking about.

"I heard"—Sariah's voice trembled—"the Wh-whistlers."

Her siblings didn't laugh. It was not a humorous subject. In fact, it was a very serious topic for the Whitman family. The "Whistlers" were something all of them had been hoping to hear—listening with great diligence—for the last six months.

"You really heard the Whistlers?" said Colter in surprise.

Sariah nodded timidly.

"I didn't hear anything." Tessa looked at Colter. "Did you?"

Colter shook his head. He turned to Sariah and put his hands on her shoulders. "Are you sure?"

"I-I think so." Then less confidently, "I don't know anymore."

All three children gazed back into the hollow.

"Maybe she's right," said Tessa, suddenly apprehensive. "Maybe we should wait for Skyler or Natasha."

"Are you serious?!" balked Colter. "If the Whistlers are back, you know what that means, right? It means—"

Tessa interrupted. "I *know* what it means. I just think we should wait for Skyler and—"

"Skyler is camping with the priests, and on Saturday Natasha won't wake up till noon." Colter turned away in exasperation and threw up his hands. "*Sisters*! If you two won't come, I'll go by myself."

"Aren't you scared?" asked Tessa, her tone deadly serious.

"Of what?" asked Colter.

Tessa dropped her shoulders and said petulantly, "You *know* what."

Colter shook his head. "No, I *don't*. And I'm not scared. You both stay here. I'm goin' in." He loped down the hill of the ravine and past the first trees that marked the traditional boundary of the hollow.

"Wait," said Tessa sharply. Drawing a breath for courage, she scampered after him.

A moment later, Colter and Tessa turned back to look at Sariah. Their sister hadn't budged. The five-year-old was standing her ground. Finally, she plopped down, cross-legged, at the lip of the ravine.

Instead of calling out, Colter sent her an "okay" sign. He wasn't sure why he didn't feel comfortable raising his voice. It just didn't seem right. Somehow, the area had become a kind of sanctuary. A holy place. And he didn't want to disturb . . . uh . . . whatever it was that made it holy. Colter thought again: *A holy place?* Maybe it was exactly the opposite. Maybe the hollow had become *un*holy—a realm where demons or Gadianton robbers lurked. Either way, no need to make unnecessary noise.

Tessa latched on to the hem of Colter's shirt as they ventured deeper into the woods, their shoes pressing perfectly sculptured footprints in the virgin mud.

"How far are we going?" asked Tessa.

"Not far," he whispered.

"Why are we whispering?" whispered Tessa.

"*Shhh*!" said Colter.

Colter knew precisely where he was going. Admittedly, he wasn't sure if he'd be able to find it. After all, everything looked so different. But he was headed to the clearing. He was going to the place where Kerra, Brock, and Grandpa Lee had witnessed all the "miracles." The place where Kiddoni the Nephite and all those other ancient warrior "ghosts" had appeared and disappeared.

A short distance later, Colter spotted the NO TRESPASSING sign. It had been knocked over in the flood. Half the letters were smeared with a muddy stew of leaves and debris, but it confirmed that they were headed in the right direction.

Tessa's heart thudded. "Colter," she squeaked, "m-maybe we should go back."

Colter stopped abruptly, gesturing for Tessa to be quiet. He listened hard. Both children remained perfectly still.

"What's wrong?" Tessa asked.

Just as she spoke, she heard the same sound that had caused Colter to stop. It was a whisper—a *dozen* whispers. The sounds "swooped" over them from all directions, indecipherable. The language was otherworldly, utterly alien. The voices seemed to originate in the woods directly behind them. They moved swiftly in a circle, like a ghostly legion.

Tessa was hyperventilating. Each breath produced a moan in her throat. "I wanna go back," she said. "Let's go back!"

Colter's heart pounded too. Then, as suddenly as the whispering began, it vanished. Both children slowly turned around, trying to home in on the source of what they'd just heard. All efforts to pinpoint additional whispers failed.

Colter faced his sister. "I'm *not* going back. You can do whatever you want."

Tessa trembled like Jell-O. She swallowed hard, worried that tears might start to flow. Colter studied the intensity of her expression and felt guilty. He was about to give in and escort her home. Heck, he could take her back to the lip of the ravine, dump her off with Sariah, and return by himself. At the last second, Tessa relented.

"Okay," she said weakly. "Just stay with me. Don't walk too fast."

Colter nodded, and then clenched his face muscles, steeling his resolve. There was no going back. If there was anything to see, he'd be the first to see it.

Morning sunlight danced wildly as they moved beneath the branches. After thirty yards, both children ground to another halt. Air caught in their lungs as their eyes lit on a mind-boggling sight. Just ahead, upon a heavy log with considerable brush piled against one side, lay a human being. He was coated from head to toe in mud, as if camouflaged to blend into the terrain. What stood out were the whites of his eyes. They were gaping wide, unblinking. Colter and Tessa edged closer. They thought they perceived a primitive mantle around his waist and coal-black hair, just like the ancient visitors who'd appeared before. Colter and Tessa were certain they were gazing upon a visitor from another century. Unfortunately, the visitor was dead.

"I'm gonna be sick," said Tessa, pressing her stomach.

Colter seemed unaffected. "That's a Nephite," he said confidently. "I *know* it."

"Do you think . . ." said Tessa diffidently, ". . . it's Kiddoni?"

Colter sent her a crooked glance, as if it was a stupid question. "How should *I* know? He must've drowned. The flood washed him here."

"The flood washed a dead Nephite into our hollow?"

"So it appears," said Colter. "We better get Dad or Grand—"

The piercing white eyes blinked. Slowly, the head of the "dead" man rolled to the side and looked straight at them. Trembling, mud-crusted fingers reached out. A sound issued from his throat—the exact sound one might have expected from a ghost: thirsty and shrill.

Colter and Tessa screamed.

CHAPTER 3

"IS YOUR FATHER GOING TO join us?" asked Elder Leota. The hulking LDS missionary from Samoa wore a smile that seemed to stretch from one end of the living room to the other.

Kerra McConnell replied nervously, "No, he's . . . job hunting."

Her younger brother, Brock, gave a snort. Kerra sent him a crusty look. After all, it *may* have been true. He *might* have been job hunting, but Kerra knew that it was more likely he was off in the hills around Leeds or St. George, Utah—thinking, daydreaming, searching for something he couldn't seem to find. Her father had held three jobs in the past six months—from construction to pruning orchards to hawking home-crafted jewelry at a local carnival. It's not that he'd been fired. Or even that he'd quit. The jobs just . . . ended. Her father always gravitated toward jobs that were temporary by nature. Over the past two weeks, Kerra wasn't sure if he'd even filled out additional applications.

Thirteen-year-old Brock didn't get his dad. He didn't understand him at *all*. Kerra noted that the boy's attitude was growing more dismissive by the day. Before six months ago, Brock had never had a father, and it was becoming apparent that he didn't want one now. Cripes, *one* person to lord over him—Kerra—was likely bad enough! *Two* disciplinarians for the young teen were probably perceived as one and a half more than he could handle. Kerra knew that what he really wanted was to move back to California. But for now, maintaining residency in southern Utah was the plan.

Eighteen-year-old Kerra had been the family's primary breadwinner for the last several months. Shortly after her birthday, she'd started waitressing at the Claim-Jumper Steakhouse a few miles from home. Last month she'd paid the rent on their Washington, Utah, duplex. Today, Saturday, was her day off. It was also the day that the Mormon missionaries made their weekly pilgrimage across town on their bicycles to teach them the gospel of Jesus Christ.

"We wish he was here," said Elder Paisley, the lanky elder from Yakima, Washington, with cheeks that seemed permanently imbued by a rosy hue. "Today is an important lesson. Maybe the *most* important."

Kerra sensed the underlying meaning of that statement, and the thought made her nervous. Today was the day the elders apparently planned to "challenge" Kerra and Brock for baptism. It was their sixth lesson. Most of the basic doctrines had been covered. It wasn't that Kerra hadn't enjoyed the elders' visits. She'd enjoyed them a lot. But . . . she remained apprehensive. She couldn't quite put her finger on why. Maybe it was the sudden change. The *permanence* of it all. The commitment to live a different kind of life than the one she'd always lived. A life where she'd always managed to rely on herself rather than some lofty, mysterious, unseen Power.

Brock was also apprehensive but for entirely different reasons. This whole weekly-appointment thing was Kerra's doing. Kerra had cornered the elders one weekend at Aunt Corinne and Uncle Drew's ward in Leeds. Dad, though he said very little, had heartily approved. The glimmer in his eye said it all. Grandpa Lee had approved as well. Heck, why wouldn't they? Dunking a *genu-wine* blood relative in the waters of baptism was a feather in the cap of every Mormon, wasn't it? Or so Brock had commented. Kerra realized her brother didn't like at *all* the idea of being someone else's feather.

Grandpa had eagerly attended the first three lessons, volunteering plenty of sagely wisdom. Brock and Kerra's dad also hadn't missed an appointment. That is, before today. For the most part, while the missionaries were in Dad's home, he had stayed quiet. Kerra felt she understood why. This whole thing—the missionaries, the Church, the gospel—carried an additional meaning and significance that the elders couldn't have understood. Kerra felt myriad emotions: questions, distresses, and some very real and visceral pain. Although she didn't know any details, she felt Dad's pains and longings were somehow similar. There were memories locked up inside her father that Kerra had no idea how to set free. Still, every word from the elders reminded her of things she sometimes wished she could forget—experiences that now seemed like memories from another life. They brought to mind people that she missed so terribly it caused pressure in her chest as if every muscle—especially her heart—tightened into an impenetrable ball. The doctrines of the LDS Church, particularly regarding the Book of Mormon, were more personal to Kerra, and certainly to her dad, than any missionaries could have realized.

For Brock, however, the dominoes of doctrine and testimony didn't fall in quite the same pattern. He had a habit of deliberately asking the elders bizarre and off-the-wall questions just to get a rise out of them. Frankly, he didn't take the lessons seriously. Kerra decided he was dealing with some kind of mental block. This became apparent whenever he sat there and mocked the entire process, an event which had occurred during virtually every lesson.

Today would be no exception.

"Dad could show up at anytime," Kerra told Elder Leota and Elder Paisley. Then she fibbed. "He said to go ahead and start without him."

They looked at one another uneasily. Finally they pursed their lips and seemed to nod in agreement. After all, Kerra was eighteen now. She needed no parental consent.

"Well," said Elder Leota in his distinctive Samoan accent, still smiling like the Grand Canyon, "today is a very important lesson. Maybe the most important lesson we've taught so far. Elder Paisley and I have discussed it and . . ."—He leaned forward—"we think you are both ready. You're ready to take the next step. We have felt the Spirit in your home. We believe you have felt it, too."

His eyes were on Kerra. Brock avoided eye contact, slouching so deeply it appeared as if the couch might swallow him.

Elder Paisley spoke more formally. "We'd like to challenge you both to become members of The Church of Jesus Christ of Latter-day Saints and take upon you the name of our Savior by being baptized by someone having authority."

Kerra and Brock were silent.

Elder Leota picked up the slack. His heart seemed as big as his smile. He said in a gentle tone, "That person can be your father, one of us, or even your grandfather or uncle. It doesn't matter. What matters is they have the priesthood. Actually, what matters *most* is whether the Spirit has confirmed to you that the Church is true. It's up to both of you to take the next step. How do you feel right now about the things that we are telling you?"

Kerra glanced at her brother, whose eyes studied the motley, pea-green, pre-nineties patterns on the living room rug. She turned back to Elder Leota. The Samoan's eyes hadn't budged; they were locked into Kerra's. His smile had softened, but only a little.

Like her brother, Kerra's gaze dropped to the carpet. "I don't know if we're ready."

The elders shifted in their seats.

Elder Paisley said to Kerra, "You said a couple weeks ago that you believed that the Book of Mormon was true. Has that feeling changed?"

Kerra looked up. She shook her head firmly. "No. That's still my belief."

"*Why* do you believe it's true?" asked Elder Leota. "Has the Spirit confirmed this?"

It was Kerra's turn to shift uncomfortably. "I . . . uh . . . Not exactly."

Elder Paisley scrunched his eyebrows. "You mean you believe in the Book of Mormon, but not by the Spirit?"

Kerra honestly did not know how to answer. Brock decided to butt in.

He challenged Elder Paisley. "Why do *you* believe it's true?"

Elder Paisley straightened his shoulders. "I know that it's true because I prayed about it. I prayed when I was sixteen years old. The Holy Ghost testified to me—"

Brock interrupted. "That seems kinda lame."

Elder Paisley blinked several times. It was a response he'd apparently never heard before. "Excuse me?"

"The Holy Ghost? What *is* that? I don't get it. That's all you got? Let me ask you this: have you ever met a Nephite?"

The elders gawked at the thirteen-year-old. After a few seconds they chuckled uncomfortably.

Kerra poked an elbow into her brother's ribs. She sent him a subtle shake of the head, a clear and present warning.

Elder Leota replied to Brock, "Do you believe it is necessary to meet a Nephite before you can know if the book is true?"

Brock shrugged. "It wouldn't hurt."

Elder Leota pursed his lips. He sat back and said, "I do not believe that meeting a Nephite is necessary before one can—"

Brock interrupted. "So you admit it. You've never met a Nephite."

Elder Leota shrugged. "In truth, it may be that I *am* a Nephite. Or perhaps it may be that some of my ancestors are Nephites or Lamanites."

Brock shook his head. "That's not what I mean. You've never seen the places they talk about in the Book of Mormon. You've never met anybody from that period of time. So how can you know anything about it? It seems to me that I might know more—"

Kerra had lightning in her eyes, *begging* him to shut up. Brock tempered his remarks. "What I mean is, you guys have no real experience. How can you know something unless you've actually . . . had a firsthand encounter with it?"

Elder Leota didn't back down in the least. "The Holy Ghost is the strongest witness that a person can receive. Stronger even than meeting a Nephite in person or visiting for yourself the places mentioned in the Book of Mormon. As it says in Ether 12:6, 'Faith is things which are hoped for and not seen; wherefore dispute not because ye see not, for ye receive no witness until after the trial of your faith.'"

Brock smirked. Then he laughed out loud. "What if I told you that I've seen things—experienced things—without having any faith at all? What if I told you—?"

"Brock!" Kerra snapped. She looked beside herself with exasperation.

Brock pretended innocence. "What?"

"You're being rude," said Kerra through her teeth.

"I just think this is ridiculous," said Brock. "We know more than these guys could ever dream. Maybe we should be teaching *them*. Yeah, we ought to be trying to convert *them*!"

Kerra turned to the elders. "He doesn't know what he's talking about. He's making up things to see if he can get your goat—as usual."

"Perhaps so," said Elder Leota. "But it seems that we also may not have done a very good job at helping you understand how to know things without the sort of 'firsthand encounter' that your brother describes. We have not sufficiently explained how the testimony of the Spirit is more powerful than what we can see with our eyes. The Savior taught, 'Blessed are ye if ye shall believe in me and be baptized, after that ye have seen me and know that I am. And again, more blessed are they who shall believe in your words because that ye shall testify that ye have seen me.'"

Elder Paisley was scrambling to find the exact reference in 3 Nephi. His companion's memorization made it unnecessary.

Elder Leota went on to explain, "I believe the Savior meant that those who can learn truth by the Spirit, rather than with their eyes, are ultimately more blessed even than those who sometimes experience great and mighty miracles."

Brock persisted. "So you think a feeling in your heart—some kind of a burning in the gut—"

"In the bosom," Elder Paisley clarified.

"Right. Wherever. You think a feeling like that is more powerful than what you can see with your own two eyes?"

Elder Leota nodded. "Our eyes can fool us. They can fail to teach us the most important lessons. It's like with Laman and Lemuel, the wayward sons of Father Lehi. They saw an angel of God, and also witnessed other powerful miracles, but none of these things convinced them that they must also learn by the Spirit. As with you and me—as with *everyone*—these two brothers needed to receive a testimony with more than their eyes. They needed to receive it with their heart, by the power of the Holy Ghost."

All of them stared at Elder Leota, including Elder Paisley, who seemed duly impressed by the words of his Polynesian comp.

Kerra pondered Elder Leota's words. It was a new idea. She wasn't certain if she completely understood. She was about to open her mouth to ask more questions when the front door burst open, as if by a gust of wind.

It was Dad, looking breathless, pale. He held an open cell phone—the same one given to him by Aunt Corinne. It was an older model. Kerra's father hadn't been around much during those years when cell phones had virtually become a part of the human anatomy. Dad closed the phone, having just finished what was obviously an important conversation, and gaped at his children.

"Kerra, Brock," he said urgently. "We have to go to your aunt and uncle's."

"Now?" asked Kerra. She indicated the elders.

"Yes, right now," said Dad. "Something has happened. Something . . . *new.*"

He didn't need to say anything more. The look on Dad's face gave Kerra a pretty good idea—or perhaps a secret hope—of what that "something" might involve.

CHAPTER 4

CORINNE WHITMAN HAD CALLED HER brother even before she dialed 911.

It was an odd choice, and she felt guilty. But the injured man that Colter and Tessa had found in the hollow—the mud-covered human being wearing ancient clothing and lacking even the strength to stand—had pronounced her brother's name. He'd also uttered another name that no one understood. His voice was weak and desperate. There was no telling if he would live or die. Corinne felt that her brother, Chris, needed to know even before the authorities.

Chris McConnell arrived on the scene with his two children, Kerra and Brock, before any paramedics and ambulances. Grandpa Lee was waiting for them in the driveway, fifty yards north of his son-in-law's house, at the place where his grandkids had ventured into the flood-washed woods. Sariah was also there, holding the hand of two-year-old Bernadette. Kerra's junker Ford Festiva screeched to a halt at Grandpa Lee's feet.

Grandpa spoke as his son and grandchildren piled out of the car.

"He's a Nephite, all right. Maybe a Lamanite. In any case, he's not from our time. And he's in bad shape."

Kerra asked, "Did he say his name?"

"No," said Grandpa. "But it's not Kiddoni. Nor is he any other Nephite or Gadianton robber we might've met last summer."

Kerra wasn't certain how to react. This stranger was seriously injured—maybe even to the point of death. Yet Kerra couldn't suppress a twinge of selfish disappointment.

Grandpa started to lead his son and two grandchildren down the ravine and into the muddy hollow. Sariah and little Bernadette were very much content to remain behind.

"How has he been hurt??" asked Dad.

"Not sure," said Grandpa Lee. "He might have been half-drowned in the flood. But there's blood on his chest. Looks bad. He's so covered in mud and muck that it's hard to tell. All we know for sure is that he knows *you*. Every time someone tries to talk to him, he *asks* for you. And someone else. Someone named Mi´con."

"Mi´con?" asked Brock.

Their father seemed to recognize the name, but he didn't take the time to explain.

"Is he conscious?" asked Dad.

Grandpa nodded. "Barely. He's delirious. Maybe seein' you will help bring him to his senses."

Kerra thought of Dad's beardless face and wondered, in a delirious state, if this man would even recognize him. How long had her father worn those awful-looking whiskers? Maybe the beard was a relatively new thing—grown only after he'd become a Gadianton prisoner.

"We hope," said Grandpa, "that you'll at least recognize *him*."

Moments later, Aunt Corinne and Uncle Drew came into view. Five of Kerra's cousins were also present. Eighteen-year-old Skyler hovered over a muddy figure stretched out across a relatively unsullied Mexican blanket. Natasha, Sherilyn, Colter, and Tessa stood nearby.

By the looks of it, the injured Nephite had only been moved a couple of feet from where Colter and Tessa had found him. His injuries must have made everyone leery about dragging him any further. As Kerra's father drew closer, Skyler and Natasha stepped aside, allowing him a full, clear view of the stranger. Kerra looked up as the sound of an ambulance droned in the distance.

Aunt Corinne became concerned. "Is there anyone at the driveway to lead them down here?"

"I'll go," volunteered Uncle Drew.

"I'll join you," said Skyler.

The two men loped through the woods to await the paramedics.

Dad knelt over the figure in the cotton and leather tunic. Despite the mud, some of its embroidery was still visible. Kerra thought they might have resembled designs on Kiddoni's warrior garb. The man's eyes were closed; his mouth hung open. If not for the unsteady rise and fall of his chest, Kerra might have thought he was already dead.

Some effort had been made—probably by Aunt Corinne—to wipe mud from his face, but such efforts weren't particularly successful. Even if this person had been Skyler or Drew, it would have still taken a moment to recognize their features. Kerra noticed a handkerchief off to the side of the Mexican blanket, partially soiled with mud. She picked up where Aunt Corinne had left off and wiped additional sediment from the stranger's face.

All at once Dad caught her hand. His eyes flew open wide. Recognition had set in.

"Ishlom?" Dad said with a gasp.

The sound of Dad's voice partially resuscitated the wounded man. His eyelids fluttered. Finally, his focus fell upon Kerra's hovering father.

"*Mi´con!*" he said in a raspy, ragged voice.

Kerra and Brock looked at Dad strangely. Who could say if it was a nickname or if he'd mistaken their father for someone else? Dad took the name in stride and grabbed Ishlom's hand.

"Ishlom, how did you get here?"

"Mi´con," he repeated, making a feeble effort to reach for Dad's other hand.

Dad took it and asked, "What happened?"

"Mi´con," he said again, almost choking on the name.

Kerra continued to wipe around his mouth and nose, as if to ease Ishlom's efforts to breathe.

"I was afraid of that," said Grandpa Lee. "He's still delirious."

Kerra glanced back toward the driveway. The tone of the siren indicated that the ambulance had arrived.

"Hang in there, old friend," said Dad. "Help is coming."

"You *know* him?" asked Brock incredulously.

His father hesitated then nodded. "Yes."

"Is he a Nephite?"

"A Lamanite," said Dad.

Brock still wasn't quite clear on what the difference was. Unlike Kerra, who read from the Book of Mormon almost nightly, Brock couldn't have said how it all fit together. Kerra had it pretty straight in her mind that Lamanites, basically, were the Nephites' enemies. But not always. She remembered that Kiddoni had explained that during *his* particular century such hostilities had abated. In any case, her father had called him "old friend."

Aunt Corinne and the others continued to observe. Ishlom remained very still, but his lips moved, repeating the name Mi´con yet again. Kerra was ready to conclude that Ishlom was too weak to say more. Suddenly he gasped out, "I escaped."

Dad tightened his grip on Ishlom's hands and leaned in closer, desperate to hear every word from the Lamanite's thirsty throat.

"You escaped from the Gadiantons?" asked Dad.

Ishlom nodded weakly. "Yes. I followed you. I knew you would come here."

"How were you injured?" Dad inquired.

"Balám," whispered Ishlom. "He unleashed . . . the Demon Balám. But I escaped."

Brock sent his sister a peculiar look and quietly repeated the phrase. "*Demon Balám?*"

Dad persisted. "One of the balám did this to you?"

Ishlom ignored the question. A smile beamed across his face. "I found you. Thanks be to God. I had begun . . . to lose hope."

"Why did you follow me?" asked Dad.

"We *need* you," said Ishlom. "The armies have not succeeded. The Nephite armies. Only you can show them . . . the secrets. Without you, they will never find . . . the others."

Dad's shoulders sank. He maintained a grip on Ishlom's hands. "Without *me*? You overestimate me, Ishlom. The jungle . . . mountains . . . I don't know your lands as well as you think."

Ishlom opened his eyes widely. "You don't understand. *She* needs you. My sister. The child."

Dad sputtered, "Th-the *child*?"

Ishlom closed his eyes, his last flickers of energy fading. He managed another weak smile. "You didn't know."

"About the child? No, Ishlom," said Dad. "What child? *Whose* child?"

Ishlom did not reply. A long, slow breath seeped from his lungs. Kerra trembled as she realized it may have been his *last* breath. The woods began to crash and crunch with the sound of footfalls. The paramedics arrived with their equipment, followed by Skyler and Uncle Drew. Dad and the others backed away, allowing the experts to check for a pulse, administer CPR, and prepare the silent, motionless body for transport. As they rushed the stretcher through the woods, Dad did his best to stay near Ishlom's side, but the paramedics discouraged his efforts. There were no signs of life. The stranger in the ancient tunic had most certainly expired.

A pallor hung over the Whitman family, Grandpa Lee, Kerra, Brock, and their father as they watched the ambulance drive away. The vehicle was soon replaced by two patrol cars and four very inquisitive officers. One of the officers, a man with a long, curled mustache, seemed to instantly recognize Kerra's father. He also recognized Drew and Corinne.

"Did the man say anything before he died?" the policeman demanded.

Dad watched as the ambulance rounded the final corner past Grandpa Lee's violin shop. The officer's question was directed at everyone, but mostly at Kerra's dad. Perhaps because everyone's eyes were watching him closely.

Dad shook his head, his mind numb, his thoughts in a whirlwind. "N-no. Just . . . rambling. Nothing . . . that I could understand."

"So the children found him exactly how he was?" asked the officer.

Colter and Tessa nodded. "Yeah. That's right."

"How did he sustain his injuries?"

The kids shook their heads. No one else could answer him either.

The officer kept pursuing. "Did anyone know him?"

Again, all eyes vacillated toward Kerra's father.

The policeman stepped closer to him. "Maybe you don't remember me, Mr. McConnell. We met last summer. I was here right after the house at the end of this driveway was trashed by . . . well . . . the way it was described back then was an 'army of Indians.'" He turned to ensure that his voice was heard by everyone. "So if anybody here has more information than what I've already been told, I'd like to hear it. Was that man in the ambulance one of these . . . 'Indians'?"

Still no one replied.

The officer's frustration was mounting. He again leaned toward Chris McConnell and asked, "Did you know that man?"

Dad hung his head. "No. No one . . . none of us . . . ever saw him before."

CHAPTER 5

KERRA WASN'T QUITE SURE WHY her father had lied to the police. In the end, she concluded it was just too difficult to explain. Even if he'd tried, who would have believed him? The description, six months earlier, of an "army of Indians" must have been something offered up by one of the Whitman children. Even then Kerra distinctly recalled that no one had quite known what to say to the cops. Everyone said as little as possible. Corinne and Drew had simply cleaned up the property and continued on with their lives.

Corinne's reunion with her brother had been equally as joyous as Grandpa Lee's reunion with his son. Still, Kerra heard it whispered several times over the last few months that Dad was somehow "different." Before his disappearance, Corinne would have described him as a boisterous soul, given to laughter and pranks. Now he was irretrievably sober and serious. Perhaps the divorce from Kerra's mother, twelve years earlier, had something to do with that, but Corinne seemed convinced that something *else* had changed him. Something he hadn't yet divulged or discussed.

For months Kerra had noted that her father wasn't happy here. Maybe he just no longer felt a part of the twenty-first century. Certainly he treasured reconnecting with his daughter and son. Yet a piece of his soul remained terribly sad and distant. Kerra wasn't the only person who noticed that he spent a great deal of time in the hollow, as if searching for another conduit, another passageway, or some other means to go back to the time of the Nephites. Grandpa Lee had tried to talk to his son about it. Even Kerra had made an effort. But Dad said very little in response. Maybe he didn't see the point. The passageway was closed. The world of the first century AD seemed lost, like a dream that slips away mere moments after awakening.

Something was tearing her father up inside. Kerra could tell. She suspected that he'd left something behind—something or someone he missed very much. Perhaps a clear explanation was there in the brief words of the dying Lamanite. But no one would know for certain unless her father decided to talk about it.

Shortly after the police drove away, and after the Whitmans and McConnells started making their way back toward the house, Kerra realized her dad was missing. In just the past few minutes he'd given everyone the slip. She felt fairly certain of where he'd gone. Kerra made her way back up the driveway to the place that led down into the muddy hollow. There, at the lip of the ravine, she closed her eyes and concentrated. She tried to utilize every portion of her eardrums. After a few seconds, her heart surged with awareness. *She could hear it!* The sound was ever so faint. Yet it was the very same sound that she'd heard six months before—the same sound she remembered from when she was a little girl. The sound she'd heard when she'd first met Kiddoni in the woods. It was that same high-pitched note, interspersed with occasional "wisps" of human voices—*whispering* voices. Or perhaps it wasn't whispering. Perhaps it was merely how thousands of people sounded at a very low volume. Or *billions* of people. Or perhaps, thought Kerra, it was the voices and breaths of every soul who'd ever crossed this path in Leeds, Utah. Maybe she was hearing the voices of every living thing on the planet. Or *beyond* the planet. The voices of the gods themselves.

Her reverie was interrupted by her brother.

"Where are you going?"

Kerra jumped. Brock had come up behind her. She quickly shook off her mesmerization and returned to reality.

"Where do you *think*?" she replied. "I'm going down there to look for Dad."

"He's cracked," said Brock, his tone deadpan. "You know that, don't you? There's something wrong with his noodle, if you know what I mean."

"There's nothing wrong with him," Kerra defended. "And even if there was, he's your *dad*. You should speak with more respect."

"I don't even know the guy," said Brock. "He's been with us for six months and I *still* feel like I don't know him."

"That's 'cause you haven't tried," said Kerra.

"Why is it up to me?" asked Brock. "Doesn't he have some responsibility in this?"

"He *has* tried," said Kerra. "I've watched him. He invites you to go with him almost everywhere. You blow him off."

"Because he never wants to *do* anything," Brock said defensively. "At least not *normal* things, like going to a movie or playing video games. He just wants to do mountain man–type stuff, like fishing or hiking or wandering through the woods."

"Most kids would be euphoric to have a dad who wanted to do those kinds of things. But not you."

"Well, that's 'cause I'm not 'most kids.' I hate it here. You *know* I hate it here."

"Oh, Brock." Kerra sighed. "Give it up. Don't you think it's time you just accepted it? We're *not* going back to L.A."

"Says you," Brock replied.

Kerra stopped and faced him. "Are you threatening to run away again? Good luck with that." She scoffed and trotted down the ravine, into the hollow. "You're all mouth, little brother. You have no friends left in California, and you know it. But go ahead. I'm sure they've still got your first-class suite waitin' for you at juvy."

Clumsily, Brock followed after her. "I'm just sayin' his eggs are slightly scrambled. What was all that about today? Who *was* that guy? Why won't Dad talk about it?"

"When he's ready, I think he *will* talk about it."

"Right. *Sure* he will," Brock sneered. "He's already told us *sooo much*. We don't know squat about where he was for twelve years. *Nobody* knows. Not a soul. It's like the guy has PTSD."

"PTSD?" asked Kerra.

"Posttraumatic stress disorder."

"Wow," Kerra teased. "Big words. Don't choke."

"I'm serious. It's like he was in Afghanistan or Auschwitz. He's shell-shocked."

Kerra became thoughtful. "Actually, you may be more right than you realize. He was a prisoner of Gadianton robbers. We know that much."

"We also know that he knew that Lamanite—Ish-whatever. And we know he lied to the cops."

"What was he supposed to say?" She impersonated her father's baritone. "'Yes, Officer, I knew him. He's a Lamanite from two thousand years ago. We were time-travel companions.' Yeah, that would've gone over real slick."

"Frankly, sis, I'm surprised you haven't pushed him harder for info. Maybe he knows a lot more about your Nephite hunk."

Kerra faced him angrily. "He's not my—" She got hold of herself and turned forward again. "Let it go, Brock. You don't know anything about anything."

Moments later, after adding new layers of reddish mud to their shoes, they set eyes on their father. He was crouched by the Mexican blanket near the place where the Lamanite was first discovered. As far as Kerra could tell, he was just glaring off into space. She paused. Kerra glanced at Brock, who'd also paused. Brock rolled his eyes and made a face, reemphasizing his opinion that Dad was "cracked."

Kerra ignored him and approached. "Dad?"

Her father came to his feet and turned around. After a few seconds he smiled. It was a weary smile. As Kerra drew closer, he held out his arms to embrace her. She accepted the hug. Brock was more reticent. His dad waved him forward with a strange urgency. Brock finally consented, and the three-way hug was complete. Afterward, Dad continued smiling at them proudly, like . . . well, like a *father*. Kerra noticed that there were tears in his eyes.

"Are you all right?" she asked.

He hastily wiped both eyes, pretending his emotions were under control. "I'm fine. Long day. Lots of . . . memories."

Kerra finally worked up the nerve. "Who was he, Dad? Who was that man who passed away?"

Dad again studied the mud-crusted blanket where the Lamanite had uttered his final words. "His name was Ishlom."

"You told us that," said Brock glumly.

Kerra gave her brother a scolding glance. Her father, however, seemed as if he finally wanted to answer some questions.

Yet his answers were disconnected, rambling. "I know I haven't spoken much . . . about those days. Where I was or . . . I've *wanted* to tell you. That is, I've wanted to tell *someone*. No one would understand. It's so . . ." He chuckled morosely and placed his palm on his stomach, as if the topic made him nauseated. "It's just such a different world. Different in every way. It's like a dream now. I almost feel like . . . like someone with amnesia, fighting to dredge up the details. Details and . . . feelings."

"It's selfish," said Kerra.

Dad studied his daughter curiously. Even Brock appeared surprised by Kerra's tone.

Her father shook his head. "I don't—"

"You're not the only one who's suffered," said Kerra. "No one has forgotten. We all remember what happened that day. Sariah and little Bernadette still have nightmares. I bet some of the older kids do, too."

Dad turned away, chagrined. "I didn't mean to leave everyone so much in the dark."

"But you have," said Brock, suddenly united with his sister.

Dad shut his eyes tightly, as if a headache was coming on. "I just . . . I have no idea where to start."

At that moment Grandpa Lee emerged from the muddy undergrowth. He made it clear that he'd overheard most of the conversation.

"Start with Ishlom." Grandpa came to a halt before his son. "Who was he?"

"A friend," his son replied. "One of the first people I met after . . . after I arrived in their century. I was wounded. His family nursed me back to health."

"He was a *Lamanite*?" Kerra asked again, hoping the word might provoke a better explanation.

"Yes," said Dad. "A craftsman. And a farmer. I became a farmer too. And a hunter. Ishlom's kinship took me in. I lived with them several years until . . ."

"Until what?" asked Kerra.

He turned away and took several steps toward the north. "Until everything changed. Their whole world. Their village was destroyed. Everyone was killed except a few of the women and children, maybe a handful of the strongest men. It was the Reds. That is, the Gadianton robbers. Ishlom's village was too close to the mountains. Too close to the place where I came through the void."

Kerra stepped toward him. "You mean the place that leads here, to this hollow?"

"That's right," said Dad. "Anyway, it was around the time that all the Nephites gathered to the land of Zarahemla—a place of fortifications very near Ishlom's village—for their own protection and defense. But for Ishlom and me, none of that mattered. We were already captives. Slaves."

"Who is Mi´con?" asked Brock.

Dad shrugged. "That's what they came to call me. Shortened from McConnell. I guess they thought it sounded more Lamanite. I mean, it sounded more comfortable on their tongue."

"What about the sister?" asked Kerra.

Dad hesitated. Kerra couldn't tell for sure if he hadn't understood her or if he didn't *want* to answer.

Kerra pressed further. "I heard Ishlom mention his sister. And a child."

Dad stared off into space. "Yes, Ishlom had a sister."

"Was she a slave?" asked Grandpa Lee. "Like you and Ishlom?"

Dad nodded.

Kerra asked her father, "Did you love this woman?"

He looked at Kerra and Brock. Then he nodded again. "I married her."

Kerra's eyebrows shot up. "You have a . . . a *wife*? A wife in the first century AD? I have . . . a *stepmother*?"

Again her father nodded, looking ashamed.

Kerra raised her voice. "Why didn't you tell us? It's been *six months*!"

Tears again pricked at Dad's eyes as he replied sharply, "What did it matter? *Tell me!* What does it matter *now*? Why talk about something that hardly seems real anymore? Something that may never be real again?"

"And the child," Grandpa continued. "Is it . . . your child?"

Dad sank down to his knees. He was trembling. "I don't know. I didn't understand what Ishlom was trying to say."

"Is it possible?" asked Grandpa Lee.

Chris looked up at his father. "Yes, it's possible. It's very possible that Paísha had a child."

"Paísha?" repeated Kerra.

Dad nodded and said solemnly, "That's her name."

"Wild," said Brock, mostly to himself. "I have a Nephite step-mom. Maybe a Nephite half-brother or -sister."

"Lamanite," his father corrected absently.

Dad hung his head, appearing even more withdrawn and distraught. Kerra's temper fizzled out. She felt she finally understood her father, at least a little. She understood why he wandered the hills, spent so many hours in the woods, and why he seemed like he was desperately searching for a way back.

Choked with emotion, Dad said, "Nothing matters. I've tried to forget it. I'm home. I have a family here. But I *can't* forget! And then this. The flood. Ishlom." He looked at Kerra and Grandpa Lee. "The rift opened. It *opened!* Just for a second. Now it's closed again. And I have no idea what makes it happen."

Kerra lifted her gaze and listened. A zephyr rustled through the foliage of the hollow. She swore she could still hear the faint "hum" of the Whistlers. It wasn't as powerful or penetrating as she remembered, but it was definitely present. She felt prodded by a weird, familiar instinct. Six months ago she'd behaved much like her father. She'd frequently return to the clearing with its fallen log and thistles, locate the spot where she'd last laid eyes on Kiddoni, and stand in different places, wandering in and out of the tangled shadows of willows and cottonwoods, kicking through the mesquite and moonflowers, striving with all her might to catch a glimpse of . . . him. Or just a nuance of something different. Something to remind her that magic could still occur in this unique and haunting place. She felt the urge to do the same thing now—move carefully about and watch the space before her, seeking some hint of an open passageway or portal.

Brock made a startling statement. "Maybe it's not closed."

All eyes turned toward him. Feeling self-conscious, he added, "What I mean is, this isn't the right place. At least not from what *I* saw. We need to find the *arch*."

"Arch?" asked Dad.

Brock pointed southward. "It's over that way." Suddenly Brock looked uncertain, confused by alterations that the flood had inflicted on the landscape. "At least I *think* it's that way."

"*What's* that way?" asked Kerra.

"The place where a fallen tree makes a tunnel. Or at least it did before the flood. It was really weird because the trunk and many of the tree's branches had green leaves, even though its roots were sticking up at one end. It was like the tree should've been dead, but it wasn't."

Brock had everyone's full attention. Dad stepped closer. "Explain it again. What did you see? When did you see it?"

"It was last summer. I followed Kiddoni. He didn't know I was following him, but I kept up with him pretty well. Then he ran under the arch and faded away."

"He vanished?" asked Grandpa Lee.

"Yeah," said Brock. "Then, when I stepped through—I mean, when I stepped under the archway—everything . . . well . . . it sort of *morphed*. It became tropical, like a rainforest. Complete with jungle birds, insects—the whole scene. I figured out later I must've stepped into Nephite times. But then when I stepped backward, I was right back in Utah."

Dad grasped his shoulder. "Can you show us this place?"

Brock nodded. "I-I think so."

Dad released him. Kerra and Grandpa Lee glanced at each other then back at Brock. The boy realized they were waiting. So with a determined expression he strained to remember the exact direction. Then he led the way as they exited the clearing.

CHAPTER 6

As she followed her brother, Kerra felt beset by an onslaught of emotions. Partly excitement, mostly apprehension. She couldn't believe it might be this easy—not after so many months of heartache and disappointment. An archway? A tunnel created by a fallen tree? She recalled no such phenomenon—not from her childhood or any other instance. Still, as she continued after Brock, the hum of the Whistlers increased in volume.

Grandpa Lee turned to her. "Did you hear that noise?"

The question struck Kerra oddly, as if Grandpa had only heard a single whistle or whisper—not a continuous drone, like Kerra.

"Hear what noise?" asked Brock.

"*That* one," he declared. "That—" He searched for an adjective. "—*ringing*! Makes me wanna check my hearing aids. That is, if I wore any."

Dad was walking softly, trying not to increase the sound of sucking mud or crackling brush. "I hear voices," he said quietly.

"I hear them too," Kerra admitted.

Brock crinkled his nose. "What are you guys talking about?"

"You can't hear that?" asked Grandpa. "That's the hum of the Whistlers if I ever heard 'em!"

Kerra recalled that her grandfather had once described her ability to perceive the various miracles and sensations within these woods as a kind of "gift." Perhaps it was a gift that Brock simply did not possess. Not that it much mattered to him. He forged ahead like a soldier on a campaign, occasionally pausing so everyone could knock the spackle-like debris from their shoes.

Brock stopped abruptly and pointed. "That's it!"

He indicated a horizontal cottonwood, dangling six feet off the ground, the trunk wedged between a tangle of black elms and thistles in a fashion that created the perfect illusion of a passageway or gate. The tree's roots on the east were exposed. Stagnant, black water pooled under the roots—a hole where the tentacles of the cottonwood's roots had once thrived, now filled by the flood's watery dregs. The hollow in this vicinity was particularly dense with brooding trees and suffocating undergrowth, except for a narrow mud-strewn trail, about as wide as the fabled Yellow Brick Road. This path led directly under the archway. Exactly as Brock had described, there were healthy sprigs and hundreds of living buds all along the upper side of the horizontal trunk. Curiously, all life was limited to the *upper* side of the trunk. The underside displayed a gnarled crust of loose, hanging bark and shreds of dangling gray moss, like a gnome's shabby beard. Life appeared limited only to areas touched by sunlight. The remainder of the cottonwood was dead, just like any other uprooted, prostrate tree.

The area—or space—under the archway captivated Kerra. Tree branches crisscrossing over Kerra's head permitted narrow shafts of sunlight to illuminate the muddy pathway. Was it an optical illusion, or did those shafts seem to *bend* as they hit an unseen barrier in the midst of that space? It was almost as if a thick pane of glass was neatly set into place under the archway. But it was translucent, diffusing and transforming the light. The forest beyond the arch was lit by numerous shimmering swaths of color, like sunlight "prismed" through a fish tank.

Kerra could feel her heart rate increase. She walked slower than the others as they approached the archway. Brock, predictably, walked the swiftest. A couple yards before he reached the barrier, he stretched out his palm, as if to "pierce" the void. Dad grabbed his shoulder and forced him to a halt.

"What are you doing?" Dad demanded.

"Same as I did before," said Brock. "I touched it and . . . It's *cool!* Don't you remember? We saw the same thing that day by the road. You turned the wheel of the car and crashed right through it! That was when the Gadiantons, like, slipped through the car's floorboards. A wall of energy shot up out of that crack in the ground."

"I remember," Dad admitted. "But—"

Brock continued animatedly. "And then that one Gadianton—the cranky one with a face like a Rottweiler—Bakaan!—we saw him beyond the crack. He tried to stab me with his spear, but it didn't hurt. It went right *through* me!"

"Yes," said Dad. "Just hold on."

"Why?" said Brock. "It's a doorway! It's a *way back!*"

Dad again stopped his son's forward progression. Sternly, he explained, "Don't be reckless, Brock. I saw a man killed passing through such a barrier. He walked into a tree that wasn't visible from his side of the rift. His flesh—his molecules—were split in half. He died in agony with a tree trunk protruding from his neck."

Kerra shuddered.

Brock swallowed, his enthusiasm sufficiently curbed. "I passed through just fine before."

"We just need to move cautiously," said Dad. "Be careful."

Grandpa Lee was practically having a conniption. "What are you both saying? You mean to say that if we walk through there, we might end up back—" His voice choked. Sweat dripped from his bushy, gray mustache and beard.

Kerra experienced a similar rush of adrenaline. She felt almost like she was panting—as if she'd just finished a mile run. She looked at the wall. The energy sparkled. She sensed flashes of color, scenes from another reality—a lush and tropical world. Maybe it was her imagination—her deepest wishes. The perception was subtle: two or three flashes out of a thousand separate photonic waves. Otherwise, the background merely appeared to be the foliage of southern Utah, slightly distorted by a watery film.

The three generations of McConnells stood thunderstruck.

"We're not prepared for this," said Kerra. "We don't have any food. Any supplies."

"It wouldn't matter," said Dad. "We wouldn't be allowed to keep it." He seemed to be talking to himself—thinking out loud—as he added, "Besides, it could close any second. It could vanish again."

"So there's no time," said Brock. "We either go or . . ."

It was Grandpa Lee—the supposed voice of age and wisdom—who declared, "I say we go. If it might disappear, this could be our last chance."

"I came back before," said Brock. "The rift could linger on for days. Maybe weeks. We'll never know unless we just . . . plunge in." He glanced at his father. "I mean, carefully, of course."

Dad studied Grandpa Lee. Kerra studied him too. Grandpa's expression, especially his ruddy cheeks, gave him a childlike appearance. He was a boy again. She'd witnessed the same overexuberant look on his grizzled face the day he first told her about the hollow and its miracles.

Dad said to Grandpa calmly, "Think about this, Dad. Maybe you should stay. It's all on foot. No trucks. No carriages."

Grandpa Lee huffed belligerently. "You think I can't walk? I was in the 7th Infantry, North Korea. The 'Chosin Frozen.' Thirty-mile retreat, thirty below zero, shells and machine gun rounds chewing up the ice fore and aft—"

His son rolled his eyes. "That was sixty years ago—"

"Your legs don't forget," Grandpa insisted.

He was a tough old bear—no doubt about it. But he was overweight, and Kerra recalled that he took medicine.

"What about your pills?" she asked.

Grandpa wore a light jacket with inner pockets. He slapped his right breast. Kerra heard a rattle. "Got 'em right here. The ones I *need* anyway. If you young bucks think yer goin' back there without *me* . . . !" He shook his head, eyes never deviating from his son.

Kerra's heart pounded. Was this really happening? Were they really on the brink of traveling back to Zarahemla? Was there a chance she'd soon set eyes upon her cherished friend, Kiddoni?

Dad rained on her parade. "I don't think *any* of you should go back. This is *my* problem. My wife and child. If any Gadiantons followed Ishlom, the jungle beyond this rift might be crawling with enemies, including the Demon Balám."

"What's that?" asked Brock.

Dad hemmed and hawed for a moment, trying to decide the best way to explain it. For Kerra, the very notion that her father might prevent her from accompanying him induced a rush of panic. She'd waited for this moment six long months. Now he was suggesting it was too *dangerous*? There was no way—no *way*—she was staying behind. No way she wasn't going through that wall. She realized there was only one way to ensure that no one would stop her.

As Dad was about to explain the Demon Balám, Kerra lunged for the archway. Despite every warning, every danger—including the possibility of being cut in half by some invisible obstacle—she thrust herself into the sparkling vortex of energy. For an instant the sound of the Whistlers became an ear-piercing shriek. Colors blurred and washed. The surface of her skin sizzled with electricity—so acutely she thought it might leave blisters. But the pain was short-lived and left no marks. And before Kerra's eyes, the hollow's dull browns transformed into eye-popping emeralds, yellows, and a rich chocolate-colored earth. The Whistlers diminished, replaced by noises that Kerra couldn't identify—small birds and unusual insects. Magnificent jungle trees, coated in velvety moss, spun overhead as Kerra gazed skyward, openmouthed, turning in a dizzy circle. *She'd done it!* She'd breached the barrier! Her heart thudded with exhilaration.

She turned back toward the place where she'd emerged. Just as on the "Utah" side, she perceived a pulsating wall of energy. But now it was framed by another archway. It was created by another fallen tree, but a different *species* of tree—maybe four times the cottonwood's breadth. Like the cottonwood, it lay horizontal, held aloft by its own "tripod" of enormous branches. Like the cottonwood, it should have been dead. But the upper side of the trunk was spiked with dozens of velvety sprigs and hundreds of healthy leaves. The rift vibrated and danced. Waves of color rippled outward from the place where she'd breached the void—that is, from the place where she'd "disturbed" the energy. The translucent surface generated an odd sound, like sizzling grease. Kerra was breathless, grateful to be alive, terrified by what she'd done—terrified *after* the fact. Squinting, she noticed through the vortex the outlines of three figures—her father, Brock, and Grandpa Lee. They gaped back in disbelief and dismay.

One figure started forward. Seconds later, her father emerged from the archway, rubbing the flesh of his arms as if he'd experienced the same electrical "sting" as Kerra. He immediately studied the terrain in fascination. Then, finally, he looked at his daughter with chagrin.

"That was very foolish," he said.

An instant later Brock popped through the wall. "Whoooa!" he declared. "I'll *never* get tired of that!"

Dad gritted his teeth, ready to offer another rebuke. The anger quickly ebbed away. Kerra waited to see if the final person would emerge. Her grandfather remained visible, his image distorted, like a fish in the waters of a strong current. He appeared to be opening and closing his fists, as if working up the final shreds of chutzpah. Another thought struck Kerra. As she watched Grandpa Lee drink in a long, last look at the hollow, she wondered, *Is he saying good-bye?* Was he bidding farewell to the world he'd always known? Kerra perished the thought, relegating the idea to her imagination.

At last Grandpa Lee burst from the rift, eyes as bright as sunbeams, grinning a cat-that-ate-the-canary grin from ear to ear. He was trembling with excitement.

"Oh my," he said, voice gasping. "*O-oh my!*"

A flash erupted behind Grandpa's shoulder. He threw up an arm to protect his face and moved away from the arch. There was a popping sound, like filaments snapping inside a lightbulb. Webs of lightning swept across the surface of the energy wall. The boiling, seething sound rose in pitch then fell off dramatically. The window darkened. Any hint of southern Utah faded and vanished. The scene was merely the backside of the jungle—the same sight that would have been visible with no vortex at all.

"Crimen-ently!" cussed Grandpa Lee. "Did I do that?"

Dad stepped back toward the archway. He raised the fingers of his right hand, tempted to touch the invisible surface, test its reaction. Brock's solution was more impetuous. He loped back toward the rift, ready to pass through. His father stopped him, like before.

"Do you have a death wish, son?" he snapped.

"I just wanna see if it's broken," Brock defended.

"It's not broken," said Kerra.

It was an unusual declaration. By all appearances, the wall of energy was, indeed, broken. What had caused it to change? Had too many people passed through? Was Grandpa Lee too *large*? Maybe the rift was like a security gate. Maybe *metal* affected the electric barrier—the metal of Grandpa's pocketknife, belt, and suspenders. Had these things thrown the barrier off balance or caused it to implode? Still, Kerra seemed unconvinced that anything was particularly amiss. She stared at the space beneath the arch, as if the colors still danced before her eyes, somehow visible to her even if invisible to others.

She'd discovered something unexpected—a trick of the eyes. She realized if she skewed her focus, crossing her eyes slightly and blurring her vision, she discerned something different from the normal jungle landscape. Not *that* different. It was, in essence, more jungle. But *different* jungle. She might have described it as *darker* jungle, an entirely separate acre of rainforest, but at a different time of day, perhaps twilight.

Kerra saw the pouty look on Brock's face and came to her father's defense. "Dad's right. Don't go through it. You don't know what'll happen. Or where it leads."

"It won't lead anywhere at *all!*" said Brock. "I'd be standing six feet away!"

Grandpa Lee sided with Dad and Kerra. He didn't perceive what Kerra perceived, but he sensed that something wasn't right.

"Let's all just move away from it, shall we?" Grandpa expedited this by placing a hand on his son's and grandson's shoulders and leading them several paces back.

Brock asked Dad, "So are we stuck here? Are we stuck the way *you* were stuck?"

Surprisingly, there was no trepidation in Brock's voice. Just irritation, the way someone might feel if the station were changed during their favorite song.

Dad shook his head. He looked baffled. He studied his daughter, seeking to connect to whatever she was sensing. Even *he* was ready to admit that Kerra possessed a gift or "radar" that no one else in their group possessed.

"The passageway has changed," Kerra stated. "I mean, it's still a passageway. But not to Utah. Not home."

"Then where does it go?" asked Brock.

"Not sure," Kerra said. "But definitely another jungle."

"You can *see* that?" asked Dad.

Kerra nodded. Then she seemed unsure and shook her head. "I don't know. I see *something*. A new landscape. But I don't know how far away. Maybe only a hundred yards."

Brock allowed his eyes to drift downward. He did a double take.

"Wait a second!"

He took a couple large steps to his right and reached down. He snatched something up from the chocolate-colored earth. Kerra saw only that the object was shiny with a string or necklace.

Everyone gathered around Brock. It was a silver pendant with a choker that was partly leather and partly stainless steel. The pendant had an engraved image surrounded by a black, plastic border: a face with wavy hair, a short beard, and a beret.

"What is it?" asked Dad.

"It's Che," Brock replied.

"Che?" Kerra repeated.

Grandpa Lee leaned closer. "Che Guevara," he said distastefully. "Communist revolutionary."

"Freedom fighter," Brock corrected.

Grandpa raised his eyebrows. "*Freedom* fight—?! You mean cold-blooded *murderer*! What are they teachin' you kids these days?"

"It's Hitch's!" said Brock. "It belonged to Hitch!"

Kerra shuddered. Torrence "Hitch" Ventura was the leader of the Shamans—the L.A. gang that had followed them to Utah in search of a stash of drugs that Brock had unwittingly transported in a leather gym bag. All Hitch's efforts to recover the drugs were dashed when Brock threw the bag into a deep well. Hitch threatened Brock with a pistol, but that's when Kiddoni had struck. He'd fired an arrow that impaled Hitch's palm.

Aunt Corinne and Grandpa Lee had reported that Hitch's fellow gangsters—Adder, Prince, and Dushane—sped off in their sports car, escaping just as the Whitmans' property was overrun by Giddianhi's army. But the fate of Hitch Ventura wasn't entirely clear. Kerra presumed that he'd caught a ride with his henchmen back to Los Angeles. She and Brock had given the cops a detailed description and even offered names, but those additional tales of an "Indian army" had sort of muddied the whole story of what had occurred and left the police flummoxed. No word had ever reached Kerra of Hitch's arrest or capture. Over the past six months she and the Whitmans had kept a sharp watch. But no member of the Shaman gang ever reappeared. Now, it seemed, they might have discovered one reason why.

"He must've crossed over," said Brock. "He's somewhere in this world."

"Probably six feet under," commented Grandpa Lee. "That is, if Nephites and Lamanites even bother to bury scoundrels."

Kerra gave a start. She was still peering into the archway. Something about the scene through the wall of energy had surprised her.

"What is it?" asked her father.

"Not sure," said Kerra. "An animal. A shadow. I heard . . . some kind of growl."

Dad's response was more intense than anyone expected. "Quickly!" he directed. "Climb!"

He meant that everyone should climb the trunk of the massive tree that created the archway. It was certainly bulkier and more accessible to climbing than any trees in the hollow. Kerra wasn't sure why her father had reacted so dramatically, yet something deep inside echoed the same anxiety. Still, how would climbing this fallen tree trunk protect them?

Despite their doubts, everyone acted with urgency. Dad helped his son, then Kerra, and finally Grandpa Lee to hoist themselves up the mossy branches, like steps on a ladder, until they reached the topside of the trunk. Dad leaped up behind them, motioning everyone to ascend the fallen tree as high as possible, to the place where it hovered directly above the arch. At this point the tree was supported by its mushrooming limbs, so thick that they formed cavernous niches and offered multiple places to hide. Kerra made her way among the limbs, balancing herself by clinging to mossy, leaf-covered sprigs. Suddenly Dad held up his hand—a signal that everyone should remain perfectly still.

Kerra and Dad were wedged in a good position to view whatever emerged from the rift. She studied her father's face, desperate to ask what he thought she'd seen or heard. She began to doubt the alarm bells in her gut. To her it was just a shadow—perhaps nothing at all. Her description of a "growl" seemed odd, too. Why had she described it like that? The more she thought about it, the more abstract it seemed. She couldn't really compare it to any sound she'd ever—

A subtle hissing, sizzling sound resonated below them. Kerra watched a living thing slowly emerge from the vortex. At first she thought it was a man—someone in a bright orange cape with a mottled hood. Then she saw the collar around its neck. The movements were lithe and sinister. It was definitely an animal—a jaguar.

Kerra caught her breath. She instinctively moved her hand to her mouth to suppress any possible sound. A jaguar!—wearing a *collar*? And an extravagant collar at that—embossed leather with jadestone. A *pet* jaguar? Who could say? In any case, it was *enormous*. Kerra wasn't certain that she'd ever set eyes on a live jaguar. Her memories of the large cats at the Los Angeles Zoo sort of blended together. Still, she wouldn't have expected a jaguar to be all that much bigger than a leopard or mountain lion. However, the enormity of this beast reminded her of a Bengal tiger. Its movements were liquid, flawless. A low growl escaped its throat, eyes moving from right to left across the breadth of the forest. Its actions seemed calculated, deliberate. It struck Kerra that it was *thinking*. Thinking like a person. Searching for something. Was it hunting? If so, *what*? Or who?

By the look on Dad's face, she realized he feared it was hunting *them*. But that seemed ridiculous unless . . . unless somehow it had sensed their presence across the rift, much the same way that she'd sensed *its* presence. But what about that collar? Kerra remembered seeing a collared jaguar in some Book of Mormon painting. The animal was lying at the feet of . . . Was it King Noah? Did such an accessory mean that this creature wasn't wild? But if it was some kind of pet, why should they fear it at all?

None of these thoughts squelched her feelings of alarm. Every muscle of this beast was rigid and tense, as if ready to pounce and deliver a lethal strike. All at once it raised its head and sniffed the air. This movement allowed Kerra to glimpse its eyes. It took every bit of self-discipline not to gasp. She'd never seen such eyes on an animal. They had a sheen of intelligence. And something else. Something black and evil. Dad pressed a finger to his lips, still pleading—urging—everyone to remain calm and still.

The creature wandered to the place where Brock had found the silver and leather choker. It sniffed the earth. Kerra glanced at Brock. He was clenching his teeth crookedly. His eyes were crossed, focusing on something at the end of his nose. Kerra realized it was an insect— a large ant. It seemingly ran in a circle around the end of his nose, like a dog searching for a place to lie down. Her brother didn't budge, but the urge to slap it away dominated every thought.

Kerra felt a terrible sting on her shin. It burned as if someone had stubbed out a cigarette against her flesh. Something had bitten her. She glanced down at her pants. Ants climbed all over her ankles and clothes! Ants were all over the tree. Her family had positioned themselves right in the middle of an ant expressway. The bite burned and throbbed, as if the pest had chomped off a dime-sized hunk. Then came another sting, lower down on her leg.

Still, Kerra did not move. Amazingly, neither did Brock. Dad and Grandpa Lee also remained like statues. The jaguar stared into the forest, scanning for prey. It seemed poised there forever. At last it turned and stalked back toward the wall of energy. Its progress was steady, yet to Kerra it moved in slow motion. At last she heard another sizzling, sucking sound. She watched until the jaguar's undulating tail slipped into the vortex and disappeared. The sizzling ended.

Immediately, Kerra began slapping, swiping, and swatting ants off her body. The relief was all-encompassing as she scratched a half dozen places where the insects had successfully devoured portions of her flesh. Brock and Grandpa were also slapping off ants. Dad's focus, however, remained riveted on the archway.

"What was it?" asked Grandpa.

"Where did it come from?" asked Brock. "A jaguar with a collar?"

"It belongs to Akuhuun," said Dad, "the son of Giddianhi, former king of the Gadiantons."

"He owns a trained jaguar?" asked Kerra.

"He owns *two* of them," said Dad. "Trained for only two things: to hunt and to kill. We've just seen one of the Demon Balám."

CHAPTER 7

CAREFULLY, STEALTHILY, DAD DIRECTED KERRA, Brock, and Grandpa to climb down from the fallen tree and then around the backside of the arch. Kerra saw her brother pause to gaze through the archway, his eyes alert and his breathing more rapid than normal. There was really nothing to see. Any evidence of an energy field or something else unusual had entirely faded, at least on *this* side of the arch. Brock still held Hitch Ventura's choker, though he'd mostly forgotten about it. He appeared unusually stressed—even more than Kerra might have expected under the circumstances. She surmised that it had to do with reality sinking into his mind. Her grandfather also appeared discomposed. The whole experience—passing into another century— had lost some of the "spirit of adventure" that they'd been anticipating. It had suddenly become a plight to survive.

Dad was surveying the terrain, deciding which direction they should travel, as Brock asked a question, his voice subdued.

"Why do they call it that? *Demon Balám.* What does it even mean?"

Dad studied Brock, at first hesitant. In the end he sighed and said, "The Gadiantons believe . . . and many of the *prisoners* of the Gadiantons believe . . . that the soul of a jaguar no longer possesses the bodies or minds of these creatures. They think it's a spell. Sorcery." He shrugged it off. "Beyond that I don't know anything about it. And I don't *want* to know."

Brock wasn't convinced by his ambivalence. "But do you believe it?"

"It doesn't matter," Dad responded sternly. "We have to leave here—*now!*"

He led them straight into the thick of the jungle, along a scant and tenuous trail that meandered northward, between the rims of the valley.

There was very little talking. Kerra couldn't shake the image of the killer jaguar from her mind. If she'd had to guess, she'd have estimated that it was four or five hundred pounds. Did jaguars normally grow so large? Perhaps a more interesting question was could they really be "trained"? Especially trained to kill human beings? She'd seen circus acts with tigers and lions. Maybe even leopards. But never jaguars. She vaguely recalled some nature show that said jaguars were too "intelligent and independent" to be domesticated. Yet somehow these evil witch doctors—these robbers of Gadianton—had done precisely that. Or at least one of them had done it—a son of Giddianhi, the Gadianton's former king. A son named Akuhuun.

Kerra pondered the things her father had said—the part about an animal being possessed by a demon. She didn't believe it. Perhaps she just didn't *want* to believe it. Besides, what kind of "demon"—if in fact such an entity existed—would possess the body of a jaguar?

"Maybe we'd be safer off the ground," said Brock.

"What are you suggesting?" asked Kerra. "That we travel by jungle vine, like Tarzan?"

Although Kerra was being facetious, her father quashed the idea anyway. "It wouldn't make any difference. Jaguars climb trees better than Tarzan."

Kerra watched her grandfather. After only a few minutes, he was already drenched in sweat. He'd abandoned his light jacket, placing his pills in a pocket of his pants. Huge circles of perspiration had formed around the armpits of his checkered, button-up shirt, and he was breathing heavily.

He finally asked his son, "Where are you taking us?"

"To Ishlom's village," Dad replied.

"His village?" asked Kerra. "I thought you said it was destroyed."

"That was two years ago," said Dad. "People in this part of the world . . . that is, in this century . . . don't normally carve out a new patch of ground in the forest. They just rebuild on the old one. If the Gadianton robbers have truly been driven from this area, as Kiddoni told you six months ago, I can only hope that remnants of Ishlom's family are beginning to resettle on their traditional home site. Perhaps we'll make contact with some people that I know."

"How long before we get there?" asked Brock.

"Before dark," said Dad, "I hope."

The trail seemed to grow less discernible with every step. Kerra turned around and studied the jungle where they'd just been. The moss-covered trees, towering branches, and undergrowth with its enormous leaves and ferns were all starting to look the same. It had only been an hour, yet she seriously doubted if they could have found the archway again. Nevertheless, her father pushed onward, as if he really was following some kind of trail. Kerra wiped her brow. The jungle was like a sauna. Sweat flowed from everyone's faces as if a water hose had been strapped up their backs and clipped atop their foreheads. Grandpa Lee started lagging behind. He paused and leaned against a tree whose bark was layered in ridge-patterned mushrooms. She stepped back to him.

"Are you sure you're—?"

Grandpa wouldn't let her finish the question. "I'm fine," he huffed. He immediately drew in a deep breath and marched past her.

Kerra's concern intensified by the hour. They had no water. No food. And the light of day was ebbing.

About this time the landscape began to change. Steep, jungle-blanketed hills on either side became less elevated. The pathway through the forest broadened. Vegetation became less dense and suffocating. With the advent of evening, the chittering of birds, insects, and other wild things in the forest enlivened and revitalized. The cacophony of sounds seemed to Kerra like a ragged symphony warming up for an exuberant concert.

A moment later they passed the first charred remains of a former Lamanite dwelling. Dad paused.

"What's wrong?" asked Grandpa.

"We're going to the leave the trail for a few minutes," said Dad.

"Why?" asked Brock, studying the forest fearfully. The last time his father had given such a firm order, a humongous jaguar had appeared. But taking cover was not Dad's motive.

"To do some shopping," he announced.

He led them past the ruined dwelling and into an area where additional burned and battered huts wallowed beneath the trees. Some of the structures were nearly invisible as the jungle foliage threatened to swallow them whole.

"I don't understand," said Kerra. "Shopping?"

"Scavenging may be a better word," said Dad. "I know this area. This neighborhood. I know it all too well."

"What are we scavenging for?" asked Brock.

Kerra felt she already knew the answer. She'd been wondering about it for hours.

Dad said, "The last thing any of us want to do in a region where the locals live in terror of Gadianton robbers is *stand out*. I assure you, our modern clothes will draw the wrong kind of attention. We're going to abandon our current wardrobes and don some garments a little more . . . *timely*."

Dad started his search in the first dwelling they encountered. Kerra was impressed at how quickly he located precisely what they needed. By the time they'd finished, Dad had explored a dozen huts—even some badly damaged by fire—and almost always located stone "keeps" along the inner walls and corners. These storage boxes were covered in a layer of dirt, followed by a second layer of reed matting, and a third layer of wood. The clothing and other property represented the worldly goods of villagers who had long since disappeared.

Dad laid a selection of men's mantles and women's skirts at his family's feet. "Take your pick. It appears that I was wrong. Ishlom's kinship may yet return here, but for the time being it appears that they have migrated to the place of safety."

"If they migrated," asked Kerra, "why would they leave so much behind?"

"That tells you they were in a hurry," said Dad.

"What about when they come back?" asked Brock, slipping a green and tawny cotton tunic—just his size—over his shoulders. "Won't they be a little irritated to find their stuff missing?"

"Most will be far more impressed with what we leave in place of what we've taken," said Dad.

"Well, I'm not leaving my shoes," said Brock. "These are Adidas Barricades. Best shoes I ever owned!"

"More likely the best shoes you ever *stole*," proclaimed Kerra.

"I *highly* advise wearing the Lamanite sandals," Dad emphasized. "If a Gadianton—or even certain Nephites—were to find you wearing shoes like those, they might not take the time to ask how such shoes are untied. They'll just chop off your foot above the ankle."

Moments later Dad unloaded an armful of traditional ancient-American sandals.

"Try 'em out," he said. "They're not bad. Just takes getting used to. They breathe better. You'll avoid foot rot. I'll show you how to wrap the straps."

Utilizing all of his knowledge of local fashion and customs, Dad successfully outfitted his father and two children. Kerra chose a feminine-looking mantle with colorful embroidery and soft blue hues. Grandpa chose a loose-hanging brown, white, and red tunic with a leather-beaded sash. The clothing promised to be much cooler than his jacket, button-up shirt, pants, and suspenders. The abundance of clothing and its diversity was surprising. So was its cleanliness. The fabrics needed some airing out, but after a couple years, Kerra would have thought that rodents or moisture would have ruined the weaving and leather. The sturdy keeps of the neighborhood's former occupants were apparently designed with just such contingencies in mind.

Brock found a fiber satchel that could be worn like a backpack. He decided to keep it and then summarily discarded his father's advice about donating his shoes. He also secretly stashed his grandfather's Skechers—in case the sandal thing didn't work out. Additionally, he kept the Che Guevara necklace/choker thing that had belonged to Hitch, his 8-GB MP3 player with one working earphone, and his pocket slim-jim that unfolded like a ruler, confident that it would surely serve some useful purpose in the first century AD.

Dad kept his cell phone. The battery was dead. Still, he knew the sleek, shiny object might come in handy for bargaining. Grandpa kept only his meds and his serviceman-issue, pocket-sized Book of Mormon—a book that he'd carried somewhere on his person virtually every day of his life. As for Kerra, she stubbornly retained her twentieth-century undergarments, and there was *nothing* in this world that could have convinced her to do otherwise.

It wasn't long after they recommenced their journey that the forest gave way to an open expanse. More signs of civilization began to appear, from the stumps of harvested trees to well-trodden foot paths. Moreover, they began to hear voices on the wind.

Grandpa took a deep whiff. "Smell that?"

Dad nodded. "Cook fires. Roasting corn."

"Will they feed us?" asked Brock. "Will they have water?"

"Yes, to both," said Dad, but he added his usual mantra. "I hope."

After another hundred yards Kerra came to a halt. A massive wall appeared across the expanse. It consisted of a deep ditch, earthworks, wooden pikes, and a long railing with a line of flickering torches and sentries marching to and fro. It looked formidable but very new and raw, as if it had been cast up in a short period of time.

Kerra's heart began to race. For a second she forgot about her thirst and hunger. She forgot practically everything. Kiddoni's features floated before her mind, beckoning her on. Was it possible that he was here, inside this fort? Six months ago Kiddoni had made the patch of jungle near the archway his personal surveillance post. He was firmly convinced that the Gadianton robbers would attack Zarahemla's troops by storming out of the mountains, passing directly past Kiddoni's position. He'd urgently sought to convince the Nephite generals that his theory was correct. They'd had their own theories and had refused to listen. In the end Kiddoni was proven right. Kerra wondered if his insight might have earned him some kind of commendation in the Nephite army. After all, he'd successfully warned his people of Giddianhi's invasion. That is, Kiddoni and *Kerra* had warned them. She'd utilized her own hearty lungs to sound the final alarm with Kiddoni's trumpet.

The last time she'd seen Kiddoni, his arm and shoulder were bound up in a sling. He'd been pierced by an arrow, fired from the bow of Kush the assassin. Surely by now Kiddoni's wound had healed. A disturbing thought struck her. Six months. Yes, it had been six months since she'd laid eyes on her Nephite warrior. But did that necessarily mean the same length of time had passed *here,* in the first century? The thought tormented her. She shut her eyes tightly and cast it off. When she'd first met Kiddoni, she was only five years old. A dozen years later, when they'd met again, a comparable period had elapsed in both centuries. She had no reason to believe anything had changed. Surely the passage of time remained synchronous. *Surely.*

Before they could draw near to the wall, the flames from two torches appeared ahead. Dad halted as numerous silhouettes bolted from the shadows. The space around them erupted with armed soldiers. The two original torches were set to a dozen other torches. The area became vibrant with flickering flames. Kerra, Brock, Dad, and Grandpa clustered together tightly as spearpoints issued from the darkness. They were surrounded. The twenty or so warriors acted volatile and edgy, as if rattled to think that strangers had penetrated the perimeter of their encampment as close as two hundred yards. Firelight glistened off their faces and flesh. Many carried shields and sported leather armor with a sort of chain mail composed of cube-cut stones with holes bored through the middle. Kerra and the others remained still, sensing that these sentries were jumpy enough to inflict fatal blows with the least provocation.

"Halt!" someone cried, entirely failing to observe that all four had already done just that.

"Who are you?" another demanded, lifting his torch higher to add additional light. "What are your kinships?"

One sentry finally discerned that the foursome included a boy and an old man. His voice softened considerably. "The sun has set. Why have you broken curfew? Don't you realize you can be arrested?"

"We didn't know about your curfew," Grandpa replied.

Dad set his eyes upon the sentry who'd raised up his torch. Despite his threatening tone, Dad spoke to him with the sentiment of a friend. "Lemech . . . it's me." The warrior squinted. He took in Chris's face. Recognition started to set in.

"Mi´con?" he asked in disbelief.

Dad nodded.

Lemech stepped closer. He lowered his weapon, looking befuddled, as if confronted by something wondrous. "Mi´con," he declared, voice more subdued. "Is it really you?"

"Do you know these people, Lemech?" another sentry stiffly inquired, still pointing his spear at the intruders.

Lemech dropped his weapon entirely. He handed off his torch to another soldier. Kerra watched as the warrior embraced her father, eyes moistening.

"Mi´con!" he exclaimed, voice choked with emotion. "My brother!"

Kerra, Brock, and Grandpa finally dared to draw a breath. A confrontation had been averted. But they were confused. *Brother?* Did that mean this man was Kerra and Brock's *uncle?* Before today, of course, no one would have known that such a relative existed. Kerra decided he was more likely a brother-in-*law*—a sibling of her stepmother, Paísha. Still, the information was disquieting. Then Kerra wondered why she should feel so surprised. Her father had lived in this century for a dozen years. Surely they'd hardly scratched the surface of his relationships and memories.

Most of the sentries had relaxed their weapons. Others wanted more details.

"Your brother?" repeated a fierce-looking soldier behind Lemech. "Why is he traveling after curfew?"

"Who are the others?" inquired a sentry with his hair tied in a high topknot, like a black bushel of grain.

"They are members of my family," said Mi´con. "This is my father, Lee McConnell. And these . . ." He paused awkwardly. ". . . are my children."

"*Children?*" asked Lemech in dismay.

Dad set his hand upon Lemech's shoulder, as if to reassure him. "Yes. If you think back, Lemech, many years ago to when we first met, you will remember that I told you about my children."

Lemech seemed to recall something; the memory was obviously vague.

"What about Paísha?" asked Lemech. "Where is my sister? And where is our brother, Ishlom?"

The corners of Dad's mouth drooped. His expression became deathly solemn. "There is much we need to discuss, Lemech. I've been away for many moons. But today I've returned. I've come directly from the Place of the Whistlers. The site of the Great Gadianton Battle."

Lemech knew the location. He looked concerned. Even though it was the site of a successful battle against their Gadianton enemies, it was still apparently a very dangerous place to visit.

Grandpa Lee cleared his throat. "May we have some water? Please. We've been, uh, wandering in this heat—walking for hours."

"This incident must be reported," said the sentry with the topknot.

"Report it, then!" said Lemech petulantly. "Tell the Captain of the Guard that I am at my tent. I will look after my kin."

CHAPTER 8

AFTER QUENCHING THEIR THIRST IN a nearby basin, Lemech led Chris, Kerra, Brock, and Grandpa Lee toward the gate of the encampment.

"What's its name?" asked Brock. "Does your fort have a name?"

"Sorrow," Lemech replied.

Brock sent Kerra a wry expression typical of whenever he felt something was stupid.

"Is that really its name?" asked Brock.

Lemech sighed. "Some call it the fortress of Lachoneus. But I know it only as Sorrow."

There were numerous dwellings and tents outside the fortifications. The population of the valley obviously didn't want to live like sardines, so they spread out beyond the bulwarks and ditches, no doubt ready to rush inside the gates at a moment's notice if an alarm was sounded.

Despite the fort's name, or nickname, to Kerra the people themselves didn't appear especially depressed. Granted, many looked tired and drained, but there was also something . . . *jubilant* about their mood.

She counted dozens of campfires surrounded by humble families with meager worldly goods. Every stitch of their belongings appeared to have been wrapped into heavy bundles, ready to be hoisted on their backs. As with the jungle, Kerra was equally mesmerized by all the sights and sounds: children playing in the fire glow, old men strumming twangy instruments or blowing into oddly shaped flutes and whistles. Many of the fathers were gathered into tight clusters, as if engaged in serious planning, while the women cooked and gossiped and sometimes sang lyrics that went along with the songs played by the old men. Mothers crooned to drowsy babes in tightly wrapped blankets. Very few of the inhabitants of this valley appeared or planned to be permanent residents. Instead, Kerra decided they were principally pilgrims. Or refugees.

They crossed a bridge into the main part of the fortress. Rains had turned the bottom of the ditch encircling the city into a mud pit. The ditch also boasted multiple layers of sharpened pikes or spears intended to discourage or skewer besiegers.

Lemech led them into the army compound. Dozens of threadbare tents and flimsy shelters crisscrossed the cityscape. Some hammocks appeared empty. A portion of Zarahemla's soldiers were out on patrol. Perhaps on campaign. Those in the compound looked stricken with boredom. Kerra heard several men arguing about trivial matters— food portions or quality, as far as she could determine. There was little laughter or merriment around the campfires. Kerra perceived long and drooping faces; men as thread-worn as their tents, chewing charred tortillas or stripping meat from animals roasting on spits.

The mood was drearier in the militarized zone than among the pilgrims. Kerra wondered if the warriors yearned to trade places with noncombatants. They might have wanted to join them in their preparations for going home. If what Kiddoni had said six months ago still held true, the main battle against the Gadianton armies was over. Now it was just a matter of mopping up those insurgents who remained, warriors too stubborn to admit defeat. Or too indoctrinated to change. Such enemies, it seemed, were still holed up in the mountains to the east and south, wreaking havoc whenever circumstances allowed. She tried to remember what was recorded in this particular section of the Book of Mormon. She'd probably read it more than any other chapters in the volume since it corresponded with the time period of Kiddoni. It seemed to her that Zarahemla's conflict with the Gadiantons did not come to an immediate end after the Great Battle wherein the Gadianton leader, Giddianhi, was slain. She couldn't recall how much longer the conflict had dragged on. Was it a year? Two years? It seemed to her that it might be a little soon for families to be packing up for any homeward migrations.

After arriving at Lemech's humble shelter and lighting a pair of lamps, Kerra, Brock, and Grandpa got their first clear look at

Lemech's face. It was a harsh face, much older than its years. Lemech's forehead was unusually high, like other Lamanites Kerra had seen. She felt certain it was some kind of alteration, perhaps an operation performed at birth. She'd read about something like that among the Mayans of Central America. Lemech's high forehead was creased with wrinkles and scars, like the roadmap of a busy metropolis. Unlike other Lamanites whom Kerra had had the displeasure of meeting—that is, *Gadianton* Lamanites—Lemech possessed no tattoos. She presumed he was a Christian, though she couldn't have said for sure.

Dad waited until everyone had gathered beneath the shelter and he had the fullness of Lemech's attention before he began to fill him in on what had transpired.

"Ishlom is dead," he said solemnly. "He died trying to find me, trying to save Paísha."

Lemech let this settle in. He sat cross-legged upon his floor mat and seemed to study the weavings beside his ankles. Kerra felt he took the information rather well. Perhaps *too* well. The man's capacity to feel grief appeared suppressed or warped. Too many awful experiences had made him stoic, detached.

"Where is Paísha now?" Lemech inquired dispassionately.

"I don't know," Dad admitted. "Ishlom passed away before he could fully explain. He said she was alive but in danger. He seemed to suggest that . . . she was in the hands of the Reds. Perhaps even under the control of the man whose followers enslaved Ishlom and me—Akuhuun, the son of Giddianhi. Akuhuun and Zemnarihah controlled dozens of captives: men and women, Nephites and Lamanites. I was a slave for two years. But I had the feeling—just an instinct—that Paísha had not been a captive for very long. Perhaps only a few weeks."

Lemech drew his eyebrows together. He looked puzzled. "Two weeks? Then where has she been for two years? Paísha chose to journey to the land of Jershon with several of our cousins. She never arrived. That was more than two years ago. I have not seen her for two and a half years."

Now it was Dad's turn to look bewildered. "But . . . Paísha escaped when Ishlom and I were taken captive. *That* was two and a half years ago. Do you mean to say that she left for Jershon right after the village was attacked?"

Lemech shook his head. Kerra felt as if her heart was being squeezed. The prospect of Lemech's next words filled her with terror.

He said, "The village was first attacked—you and Ishlom were taken captive—*four* years ago, my brother. I have not seen *your* face for four long years."

Dad gaped in consternation. His eyes were swimming as he pondered what this meant. Kerra felt as if all the oxygen had been sucked from the tent. She did the math in her brain—worked it out before panic set in and her mind froze.

Eighteen months. As best as she could figure, that was the differential between her perspective and Kiddoni's perspective. He was now eighteen months older than before. For Kerra, six months had passed. For Kiddoni, it had been at least two years. A difference of eighteen months. She squeezed her eyelids tightly. *Was that right?* Panic was setting in. She wasn't sure of anything. She realized her fingernails were digging into the flesh of her knees.

Lemech continued. "What you have said still offers some hope. Until this moment I was certain that she was dead. Her fate was an utter mystery, as well as the fate of others. Including . . . your son."

Kerra snapped back to alertness. *What did he just say?* Rain pitter-pattered against the canvas. Everything was quiet except for the percussion of raindrops.

For her father, it was confirmation of the few scant words that Ishlom spoke before his death. He did, in fact, have another child—a son. Grandpa had another grandson. Brock and Kerra did, indeed, have a half-brother. A *Lamanite* half-brother. A sibling from a completely different century.

"When," asked Dad, swallowing, "was the child born?"

"Six moons after the raid that destroyed our village," said Lemech. "Six months after you and Ishlom . . . were taken." He asked reticently, "Were you even aware . . . ? Did you know that Paísha was . . . ?"

"We wondered," Dad replied. "We expressed our suspicions . . . our hopes . . . but . . ."

Dad shuddered. Kerra suppressed her own emotions long enough to glimpse her father's eyes. She didn't have to experience his horrible memories. She could see them all on his face. Everything in her dad's life had been shattered the day the robbers had attacked. All his plans and dreams. Even now his hopes hung by a thread. Perhaps merely by a wisp of smoke.

"He'd be about almost . . . no, he *would* be . . . four years old now," said Lemech. "That is . . . if the Gadiantons—"

"He's alive," said Dad quietly.

"We've heard rumors," said Lemech, "—terrible rumors . . . that Reds do not spare the young. Too much trouble. They serve no—"

Dad's head snapped up. "He's *alive*! Ishlom would not have said what he said if . . ."

He stopped. His expression changed. He realized anything that Ishlom had said was now *two years old*. It was past history. Dad looked faint. Grandpa went to him before his knees could buckle. He helped him sit at the edge of Lemech's floor mat. Dad's chin rested on his chest. His fists remained clenched, but all his efforts at sounding brave or confident were clearly waning.

Then he found a renewed spark of courage and said to Lemech, "An infant—a toddler—*would* serve a useful purpose. I lived in the squalor of Gadianton encampments for two years. I know how they think. They manipulate the slaves against each other. The men will work to protect the women. The women will serve to protect each other. A mother could certainly be manipulated to work if it protected her child. Paísha is alive. I know it. And so is my son."

Lemech asked, "How many Nephite and Lamanite captives are there?"

Dad looked uncertain. "There were . . . seventy. Perhaps a hundred. But that was two years ago. And these were the ones who resided in Akuhuun's camp. There were other encampments, including those of Zemnarihah. Other places of refuge surely have other captives. But as I've said, this is how it was before the Great Battle. Before Akuhuun's father, Giddianhi, was slain."

Lemech sat back. He spoke carefully. "The whereabouts of Akuhuun or Zemnarihah are not known to the Nephite leaders. Both Gadianton leaders seek to unify the scattered bands hiding in the mountains. Some believe the only reason they have not attacked us in our stronghold is because of a Gadianton power void. Akuhuun and Zemnarihah compete for the loyalty of the Gadianton army. It would be *better* if they attacked. Better if they came to *us*. Gidgiddoni has always pursued a disciplined strategy that our warriors should remain close to our fortifications, but in the past few months there has been enormous pressure to send regiments into the wilderness. There have been a few skirmishes, but I don't think any of our battalions have returned victorious. Some have come back without engaging any enemy fighters. And some . . . have not returned at all. A few have begun to believe that the son of Giddianhi—Lord Akuhuun—has unearthly powers. They say his capacity for evil greatly transcends his father's. It is said that Akuhuun controls the elements of wind and fire, that he moves like a phantom through the mist, and that he has at his command supernatural soldiers who transform into beasts. They are called Demon Balám."

That phrase again: *demon jaguars.* Kerra, Brock, and Grandpa Lee glanced at one another, recalling the creature that had materialized out of the rift. Kerra's father gave no reaction whatsoever. He didn't appear interested in confirming or denying these rumors. He remained focused on Lemech's speech.

Lemech continued. "Many of Zarahemla's soldiers have begun to believe these superstitions, especially the non-Christians." He shrugged and confessed, "Maybe a few Christians believe them too. A lot of good men have failed to return from the mountains." Lemech shook himself, as if shrugging off an uncomfortable chill. "Ah, forget such nonsense! I think we are just weary. The army wants to go home. If the Reds wish to live in the wilderness, let them. Let them practice their sorceries. They do not plant. They do not harvest. They survive on meat and game, which every day grows more scarce. Inevitably they will starve. We see our families preparing to journey home to the lands of our forefathers. They hope Lachoneus will announce their departure any day—any hour. We soldiers yearn to join them. But until the Gadiantons are vanquished—until our leaders know that the Reds cannot regroup—the captains will not release us." Lemech's eyes narrowed thoughtfully. "I wonder, Mi´con, if there are things you know that might aid Judge Lachoneus and Captain Gidgiddoni. Things that might help our army complete its mission. Do you know Akuhuun or Zemnarihah's secret hiding places in the wilderness?"

Dad nodded but falteringly. "I know some of them. Perhaps quite a few. Often we were blindfolded and bound as we were moved about. But not always. Not when the terrain was too difficult. I believe I know many of their secret places. As I have said, much time has passed. By no means do I know *all* of them."

Lemech pondered this. Then he asked, "What are your intentions, Brother Mi´con? You have found your family. Your *original* family. After four years, why did you come back here, to the fortress of Sorrow?"

Dad shook his head. "It's called Ishkim. Not Sorrow. This land and its village are named for your father."

Lemech looked away. "My father is dead. So is my mother. And my sons. Ishkim is gone. The ashes of our village have been stirred back into the earth. There will never be another village named for my kinship. The clan of my fathers is dead. Only my sister, Paísha, remains. Except that by now she, too, may—"

"*No,*" Dad interrupted. He seized Lemech's arm. "They are not all gone. You said yourself that I have a son. *He* is your kin. Just as *I* am your kin. But that's not all, Lemech. Your eldest son, Menkom, still lives."

Lemech's expression froze. He searched his brother-in-law's eyes. He seized Mi´con's arm in return, mouth opening and closing, tongue unable to speak. Finally he stuttered, "How can you—? A-are you—? H-how do you know this?"

Dad backpedaled a little. "I guess I don't. I don't know anything for certain. I know only that he was alive two years ago. He tried to escape with me, but . . ."

"But what?" asked Lemech, breathless.

Dad sighed. "We were separated. I suspect . . . I *believe* . . . he was recaptured."

Lemech's eyes went blank. Quickly his tear ducts overflowed. He started trembling. Dad tried to steady him. It was almost too much for Lemech to take in. Kerra realized he'd abandoned all hope of ever hearing such news. To hear it now—after four long years—shook him to the core. He was on the verge of dismissing it all, lashing out angrily, but Dad's steady hand had the desired effect.

"You have to believe," said Dad, "just as *I* believe. They *are* alive— *all* of them. Just waiting for the warriors of Zarahemla. Waiting to be rescued."

Lemech shut his eyes and drew several deep breaths, calming himself. When his eyes reopened, he appeared to have made a decision.

"Wait here," he instructed. He looked at Kerra and the others. "All of you, wait here. I will speak to the Captain of the Guard. I will tell him everything that you have said."

With that, Lemech quickly slipped into the darkness. Kerra, Brock, Grandpa, and Dad sat beneath the meager shelter, still listening to the purr of the rain. They ate some tortillas and dried berries that Lemech had left, easing the hunger that burned in their stomachs.

Grandpa asked Lemech's question again. "What *are* your intentions, Chris? What are you planning to do?"

Dad swallowed a bite of food then said, "I will find my wife and child."

Kerra asked, "What are you expecting *us* to do?"

Dad looked off into the night. "I'm not sure. You'll stay here, I suppose."

"Stay *here*?!" Brock protested. "You've gotta be kidding?!"

Dad made a crooked grin. "You want to go with me? You still have a yearning for adventure?"

He'd misinterpreted Brock. His son came to his feet. "Of course not! I wanna go *home*! I wanna go back to the archway in the forest."

"Why?" asked Kerra. "Right now it won't take you anywhere near where you wanna go."

"Then I'll wait there till it does," said Brock. "We'll camp. We'll wait for a disturbance. Maybe we'll *cause* a disturbance."

Grandpa slapped Dad's knee. "Well, I'm with you, Chris. If it means saving my little grandson, I'll help in any way I can."

Dad furrowed his brow. "If there's anyone who ought to take Brock's suggestion, it's you, Dad. You looked bad today. You barely kept up."

Grandpa Lee scoffed. "I'm just gettin' my wind. Might take a day or two. That's all. I'll be fine."

Mi´con opened his mouth to argue. He knew his father too well. It was futile. His mind was set. Kerra sensed that her father was already contemplating some way—for Grandpa's own good—that he might be left behind.

That left only Kerra's thoughts undeclared. She honestly didn't know what to say. She kept her thoughts to herself, awaiting Lemech's return. She caught Dad watching her. *He knows what I'm thinking,* thought Kerra. It really didn't take much imagination. Her heart hadn't stopped pounding since she'd learned that the age difference between her and Kiddoni had increased by eighteen months. She felt sick inside. And excruciatingly frustrated. With all the other earth-shaking subjects of conversation, she'd failed to ask the one question that burned in her mind. And it seemed there was more than a good chance that Lemech would know the answer. Lemech had grown up in this area. As far as she could determine, so had Kiddoni. Kiddoni might have been raised right alongside Lemech's clan. Maybe they were friends. The chances seemed extraordinarily good that Lemech knew precisely where Kiddoni was.

She wondered why she hadn't already asked. Such a brief question. Had she hesitated out of fear? Lemech had mentioned the loss of "a lot of good men"—warriors killed or missing while pursuing Gadiantons into their "secret places." Maybe she feared what Lemech might report. No, Kerra dismissed this. She wasn't afraid. She'd hesitated out of respect. The timing wasn't right. She'd pose the question to her new "uncle" as soon as he returned. They expected him at any moment.

Unfortunately, it didn't turn out like that. An hour later an unfamiliar voice shouted her father's Lamanite name.

"Mi´con! I'm looking for Mi´con, brother of Lemech!"

Dad emerged from the tent, followed by the others.

"I'm Mi´con," said Dad.

A soldier in red feathers and regalia quickly approached. "I'm Shiloah, Captain of the Guard. You and your family are to come with me."

"Where's Lemech?" asked Dad.

"With the Chief Captain," he responded. "You've been summoned to the tent of Gidgiddoni, commander of the armies of Zarahemla."

CHAPTER 9

THE TENT OF GIDGIDDONI WAS not notably more impressive than the tent of Lemech, at least as far the quality of canvas. There was just more of it. The Chief Captain's tent was a patchwork of textiles, brick, mud, branches, and thatch. There were plenty of lamps—enough that it made the army's headquarters easy to locate in the dark. The interior was roomy enough. It might have sheltered a hundred men. For now, however, the captain's attendants and bodyguards remained outside. When Dad, Kerra, Brock, Grandpa, and Shiloah entered, only three other persons stood within. One was Lemech. As for the other two, Kerra could only wager a guess.

Grandpa Lee seemed to appreciate the momentousness of this occasion more than anyone else. He pointed at a squat man in the center of the room, adorned in bright jadestone and similarly colored feathers, his limbs encircled with bands of silver and a necklace with a large silver medallion accented with mother-of-pearl and black onyx in the shape of an eagle. Grandpa whispered into Dad's ear, "That's him. That's Captain Gidgiddoni. Possibly the greatest military mind in Nephite history."

"Actually, that's Judge Lachoneus," Dad corrected. "The *other* man is Gidgiddoni."

Dad indicated the tallest of the three. The person was dressed much more modestly in a leather cuirass, dark tunic, and the sandals of a common Nephite soldier. Grandpa gaped at his son. He seemed incensed that he'd never mentioned his acquaintance with two of the most distinguished figures in Book of Mormon history. Then again, everything they'd learned in the past twenty-four hours about Chris McConnell—or *Mi'con*—might have filled an entire volume.

Kerra was not unfamiliar with the names of these two leaders. She recalled that the book of Helaman had referred to Gidgiddoni and Lachoneus as "prophets." It was the first time she'd been in the presence of anyone holding such a title. She wasn't certain what she ought to expect. All that she knew about "prophets" had come from old movies like *The Ten Commandments*.

Kerra found the real McCoy to be far less pretentious than expected. Shiloah knelt before them. It was apparently a traditional gesture of respect, yet both men seemed oddly impatient with such fanfare. They cordially dismissed the Captain of the Guard. Kerra and Brock wondered if they should kneel too, but no one indicated that this was necessary. The plainly dressed Gidgiddoni approached Kerra's dad. He was muscular with a remarkably thick neck. His jaw was slightly crooked, as if a past injury had incorrectly healed. Or maybe he just preferred to set it that way, out of habit. Kerra judged right away that he was not a patient man. His eyes had difficulty focusing on any one thing for long, as if he preferred to get to the heart of an issue as quickly as possible. Gidgiddoni greeted her father with a formal embrace. Afterward, he stared at him quizzically.

"Have we met before?"

"Once," Dad confirmed. "At the start of the Gadianton uprising. I was introduced to you by Ishkim, Lemech's father, after I was accepted into his clan. I trained as a warrior with the local militia before Ishkim's village was attacked. You inspected our unit while deciding upon a final gathering place for Zarahemla's citizens."

Kerra and Brock were mesmerized. Their father had already *met* this man? He'd trained as a *warrior*? What else might they learn before this day ended?

It was Lachoneus, the Chief Judge, who responded. "Yes, I remember now." He also embraced Mi′con, but Kerra perceived that he did so with reluctance and suspicion. "I remember it well. Your race was unfamiliar to me." He looked Mi′con up and down. "It is *still* unfamiliar. I've never met someone with features like yours." He took in Grandpa Lee, Kerra, and Brock. "Or like those of your family."

"I've led a unique life," Dad replied, "and one filled with much tragedy and distress."

It was a clever way, thought Kerra, of diverting the subject.

"We understand," said Captain Gidgiddoni. "Most of the people of Zarahemla could express similar feelings. We are told that you were held captive for two years by Akuhuun, son of Giddianhi, before you escaped. We are told that your wife and child are still enslaved."

Dad nodded. "Yes. I learned this only recently, from the lips of a dying man."

"That man was your brother-in-law, Ishlom, son of Ishkim. Is that right?" asked Lachoneus.

"Yes," said Dad, glancing at Lemech.

Gidgiddoni also referred to his brother-in-law and said, "Lemech, the eldest son of Ishkim, tells us that you might know the secret resorts of Akuhuun and possibly other Gadianton bands still holed up in the mountains."

"Possibly," said Dad, sounding wary.

Lachoneus's next question had an accusing tone. "Is it true that you escaped two years ago?"

Dad hesitated. To him only six months had elapsed. But would that have made any difference? "That's right," he replied.

"Why did you not immediately return to the camp of Zarahemla and reveal everything that you knew about Akuhuun to our forces?"

Dad squared his shoulders. "If I had been able to return, I would have. I would have come here to find my wife, Paísha, and my infant son. I would have striven to save them from the fate that has now befallen them. Circumstances beyond my control prevented this from happening."

"Circumstances beyond your control?" said Lachoneus skeptically. "I think you better explain that. Do you mean that you were *forced* to return to your homeland? *Forced* to reunite with your other family? Your *original* family?"

Lachoneus's implication wasn't clear. Maybe it was a subtle accusation of bigamy. In any event, the Chief Judge obviously didn't trust Mi´con or his story.

Dad's voice remained even-toned and unyielding. "Judge Lachoneus, that is *precisely* what I mean. For all these months I have yearned with every drop of my blood to return to this land. Ishlom's appearance—his death—made that return possible."

"His appearance and death . . . made your return *possible?*" asked Lachoneus, noting a curious absence of logic.

Kerra snarled under her breath. For a prophet, Judge Lachoneus seemed a hard-nosed, unsympathetic administrator. She didn't want to pass a wrong judgment on him. From his point of view, skepticism was certainly understandable. Without getting into the intricacies of whispering voices, energy walls, and time portals, how could he be expected to swallow Dad's story? To him it sounded like the standard hard-luck tale of a soldier gone AWOL.

Dad wisely avoided trying to explain the archway and rift. He lifted his chin and said fiercely, "I am a man of honor, and I would not have deliberately kept *any* information from—"

The speech was cut short. Gidgiddoni put a hand on Lachoneus's silver armband to dispel the contention, but he directed his remarks at Dad. "No one is suggesting that you are not a man of honor, Mi´con. If you say that you were prevented from returning, then we accept your word." He glanced at Lachoneus. "*I* accept your word."

Lachoneus puffed his cheeks in and out. Finally, he looked down, conceding that he may have misspoken. Or perhaps he realized they simply had no choice. Mi´con was here now. And he definitely had knowledge that no one else seemed to possess. Kerra took advantage of this brief lull in conversation and finally broached the subject that was consuming her mind.

"I confirm what my father is saying," she began. "My brother and grandfather will confirm it too. If my dad could have returned earlier, he'd have done so. Not a day went by that he didn't wish to return. It was the same for me. I would have come with him. I am *also* looking for someone. Someone very important to me. His name is Kiddoni. He is a Nephite warrior."

Gidgiddoni, Lachoneus, and Lemech considered Kerra carefully. She couldn't read their expressions.

She pursued further. "It was Kiddoni who warned the armies of Zarahemla that the Gadianton warriors were invading. During the Great Battle his shoulder was pierced by an arrow."

Lemech cleared his throat and said soberly, respectfully, "I knew Kiddoni. I knew his clan. His family dwelled peacefully with my family here in this valley for more than a generation."

"I also knew Kiddoni," said Gidgiddoni. "I promoted him to the rank of battalion commander following the death of Giddianhi, shortly after his wound had healed."

Kerra's heart started to ache. She burst into a cold sweat. Why did they say *knew*? Why had they spoken in the past tense?

She swallowed hard, voice quivering. "Where is he?"

"His battalion," said Gidgiddoni mournfully, "is missing."

Kerra waited for more. The Nephite captain didn't seem to have anything to add.

"Missing?" Kerra repeated.

Lachoneus, his gruff personality having faded and softened, explained, "Yes. His battalion has been missing for more than four months."

Grandpa Lee inquired, "How many men comprise a battalion?"

"Three hundred," said Gidgiddoni.

Kerra sounded as if she was starting to hyperventilate as she asked, "How can three hundred men just be missing?"

Dad went to her and offered support.

Gidgiddoni replied, "We have lost three battalions in the last year. Kiddoni's battalion is the latest."

"What direction did they travel?" asked Dad.

"South," said Lachoneus, "upriver, into the wilderness of Hermounts."

"It makes no sense," said Grandpa Lee. "There must be some evidence. Bodies. Weapons. Nine hundred men don't just vanish into thin air."

Lachoneus sighed. Gidgiddoni gritted his teeth. It was plainly an issue that had caused both men—in fact, every citizen of Zarahemla—considerable stress and anxiety.

But for Kerra it was something else. More than just stress or anxiety. It was like a part of herself withering, fading away. For most of her life, Kiddoni—that is, her *memory* of Kiddoni—had been more like dream. For a brief period—so very brief—the dream had become reality. Now it was becoming . . . she didn't even know. Kiddoni had made the puzzle fit: the pointless puzzle of her life. A world without him made no sense, even a world with a gap of twenty centuries. Kiddoni was *not* gone, she decided. He was not dead. If Kiddoni had perished in the last four months, the puzzle of her life became pointless again. Absolutely unintelligible.

"As I mentioned before," said Lemech, "many of the soldiers attribute such losses to the sorceries and spells of the Reds."

Gidgiddoni's temper flared. "That is nonsense. I don't want to hear any more of that kind of tripe, especially from a warrior of Zarahemla. Until the full fate of these battalions is known and documented, you will do everything possible to contain such rumors."

Lemech bit his cheek and looked away. Tears slipped from Kerra's eyes. It felt like some kind of mechanism was inside her with someone relentlessly spinning the crank.

Dad said to Gidgiddoni, "Those mountains are as treacherous as any terrain I've ever encountered. Other factors may explain the disappearance of so many men."

"Other factors?" said Lachoneus.

Dad opened his mouth but then looked to Grandpa Lee. Grandpa actually looked to Kerra. Kerra added nothing. Dad appeared uneasy, as if he'd stuck his foot in his mouth. Kerra wasn't certain what her father might have wanted to say. Was he about to say that "other factors" might include time portals to other centuries? It seemed a stretch. Nothing that anyone had witnessed in the wooded hollow near Leeds, Utah, would have explained the disappearance of nine hundred men. Finally, Dad declared, "I only mean that it's a complex land with many hidden valleys and corridors. An army might find itself lost for months."

"Is it the same region where you were enslaved for two years?" asked Lachoneus.

Mi´con nodded. "Yes, I think so."

For several moments Gidgiddoni had been in a state of quiet contemplation. He finally revealed his thoughts. "If you returned to this wilderness," he asked Mi´con, "could you lead a battalion of Nephite and Lamanite warriors to the secret hiding places of Akuhuun and his followers? Could you do so in such a way that the Gadiantons might be taken by surprise? A way that our captive men and women might be set free?"

Dad looked overwhelmed. Breathlessly, he said, "My guess—my *suspicion*—is that a small party of men might secretly infiltrate such a region better than an entire battalion."

"We're not interested in just 'infiltrating,'" said Lachoneus. "The Gadianton robbers must be crushed. Their disease must be wiped off the face of the land. Otherwise there will never be peace in Zarahemla.

Our cities and villages will continue to be harassed. Our armies will have to remain on constant alert for marauders. Our crops and food supplies will be forever threatened. Our women and children will be in perpetual—"

Gidgiddoni raised his hand to cut off the Chief Judge. He sent Lachoneus an apologetic look then focused again on Mi´con. "I must ask you a more direct question. Akuhuun, the son of Giddianhi— would you recognize him on sight?"

Dad drew a deep breath. "Yeah. I would recognize him."

Kerra saw her father shudder.

"I assure you," said Gidgiddoni soberly, "this is no small thing. You're the only person in these quarters who has ever laid eyes on him. You may be the only man who has seen him among all of the soldiers of this army. So I ask you, will you lead a battalion of warriors into the wilderness of Hermounts to find Akuhuun? And also to rescue your wife and son?"

Dad couldn't hide his uncertainty. "I have never commanded a batta—"

Gidgiddoni shook his head. "I'm sorry. You misunderstand me. By 'lead' I do not mean *command*. You would not be the Battalion Commander. Rather, you would be its guide. Its scout."

Dad's expression changed. He looked relieved. He now pondered the question in all seriousness. "I may know a way that a battalion can enter the region in relative secrecy. But I would have to backtrack to the area where we began our journey. You already know this ground. It's the same place where the Nephite army fought against the blood-painted forces of Giddianhi two years ago."

"You traveled here this morning from the same ground as the Great Battle?" asked Gidgiddoni.

"Yes," Dad confirmed.

Kerra wondered why Gidgiddoni had asked this question, and in such an unusual tone. Did he know something about the mysterious powers at work in this area? Did he know about the archway or the conduits of energy? If so, the Chief Captain never revealed it.

"With God's help," Dad continued, "I will find a place very near this area where I can leave my children in a state of relative safety. From there, our battalion can embark directly into Gadianton-held territory."

Lachoneus looked deeply concerned. He said to Gidgiddoni, "Who would command this battalion? Under your direction, our best commanders have been asked to remain close to our fortifications."

Gidgiddoni pondered this and said with regret, "I would command the battalion myself, but our situation in this valley remains tenuous. I must complete the fortifications that are only beginning to fully take shape. It is to my eternal regret that I have allowed *any* of our battalions to venture so deeply into the wilderness. I have conceded to the demands of our citizens who believe such strategies may bring this war to a speedy conclusion, and we have repeatedly paid a heavy price for such folly. It is my conviction that the robbers will soon become so deprived of food and provisions that they will be compelled to lay siege to our strongholds. They will come to *us*. And still the voices pressuring us to seek out the Gadiantons in their places of hiding increase day by day. Our people have grown dangerously restless. They only wish to return to their lands and fields. In time, stopping their homeward migration may become as difficult as stopping a migration of butterflies. So, in a final effort to quell such restlessness, I will allow one last battalion to leave these precincts."

"Who would be our commander?" asked Lemech, making it clear that he was its first volunteer.

Gidgiddoni looked at Lachoneus. "My nephew."

The Chief Judge's eyes widened. It was obvious this suggestion did not stimulate overwhelming confidence.

Lemech replied carefully, "Your nephew . . . the *drunk*?"

Gidgiddoni flinched. His eyes darkened while Lemech's cheeks paled, probably wishing he'd kept his opinion to himself.

Gidgiddoni said fiercely, "My nephew is one of the finest warriors in this army." He turned to Mi´con. "You revealed to us that your life has had much tragedy and distress. The same holds true for my nephew. His parents and siblings—my own brother, nieces, and nephews—were tortured and slain by Gadianton assassins. It happened shortly after my nephew returned from a campaign with the Rattlesnake Battalion. He'd rooted out many members of a particularly rapacious band of Gadiantons in the East Wilderness whose warriors are loyal to Akuhuun. My nephew suffered terrible losses—some of his bravest comrades. I am told he personally slew many high-ranking

Gadianton robbers with his own sword, including Zemnarihah's brother, Gamnor. However, some slipped away. Afterward, they sought vengeance against my nephew. In addition to my brother and his family, his wife-to-be, too, was murdered by assassins—a girl whom he loved since childhood." He added solemnly, "He has been in mourning ever since. Something like this, a fresh campaign, something of such import, might shake him from his grief."

Lemech asked the Chief Captain, "May I speak freely?"

Gidgiddoni's shoulders slumped. He wasn't eager to hear what Lemech had to say but felt he had no choice. "You may," he replied tiredly.

"Your nephew has lost respect. The army of Zarahemla believes his judgment is unsound. There are things that happened in the East Wilderness. Things that few soldiers will discuss. No battalion of men will follow him—not on such a dangerous campaign. In his grief—his bitterness and drunkenness—he has abused many people, brawling in public, nearly killing several men—"

Gidgiddoni interrupted. "I am perfectly aware of my nephew's mistakes—"

Lemech continued vigorously. "Not many would agree that his Rattlesnake warriors led a successful campaign. They believe his tactics were . . . revolting. Perverse. Moreover, I have heard that your nephew is a man of . . ." He struggled to find an appropriate description and settled on, ". . . broken mind. They say his is unstable. It seems only a matter of time before his violent nature causes—"

Gidgiddoni had heard enough. "Lemech, I do not accept your characterization. He is *not* a man of 'broken mind.' He is a strict commander. If you knew him the way that *I* know him . . ." Gidgiddoni paused. He seemed to feel awkward. Clearly he did not wish to make this personal. This was a *military* decision. He finally added, "His mistakes have been dealt with according to our laws. There has been no special treatment."

Judge Lachoneus inquired, "Is he still in the brig?"

"He was released a few days ago," said Gidgiddoni. "And if he were to seriously hurt someone—deliberately or accidentally—the penalty would be swift and harsh. The fact that he is my kin would not protect him from our laws."

"What about in the wilds?" said Lemech. "If he is to be our commander in the wilderness of Hermounts then, out there, he would *be* the law."

"I have heard your concerns," said Gidgiddoni impatiently. "I will give the matter due diligence. Find Shiloah. Have the Captain of the Guard summon my nephew to meet here tomorrow morning. I will assess his . . . demeanor." He sent Lemech a look of warning. "Afterward, my decision will be final."

Brock felt intrigued. Without ever having laid eyes on this supposed ill-tempered drunkard, he looked forward to meeting him. Honestly, such a character reminded him of the riff-raff he used to hang with in L.A. But what was his name? No one seemed inclined to utter it, as if the mere syllables carried a curse, like Voldemort or Sauron or some other evil moniker that might turn someone into a pillar of salt.

Boldly, Brock asked the Chief Captain, "What is he called? I mean, does your nephew have a name?"

Gidgiddoni eyed Brock, as if noticing the youngster for the first time.

"Of course," said the Chief Captain. "He is my namesake. My brother gave me this honor at his naming ceremony. He is called Gidgiddonihah."

CHAPTER 10

A DISCUSSION OF GIDGIDDONIHAH, THE Chief Captain's nephew, continued around the campfire after returning to Lemech's tent. It lasted late into the night. Dad's brother-in-law had a distinctly negative opinion, but other soldiers, whose tents were near enough to overhear the conversation, offered alternative perspectives.

Gidgiddonihah, they said, was a very young warrior—about twenty years old. The same age, thought Kerra, as Kiddoni. His drink of preference, according to the bawdy gathering, was a strong grog derived from corn and sweet potatoes. Whenever Kerra sensed prejudice, that prejudice was surprisingly visceral. For now she was more interested in his credentials as a battalion commander. Her questions tried to glean additional info about the tragedies heaped on his family, particularly the murder of his fiancée. Such events, both fans and detractors claimed, had left him deeply embittered, unapproachable, and even—in the view of some—dangerous.

Virtually everyone held the opinion that he was an extraordinary warrior. Several went so far as call him "the most lethal soldier in all the armies of Zarahemla." Still, certain decisions he'd made during his campaign in the East Wilderness had left a rotten taste in many mouths and raised serious doubts about his future leadership potential. Despite Kerra's efforts to learn more about exactly what had occurred, no one was inclined to discuss it. She suspected that most were just going off vague rumors. She couldn't have said if a single person in the gathering had firsthand knowledge of anything regarding the matter.

Mostly what Kerra learned were the bare-bones facts: Of the three hundred or so men of the Rattlesnake Battalion, fully one-third had been slain. Another third had returned with harsh disciplinary sanctions hanging over their heads—sanctions brought upon them by their commander, Gidgiddonihah. Charges ranged from cowardice to insubordination to mutiny—some that carried the penalty of death. However, by the time such charges were to have been recorded, Gidgiddonihah experienced a change of heart. Because of the severe loss of life and the sheer number of delinquent warriors, most penalties were reduced or expunged. Gidgiddonihah said he did not wish to compound the tragedy, proclaiming that his men "had witnessed enough death and bloodshed."

This show of mercy did little to mollify ill will in the ranks. Many soldiers of Zarahemla considered Gidgiddonihah a tyrant. Some believed his actions had actually *caused* the battalion's massive losses. A few of the men, however, painted a very different picture. They said if it hadn't been for Gidgiddonihah—his controversial decisions and ruthless counteroffensive—*no* soldiers would have survived. The Rattlesnake Battalion would have ceased to exist, much like the other three missing battalions. As it was, Gidgiddonihah's campaign in the East Wilderness had virtually erased any sizable threat from robber bands in that district. Nevertheless, Gidgiddonihah's success had provoked an unprecedented crusade of revenge.

The assassination of Gidgiddonihah's family members began shortly after the Rattlesnake Battalion's return. His fiancée, Chani, was the last to be slain. One of his lieutenants had caught a glimpse of Chani's fleeing assassin and offered his commander a detailed description. Gidgiddonihah had supposedly branded those details onto his memory. A rumor was even started that some of Gidgiddonihah's own soldiers had participated in this horror. Even Gid dismissed these rumors, but as soon as word of it reached his uncle, the Chief Captain, he relieved his nephew of command. Gidgiddoni announced that Gidgiddonihah's discharge was for his own protection and the protection of his men. Privately, Lachoneus and others believed it was to prevent the headstrong commander from unleashing a wave of vengeance so rabid and reckless that it might ensure his destruction. The army's rumor mill concluded that Gidgiddonihah was being deliberately punished. Some weeks later, after Gidgiddonihah was imprisoned after a drunken brawl that injured four of his harshest critics, these rumors seemed verified.

He'd languished in the army's brig for two full months. His uncle had approved his release only a few days earlier. According to Lemech and his comrades, the former battalion commander hadn't experienced a sober moment since.

Dad, Kerra, and Brock requested to be present when Shiloah, the Captain of the Guard, approached Gidgiddonihah at his tent the following morning. Shiloah was not looking forward to the task. He almost delegated the responsibility to an underling. He realized, however, that if the commander failed to appear, the reprimand might be severe. Besides, watching the reaction of these strange newcomers to the sight of the broken-down warrior/nephew of Captain Gidgiddoni might be sadistically entertaining.

Grandpa Lee had also expressed a desire to join the others, but he'd overslept. Dad refused to rouse him, feeling that Grandpa Lee needed all the slumber possible if it would help him "catch his wind."

At approximately 7:00 AM, Kerra, Brock, and Dad, along with the Captain of the Guard, were poised outside a tent on the outskirts of the army's encampment. Shiloah had recruited two of his burlier guardsmen to come along in case Gidgiddonihah became unruly or uncooperative. There was a stream behind the commander's tent, running southward toward the local refuse dump. The stench was foul, attracting flies and other vermin.

Brock plugged his nose and whispered to Kerra, "He'll smell just like a Gadianton. This means when we reach the wilderness, he'll help us to fit right in."

Dad, Brock, and Kerra glued their gaze to the doorway of the tent. Kerra felt far more suspense than she'd expected. *Please*, she prayed, *let the Chief Captain's appraisal of his nephew be accurate.* The life of Kiddoni, as well as her stepmother and half-brother, depended upon this individual's skills and abilities. According to the Book of Mormon, Captain Gidgiddoni was an inspired man. He wouldn't just assign such a mission to any random commander. According to every opinion expressed, they were being sent into the very nest of the most ruthless robbers still at large in Zarahemla.

Kerra tried to temper her expectations. Nobody looked especially great at this hour of the morning. She couldn't expect the man who emerged to evoke immediate confidence. Still, she hoped she might perceive someone whose persona at least hinted at something noble and powerful.

Shiloah and his two attendants approached the tent entrance.

"Gidgiddonihah!" shouted Shiloah.

He waited only a few seconds before pushing aside the flap and entering. His attendants followed. A moment later, Shiloah stepped back outside, looking in all directions.

"Gidgiddonihah!" he cried again.

Kerra groaned inwardly. Their eminent leader wasn't even home. She felt deflated.

Brock heard something and glanced into the undergrowth behind him. While the others remained focused on Shiloah and his attendants, Brock took several steps into the weeds.

A body appeared before him. A *dead* body—or that's how it appeared. It was facedown, motionless. Then Brock heard something. A breath? A grunt? The man wore only a loincloth. Otherwise his skin was totally exposed to insects and the bright morning sun. He was muscular but covered with dirt. Could this be him? Was it possible that here lay the mightiest warrior of all of Zarahemla?

Brock scrunched down just a foot south of the man's head. The figure's back elevated up and down. *Definitely breathing*, thought Brock. He started to raise his hand. His intent was to nudge the man's shoulder, hardly expecting any reaction. The dude was obviously plastered. It might take a barrel of ice water to rouse him.

Brock's fingers had barely made contact with the man's flesh—honestly, he wasn't certain he'd actually *touched* him. The next events occurred so swiftly Brock couldn't have described it. When he experienced his next cognizant thought, Brock was lying flat on his back, a metal hatchet blade against his throat. He sucked a deep breath. There wasn't even time for his life to pass before his eyes. He tried to focus on his attacker's face. His attacker was doing much the same thing, opening and closing his blood-red eyes, shaking his jowls, trying to determine exactly who or what trembled at the edge of his blade. Brock couldn't quite figure out how a man who'd just reacted with the speed of a black mamba suddenly looked so unsteady on his feet.

"Who are you?" the man asked, voice slurred.

"N-no one!" Brock squealed. "A kid!"

Kerra and Dad were now close at hand. Shiloah and his attendants had also moved in.

"Gidgiddonihah!" Shiloah cried. "Let him go!"

Simultaneously, Dad pleaded, "My son meant no harm. *Please!*"

Gidgiddonihah made a careful, bleary-eyed appraisal of everyone standing about. After a moment he removed the hatchet from Brock's throat and straightened his back. Shiloah and his attendants edged closer, but they weren't about to move in. Gidgiddonihah was still armed with his gleaming copper hatchet, and whatever his condition, he was clearly adept at using it.

Kerra studied the man's face. He wasn't particularly handsome. Then again, how could she tell? Half inebriated. Eyes red and swollen. Dark hair a rat's nest. Gidgiddonihah used his wrist to wipe crusted spittle from his chin. Dirt and weeds were stuck to his forehead and all down the front of his chest. Still, thought Kerra, he had a distinctive face. Not flawless. Not prettily sculpted. If anything was unappealing, it was probably his nose—flat and squat with large nostrils. But no. On reassessment, Kerra decided it *worked*. It fit him perfectly, giving him precisely the character and charisma she'd first hoped for and imagined.

He sported a thick sheen of facial hair, unusually dark, especially since most Nephites and Lamanites had little facial hair to begin with. Gidgiddonihah had what might have amounted to three days' growth for her *father*. For a Nephite, perhaps it was two or three *weeks'* worth of scrub.

As it clicked in Brock's mind that he wasn't about to die, he scrambled like a rabbit to get far away.

"Gidgiddonihah," Shiloah repeated, "you have been summoned by your uncle. We are here to escort you to the tent of Captain Gidgiddoni."

He looked up at Shiloah, eyes blank, as if he hadn't understood. Or didn't care. He focused on something beyond those gathered around him and began walking forward. Shiloah and his attendants gave him plenty of room. That hatchet remained tight in his fist. Gidgiddonihah obliviously bypassed Shiloah, Kerra, and his own tent. He was headed toward the stream.

The current running behind his tent was moderately clean for the next twenty yards, until it mingled with the community's refuse.

Gidgiddonihah dropped his weapon on the bank and tromped, without hesitation, into the cool water until he'd reached the middle. He faced upstream, shut his eyes, and held out his arms as if challenging an oncoming train. He timbered forward like a felled redwood, sending up a huge splash and disappearing beneath the surface. He didn't come up right away. He seemed perfectly happy facedown under the current.

Shiloah and his men didn't want to miss such an opportune moment to fulfill their orders. The attendants rushed into the stream while Shiloah retrieved the abandoned hatchet. Shiloah's guards positioned themselves on either side of the submerged warrior. After waiting another ten seconds, perhaps fearing the Chief Captain's nephew was drowning, they reached under the surface to hoist him to his feet.

As they grasped his shoulders, Gidgiddonihah sprang back to life. Water exploded as the warrior twisted to the left and right, popping a fist and one elbow. In seconds both men were flat on their backs, floating listlessly in the current. Gidgiddonihah was the only man left standing.

Disoriented, both attendants finally crawled to the bank and tried to assert a new aggressive posture—from fifteen feet away. Kerra couldn't help grinning. The battalion commander stood in the water, poised like a tiger. *No*, thought Kerra—*like a jaguar*. It seemed remarkable to her how every muscle and movement reminded her of the animal that had emerged from the vortex. The attendants huffed and spat, mad as hornets, although neither of them dared step back in range of Gidgiddonihah's fists.

Shiloah shouted angrily, "Don't make another move! Attack these men again and I'll have you thrown back into the brig! We are here on Gidgiddoni's orders! You are to accompany us to his tent *now!*"

Gidgiddonihah seemed, for the first time, to fully notice the people standing around him. His speech slightly slurred, he repeated, "Gidgiddoni?"

"Your uncle the Chief Captain!" Shiloah blustered.

Gidgiddonihah raised his eyebrows. "Oh." He smiled crookedly. "Why didn't you just say so?"

CHAPTER 11

"I LIKE HIM," SAID BROCK.

"He's a walking disaster," said Dad.

Grandpa said grumpily, "I'd love to offer my opinion, but *nobody woke me up!*"

They'd been waiting outside the Chief Captain's headquarters for ten minutes. Shiloah and his men had entered the tent with Gidgiddonihah. This time Dad and the others were not invited to follow and hear what was said. Kerra imagined that they were enthusiastically recounting Gidgiddonihah's misdeeds from earlier that morning. Moments later Shiloah and his guards reemerged, looking crestfallen and embittered.

"What's happening?" Dad inquired.

"He's being briefed," Shiloah replied.

The attendants laughed at their superior's answer, but without mirth.

"Good luck with your . . . *expedition*," spat the Captain of the Guard. He and his men continued on without expressing another syllable, evidently grateful just to be done with the matter. Kerra presumed that all three men would be glad never to set eyes on the Chief Captain's nephew again.

Lachoneus was not inside the tent with Captain Gidgiddoni and Commander Gidgiddonihah. Another important meeting was taking place about seventy-five yards to the west, in an open area that looked like a traditional meeting place for the Chief Judge and his lesser judges, alongside the tribal and kinship leaders of Zarahemla. At present there were about two hundred or so Nephites and Lamanites, many of them wrinkled and long in the tooth. From where Kerra sat she could only make out snatches of certain sentences and phrases, but it was plainly a heated discussion. Lachoneus was making it clear in no uncertain terms that families were *not* to begin any homeward migrations until further notice.

It was apparently heartbreaking news. The outcry was intense. Tribal leaders had somehow gotten it into their heads that the Gadianton insurgents were on their last legs—on the verge of starvation. Rumors were also rampant about infighting between Gadiantons loyal to Akuhuun or Zemnarihah. They had begun to seriously question the Reds' ability to organize an effective assault. "Besides," said one clan leader, "they are holed up in the uninhabitable wilderness! We only desire to return to the lands and cities of our inheritance!"

"The roads remain unsafe," warned Lachoneus. "The Gadianton robbers are as strong today as one year ago—perhaps stronger!" He reminded them of the three battalions that had disappeared in the mountains and further warned that, "Any families who attempt to leave the places of security established by our army or who take important provisions from the encampment will be rounded up by the warriors of Zarahemla! Clan leaders will be summarily punished!"

Some of the fervor died down after that. The mood remained grim and tense, but voices decreased in volume. Lachoneus began to answer as best he could many questions regarding how soon the situation might change, what plans the army was undertaking to resolve the crisis, and other matters and complaints that were probably typical of these kinds of meetings.

A full hour had passed as they waited in the increasingly oppressive heat.

Dad turned to Kerra. "We haven't heard your opinion yet. What do *you* think of our battalion commander?"

Kerra pondered the question. "I'm not sure. I think he's a very skilled soldier."

"That doesn't make him a qualified commander," said Grandpa Lee. "Did he really nearly cut off my grandson's head?"

Brock waved it off. "Ah, I just startled him."

"And then you practically wet your pants," added Kerra.

"Another exaggeration."

"So why do *you* like him?" Dad asked his son.

"He reminds me of that eye-patch dude in *True Grit*," said Brock. "The John Wayne version. Not that newer piece of crud."

"John Wayne." Dad rolled his eyes. "Oh, brother."

"Sure," said Brock. "Not a perfect hero by any means. But with *grit*. Lots of grit."

"You watch too many movies," said Dad.

"Thank you," said Brock.

Dad continued. "We don't need grit. We need *integrity*. This is my wife and son. It's the lives of my wife, my daughter, and *both* of my sons. A lot of other sons and daughters, too. If this man is just an ill-tempered, reckless drunk who deserves no respect from his troops, he could easily get us all killed."

"His *uncle* has integrity," said Kerra. "His uncle is a prophet."

Dad, Brock, and Grandpa looked at her with surprise. Kerra realized any kind of religious sentiment from her lips sounded peculiar and out of character.

She tempered her statement slightly. "At least there are a lot of people who *believe* he's a prophet. Gidgiddoni wouldn't make this decision lightly. If he believes his nephew is up to the task . . . I think we should give Gidgiddonihah a chance."

"Gid," said Brock, testing the name in the air. "I'm calling him Gid. The other's too dang long."

"I'd be careful about that," said Grandpa. "Not so sure it's a good idea, unless you want him to *really* chop—"

At that instant Gidgiddonihah emerged from his uncle's tent. He was closely followed by two soldiers whom Kerra and the others hadn't seen before—young soldiers. *Very* young. One of them was definitely younger than Kerra—fifteen or sixteen. These warriors fought to keep up with Gid. Dad tried to step into the commander's path, determined to introduce himself and find out more about the expedition. Kerra could tell by Gidgiddonihah's pace—and the fact that he gave her father no eye contact—that he had no intention of stopping. She thought Dad might permit the commander to barrel over the top of him, but Dad stopped just short of a collision. Gidgiddonihah stormed on by. At the last second, however, he *did* make eye contact. Not with Dad. But with Kerra.

It was an obvious double take. Gid even faltered in his step. Kerra tolerated the eye contact for about two seconds then looked away. She wasn't sure why he suddenly found her so curious. She'd been less than ten feet away for most of the morning as he was escorted to Gidgiddoni's tent. She presumed he'd finally sobered up enough to notice. But as soon as Kerra averted her gaze, Gidgiddonihah did the same. He continued toward some unknown destination without further delay.

Kerra noticed Brock smiling at her. The little twerp had seen the whole thing. She ignored him—almost violently.

The two young soldiers who'd been following Gid halted in their pursuit, pausing alongside Dad and the others.

"What's the situation?" Dad asked them.

"What's wrong with him?" asked Grandpa Lee, nudging toward Gidgiddonihah.

"Don't let my cousin vex you," said the older of the two soldiers. "I am Manazzeh, son of Gidgiddoni. This is my brother, Chemnon."

"Nice to meet you," said Dad, scrutinizing them carefully. "The Chief Captain is your father?"

Manazzeh nodded. The young man was close to Kerra's age, which meant he was only a year or two younger than Gidgiddonihah. Still, he carried himself in a way that seemed to represent himself as Gid's equal. He had a muscular build like his father, but his short, thick hair stood almost straight up from his head, like a large, black cowlick. His brother, on the other hand, wore a haircut that reminded Kerra of a young Beatle, except for an overly long tail in the back. If the tail hadn't been so straight and sleek, she might have called it a mullet.

"My father has ordered us to accompany your battalion," said the older brother, Manazzeh.

"I take it that the commander wasn't too happy about that," observed Grandpa.

The younger brother, Chemnon, grunted. "Gidgiddonihah isn't too happy about much of anything right now."

"Is he going to lead the battalion?" asked Brock.

Chemnon noticed Brock. The young officer made a small smile and tousled Brock's hair. Brock didn't appreciate this. Even Kerra felt it was patronizing. After all he was only Brock's elder by a couple of years.

Chemnon replied, "Oh yes. He'll lead the battalion. He's going now to organize the other Rattlesnake platoon leaders. My father wanted us to stand with him, but . . . apparently my cousin doesn't believe that will be necessary."

"I thought your cousin wasn't particularly popular among the troops," said Kerra.

Even before she'd opened her mouth, Manazzeh and Chemnon stole frequent glances in her direction. Now that she'd spoken, they offered her their full attention.

"Among some, perhaps," said Manazzeh. "But there are others who would march with him to the death. You are Mi´con's daughter, the girl who will march with us as far as the Great Battleground?"

Kerra nodded but not convincingly. She hadn't quite decided how far she intended to march. She'd figure that out later.

"I wanted to introduce myself to the commander," said Dad peevishly.

"He already knows who you are," said Manazzeh.

This incensed Dad all the more. "Then why brush me off? I'm supposed to be his guide. Shouldn't he want to talk to me?"

Kerra suspected her father's offense also had something to do with Gidgiddonihah's age. The officer was, after all, only twenty years old. What forty-plus-year-old *wouldn't* be put off by the impudence of a twenty-year-old? Especially one who'd been assigned as his superior?

"He'll talk to you," Manazzeh assured, "in his own time. He's still getting used to the whole idea. Actually, I'm not sure he likes being a commander. My cousin is more of a lone wolf."

A new voice boomed. "That's not true."

It was their father, Captain Gidgiddoni, having emerged from his tent, approaching from behind.

He glared at his older son with disapproval. "Gidgiddonihah is a fine commander. He has great talent and even stronger instincts. Moreover, he is a true soldier who would never reject a commission from his Chief Captain."

Manazzeh looked shamefully toward the ground, embarrassed that his father had overheard. Kerra, however, sensed that Gidgiddoni's words didn't quite gel.

She said to the Captain, "If you feel he's such a fine commander, why have you asked your sons to accompany us?"

It was a cheeky question. Gidgiddoni was slightly taken aback. He quickly regained his authoritative composure. "Because my sons will one day lead armies of their own. And there is much that they could learn from a warrior like Gidgiddonihah."

He glanced from one son to the other to make sure they'd heard him clearly. Kerra stared at the Chief Captain. His statement wasn't convincing. She still wasn't satisfied. Something told her that his sons were somehow meant to keep his nephew in line.

"When are we leaving?" asked Brock.

"If all comes together as planned, you will leave tomorrow morning," said Gidgiddoni.

"That soon?" asked Grandpa. "Is that possible?"

"Of course," said Manazzeh.

"We're Nephites," said Chemnon.

Both sons looked straight at Kerra as they said this. *Oh, brother*, she thought. Were there really girls in this world who enjoyed such superficial attention? It was nauseating. Neither of these teenagers seemed to care too deeply about who she was or why she was here.

The Chief Captain ignored his sons' bravado and spoke to Dad seriously. "Your mission to Hermounts is critical to our cause. For several years now we have known that there is an internal struggle within the Gadianton sect. Ever since the death of Giddianhi, two separate forces have been vying for power, neither prevailing. The forces of Zemnarihah, who was always Giddianhi's second-in-command and heir apparent, and those of Akuhuun, Giddianhi's only son who came to prominence quite unexpectedly after his father's death. Before that he was sort of a mystical figure, kept to himself, and did not aspire to leadership and power. Obviously all that has changed. It is vital that one of these forces succeeds and the other fails. No one understands these dynamics better than Commander Gidgiddonihah."

"Which force," asked Grandpa Lee, "are you hoping will fail?"

Gidgiddoni smiled faintly, eyes radiating a dark confidence, almost as if the information that answered this question had come to him . . . as a revelation.

The Chief Captain said to Grandpa Lee, "I have a feeling that Mi´con knows the answer to that question as well as any other warrior of Zarahemla. I will let him answer it for you." He straightened up. "I must attend to other matters. My sons will direct your preparations. I'll see you off at first light."

CHAPTER 12

THERE WASN'T MUCH FANFARE.

As a matter of fact, Kerra almost had the feeling that this new expedition into the wilderness was something of a secret. It was, after all, an expedition that went directly against Gidgiddoni's military philosophy. For more than two years he'd strived to draw the enemy to *him*. He did not want to hunt Gadiantons. He wanted them, in essence, to knock on his door. It was clear that this whole policy shift of sending battalions into the wilderness was a foolish mistake—an attempt to appease certain civilian pressures—and it weighed heavily on his conscience. This mission, with God's help, would be the last time any such effort would be necessary.

Captain Gidgiddoni organized the sendoff about a half mile into the forest and only a few minutes after sunrise. Approximately three hundred men, most of them less than eager, lined up for an inspection conducted by Captain Gidgiddoni and his nephew, Gidgiddonihah.

Gid appeared equally unenthusiastic. Then again, thought Kerra, "unenthusiastic" might not have been the right word. Oh, it was accurate enough. It's just that his *reasons* had little in common with his men's. Kerra suspected it was *because* of the men that Gid regretted being here. The misgivings, and even the outright *loathing*, that most of these warriors felt for Gidgiddonihah was so thick that it could almost be sliced with a knife. And it still wasn't clear to Kerra why they felt this way. What exactly *had* occurred in the East Wilderness a few months earlier that had left these warriors with such a bad taste in their mouths? Kerra was determined to find out the full rationale the first chance she got.

Captain Gidgiddoni walked among the ranks before their departure. "You have been chosen," he began, "for one of the most important campaigns of this long war. I have full confidence that my nephew is, without reservation, the right person to lead you. I have obtained this confidence not only from my long career as a military strategist, serving under Captain Moronihah, son of Moroni, but also from my faith in the Lord Jesus Christ."

Kerra crinkled an eyebrow. That was laying it on a bit thick, wasn't it? Religious references from a military commander struck her as odd. Gidgiddoni was pulling out all the stops in an effort to heal the prevailing prejudice toward his nephew. It seemed manipulative—using religion this way. Then Kerra reminded herself: To these soldiers, Gidgiddoni was not just their Chief Captain. He was their *prophet*.

Gidgiddoni continued. "If any of you have ever trusted the spirit of revelation which I have exercised in leading the armies of Zarahemla, I ask you to trust in that gift now. I have organized this campaign and assigned its leaders exercising all of my powers in this sacred office. So I make a promise. I promise that if you will exercise *your* faith in Christ, and your faith in me as His representative, this mission will succeed, the wicked ambitions of the Gadianton armies will be thwarted as a direct result of your service, and the fervent desires of your families to return home to their lands will be fulfilled."

Kerra glanced over to see how Gid was reacting to this speech. The Chief Captain's nephew appeared no less surprised by his uncle's bluntness than the rest of the soldiers. It was a bold promise. Her father and grandfather looked deeply moved. Even Brock was beaming with pride, and he wasn't even a soldier! He didn't have a city or village to return home *to*!

But wait a minute. That wasn't true. Kerra realized that Gidgiddoni's promise not only applied to the warriors. It applied to *her* and her family. *They* would be permitted to return home as well. She couldn't have said why she felt so certain of this, but she'd rarely felt so sure about anything.

A fleeting expression of gratitude crossed Gidgiddonihah's face—gratitude that his uncle had made some effort to establish a bond of loyalty. He may not have believed it would work, but at least the effort had been made. Gid's expression quickly changed. Back to business. He followed up the Chief Captain's speech with two words: "*Move out!*"

The command was repeated multiple times by Gid's second-in-command—a veteran warrior named Pek who wore a thick leather cuirass that left his shoulders bare. It seemed that he did this deliberately to display a deep, ragged scar on the left side, running from his neck to the curve of his shoulder. Gidgiddonihah's men of the reconstituted Rattlesnake Battalion marched in a double-file line along the same basic course that Kerra, Brock, Dad, and Grandpa had taken two days before.

It was a hot, greasy day. Water was treated as a precious commodity. A Nephite battalion consisted not only of fighting men, but also men who served as porters, cooks, physicians, and other specialists. Kerra noticed five men carrying barrels or kegs, each seemingly carved from a single piece of wood. Liquid could be heard sloshing inside.

Brock asked a porter, "What's in the barrels?"

"Corn grog," the man replied. With a twisted smile he added, "Our illustrious leader is known to be . . . thirsty."

The other four porters laughed. Kerra didn't find the joke funny at all. Had his uncle's message about the seriousness of this mission fully penetrated his nephew's ears? And yet no one man could possibly consume that much alcohol. What other purpose might it serve?

The warriors were subdivided into archers, spear throwers, dart throwers, and infantrymen who carried obsidian-edged clubs or swords. Dad and Grandpa marched alongside Lemech and several of Lemech's comrades, some of whom Dad had known from the past.

Gidgiddonihah marched at the head of the column. For the most part he was alone and deep in thought, although his personal guard and aides were always about. Somehow, Brock found his way to the front. He walked somewhat behind Gid as the commander drew a leather canteen from his belt and took a long draught. Brock noticed *two* canteens on Gid's belt, along with numerous weapons. He caught a strong whiff of a familiar substance as he came up behind the commander.

"What's in the canteen, uh, your honor, sir??" he asked impishly.

Gid considered him narrowly and said, "Medicine."

"Ah," said Brock. "The kind that washes wounds?"

He replied, half to himself, "Sure. And washes away bad memories."

"Hmm," said Brock. "I got a few of those myself. Maybe you and I could find a time to wash away some bad memories together."

Gidgiddonihah didn't find him quaint or clever. He summoned a pair of guards. "Take the boy back into the ranks."

Brock frowned petulantly. He soon found himself again marching alongside his father, grandfather, and sister.

Once more Kerra's dad expressed irritation that Gid hadn't yet sought an audience. Again Manazzeh and Chemnon reassured him that such a consultation was forthcoming, probably as soon as they reached the day's destination. That destination was the same location where this whole adventure had begun: the area very near to the mysterious archway. To the warriors it was the "Great Battleground"—the place where the former Gadianton leader, Giddianhi, had been defeated and slain. Word was that this single battle was the most violent, the most destructive, in all of Nephite history, with more casualties than any prior conflict. Kerra had read the entire Book of Mormon. She'd soaked in its numerous battles and conflicts, so this idea was a little difficult to imagine, especially as she realized that she'd *been* there. She'd listened to all the fighting and death throughout a very long, sleepless night in the company of her brother and newfound father.

She sensed an oppressive, almost paralyzing, tension among the hundreds of marching soldiers around her. Despite all their bluster and bravado, these men were frightened. She was sure of it. It didn't seem to matter that Gidgiddoni had won a so-called "Great Battle" in this district two years earlier. That event seemed far in the past. Such a grand victory did not necessarily fill the warriors' minds with comfort or confidence. At least not today.

She tried in vain to comprehend the many forces that, over the last several years, had turned this ancient society upside down. Within a single generation an extraordinary number of people had apparently abandoned their principal religion—which Kerra understood to be Christianity—and joined ranks with something else: a philosophy of secrets and shadows that for some reason had satisfied the needs of these defectors and apostates in a way that the Christianity of their youth had not. Such a shocking percentage of people had embraced this newfangled cult that it seemingly took the rest of the populace by complete surprise. The movement had eventually transformed the entire Nephite world, inspiring mass migrations and urgent building projects for self-preservation and defense. Kerra realized, in a real way, the campaign in which she was presently involved was a kind of desperate "Hail Mary" play for Gidgiddoni and Lachoneus. These brilliant leaders somehow hoped and prayed that this one campaign might turn the tide of a war that, for the time being, had lapsed into a treacherous stalemate.

She tried to dismiss all of these thoughts from her head. Politics was not her cup of tea. The subject frayed her nerves and upset her stomach. Instead, she strived to think about something more lighthearted, more romantic—the fact that their destination was *also* the place where Kiddoni had come to play with her as a child. It was the very same area where, as a young warrior, Kiddoni had elected to stand guard against an impending Red invasion, all the while secretly hoping that Sakerra McConnell might reappear in the mist and fog. These thoughts buoyed her up, and reminded her that even at the heart of the most tumultuous events, it all came down to the singular stories, hopes, and struggles of individual souls and their valiant efforts, in the midst of every heartwrenching tragedy, to simply carry on.

A few miles into the journey, Kerra looked to her left and saw Chemnon, the younger of the Chief Captain's sons, marching beside her. Manazzeh, the older son, was also near, though for now he hung back. Chemnon walked so close to her that they might have named each other's aftershave. Kerra tried to ignore him, but Chemnon made that impossible.

"You know," he began, "with every step our course grows more and more perilous."

"I just traveled through here two days ago," said Kerra. "We saw no perils. Nothing dangerous. Not even animals." She was referring to general wildlife, neglecting to mention the Demon Balám.

"Why do you suppose that is?" asked Chemnon.

"What?"

"Why do you suppose you have seen no animals? At least, no game?"

Sarcastically, Kerra replied, "Because, uh, the undergrowth is really, really thick?"

Chemnon shook his head. "That's not the reason. All edible game is gone. Tapirs, peccaries, coatimundi, kinkajous, deer, monkeys, agouti, opossums, turkeys, pheasants—even rabbits and squirrels. Everything, *gone*. The forest is virtually empty."

"Okay," said Kerra, pretending it was a riddle. "I give up. Why?"

"How do you think the Reds have survived for so long? They are meat eaters. Savages. They do not plant or harvest. They have made the wilderness barren of most things wild. As you will soon see, the animals are nearly gone from these woods as well as deeper into the forest. Because of this, we presume that they move freely in and around our places of safety. Robber patrols could be anywhere. Behind any tree."

Kerra sent him a dubious expression. "Are you trying to scare me, Chemnon?"

Chemnon shrugged. "You're the only female in this battalion. You should have a bodyguard. A warrior assigned exclusively to your protection. You should probably have many, but . . . at least one."

Coyly, Kerra asked, "Are you volunteering for the job?"

He proudly lifted his chin. "I do not think you could do better."

"Actually," said Kerra, "my brother, Brock, is already doing a pretty good job. And I think he's a little taller than you. Isn't he?"

Chemnon chuckled. The sound was a little warped. It took a few additional seconds before Kerra's insult fully sank in. At last his cheeks flushed. He glanced back at Brock—two years younger, no military training, not even toting a weapon. Then he looked back at Kerra, umbrage etched in every muscle of his face. In reality, Kerra couldn't have said who was taller. Not that it mattered. In a sobering instant Chemnon realized she thought of him as a spoiled, immature, presumptuous teenager, which was probably accurate, although he was loathe to admit it. The young warrior frowned heavily.

"I will watch over you anyway," he grunted. Chemnon marched on ahead, attempting to conceal a bright crimson blush.

Kerra heard laughter from Chemnon's older brother. Gracelessly, Manazzeh moved into the spot abandoned by his younger brother.

Recomposing himself, he said, "I must apologize for Chemnon's churlishness. He is very young and . . . inexperienced."

"Ah," said Kerra. "So I take it that you're much older and more 'expert'?"

Her sarcasm caused his smile to wilt. He admitted, "Not really. But there are things that I know about you, Sakerra McConnell, that Chemnon does not."

Hearing him pronounce her full name was disconcerting. She responded defensively, "Where did you hear that?"

"I believe you and I have a mutual friend: Commander Kiddoni."

She faltered. "You know Kiddoni?"

He nodded, pleased to have gained her full attention. "I do."

"How do you know him?"

"I know all the commanders. I know him well enough that I have heard him speak of you."

"He spoke of me?"

Manazzeh cocked his head, striving to recall Kiddoni's exact phrases. "His 'lovely Sakerra.' His 'angel in the forest.' He said that he met you here, in these woods." Manazzeh shrugged. "Actually, that's pretty much the whole of what he said. I confess, he didn't dwell on the subject. Some of his comrades teased him about it. I never did, though. I knew it was a sensitive subject. Also a sad one. I think he missed you. And he felt great aggravation. He didn't seem to understand why he couldn't be with you. Or possibly . . . why you went away."

"I *didn't* go away," snapped Kerra. She regained her composure. "I mean . . . I always intended to come back and find him. That's why I'm here now. I came back."

Manazzeh nodded. He looked at the ground. "I was very sorry when I heard about what happened to his battalion. And to him."

Kerra watched his eyes, unsure if he was sincere. "How do you know that *anything* happened to him?"

Manazzeh shrugged. "I suppose no one can know for certain. No one that was not an eyewitness of the events. We know only that Kiddoni vanished, along with three hundred warriors of the Jade Battalion. Honestly, after four moons . . . it is probably natural that many have concluded the worst."

"Has anyone ever searched for him?" asked Kerra.

"Of course," said Manazzeh. He glanced around and lowered his voice. "But we've never been certain which direction his forces went. Reports are conflicting. Indeed, some claim that he followed this very trail into Hermounts. If that's true, we may be the first search party to pursue Kiddoni's actual course—the trail of the Jade Battalion—deep enough into these mountains."

"Why do you lower your voice?" Kerra asked.

Manazzeh appeared perturbed that Kerra had *not* lowered *hers*. He continued to speak softly. "Because there's no reason to arouse more fear or anxiety than what already exists. A genuine concern prevails that many of these men will desert in the night. Or worse."

"Worse? You mean mutiny?"

Manazzeh continued to glance around, but he did not answer, which was answer enough.

"Because of Gidgiddonihah?" asked Kerra.

"That's one reason, yes," Manazzeh confessed. "They don't want to end up like those who served with him during his *last* campaign."

"You mean . . . dead?"

"Not just dead. No warrior is ashamed to die," Manazzeh exaggerated. "They don't want to end up like the corpses."

Kerra furrowed her brow. "The *corpses*? You mean bodies? I don't follow. What happened to the corpses?"

"He burned them," Manazzeh said softly, as if it was a terrible secret.

Kerra waited for something more. "And?"

Manazzeh looked surprised. "*And*? Is that not enough? Did you not hear me? He *burned* them! I am told that he may have also mutilated some of them. Cut them up. He desecrated the dead! Does that not offend you?"

"Should it?" asked Kerra obliviously.

Manazzeh couldn't fathom her lack of disgust. "Most of us in this army are stalwart Christians, like my father. We believe in the resurrection of the mortal body—a miracle that will be brought to pass by the Messiah. The body is sacred. It is the tabernacle of God. We do not burn or desecrate the temple of God. We *bury* the bodies of the dead. We return them to the soil with all dignity and holiness."

Kerra still strived to comprehend his reasoning and passion. "Let me see if I got this straight. The hatred and distrust that the soldiers feel toward Gidgiddonihah . . . is because he cut up and burned the bodies of the dead warriors under his command instead of burying them?"

Manazzeh remained aghast. "Obviously you are not Christian and do not understand our ways."

Kerra shrugged. "Not officially, I suppose. I'm not baptized. But I know lots of Christians in my country. And I'm not sure they'd feel the same level of . . . outrage. Or at least they wouldn't take the offense quite so seriously."

"Then they cannot be true Christians," rebutted Manazzeh. "Our attitude about the body and our customs regarding the dead is what separates us from the savages. Gidgiddonihah violated those customs. If he'd acted according to my father's guidelines, every corpse would have been returned to its family for proper burial. Granted, this is not always possible in war. Having lost so many warriors, maybe it wasn't practical for them *all* to be returned. But the report I heard was that Gidgiddonihah commanded that every corpse should be burned—one by one—often in the very place where the soldier fell."

"And that's why they despise him?" asked Kerra.

"Such an order is an abomination," declared Manazzeh. "Many of those casualties had brothers and kinsmen in the Rattlesnake Battalion. The commander's acts were unforgivable."

"Maybe he had a reason," said Kerra.

"What possible—?!" Manazzeh swallowed his temper. "If there was a reason, he never revealed it."

"He must have revealed it to your father. Otherwise, your father wouldn't have offered him this command."

Manazzeh smiled begrudgingly. "My father loves Gidgiddonihah. Gidgiddonihah is his namesake, the son of his only brother, who was recently murdered, probably as a direct result of his nephew's actions. My father has always been delighted and overwhelmed by the talents and skills that Gidgiddonihah exhibits as a warrior."

"Sooo . . . you think your father's judgments were clouded? You think he's so delighted and overwhelmed with Gidgiddonihah's talents and skills that he would unwisely give him command over such a crucial mission? That he would readily sacrifice an entire battalion that clearly despises their commander?"

Manazzeh tried to backtrack. He seemed befuddled. "No, my—my father has always acted—*always* acted with sound judgment. But he is only a man. Only human. He is . . ." His mind couldn't muster additional words.

Kerra said, "It sounds like, at least regarding the parameters of this mission, you may not know your father very well. Or your cousin."

Manazzeh pursed his lips. He clenched his teeth and nodded—a gesture which seemed to say "excuse me a moment." He joined his brother further up the column.

Kerra sighed. She'd silenced and offended two of the unit's more prestigious members. *Ah, whatever,* she thought. If it meant that she'd no longer have to deal with their petty flirtations or be further treated like a helpless female, the episode may have been worth it. In any case, she shrugged it off, preferring to focus her anxieties on Kiddoni. And on her family. And on the dreadful mysteries that lay ahead.

CHAPTER 13

THE MARCH LASTED UNTIL LATE in the afternoon. The forest grew increasingly dense and ominous while the valley slopes seemed to constrict on all sides. The stream that cut through this valley was sometimes silent and sometimes rumbling over turbulent cascades. Kerra finally began to recognize landmarks in the thick, shadowed woods. As twilight descended, the snarled jungle canopy overhead produced countless illusions: peering eyes, groping fingers, and snarling fangs. Some of those illusions may have been real. Weren't these woods once the home of countless howler and spider monkeys? But if that was true, where were the typical mating calls and other communications that Kerra had once heard Kiddoni describe? Perhaps Chemnon was right. The forest truly was almost devoid of game. The quiet struck Kerra as alarming. Her heart thudded as her mind rehearsed Chemnon's creepy description of Gadianton spies skulking behind every tree and slaying for meat every living thing that moved through Zarahemla's jungles.

Suddenly Kerra heard a loud twang. She looked ahead. Men were converging on one of their warriors who'd fired an arrow into the woods.

"I saw one!" he shrieked, making no effort to soften his voice.

Pek, Gid's second-in-command, arrived on the scene. Kerra, Brock, Dad, and Grandpa Lee drew close enough to hear the conversation.

"He was right there!" the warrior proclaimed. "Behind that trunk!"

Pek gestured for him to lower his voice. The man's muscles were taut with anxiety. His energy had a contagious effect on everyone in his midst. Another twang! A second bowman sent an arrow whistling toward the trees.

A half dozen men were now pointing toward the thick brush, announcing the sighting of a Red spy. The sound of rustling in the foliage confirmed that some kind of intruder was now in full retreat.

"Seven men!" barked Pek. "I need seven volunteers to join me in pursuit!"

"NO!" boomed another voice. It was Gidgiddonihah, finally arriving on the scene. "No one will pursue!"

"But, Commander," Pek protested, "we can still catch—"

"*No one!*" repeated Gidgiddonihah, his teeth clenched. "The battalion stays together. Form a tight circle among the trees. We'll bivouac here for the night. Raise your tents!"

Gid's burning gaze crossed twenty or thirty bewildered warriors. The men's mouths were agape, fingers *itching* to shed enemy blood. But Gidgiddonihah's jaw remained set. His orders were clear. Finally, he turned and walked back to the front of the column.

Men spat indignantly into the dirt. Kerra heard murmurs of disapproval. But no one seemed inclined to disobey. In a way, this surprised Kerra. Gidgiddonihah was only twenty years old. More than half the army was older than their commander. And yet the Chief Captain's nephew carried an aura of authority that Kerra had never before experienced or witnessed. He might as well have been eighty. His demeanor of supremacy was all-pervasive.

Pek at first acted just as confounded by Gidgiddonihah's decision as the other warriors, but he wasn't about to tolerate insubordination.

"You heard the commander!" he raged. "Raise your tents! Tie off your hammocks! We sleep here tonight. This is sacred ground, soldiers! You are standing upon the soil of the Great Gadianton Battle. We will sleep tonight among the hero spirits of our fallen kinsmen!"

They had reached the area where Lord Giddianhi had been slain two years before—the same area where Kerra had once played an anonymous but pivotal role. It was very near this place—albeit in a parallel dimension, a different century—where she'd retrieved Kiddoni's horn from a fissure in the earth and sounded an alarm that reverberated above the jungle canopy and called forth the forces of Zarahemla. From Kerra's perspective, she'd never left southern Utah. Yet even in *this* dimension—that is, the tropical forest of the first century AD—not much evidence remained of this epic struggle. There were a few broken weapons in the underbrush, a scattering of half-healed gouges and gashes in the mossy bark of various trees. Two years of jungle growth, Kerra realized, was comparable to *decades* in other environments. She estimated that they were still several hundred yards short of the archway where they'd located Hitch's necklace, the rift where the Demon Balám had emerged. The Great Battleground encompassed more territory than Kerra had first realized.

She looked at her brother, father, and grandfather. She could tell the archway was very much on their minds. Like them, she ignored any tremor of foreboding in her heart and helped to set up camp alongside the other warriors of the Rattlesnake Battalion.

Before the job was finished, Manazzeh's prediction was at last fulfilled. That is, the commander's senior aide finally arrived, requesting Mi'con to follow him to Gidgiddonihah's tent. To Kerra's surprise, he also beckoned her.

"Me?" Kerra asked, looking over her shoulder to see if the aide had motioned toward someone else.

"The commander has summoned *both* of you," he confirmed.

Brock and Grandpa watched with concern as Dad took Kerra's hand. The two of them followed the aide, whose name was Hamnish, to the center of the encampment, where the commander had established his temporary headquarters. As they approached the three-sided enclosure with a canvas roof, Kerra felt apprehensive. Thus far no one in her family, except Brock, had exchanged a single syllable with the crusty nephew of Gidgiddoni. Kerra also noted, disparagingly, that the five kegs of corn grog had been carefully lined up along one of the tent's outer walls.

As Kerra looked into the enclosure, she saw the commander sitting cross-legged in the middle. She noted the presence of three other men: the sons of Gidgiddoni—Manazzeh and Chemnon—and also Pek, Gid's principal lieutenant. After Dad and Kerra were brought inside, Gidgiddonihah instructed his aide, "See that we are not disturbed, Hamnish. This is a private conference."

Hamnish nodded and departed. Kerra realized with some dismay that her father was the oldest person there. Pek came in second, in his late twenties. Otherwise, it appeared that this invasion had been left in the hands of very young warriors indeed.

Gidgiddonihah didn't make eye contact with Dad or Kerra right away. He arose and stepped to the edge of the tent, watching until his aide was far enough away to be out of hearing. It was a curious thing. After all, Hamnish was a senior aide. Would it have been so terrible if he had overheard? Others had noted the commander's unusual behavior. It made them all visibly nervous.

Finally, Gidgiddonihah—the cunning warrior whose movements were as lithe as a jaguar's, the unstable drunk whose life of late was so saturated with grief—returned to the center of the tent and faced his audience.

"What we discuss this night," he began, "cannot leave this tent. Only the five of you seated here now will be told the details of what I'm about to disclose. Afterward, I'll select a few others who will be *partially* informed. But before I start I must have your oaths. You must agree to obey my command and keep this meeting private— at least until the events described are set in motion." He turned to Manazzeh and Chemnon. "I must hear an oath especially from the two of you, my cousins. I know you have felt puzzled, even dismayed, by your father's orders that you must accompany this battalion. I tried to dissuade him, but as always, his reasoning was sound. Your father specifically directed me to include you in this conference. He wanted you to be fully aware of what is about to transpire. The roles that you will both play are pivotal to our success. However, you will not be directly involved in the actions that I will undertake."

Manazzeh and Chemnon gaped at him, eyes blinking. Kerra felt the tension ratchet up several notches. This wasn't at all how anyone had expected Gidgiddonihah to begin his speech.

Gingerly, Manazzeh asked, "Are you sober, my cousin?"

Gid narrowed his eyes, ground his teeth. "Of *course* I'm sober. Don't patronize me, Manazzeh. I must have your oath."

Pek responded before drawing another breath. "You have *my* oath, Commander. I swear before heaven and earth to obey your command and not disclose whatever you say until I'm granted permission."

"Thank you, Pek," said Gid.

Dad lifted his hand. "Wait-wait-wait a second," he stammered. "I wasn't prepared for this. What's all this about?"

Gidgiddonihah stepped up to him. "Your name is Mi´con and

you were a captive of Akuhuun, the son of Giddianhi, for two years in this wilderness. Is that correct?"

Dad nodded.

He scrunched down to look directly into Dad's eyes. "You, your daughter, and your other family members are the only individuals in this battalion who I know nothing about. I'm told that it's because of information you provided—things you said—that my uncle organized this expedition in the first place. If it were me, I would have never allowed strangers—and more particularly, a woman—to play *any* significant role in a mission of this magnitude. But . . ." He stood up tall again. ". . . I trust my uncle. And since it is his command, I will obey."

Kerra cleared her throat. "Maybe we ought to know a little more about what's happening before we go swearing any oaths."

Gidgiddonihah grinned crookedly. "My uncle said you were a brazen one. He likes you very much."

"Groovy," Kerra deadpanned. "Your uncle likes me. I'm flattered. Why include me in this company at all? What can I possibly contribute?"

Gid pursed his lips, genuinely stymied. "The answer to that isn't entirely evident or transparent to me," he admitted. "But I hope that I will comprehend soon enough. And I know better than to dismiss my uncle's sagacity. So do I have your oath?"

She shook her head. "Not yet."

Gid's mouth sagged. Kerra remained inflexible.

Manazzeh spoke. "My brother and I will certainly give you our oaths, Cousin Gidgiddonihah. We'll obey you as the commander of this battalion. But why didn't our father inform us about any . . . *unconventional* strategies . . . before we left the fortifications? He has never kept the truth from us before."

"And neither does he keep it from you now," said Gid. "It's merely a matter of timing. Your father knows you well. He knows that you are both very headstrong. And he knows that you have both misunderstood, and even publicly decried, decisions that I made during my last campaign into the East Wilderness."

Manazzeh glanced at Kerra. She'd voiced this exact notion only hours ago.

Chemnon piped in. "As my brother said, you have our oaths. And you have our loyalty. Now say what you have brought us here to say."

Gidgiddonihah focused again on Mi'con.

Dad nodded, albeit clumsily. "I give you my word. My *oath*. But I hope that whatever you have to tell us makes clear sense. The lives of my loved ones depend on it."

A stony chill settled into Gid's expression. He was almost angry as he replied, "I know how that feels. I know how it feels to have loved ones who depend upon you. And I know how it feels to utterly fail them."

His gaze was so penetrating that Dad looked away. Gid initiated one last stare-down, this time with Kerra, but she only glared back. She wasn't budging. Gidgiddonihah made a slight hiss. He seemed to decide that hearing her oath wasn't imperative at the moment. Maybe, Kerra wondered, he didn't think a woman's oath was worth much to begin with.

Gid directed his next words to Kerra's father. "You said something to my uncle two days ago. You advised him that it might be better if a small party of men secretly infiltrated the regions of Hermounts rather than sending an entire battalion. Why did you offer this advice?"

Dad looked uncomfortable. He finally replied, "Well . . . because of the lay of the land. And because of the tactics of the Gadianton robbers."

"What tactics?" asked Gid, his eyes like lasers. Kerra sensed that the commander already held strong opinions. Her dad was being tested.

"They have lookouts posted everywhere," said Mi'con. "And secret methods of conveying information a very long distance in a short amount of time. I feared that a battalion . . ." He faltered, worried that he might be overstepping his bounds.

"No, don't stop," said Gid. "Go on. What are your fears?"

Dad released a slow breath then blurted out, "I fear a battalion is too conspicuous. It draws too much attention. Your uncle has conducted this war by utilizing the correct strategies all along. He has sought to draw the Gadiantons to *him*. Unfortunately, it has meant that captives, like myself, were all but ignored and forgotten, but I concede that the basic strategy has been sound. Lately, that strategy has been altered. I fear that a unit of this size makes us all sitting ducks."

Gid smiled, deeply pleased by Dad's words. "Your instincts are dead on, Mi´con. I think Gidgiddoni deeply regrets allowing himself to be pressured by some of the local clan leaders into launching any campaigns whatsoever into wilderness areas. Although, admittedly, some valuable intelligence has been gained by these actions, the cost has been far too high. In fact, Mi´con, I suspect a scenario like the one you have described is being set into motion right now, as we sit in this tent. Those robbers that we sighted an hour ago *wanted* to be seen. They *allowed* us to pinpoint them. If I've learned anything about Gadiantons, it's that if they don't *wish* to be discovered, they are *not* discovered." He turned to Pek. "If I had let you take seven warriors into the woods, you and those seven men would now be dead. I'm certain of it. I'll wager that at this moment the surrounding jungle is hiding twenty or thirty of Akuhuun's spies. Not enough to fight us, but enough that we can't flare a nostril without someone reporting it to Akuhuun or Zemnarihah. From here on out they'll know exactly where we are and what we're doing. I guarantee that within the last hour—maybe even as of late this morning—a rabble of spies was sent scurrying up the valley to call forth additional troops. If our battalion were to remain here, or even if we continued marching southward, we would be utterly slaughtered in two days or less—just like the other three battalions that left the safety of our fortifications."

Manazzeh was shaking his head. He looked genuinely perplexed. "It doesn't make sense. My father is no fool. He organized this battalion and sent us into this wilderness—"

Gid interrupted. "You're right, Manazzeh. He *is* no fool. He is perfectly aware of our predicament. That's why every directive I'm about to disclose has your father's full endorsement."

"That cannot be," said Chemnon. "We were *with* you yesterday morning. He never outlined an alternate plan. When did he issue these new orders?"

"Yesterday *evening*," said Gid. "We discussed our strategy until the sixth hour of the night."

"I don't believe it," said Manazzeh stubbornly. "Why would he do this?"

"You'll have to ask him that yourself," said Gid, "after you return. Don't pretend to be ignorant, Manazzeh. Your father knows perfectly well the weaknesses of his sons."

Manazzeh stiffened his jaw angrily. "What exactly did you and my father 'discuss' until the sixth hour of the night?"

"The entire strategy," said Gid. "We discussed today's march and the plan to pitch our tents here, on the very ground where we celebrated our great victory two years ago. It's all part of a diversion. Your father's hope—and my intent—is that this diversion will allow a small party of warriors to slip quietly into the mountains to locate the robbers' roost—the headquarters of Akuhuun."

"What then?" asked Chemnon.

"What do you think?" replied Gid solemnly. "I will kill him. Akuhuun must be eliminated at any cost."

Manazzeh was nearly beside himself. "You mean to say this whole expedition—today's march—was organized just so a small band of assassins could sneak away undetected into the wilderness of Hermounts?"

"Yes," said Gidgiddonihah calmly.

"Wh-who," asked Mi′con, "are the assassins?"

Gid looked at him and declared, "*I* am the principal assassin. Also Pek, my lieutenant. And two or three others. But no more. And as I say, no one else will be told the complete details of our mission until we're much closer to our destination. For this mission, our strength is not in numbers. It's in stealth. It's in *invisibility*."

Chemnon remained befuddled. "And this was our father's plan all *along*?"

"Very good, Chemnon," said Gid caustically. "Welcome to the conversation."

"What about my brother and me?" asked Manazzeh. "Are we to be a part of this assassination squad?"

"No," said Gid. "Tomorrow you and Chemnon will take command of the Rattlesnake Battalion after my . . . disappearance. You will tell the men that I was ordered by my uncle to return. This news will likely be received with delight and relief. Afterward, you will make preparations as if to continue marching up the valley, and then you will take a circuitous route, turn the battalion around, and get these men back to Lachoneus's fortifications as rapidly as possible. During all the fanfare, I will escape with my team."

Again, Kerra's father guardedly raised his hand. "What, exactly, is my role?"

"It has not changed," said Gid. "I am told, Mi'con, that you know these mountains better than any individual in this battalion. Moreover, you're apparently the only soul here who has ever laid eyes on Akuhuun. It is my uncle's wish—and mine—that you will continue to act as our guide. Lead me and my men to our target. Do this and I promise that I will do everything to protect your life and the life of your daughter. I will also do all in my power to liberate your loved ones and any other Nephite or Lamanite captives that we might discover."

Mi'con continued to gape. So did Kerra. Neither responded right away.

Manazzeh interjected, "I still don't understand the objective. Assassinate *Akuhuun*? What *difference* will it make?"

"*Every* difference," said Gid, wrestling with a growing impatience. "As everyone here knows, there are two factions currently vying for control of the robber bands. Or rather, two *men*. Because of this infighting, the Reds have failed to launch any meaningful assault against our strongholds for two years. However, I believe that power struggle is shifting. It's moving away from Zemnarihah and toward Akuhuun. Your father and I agree that we cannot permit this to happen."

"Cannot *permit*?" Chemnon repeated agitatedly. "What does it matter? Both men are equally despicable."

"No," Gid countered in a powerful tone. "They are not equal in any way. Zemnarihah, like Giddianhi, represents an older robber tradition of secret oaths and stealthy combinations. Despicable as Zemnarihah is, his strategies are not as progressive and diabolical as the *new* strategies of Akuhuun, son of Giddianhi. Zemnarihah still believes that he can beat us in a direct confrontation—a battle to the death. If not for Akuhuun, I think such a campaign would have already been waged. And such an effort, we believe, would have ended this war with a sound victory for Zarahemla's armies. But Akuhuun is a different sort of man from his father and from Zemnarihah. He's smarter. Craftier. More dangerous. He operates on a different set of values. He dismisses Zemnarihah as weak, impetuous, and ill-tempered. Akuhuun, on the other hand, is much more careful. More patient. In all honesty, he thinks too much like my uncle. He seeks to wear down the Nephite and Lamanite populace by attrition."

"*Attrition*?!" balked Manazzeh. "Nonsense! Can the Reds survive on empty stomachs? These forests are barren. There is no more game!"

"Precisely," said Gid. "But such conditions are not as crippling to Akuhuun. His followers are more austere. More disciplined. We believe Akuhuun will be considerably more difficult to defeat than Zemnarihah. It might take years. And before Akuhuun and his forces could be drawn out of hiding to fight a decisive contest, our own food stores and provisions could become depleted. Even now our people are on the cusp of revolt. They're willing to abandon Lachoneus's strongholds, believing the Gadiantons are satisfied to remain in the mountains—believing they've grown *accustomed* to their dreary and meager existence. Meanwhile, Zarahemla's citizens yearn to go home. But if my uncle and the Chief Judge were to give in to such pressures, it would guarantee our nation's utter destruction. It would abolish our entire way of life."

"What is so 'new' and unique about Akuhuun's strategies?" asked Chemnon.

Gid glanced at Kerra. "I don't wish to describe them at this moment. But I can assure you, I have experienced them firsthand. I saw for myself, in the East Wilderness, Akuhuun's willingness to commit atrocities of a character and nature never before witnessed by the descendants of Lehi. These same strategies, I believe, were launched against the three battalions that are now missing."

Manazzeh scoffed. "You have asked us to lead these men tomorrow in a charade that will provoke resentment and confusion—not delight. How can we do what you have asked if we don't understand the reasons?" He added darkly, "I'm sure you're aware, cousin, that many soldiers claim that unspeakable atrocities were committed by *you*. How can you justify the things that you ordered your men to do in the East Wilderness? I've heard about your actions from many witnesses. I've heard them describe how you desecrated the dead. How you ordered your platoon leaders to mutilate and burn the bodies of our fallen warriors. Is it true? Tell us once and for all!"

Gid glared back at his cousin with terrible fury. He finally seethed, "It's true. Every word of it. But why, Manazzeh, have you never asked *me* for an explanation? You want a description, cousin? All right. I'll give you a description, despite the presence of a woman and despite your bullheaded distrust and arrogance. Yes, I ordered our casualties burned. Also, at times, mutilated. But I did it for a very specific reason. I did it because the warriors of Akuhuun were *harvesting our dead!* Do you understand? You are correct that these forests are barren of game. So how is it that you think Akuhuun and his ilk continue to survive? How do you imagine that the bodies of our missing soldiers are being used? If you are to fully comprehend the depravity of a man like Akuhuun, you must abandon all of your preconceptions of military chivalry and humanity. Three missing battalions! Nine-hundred soldiers! And not a single corpse recovered! Why do you suppose that is, cousin? How long do you think it took your father to discern the awful truth? I promise you, he now understands. He understands exactly the actions that I undertook in the East Wilderness. And he knows that I would order my men to do it *again.* He knows if the circumstances were to be repeated, I would order *you* to perform precisely the same atrocities. These barrels of grog outside this tent—why did you think that I brought them? Did you think that I meant to drink myself into a mindless stupor here in the jungle night after night? No, my cousins. I brought these barrels for *you*—in case the very worst occurs. In case this battalion, like the others, finds itself confronted with total annihilation. If so, you will use those barrels to immolate the bodies of the dead. You will set them all aflame. We will not allow the armies of Akuhuun to feed on the flesh of our brethren and comrades-in-arms. So now—at last—do you understand?"

Manazzeh and Chemnon, along with all others inside the tent, sat there dumbstruck. Kerra's mind found it difficult to absorb what Gidgiddonihah had described. It was so repugnant, so repulsive, that his words seemed to penetrate her viscera as well as her ears. Actually, his description was so incomprehensible that she almost felt her ears didn't hear it at all. It was as if she *watched* herself from a distance take in Gid's revelations, like an observer, a third party. She absorbed the awful horror as if from a nightmare.

Finally, Manazzeh nodded.

Gidgiddonihah continued. "I presume you also understand why Akuhuun must fail in his ultimate quest to win the hearts and minds of the robber bands and usurp the authority of Zemnarihah. I presume you understand why he *must* be slain."

"I understand, Gidgiddonihah," said Manazzeh flatly, dejectedly.

Kerra was still trying to digest all of the facts. Three lost battalions. Nine hundred missing warriors. One of them . . . Kiddoni. *No,* she told herself again. Despite everything the commander had laid out—even realizing that Gid himself might have tried to persuade her otherwise—she refused to accept that Kiddoni had suffered the fate that Gid had described. Something inside her whispered otherwise. She glanced at her father. He appeared stricken by his own inner turmoil, pondering what destiny may have awaited—or had already overtaken—his wife and son.

"Now," Gid concluded, "I presume you also understand why none of this can be told to our troops. For now, our plans must be kept very quiet and close to the chest. So I'll ask one last time: do I have your oaths?"

CHAPTER 14

KERRA LAY IN HER ROPE hammock, wide awake, staring up at a cloud-obscured moon. There had only been enough canvas to construct a partial roof. The cumulus layer was thick, though no rain had yet begun tapping the sectional ceiling. Everyone else in the tent, Kerra presumed, was fast asleep. She could hear her grandfather snoring like a tractor three hammocks away. For Kerra, sleep was as far from her eyes as the distant stars.

Yes, she'd finally given the commander her oath. She had the strong premonition that if she hadn't, something drastic would have taken place. Her insolence would not have been further tolerated. Gid might have ordered Pek to have her bound, gagged, and hidden away somewhere. Maybe she'd have simply been slain. The clandestine nature of Gidgiddonihah's mission was serious business. These guys were not messing around.

Despite an accumulation of blankets, Kerra couldn't stop shivering. The chill crept in from underneath the hammock's netting. It wasn't merely the cold that tormented her. Whenever she closed her eyes she saw glimpses of Kiddoni's face. Most often she pictured her last image of him from that day in the clearing, just before his visage had faded entirely. If it wasn't for the spark of hope still smoldering inside her, she'd have never consented to *any* oath. She'd have never agreed to join Gidgiddonihah's coterie of assassins. It still wasn't clear to her why they'd asked her to accompany them in the first place. She'd never agree to carry a weapon. She'd be too afraid of accidentally severing her own limb. She could only speculate that it had something to do with her "gifts."

Her grandfather had first pointed them out. She still couldn't quite comprehend his arcane and mysterious description. Grandpa Lee had insisted that she possessed certain gifts or abilities related to the hollow, the Whistlers, and the rifts of time and space. He'd told her that she could "hear things, feel things that few others could." But even if she'd grasped the practical application of such gifts, how would Gidgiddonihah have known or figured out that she possessed them?

His uncle, Gidgiddoni, she decided. It was the only explanation. Somehow the Chief Captain had discerned the same things as her grandfather. Something or someone had whispered it to his mind. A revelation. A transmission of the Spirit. Or whatever the heck Mormons called it. She squeezed her eyes tightly, pressing her head between her forearms. Six months ago she'd have laughingly rejected all of this nonsense. Even now it remained as foggy as the cloud-covered moon. She wondered if she'd actually been *happier* six months ago, before all of this hallelujah Jesus stuff and mind-bending time-travel gobbledygook had invaded her consciousness.

She thought again of Kiddoni. Only with Kiddoni did any of this make sense. But not if he was dead. Only if he was alive.

Kerra heard her brother stir in the hammock beside her. The encampment was perfectly dark. Not a single flame had been permitted to burn after sundown. Despite this, she perceived Brock's shadowy profile as he climbed out from under his bedding and started to exit the tent.

"Where are you going?" Kerra whispered.

Brock was startled by her voice. He whispered back, "Where do you think?"

"The bathroom?"

"Duh."

Kerra rolled out of her hammock. "I'll go with you."

"You're joking! In what way, exactly, do you think you're gonna help?"

"Quit your whining. It's not like I can see anything."

"And it's not like I'm three years old!"

"I don't care. I'm going with you."

She followed him across the encampment, dodging the shapes of neighboring tents and hammocks until they arrived at the edge of the forest. Kerra felt the moist, cool soil beneath her toes. She glared out at the silent wilderness, remembering, of course, what Gid had said about a handful of Gadianton spies keeping a persistent vigil somewhere in the murky darkness. In reality, Kerra felt that the jungle was surprisingly quiet. Yesterday at sunset, even though they were much closer to Lachoneus's fortifications, the forest had become a veritable carnival of commotion with monkeys honking and birds chattering, as if warning friends and family that darkness was fast approaching, and, "in case of emergency, please make note of the place where I'm sleeping." Now the forest seemed void of virtually every living thing.

"Turn around," Brock directed.

"What?"

"I said turn your back!"

"Are you serious? I can't even tell what direction you're facing."

"Just do it!"

She groaned and turned, choosing not to argue, despite the darkness giving him all the privacy he needed.

Before Brock had finished, a warrior urgently approached from the west and barked, "Who's there?!"

It was Lemech's voice. Dad's brother-in-law was back on sentry duty, much as he'd been on the first night when they'd arrived at the outskirts of the village of Sorrow.

"It's us," said Kerra. "The son and daughter of Mi´con. My brother had to, uh—"

No need to explain. The audible stream said it all.

"Get back to the tent," Lemech urged in a subdued tone. "It isn't safe."

"Safe?" asked Kerra.

Lemech seemed greatly agitated as he studied the forest. "I've heard things. Hard to say. But it's not natural. Not the kind of—"

He stopped midsentence as a tiny flame ignited some distance out in the woods. It was as if someone had flicked a cigarette lighter. This flare hovered in midair, like a dancing firefly, thirty or forty yards out. The flame began to expand. Within seconds, dozens of additional fireballs blazed into life throughout the blackness. A bowstring snapped. One of the fireballs whistled over Kerra and Brock's heads, landing somewhere in the encampment.

"An attack!" shouted Lemech. "*We're under attack!!*"

Kerra's flesh felt like it had been immersed in ice. She began to run back toward her father's tent; Brock was on her heels. Chaos was erupting in all directions. Fire-tipped arrows were landing throughout the camp, ripping through canvas, even piercing sleeping warriors. The projectiles somehow burst upon impact, setting ablaze everything for yards in all directions.

Kerra's thoughts were in a daze. Her brain kept repeating: *Gidgiddonihah was wrong. He said two days. He misjudged the enemy. He miscalculated. He was* wrong!

As she entered the tent, her father and grandfather were already on their feet. Part of the canvas was burning. Dad noticed his son and daughter's feet in the firelight, caked with dirt.

"Tie on your sandals!" he yelled. "You should've never taken them off!"

Another arrow hit the ground just a few feet behind Brock and Kerra. It nearly skewered Lemech, who'd also followed them to the tent. Some kind of incendiary pouch was attached to each arrowhead, splattering at the point of impact like napalm. Kerra quickly tied on her sandals. Brock, however, retrieved his satchel and pulled out his Adidas sneakers.

Shouts of panic began to dominate the darkness. The Rattlesnake Battalion had apparently been taken by complete surprise. No one had expected Akuhuun's army to be this organized—this close at hand. How many Reds were out there? How was such an attack even possible? Gidgiddonihah's expedition hadn't even *existed* two days ago! *No* one could have organized a counteroffensive so quickly. Was it merely the worst possible luck that Gadianton troops were already entrenched nearby? Or was Akuhuun, the son of Giddianhi, some kind of military genius the like of which the Nephite defenders had never encountered?

A massive explosion rang in Kerra's ears. She and the others raised their eyes toward the west. The blast created a fountain of fire as tall as the jungle canopy. For several seconds the landscape was illuminated by a brilliant light. Pandemonium reigned among the Nephite and Lamanite soldiers. Members of the Rattlesnake Battalion ran helter-skelter in every direction.

And then, in the firelight, Kerra began to perceive *other* warriors—half-naked wraiths whose skin was slathered in blood. They were pouring into the camp from the forest like an army of cockroaches. A second blast resounded, and then a third! The ground shook. Kerra realized the detonations had originated near Gidgiddonihah's tent. Only one phenomenon could have caused this—the commander's five barrels of grog. Kerra felt sure that these barrels had just erupted like volcanoes. Her spirits plummeted. Had the robbers just managed to slay Gidgiddonihah? It would be a stunning paradox if Akuhuun had managed to assassinate Gid only hours after the commander had unfolded a secret plan to assassinate Akuhuun.

As this thought grazed Kerra's mind, lo and behold, Commander Gidgiddonihah appeared at the front of the tent. He was accompanied by Pek and Hamnish. The three officers were heavily armed. Kerra exhaled with relief, but a fresh wave of distress gripped her as Gid approached and focused every particle of his attention upon her.

"You *know* things," he declared, his tone almost accusing. "My uncle was convinced that you have unique capacities—powerful gifts. *Is it true?*"

"I-I-I'm not sure what he meant!" stuttered Kerra.

Grandpa Lee interjected and said to Kerra, "*Sure* you do. You know *exactly* what he meant."

That was enough for Gid. He leaned almost nose to nose with her and commanded, "Get us out of here! Lead the way!"

Kerra stood there, frozen in bewilderment. Everybody—her family, the battalion commander, two of his officers, and Dad's brother-in-law Lemech—glared at her in stunning expectation. They were awaiting her direction—her *leadership*. Who did they think she was? A prophetess? A clairvoyant? It was all so twisted! How could she possibly—?

An idea suddenly popped into her head. The archway. Dad, or even Brock, could have led them there. But nobody was looking to Dad or Brock or Grandpa Lee. They were gaping at her. She squared her shoulders with resolve and mustered her courage.

"Follow me!"

Kerra fled the tent, heading southward. In the melee of fiery arrows and screaming soldiers, she only glanced back once to see who was keeping up. Everybody was solidly on her heels. That is, everyone who'd been inside the tent. Gidgiddonihah was closest, with Grandpa and Brock taking up the rear. Lemech paused as he spotted a fellow Lamanite.

"Helorum!" He waved to his comrade. "Over here!"

Kerra recognized him as the sentry with a high topknot who, a couple nights ago, had accosted them with a spear. Gid looked around at those following Kerra. He seemed to groan with exasperation, his disapproval directed in particular at Brock and his elderly grandfather. However, he decided this was not the proper time to raise a protest.

Kerra reached the edge of the forest. Shadows dashed among the trees and additional "fireflies"—or rather, flaming arrows—launched toward the encampment. Kerra realized the Gadianton attackers were primarily converging from three directions. The camp's southern flank had thus far been spared by the invaders. Maybe they hoped such a stratagem would force any fleeing Rattlesnake warriors to head south, into a crushing trap. A possible new explanation revealed itself in the form of a dark and menacing silhouette. An animal lunged from the brush at the south end of the encampment. It released a gut-twisting growl and pounced toward a target at the rear of Kerra's company. Her heart skipped a beat: Brock and Grandpa had been at the rear.

Someone screamed. In the confusion it was hard to tell who'd been attacked. But then Kerra saw Brock and Grandpa Lee scrambling toward her. Other members of her group were turned away, several tripping backward as they watched the scene unfold. A brief parting of bodies revealed the awful spectacle. A jaguar the size of an African lioness had clamped its jaws around a man's skull. Kerra recognized the topknot hanging to one side. It was Lemech's comrade, Helorum. The victim's fingers clenched the fur at the jaguar's throat, but in futility. Kerra realized that this was *not* the same beast they'd encountered at the archway two days earlier. This balám had no mottling of orange fur. Its coat was solid black—like ebony. She heard a terrible crack. Helorum's arms dropped. His body went limp.

The creature tossed aside Helorum's body and lunged for the next closest victim. It was *Brock*! Kerra's lungs seemed to seize inside her chest. Her brother was about to die!

He threw up his arms—an insignificant defense—and cried, "*Noooo!*"

Something extraordinary occurred. The jaguar stopped. It had fully drawn to a halt, its yellow eyes studying the thirteen-year-old boy with an odd look—the most peculiar expression that Kerra had ever seen on an animal, as if . . . it had *understood* him. Brock was on his knees, arms continuing to shield his head. Kerra still couldn't draw a breath. She watched as the beast bounded in a different direction, toward the center of the encampment. Brock remained momentarily paralyzed. Grandpa dragged him to his feet.

The group was on the move again—all but Kerra. Grandpa Lee and Brock raced past her, but Kerra's legs seemed staked to the ground, her mind mystified by the behavior of the Demon Balám. She couldn't shake the feeling that it had understood Brock's cry. For some unfathomable reason, it *obeyed.*

Dad grabbed his daughter's arm and yanked her into the forest. Gidgiddonihah, perhaps judging that Kerra was the least expendable member of the group, grabbed her *other* arm. She took large, loping steps to keep pace with the two men.

Shadows lunged out of the darkness—*lots* of them! Dad and Gid released Kerra. She tripped onto her face, sliding to a stop in a bed of ferns. Dazed and terrified, she raised her head, trying to get a grip on what was happening.

A brief parting of clouds over the three-quarter moon revealed that her group had charged headlong into a nest of Gadianton fighters. Kerra's gaze found Gidgiddonihah. His polished leather cuirass emitted a distinct shine in the moonlight. He was surrounded by at least seven blood-slathered warriors, ferociously hollering and jabbing with spears and knives. Pek, Lemech, Hamnish, and her father also fought—but with single opponents. The vast majority homed in on Gid, as if a neon sign flashed above his head reading, "*Battalion commander. Kill him!*"

Kerra watched Gidgiddonihah's movements in morbid fascination. She'd never seen anything like it. Not even Kiddoni, when he'd fought Kush and his cronies, had moved with such . . . *poetry!* That's what it was—a twisted, primeval kind of artistry. How else could it be described? What Gid did with his weapons was an art form. It defined him—defined his very reason for being. The commander's right hand wielded a copper hatchet while his left swung a club with ragged obsidian teeth. He fought like a mythical paladin, a warrior programmed by intuition, reflex, and nerves.

Gidgiddonihah made short work of four opponents in virtual synchronicity—using their momentum against them. Things moved so fast that Kerra couldn't recount the precise order of events. The commander knew naturally—instinctively—which opponent had the greatest skill or posed the most lethal threat, and he took them out in that order. An archer at the back of the mob tried to nock an arrow, but Gid flung his hatchet. The opponent hadn't even drawn his bowstring before the hatchet struck. Kerra rolled out of the way as the archer collapsed beside her in the ferns. She stared aghast at the tattooed, blood-slathered body.

She caught the flash of a blade. A powerful hand seized her by the hair. Her neck was being drawn toward a knife! That's when Gidgiddonihah struck again. Her would-be slayer made an awful gasp and fell limp. It was an understatement to say that Kerra was astonished. She hadn't even realized that Gid's last three opponents were subdued. All of them were lying in heaps upon the ground. The commander stood over her momentarily, studying her to see if she'd suffered any injury—that is, other than shock. Kerra's father and grandfather hoisted her to her feet, yet her eyes remained locked on Gid.

The skirmish had ended nearly as speedily as it began. Eleven robbers lay motionless or convulsing in death throes. Another corpse lay crumpled behind Kerra, at the base of a tree. It was Hamnish, Gid's senior aide. Pek mournfully closed his comrade's eyelids. Kerra had no time whatsoever to internalize or express emotion. She felt numb, like an android. More Gadianton wraiths could be heard whooping like banshees, as if converging from multiple directions.

Gid whispered harshly in Kerra's face: "*Which way?!*"

His voice shook her from her stupor. Kerra's legs started moving. She took off like a shot, heading southward. All of the running had evoked a side ache. She ignored the cramp, pressed her hand against it, and pushed on. Like Gid, she felt she was now operating on primal instinct. The remaining members of the company hastily followed. Gid and Pek remained close on either side of her, leery of additional assassins in the shadows.

A moment later they reached their intended destination—the archway of the massive fallen ceiba tree. Kerra altered her course slightly. Everyone adjusted with her and found themselves planted on the patch of ground where the other Demon Balám had stood two days earlier—the place where Brock had found Hitch's necklace. Gid and the others seemed confused by Kerra's hesitation. Dad and Grandpa came up behind her, staring intently into the space below the arch. Brock stepped in front of her, gazing in the same direction.

The commander's temper flared. "What are we doing?! Why have we come to a halt?!"

Grandpa Lee, Pek, and Lemech kept their wits sharp as unseen villains bounded through the underbrush to the east and west of their position, yelping loudly, apparently rushing toward the Nephite encampment.

Gid finally realized that most members of his company had their attention focused toward the space below the toppled tree trunk. "What is it? An uprooted ceiba? What is everyone staring at?"

Kerra raised her finger and pointed.

Gidgiddonihah followed her finger then turned back to her indignantly. Then he did a double take. Finally he, too, recognized the perplexity of the scene. Everyone in their group stood transfixed. The space below the archway appeared somehow fitted into place, like a 3D picture frame. It wobbled in and out of focus in a pattern that reminded Kerra of waves on a pond. Far more striking was the tableau *beyond* the wall of energy. It was jungle—perhaps not so different from the jungle that surrounded them—except that it *was* different. The vertical trunks of trees above and below the archway created by the toppled ceiba did not match up. Also, a crooked bluff cut a distinctive line a hundred yards in the distance. This bluff's upper edge was not visible in the forest around them. It was only perceptible when peering into the "frame" of the archway. However, if these had been the *only* abnormalities, most members of the company might have missed the phenomenon. What *no* one could ignore was the disparity in the light. In *their* forest—that is, in the neighborhood where Gadianton robbers could be heard bounding through the undergrowth—it was still the darkest hour of night. Clouds had again veiled the three-quarter moon.

But beyond the arch every surface was painted with a reddish glow, whether it was leaves or bark or earth. Beyond the archway, it was *not* the darkest hour of night. Beyond the toppled ceiba trunk, it was nearly sunrise. Even an interval of five or ten seconds was enough to sufficiently perceive that the light was *increasing*, not decreasing.

"What is this magic?" uttered Pek. "Why is there daylight beyond the fallen ceiba?"

"An entryway," whispered Lemech, "into the realms of the afterlife."

"Not exactly," said Grandpa Lee. "It's a doorway, all right. But it won't you lead to any Pearly Gates."

"Doorway to *what?*" demanded Gid. He faced Kerra. "What happens if we go through . . . er, step underneath . . . if we walk through the space below that fallen trunk?"

She faced Gidgiddonihah but didn't reply. Her mouth fell open, but an adequate response was not forthcoming. She faced straight ahead and made a small shrug as if to say, *Only one way to find out.* However, she knew the prospect of passing through this portal was anything but casual. She thought of Gid's uncle—of his request that Kerra join his nephew's secret mission. If Captain Gidgiddoni really *was* inspired, this—she felt certain—was *part* of it. Perhaps just the *first* part.

Bracing herself, Kerra walked toward the wall.

"Kerra!" her father shouted. He spoke just as she breached the rift. In Kerra's ears the first syllable of her name sounded normal enough, but the last syllable was echoic and distorted, impacting her eardrums from multiple directions—shrill, muffled, and far, far away.

She emerged on the other side and perceived an immediate transformation in the environment. The air was warmer. More humid. Indeed, it was not Utah. As she'd surmised two days earlier, the passage led to another jungle, possibly another part of the wilderness of Hermounts. The blurriness of the scene that she'd initially perceived beyond the archway was not exclusively created by a distortion in the rift. A low mist hung over the landscape, perhaps rising from a water source beyond the bluff. Along with the morning racket of birds and insects, she detected the distant roar of a waterfall.

Kerra turned around and faced the place where she had emerged. The eastern sky in this general direction was an electrifying red, like the froth of a shaken bottle of strawberry soda. The sun still lingered behind the mountains. It would be perhaps half an hour before its rays would break the horizon.

Kerra peered back across the rift. Interestingly, there was no arch-shaped tree trunk forming the gateway on this side of the portal. There was only a wall of stone. *Was it a cave?* She squinted and distinguished the hazy, distended silhouettes of Gid, her father, and several others beyond the vortex, still shrouded by darkness, gawking at her in jaw-dangling amazement. But no, the surface of the rift was not a cave. This energy barrier was set inside a framework of solid rock, six feet high and about twelve feet across, tapering sharply at either end. In reality, it was shaped similarly to the space beneath the archway, only it was a surface of smooth stone. What kind of stone was it? Amid the shimmers and sparks she perceived a shiny, semi-transparent green along with a hint of blue. There were also white and red striations. *Jade*, Kerra realized. It was a wall of pure jade, utterly impenetrable, except for the extraordinary circumstances created by the present miracle. Despite her breathlessness—both from running and sheer astonishment—the sight was strangely hypnotizing. She felt compelled to break her gaze or blink every few seconds to prevent herself from being drawn in by the complex patterns and waves. She'd seen nothing like this in the hollow near Leeds, Utah. Somehow, inexplicably, a flat surface of solid jade had been transformed into a remarkable passageway.

The next person to enter the rift was Pek, Gid's lieutenant. He seemed to be verifying the "safeness" of this phenomenon for the sake of his boss. However, Gid was not the type to wait for a subordinate's report. He marched immediately behind Pek, unwilling to let anyone take a risk that he wasn't willing to take himself. Dad, Brock, and Grandpa Lee soon followed. The last to emerge from the jadestone barrier was Lemech.

All members of the company looked around in consternation—some mesmerized and others, like Lemech, breathless with terror. Gidgiddonihah turned and peered back into the vortex. There were no longer any silhouettes of living men in the jungle on the opposite side, so the area beyond the wall now resembled a black hole in outer space.

The commander turned anxiously to Kerra. "Where are we?"

She shook her head. "If I were to guess, I'd say we're still in the same wilderness, just a different neighborhood—region—and perhaps with a slight alteration in time. It could be sixteen hours earlier . . . four hours later. I don't know."

Pek acted incensed, as if he'd been somehow accursed. "How is this possible? What sorcery has been inflicted upon us?"

"Not sorcery," said Kerra. "Just science. Er, nature."

"Explain," said Pek.

"I can't explain how it works," she replied. "I'd need a PhD in physics. Even *then*—"

Her father interrupted. His eyes were drinking in the landscape in all directions. "I know this place! I think it's . . . Yesss! I know *exactly* where we are!"

"Where?" asked Gid.

"Hermounts," said Dad. "But considerably farther up the valley. Perhaps two days south of our last encampment. At *least* two days."

"That cannot be," said Lemech. "How can such a thing as . . . as *this* . . . occur?"

"I can't explain it," said Dad. "But that's our location. Just over that bluff there's a steep ridge, about two hundred feet high. And several waterfalls." He looked squarely at Gid. "I'm afraid we're deep in Gadianton territory."

"Grrrreat," Brock muttered.

Gid's eyes swam with alternating emotions. Perplexity. Incredulity. And finally an emotion that Kerra couldn't quite read. The commander asked Dad, "Do you know, from here, how to reach the secret headquarters of Akuhuun, son of Giddianhi?"

Dad scanned the terrain a final time. "Yes. I do. Or at least *one* of them. Akuhuun and his minions never stayed in a single location for very long."

Gid's eyes seemed to illuminate with a fresh sparkle. Kerra wondered if he'd experienced a religious epiphany, perhaps interpreting this event as neither sorcery *nor* science, but a miracle from God.

As Gid glanced back at Brock and Grandpa Lee, his emotions changed again—to frustration. "You two cannot stay," he growled. He indicated the jade wall and the dark jungle beyond. "You must go back. It's too dangerous here."

Brock hiked up his eyebrows. "And it's less dangerous *there?*"

Lines creased Gid's forehead. It was a noteworthy point. The Rattlesnake Battalion was under brutal assault. Brock and the others had watched a man slain by a monstrous black jaguar. How could he refute the boy's argument?

Gid rambled on. "Manazzeh and Chemnon—the sons of Gidgiddoni—are now in command of the Rattlesnake Battalion. They will organize our forces. They will regroup and regain the upper hand. Afterward our forces will retreat. They'll guide our men back to the fortifications of Lachoneus."

Even as Gid was rambling, Kerra stared back into the rift. She perceived the shadows of two men in the jungle darkness—agitated, pointing, and gaping back. The surface of the rift was in flux. The waves of energy were contorting violently. The crystalline jade appeared more *vibrant*, more visible. Kerra caught her breath. She'd witnessed this before—that is, these kinds of patterns. She seen them the very last time she laid eyes on Kiddoni, just before he disappeared forever.

The rift was going away. It was *dissipating!*

Suddenly the silhouettes on the opposite side of the jadestone wall lunged forward. The first man stumbled out of the darkness. It was Chemnon, Gidgiddoni's fifteen-year-old son. Something was wrong. He screeched in pain. Manazzeh emerged behind him, teeth also clenched in agony. But Manazzeh didn't make it through— not entirely. He halted abruptly, as if an enemy had seized his foot. Manazzeh slammed forward onto his chest. Simultaneously Kerra watched the energy wall seemingly "fold in" on itself. Just as Manazzeh breached the wall, the shimmering and sparkling effect upon the smooth stone surface evaporated altogether.

Dad and others rushed to help both men. Chemnon's cheeks, shoulders and legs were covered in ghastly scrapes, as if thrashed by sandpaper. Blisters were forming on his forearms.

It was the same for Manazzeh. Scrapes and scratches crisscrossed his flesh, as if he'd lunged through a gauntlet of thorns. His uniform was shredded in places. Moreover, his right foot had not quite managed to breach the vortex before the phenomenon sucked away. He writhed in anguish. So did Chemnon, but by contrast the younger brother's circumstances weren't nearly as serious.

Kerra examined the place where Manazzeh's right foot was captured—embedded—in the jadestone wall. He repeatedly wrenched his leg, desperate to escape. All at once the foot broke free—intact, or so it appeared. He no longer wore a sandal. Most of the leather and straps appeared to have molded or melted into the jade. A few broken straps were tangled around his shin. His toes and ankle were bleeding. A portion of jade where Manazzeh's foot had escaped clattered to the ground like shards of greenish glass. At the very place where each of Gidgiddoni's sons had emerged, the jade was no longer smooth, sheer, or hard. Its properties had altered. It now had the appearance of shale—loosely interconnected. The once-solid surface could be scraped away with the fingers. Somehow, the molecular bonds had been stirred. But this was only evident at the precise points where each soldier had burst through. Otherwise it remained a wall of smooth, solid jade.

Manazzeh gritted his teeth, seemingly determined not to cry out like his brother. However, after he saw his foot, he could no longer withhold his emotions and released a wail. Dad and Grandpa Lee held him to prevent his hands from examining or complicating the injuries. Pek and Lemech held Chemnon.

Kerra was covered in perspiration. She trembled in horror. As a kid she'd watched an old movie called *The Fly*. In the movie the lead character's genes were spliced with a housefly—half man/half insect. Had something similar happened to Manazzeh and Chemnon? Had Manazzeh's foot been "splinched?" Had it fused with molecules of jade? She recalled her father describing something like this—men who'd barged carelessly through a rift, colliding with unseen obstacles and dying in torment as a tree limb protruded from their chest.

Still, Kerra's intuition rejected this. It didn't seem to adequately explain the event. Manazzeh's foot was intact. Its shape hadn't changed. There were still five toes, toenails. However, much of the skin had been peeled away. Kerra concluded that if any "splicing" had taken place, only the epidermis had been affected. Both young men had breached the rift in the nick of time. A couple seconds later and their bodies might have been fused inside the jadestone forever, faces protruding like Han Solo's in a block of carbonite.

Gidgiddonihah stood over them, torn with emotions. He wanted to sympathize with their dire predicament. In the end, his instincts as a commander won out. He asked angrily, "Why are you both here?"

Chemnon replied, teeth chattering. "W-we saw you enter the f-forest. We followed."

"Your orders were to stay with the men! You were to lead the battalion back to Lachoneus!"

"*What* battalion?" Manazzeh replied, voice choked. "It was a slaughter, just as you predicted. Only you seriously misjudged the timing—by *two days!*"

Gid appeared stricken, as if he'd taken a blow to the stomach. He turned away, but Kerra still saw his face. His eyes were wide—a mask of panic and dread. His legs wobbled. He sat down heavily on the ground, still facing away from the other members of the company.

"He beat me," Gid mumbled. "I underestimated him—again. Akuhuun beat me! Three hundred men! What have I done? *What have I done?!*"

CHAPTER 15

COMMANDER GID WANDERED TOWARD THE bluff by himself. He said he wanted to get the lay of the land, but Kerra suspected he wanted to be alone with his thoughts, if just for a few minutes. It was clear that the events of the last hour had left him grief-stricken, perhaps doubting his abilities. However, Kerra knew he'd soon realize this was no time for self-pity. His battalion was lost. Tragically, Kerra doubted that *anyone* besides the nine people in their company had survived.

"What about the promise?" asked Brock. "What about Captain Gidgiddoni's promise that the battalion would be protected? That everyone would be okay?"

"That wasn't Gidgiddoni's promise," said Dad solemnly.

Brock inflated his lungs, ready to argue. But then Grandpa stepped into the conversation. "Your dad's right. Captain Gidgiddoni's promise was quite specific, and it didn't say that everyone would make it out alive."

Kerra strained to remember the exact words. She realized, indeed, that Brock had misinterpreted the Chief Captain's speech. His promise was that if the warriors exercised their faith, the battalion's mission would succeed, the wicked ambitions of the Gadiantons would be thwarted, and the desires of their families to return home would be fulfilled. Odd. The sheer power of the speech made it an easy thing to misinterpret. In retrospect, the call for exercising faith had not been nullified. It remained in effect. If the promise of Gidgiddonihah's uncle, the prophet, was to be believed, the responsibility of keeping those fires of faith burning had now fallen entirely upon *them*.

Purely from a military standpoint, Kerra realized, the battalion had served its core and vital purpose. The distraction—the carnage—had allowed Gid's team to slip deeper into the wilderness, unnoticed. The strategy had proved more successful than anyone might have hoped. Not only had they escaped undetected, they'd circumvented two full days of traveling. No one could yet judge the full import of what had occurred, but those two days might have been paramount. It might have proven a gargantuan challenge to evade the imbedded network of spies and sentries that Akuhuun had placed in the vicinity of the Great Battleground. Now much of that network had been avoided. Much, but certainly not all.

From a military standpoint. That phrase suddenly struck Kerra as dreadfully callous and cold. Nearly three hundred warriors were dead—men whom Kerra had marched beside only hours ago. How could success "from a military standpoint" ever justify that kind of gut-wrenching sacrifice? Then again, how often could an individual person ever really grasp the nobler goal, the loftier purpose, or the greater glory of any such sacrifice, especially when the moment itself evoked only pain and regret? These paradoxes and dichotomies, she presumed, were the emotions that Gidgiddonihah was struggling with right now.

Pek had accompanied the commander partway toward the bluff. After a few minutes, he doubled back to make an announcement to the group.

"Commander Gidgiddonihah has ordered our company to divide," said Pek. "Manazzeh, on account of his injuries, will remain behind." He faced Manazzeh. "We will locate a hiding place nearby where you will hole up and await further word. The boy, Brock, will remain with you, along with Lee´con."

Lee´con, Kerra repeated in her thoughts. It was the moniker they'd come up with for Grandpa Lee. Sort of a natural amalgamation of Lee and McConnell, similar to her father's nickname.

Brock protested. "Maybe we don't *want* to be left behind. Maybe I can help."

Remarkable, thought Kerra. Two days ago her brother was perfectly happy to remain in the background. She suspected the sons of Captain Gidgiddoni had played a part in changing that. Male ego.

Was it always so predictable? Brock didn't like feeling one-upped by two guys just a few years older than himself.

Chemnon took it upon himself to put Brock in his place. "You're not a soldier," he reminded him. "You'd only slow us down."

Oh, brother, thought Kerra. Such an inspired remark! Clearly Chemnon was still smarting over Kerra's quip yesterday about her brother being taller and perhaps a superior bodyguard. By all appearances, Chemnon was a typical, petty, testosterone-driven fifteen-year-old.

It was Pek who put a needle to Chemnon's inflated aspirations. He told Gidgiddoni's younger son, "You will *also* remain behind."

Chemnon huffed with indignation. "That makes no sense. I am not injured. These are just scratches. Why would I be—?"

"Gidgiddonihah's orders," Pek interrupted. "You'll remain with your brother."

Chemnon pursed his lips, incensed. He probably thought Gid was still furious over his and Manazzeh's abandonment of the battalion. Or, thought Kerra, Gid didn't want to be responsible for his uncle's sons being butchered and eaten by Gadianton cannibals. The commander already felt the terrible burden of three hundred lost lives. No need to compound his already excruciating guilt.

"The commander is attempting to locate a place of security," said Pek. "He wants us to fashion a crutch for Manazzeh."

Lemech set about to accomplish this task.

Manazzeh lay flat on his back before the jadestone wall, still recovering from the shock. Dad had saved a strip of cloth from one of the burned-out huts they'd encountered their first day in the new century. He'd carefully wrapped Manazzeh's bleeding foot. Brock, however, approached Manazzeh with something more intriguing. He pulled Grandpa's tennis shoes from his leather satchel.

"This might help," said Brock, "if they fit."

"What are they?" asked Manazzeh.

"What *are* they?" Brock brought forward his right foot, offering a grandiose display of his Adidas Barricades. "They're shoes. Not as cool as mine. But they'll do."

Grandpa looked at his grandson with perplexity. "You kept my shoes?"

"An afterthought," said Brock. "I felt you might live to regret throwing them away."

"Good afterthought," said Grandpa. "I got blisters on each ankle the size of silver dollars. But . . ." He looked at Manazzeh, then back at the shoes.

Brock did not hand them over until Grandpa gave his consent.

Finally, Grandpa Lee made a scoffing sound and waved it off. Manazzeh's needs obviously exceeded his own.

"Before we put 'em on," Brock told Manazzeh, "put *these* on."

Grandpa watched his grandson pull out his old pair of socks. "What *else* of mine do you have in that bag?" he grumbled.

"That's it," Brock replied. "Except for . . ." He examined the sack. His slim-jim was there, but . . . "Hey! Where's my MP3 player?"

"M-P-3?" asked Chemnon.

Brock cursed then turned to his sister. "Did you take my player?"

"No," said Kerra.

"Well, that sucks," said Brock. "Must've fallen out on the trail."

Manazzeh examined the shoes inside and out—dark brown Skechers with an inch-thick tread. "They appear . . . constricting. I could never tie them on. The pain would be . . . unbearable."

"Just *try*," Brock urged. "You can make the laces as loose as you want. I'll help."

Kerra studied the jadestone wall. The luminescent greens with artful striations would have attracted the eye of any rock enthusiast. Evidence revealed that this stone had once been hacked and quarried, perhaps centuries ago. What else could explain the sheered-off contour of its face? The question was, how was this flat surface transformed into a doorway in time, warping the laws of physics? Was it the nature of the cut? The quality of the jade? Was it this particular place in the universe? This latitude and longitude? What had allowed it to become an intermittent passageway through the realms of time and space? Moreover, what had reawakened the miracle, and what made it go dormant? Kerra vividly recalled that the Demon Balám had used this doorway. Stealthily, the orange-and-black jaguar with an embroidered jade collar had breached the rift and reappeared in the region of the Great Battleground. As Kerra looked at the jade-stone wall, she experienced a brief vision of the vortex reformulating, the Demon Balám's reappearance, claws slashing, and jaws clamping down on her skull. She shook off the gruesome image.

Another strange idea occurred to her. She wondered if, somehow, the presence of this rift explained how Akuhuun had so quickly and successfully assembled his armies for last night's ambush. This particular doorway was rather small. But what if Akuhuun had utilized *numerous* rifts to move his warriors into position?

During the Great Battle between the forces of Giddianhi and Gidgiddoni—which by Kerra's reckoning had taken place six months ago—she recalled *many* "rifts" or places in the forest where Nephite and Gadianton warriors had "crossed over." Most of these warriors didn't realize that they'd crossed *anywhere*. The sudden appearance of Aunt Corinne and Uncle Drew's home in the middle of what had previously been familiar ground had seemed a strange anomaly. Yet few of the Gadiantons or Nephites had interpreted it as something miraculous. Some warriors, Kerra had observed, didn't register anything unusual at all. They perceived their surroundings exactly as they'd been before. According to their perception, they'd never left the precincts of Zarahemla. To those in the twenty-first century, these warriors had seemed like ghosts, haunting an unfamiliar—if limited—domain. Some of them, like Kiddoni on the day he and Kerra had first reunited, could collide and pass right through the molecules of someone in modern times, like a pair of intermingled holograms or mists of vapor. At other times, a slight alteration in physics had permitted such individuals from different centuries to interact in a perfectly normal manner—their sense of touch intact—even though they perceived their surroundings differently.

Kerra couldn't begin to understand or predict what controlled these abnormalities. The physics seemed incredibly fragile and complex. Nevertheless, she felt strongly that Akuhuun had exploited this phenomenon to his advantage. Perhaps he'd done so on four different occasions, allowing his blood-stained warriors to annihilate four Nephite battalions. If this was true, Gid needed to know it. Such information might relieve some of his mental self-flagellation. The Rattlesnake Battalion had been facing something that *no* one comprehended—something that Gid's warriors couldn't have possibly defended against.

As Kerra pondered these concepts, she wondered if she was start-ing to understand why Gid's uncle had enlisted her in this quest. The concept continued to overwhelm and intimidate her. Her grandfa-ther's words from six months ago continued to repeat in her mind: "You have the *gift*, my girl. Even when you were little you could hear things, *feel* things, that not many others can . . . It's the same gift that draws you to those woods."

Hear things. Feel things. Sense things.

If she thought about it too much, it made her delirious. Whatever gifts her grandfather felt she possessed, she couldn't imagine how her powers of perception were any more "honed" than Dad's. Or Brock's. Or even Grandpa's! Whatever Grandpa may have said, Kerra felt sure that he had definite "gifts" of his own.

She'd noticed that her name was not mentioned as one of those who would remain behind with Manazzeh. Apparently Gidgiddonihah *specifically* wanted her to join them for the rest of the mission. It seemed ludicrous. She felt more like a liability, a monkey wrench, a guarantee that everybody would end up imprisoned and slaughtered. She pondered Gid's words from last night: *I know better than to dismiss my uncle's sagacity.*

For now, Kerra would rely on those words. The so-called wisdom of Gidgiddoni. What else was there to rely upon? Perhaps it was the beginning of something she might have called faith.

Kerra looked toward the commander. He knelt about seventy yards away, at the edge of the bluff. Beyond him was a narrow valley, perhaps more of a gulley. The air echoed with the drone of multiple waterfalls.

Kerra started walking toward Gid, drawing stares from Pek and her father. She crossed a leafy field and traversed a rocky knoll. Gid was wiping his stained copper hatchet against the grass, cleaning off the blood, she presumed. His uniform was mostly of thick, hardened leather, but a soft cloth hung down from his left hip, perhaps strictly for polishing his weapons. As he polished away, his mind appeared absorbed in other thoughts.

He looked up quickly as Kerra approached and returned the hatchet to his belt, possibly believing such an activity was uncouth in the presence of a woman. He stared across the valley, teeming with vegetation, so much so that it hid the cascading falls from view. Only part of a stream was visible—a sleepy section reflecting the golden sunrise. A mile farther up the gulley, southward, the saddle of a hill opened up to a wide, jungle-covered expanse, presently obscured in mist.

Gid continued facing forward. "What do you want?"

She was unsure how to start. "I-uh-wanted to explain . . . about the passageway. The rift. And . . ."

"And what?"

"Also . . . I wanted to thank you."

"Why?"

"You saved my life. Back there. In the dark."

Gid grunted, as if the compliment deserved no other acknowledgment. "What did you want to explain?"

"Well . . ." Kerra began. She felt flustered. In many ways Gidgiddonihah reminded her of Kiddoni. They were both highly disciplined warriors. Gid may not have been as handsome, but . . . he was considerably more intimidating. "If you haven't already guessed, my father, grandfather, brother, and I . . . We're not from here." She pointed toward the jadestone. "We came through that rift. I mean . . . not exactly *that* rift, but . . . a rift sort of like it. We're from a different place. A different land."

Gid waited for more. "What is that to me?"

Kerra blurted it out. "Also a different *time*. I mean . . . a different era of history."

Gid studied her. He turned back toward the valley, eyes glazing over, thoughts still far away. "I do not pretend to understand all things. I've learned to accept my fate, no matter where it leads. Or rather, I've been *forced* to accept it. God causes miracles. God withholds miracles. I am no longer . . . surprised."

She scrunched her eyebrows. It was an odd speech. Lonely and cynical. "I just wanted to explain. Last night's attack . . . there may be nothing you could have done to prevent it. The Gadiantons may be using these passages."

"How?"

She shrugged. "I'm not sure. Not exactly. They've obviously lived here for quite some time. They may have discovered them on their own or—"

"*Or*—" Gid interrupted, suddenly intrigued, "—or else these passages may have been *shown* to them—through sorcery. These 'rifts'—as you call them—may have been revealed by the Enemy of Us All."

She tilted her head. Such a conclusion wasn't unreasonable. She bit the inside of her cheek and nodded. "Possibly. But—"

Gid interrupted again, narrowing his gaze. "Are you a sorceress, Ke'con?"

She widened her eyes, laughing uncomfortably. "Um, no. No, I'm not—"

"Of course you're not," said Gid, dismissing his own accusation as a matter of deduction. "Or my uncle would not have recommended you."

"And call me Kerra," she insisted. "Or Sakerra. I don't like the abbreviation thing, like you did to the names of my father and grand—"

Gid stayed on subject. "If you are not a sorceress, how is it that you know how to find . . . or *use* . . . these passages?"

"I couldn't say," said Kerra. "You'd have to ask my grandfather."

"Why would I have to ask Lee'con?"

"Well, he thinks I have some kind of—" She wriggled her fingers mystically. "—*gift*. I'm not really sure."

"Gift? As in *spiritual* gift?"

"Something like that."

Gid looked at her seriously. "Do *you* believe you have this gift?"

"Sometimes," Kerra admitted uneasily. "Honestly, I . . ." She gave up and just admitted, "Yes. There are times. Yes, I think I do."

Gid's gaze was so penetrating that Kerra squirmed inside. Still, she refused to be daunted. The commander leaned in close—so close she could feel his heated breath in the cool humidity. In spite of it, she did not back off or lean away.

Gid said, "I will tell you something, Kerra-Sakerra . . . I do not expect to leave this wilderness alive. I expect to die on this mission. But I also expect to succeed in my objective. And, because of your help, I promise that I will do everything in my power to ensure that you and your family escape alive and . . . *intact*. I ask only for your loyalty. Your *honesty*. So do *not* lie to me. If you do not possess the powers that you proclaim, tell me now so that I do not die in vain."

Kerra swallowed then stiffened her jaw. "If I'm lying, you'll probably fail in your mission anyway. Right?"

His expression softened slightly. Only for an instant. "Yes, probably. Possibly. But I would still like to hear your answer."

"I've *already* answered you," she said. "Is it your habit to demand numerous answers to the same question?"

He formed a crooked grin. "Yes."

Kerra didn't blink. Neither did she answer him again. After an interminable span, Gid broke off his searing gaze. She'd won the staredown. Or so it appeared. Gid started walking back toward the other members of the company.

"Let's keep moving," he announced. "We'll find a hiding place for Manazzeh and the others at the base of this gulley."

Kerra remained standing alone at the edge of the bluff. She wouldn't have to wait here alone for long. By the looks of it, the best route into the gulley descended at precisely the place where she was standing. She watched Gid walk away, contemplating his statement—his premonition—that he would not survive. If that was true—if he was predicting his own demise—exactly how did he expect to help her and the *others* survive? It seemed a cocky, bombastic contradiction. Indeed, she'd never met anyone like Gidgiddonihah. On the other hand, she was also certain that Gid had never met anyone like her.

The gulley encompassed a considerable amount of territory. Many features were cloaked by greenery and mist. Gidgiddonihah's company worked their way along a muddy trail and through moist, leafy foliage. The going was painfully tedious with Pek and Chemnon assisting Manazzeh with every step. Brock was inclined to pat himself on the back for the idea of offering him Grandpa's shoes. The laces were tied loosely. Nevertheless, *without* them, Brock was sure they'd have been forced to carry Manazzeh. Grandpa's Skechers allowed Manazzeh to utilize a crude crutch. He even managed to put some weight on the injury, which to his brother seemed miraculous.

"Where did you obtain such footwear?" Chemnon inquired.

"Ancient Chinese secret," said Brock.

"Chinese?"

"Put it this way. If I told ya, I'd have to kill ya."

Chemnon smirked. "As if that were possible."

"We obtained them a long, long time ago, in a galaxy far, far away."

"Nonsense."

"If I revealed the secret, the manufacturer would hunt me down like a dog. Corporate espionage is a serious crime."

"You're taunting me, aren't you?"

"Nahh!" said Brock. "Ya think so? Oh, wait. Yes. Absolutely."

Chemnon reddened with fury. He said to Gid, "Is his presence so necessary?"

"Keep silent," Gid commanded. "These valleys carry even the slightest sound a very great distance."

Brock continued to taunt Chemnon with facial expressions—everything short of sticking out his tongue. The younger son of Gidgiddoni finally faced away in frustration.

Soon they arrived at the base of the gulley. A stone's throw further and the foliage parted. They'd reached the bank of the stream. Kerra glanced south and feasted her eyes on three of the waterfalls that they'd been hearing all morning. These falls cascaded over three embankments, each twenty feet higher than its predecessor. Below the third falls, which happened to be the same plateau upon which they stood, a crevasse meandered along the face of the cliff. One end of this cliff crept behind the third waterfall then extended far to the right, finally ending in a tangle of vines. An area across the stream and beneath this cliff face appeared dry and hospitable. It was also private. Unless someone had willfully followed them into the gulley, the likeliness of being discovered appeared quite slim, especially since a *fourth* waterfall—the tallest of them all—rumbled over a precipice a mere thirty yards downstream, making this shelf largely inaccessible. Kerra found her eyes drawn downstream, toward this final waterfall. The sight of it sent a peculiar sensation down her spine. She wasn't sure why. Finally, she shrugged it off, worried that she was becoming prone to imagining things that simply were not there.

"We'll divide up here," said Gidgiddonihah. "Manazzeh, Chemnon, and the others will hide beneath that ridge, inside that crevasse. After our mission is complete, we'll return."

Brock assessed the current. "You want us to cross the stream? Better hope we don't slip in and get sucked over the next waterfall."

"I see stones over there," said Pek, pointing at a pool just below the third waterfall.

"Stones?" said Grandpa. "A walkway? In other words, we're apparently not the first explorers to discover this little paradise. Best keep on our toes."

"How long are we expected to wait?" asked Chemnon.

All eyes turned to Dad for an answer.

He pointed toward the highest fall. "We'll make our way to that summit and continue south. With any luck, we'll reach the largest encampment of prisoners in a day or two. This is the same camp where I lived for two years."

Gid turned to Chemnon. "That's your answer. A day to reach our destination. A day to accomplish our task. Another day to return. Three days total. Four at the most."

"We'll give you five," said Manazzeh. "Five days to send us word. After that . . . we'll embark for home, taking the shortest route."

"I wouldn't advise that," said Pek. "I'd seek a roundabout path, or you'll surely collide with Akuhuun's army, fresh from last night's victory."

Kerra looked at Gid. He made no comment. He knew that just a short while ago Kerra had postulated an entirely different theory for how the Gadiantons moved about. Still, whether or not it was true, Pek's advice was sound. Heck, her theory might've been dead wrong. Gid's silence on the matter seemed appropriate.

"We have no provisions," said Chemnon. "If these forests are barren of game, like other parts of Hermounts, we won't find much to eat. Five days. After that, we cannot remain."

Gid nodded. "Understood. Five days."

It was time to separate. Dad embraced his father and his son. Kerra embraced them as well.

Grandpa whispered in his granddaughter's ear. "You're the key, sweetheart. You realize that, don't you?"

She still had grave reservations about such concepts, but she nodded anyway, for Grandpa's sake.

"If you have doubts," Grandpa added, "you know how to resolve them. Right?"

She scrunched her forehead. Then it hit her. He was talking about religion. Prayer and fasting and whatever.

"Right," she responded obliquely. "Be careful crossing that stream, Grandpa." She glanced toward the final waterfall. "There's something . . . weird . . . over there."

Grandpa's bushy eyebrows popped up. "*Weird*? Don't worry, grand-daughter. I have no plans of riding any waterfalls today."

The journey to the summit began. Kerra glanced back often as they ascended the slippery trail. Her heart felt squeezed and pinched. She realized she might never lay eyes upon her brother and grandfather again. She shuddered. The thought was almost too much to bear. Lemech glanced at Kerra and noticed tears in her eyes.

"None of that," he said. His tone was kindly, but stern. Kerra quickly realized his motives were not compassionate.

"Fear draws evil," explained her father's superstitious brother-in-law. "Anxiety calls forth the devil's demons. If you're afraid, don't ever show it. There are always dark powers that gain strength from our fear."

She gaped at Lemech, wondering how his superstitions might relate to Grandpa Lee's challenge for her to call upon God in prayer. Were the two tactics really all that different? In any case, how could a person hide their fear? Did Lemech really think the devil was that stupid and would fall for such ruses? Fear was fear, and if any being knew when we were afraid, it was the devil.

Moreover, why should she resolve her doubts by begging to God? If doubts persisted, why would Heavenly Father take them away? Maybe doubts were good. They kept you honest and alert. They kept you humble. Everything she'd learned about faith—statements from Kiddoni, her aunt, her uncle, her father, the LDS missionaries—seemed jumbled somehow. Her grandfather once said that God knew what people were going to pray for even *before* they prayed. If that was true, then for Pete's sake, what was the *point*? Did God just like hearing people grovel and nag and plead? The notion flew in the face of every philosophy she'd ever used to guide her life: the conviction that she was on her *own* in this miserable world. If she wanted something, then she better darn well—by herself—figure out how to get it. It seemed a much healthier way to conduct her life. Prayer. The very idea seemed weak. Pointless. Still, there was one thing she'd never done.

She'd never actually tried it.

CHAPTER 16

TERRIFIC, THOUGHT BROCK.

Wasn't this every kid's fantasy? Being stuck in a cave with two prima donna Nephites and his elderly grandfather? Oh, and add to that being *hungry*! No, we couldn't forget *that*!

Brock hadn't eaten since last night. Of course, by his perception, last night was only two hours ago. So why in blazes didn't he feel tired? He'd by no means had a full night's sleep. When people anticipate being bored, the first thing on their minds is sleep, right? Besides, the heat and humidity were getting so thick you could practically make designs in the air with your finger. A siesta should've sounded good. But Brock McConnell paced like a caged leopard, like he'd devoured a full container of No-Doz. He couldn't have slept if his life had depended on it.

Maybe it was just his traumatic lack of a pillow. Or a blanket. Yet such inconveniences didn't seem to affect Grandpa. The old warhorse simply rustled up some soft grass and leaves, located a cool sandbank, and appeared to be settling in for a long snooze.

For Brock, the thing that kept him awake might've been the look of that pristine pool at the base of the falls. It beckoned to him like one of those siren women from Greek mythology. Grandpa had warned him about the current and the dangerous waterfall beyond, but the stones they'd used to cross the stream had created a nice security barrier—a place to cling to as a last resort. Nah, Grandpappy's warning had been overstated. Brock was definitely goin' in. However, as he was about to remove his shirt, Chemnon popped his fantasy like a soap bubble.

"First things first," said the Nephite. "We must gather provisions, construct a shelter."

"I thought this crevasse was our shelter," said Brock.

"Don't underestimate the night chill at this altitude," said Manazzeh. "My brother is right. We need to construct a proper wind break. We must find food."

"Yesterday you said there *wasn't* any food," Brock reminded him.

"This could be true," said Manazzeh. "There may not be much. But we have to try."

"I'm all for it," said Grandpa Lee, rousing from his sandy crib. "Brock and I will help in any way we can. But if you expect us to use one of them bows to rustle up some grub, you might be disappointed. I hunted some with a bow when I was a kid, but I was never much good at it."

"How are you with a sling?" asked Chemnon.

"Uh . . . not much better, I'm afraid."

"Do they not hunt where you're from?" asked Manazzeh.

"Some are hunters; some are gatherers," said Brock. "Grandpa and I come from a long line of gatherers."

"Are you competent with *any* weapons?" asked Chemnon.

"Of course," said Brock. He indicated Manazzeh's obsidian-edged sword. "I can swing that puppy well enough."

Chemnon huffed sarcastically. "That will help—so long as I can always coerce the deer to run at you in a straight line."

Brock retrieved the sword anyway. Manazzeh winced from another wave of pain and did not resist.

"If you wanna hunt, let's hunt," said Brock. "If nothing else, I'll be like a pointer hound. I'll spot the game and you can shoot it." He demonstrated by lifting one leg and positioning his arms, looking far more like a figure in an Egyptian mural than an Irish setter.

Chemnon rolled his eyes. "Fine. Let's hunt."

* * *

Dad drew to a halt as a structure appeared ahead, looming just above the jungle trees. It was a *big* structure, utterly in ruins. A massive entryway faced them, like a cave. There were multiple terraces. The dust of many centuries had settled on every surface. In some places the dust had grown so thick nature had adopted it as a bed of soil for trees, ferns, and vines.

"A pyramid," Kerra said quietly.

If so, it was the most "disguised" pyramid she'd ever imagined. Members of the company glanced around and distinguished numerous additional mounds, some as big as houses. If this spot of real estate had once been a city, the jungle had reclaimed it long ago. Exposed stone was a rarity, except for the entryway and a few other surfaces on and around the temple's base. Tree roots groped at the edges of these buried edifices like arthritic fingers.

Gidgiddonihah, Lemech, and Pek looked at Dad for instructions. It wasn't the first time he'd paused over the past few hours, striving to find his bearings. He looked genuinely confused. This, too, was an unfamiliar locale.

Dad was lost. Kerra knew it. And now Gid knew it too.

Nevertheless, Dad nodded studiously and said, "This is good. It's perfect. The temple is higher than the jungle canopy. I can climb it and get a more precise lay of the land."

Gid's expression was dubious, disappointed. Every passing minute further emphasized the precariousness of their circumstances. They were in the middle of unfamiliar terrain in a very dangerous region of Zarahemla. Wandering aimlessly in a place like this might cause disorientation so serious that they'd never find their way back to the falls.

Dad wasted no time. He barged forward to the base of the pyramid to begin his climb.

Gid nudged Lemech and Pek to follow. With sour expressions, they obeyed their commander.

Kerra and Gidgiddonihah walked to the base of the temple's entryway. Nearly all of it was encased in soil and leaves except for a ten-foot-wide path that led to the structure's cavernous interior. Once, this path might have extended twenty yards in either direction, across the entire width of the pyramid. For now the edifice reminded Kerra of a living thing plagued by tumors—tumors that sprouted tufts of hair in the form of grass and vines.

Gid gazed upward and studied a couple of visible carvings along the entrance's top flange—abstract representations of animals—some real, some mythical. There were jaguars, rattlesnakes, and even a one-eyed behemoth with a dangling tongue. At one time such sculptures had been brightly painted, but most of the color had been long since worn away by the elements.

"Jaredites," said Gid, identifying the temple's architects. "The *original* inhabitants of Zarahemla."

"How old?" asked Kerra.

He shrugged. "Who can say? Thousands of years. Maybe as old as Mahonri Moriancumr himself."

Kerra took a seat on the steps. "This seems like a rugged area to build a city, so high in the mountains."

"As you can see," said Gid, "the inhabitants did not remain."

"Someday," said Kerra, "my people will scrape away all the dirt, trees, and muck from these stones and charge a couple greenbacks to any soul who wants to see it."

"Why?" asked Gid.

She leaned back on her hands. "That's just what people from my century do whenever they find ruins from an ancient civilization."

"This is an evil place," said Gid. "Though it may have been first constructed by Jared's descendants, such people did not remain on the holy ground of Christ's followers. Later generations corrupted this edifice. The whole structure should now be razed to the dust, not transformed into a monument for visitors who will part with their substance to celebrate its splendor. Many of the symbols carved along that rim are the same as those used by Gadianton's satanic priests today." He pointed. "That one extols the glory of death by sacrifice." He pointed to another glyph. "That carving, if you can't already tell, is a beating heart after being removed from the cavity of a man's chest. As you have already observed, no people would normally build in such a rugged place. They either came here to escape evil, or they came here to embrace it. I suspect the last inhabitants took refuge here for the same reasons as today's Reds—to hide from the civilized, God-fearing peoples of the most accessible parts of the land. Robber bands would then organize attacks from these places and glut themselves on the labors of the righteous."

It was a passionate speech. Kerra feared his interpretation was oversimplified. She patted the stone. "Well, you gotta admit, it was once a pretty studly-looking pyramid. If Gadiantons are so lazy—refusing to farm or grow food—where'd they find the energy to maintain something like this?"

"They *didn't*," spat Gid. "They used slaves, the same way they used your father for two years. The same way they are now using your stepmother and half-brother, or even Lemech's son, and many other Nephite and Lamanite captives."

Kerra's sense of irony dissipated. She nodded and whispered, "Also Kiddoni."

She'd thought her voice was soft enough that Gid wouldn't hear, but the gaping entryway echoed the slightest sounds.

"Yes," Gid confirmed. "That is, if he lived, along with any other battalion commanders. They, too, would have been forced to become slaves."

Kerra blushed. She wasn't aware that Gid knew anything about her and Kiddoni. Apparently Gid's uncle, or perhaps Kerra's dad, had filled him in on some of the more juicy details.

Gid stepped around in front of Kerra. "I know that many have advised you to abandon all hope regarding Kiddoni. I will not tell you this. If the Reds can capture a battalion commander alive and make an example of him, I believe they will do so. At least . . . for a period of time."

"A period of time?" asked Kerra.

"Eventually, they would likely execute him, especially if it's on a festival day that honors their demons, like the Kawak monster, or some other wraith who is only appeased by human flesh."

"When are these 'festival' days?" asked Kerra darkly.

Gid smiled morosely. "I wouldn't worry. Their most holy day—that is, their most *un*holy day—is the summer solstice, which will not occur for many weeks."

Kerra pondered this. It was comforting . . . sort of. There still seemed to be so many things to fear.

Gid observed, "I can tell that you care for him a great deal."

Kerra nodded and shrugged. "I've known him since childhood. He . . . 'found' me . . . on the other side of a rift. We've been close friends for as long as I can remember."

"But not betrothed?"

"What?" said Kerra. She furrowed her brow, irritated. "How do you mean?"

"I mean, did your families agree that you should marry? Are you his 'intended' bride?"

"I don't 'intend' to be *anybody's* bride," she quipped. "Where I'm from it doesn't work like that."

"Do young girls not marry where you are from?"

"Of course we marry. We're just not betrothed from birth—especially by our parents."

"I see," said Gid. "Well . . . Kiddoni would be a fool to let you slip through his fingers. You are quite beautiful."

"Thanks," said Kerra. She didn't say, "*I think*," but by her tone those words could have easily been added.

The commander sat near her on the stairs, two steps lower. "You act as though you have not heard this compliment."

"I've heard it," said Kerra. "I just never know how to take it. Beauty is . . . I dunno . . . synthetic. Unoriginal. Empty. It makes many people hate you—people you've never met. And it makes other people love you in a way that means absolutely nothing. All in all, it doesn't account for much."

Gid chuckled. "It's funny. You sound very much like my fiancée. She voiced . . . similar feelings. She called beauty 'the devil's best temptation for vice and sloth.' Even though she . . . she was also very beautiful."

Gid's eyes glazed over again. He made a tiny shudder, attempting to dismiss the memory to some far corner of his mind.

Kerra refused to let him tuck it away. "You must have also cared for *her* a great deal."

"I *loved* her," said Gid tersely, without hesitation. "I loved her from the first day that I laid eyes on her, when I was nine years old. Her name was Chani. Her family visited us. It was all very formal. After I was introduced to her, she wept and ran away." Gid smiled. "Her parents were furious. But over time, the two of us became friends. And eventually, I won her heart. Unexpectedly, I won the heart of another at the same time."

"Oh?"

"Her little sister, Rebha," said Gid. "She is no less beautiful than Chani."

"You must be a real lady-killer, Gidgiddonihah."

There was the slightest—the *absolute* slightest—hint of a blush on Gid's cheeks. "Rebha was jealous of her older sister. She often tried to steal my attention. For a while it was quite the family scandal." He was grinning crookedly. Nevertheless, seeing the young war commander smile in any way, thought Kerra, was a truly wonderful thing.

Tentatively, Kerra inquired, "Rebha . . . is she . . . ?"

Gid discerned her question and replied, "Yes. She's alive and well. But she is in mourning, like her parents and siblings."

"I suspect," said Kerra, "you may have reciprocated some of Rebha's feelings. Perhaps some of those old fires could someday be rekindled."

Gid sent her a hard look, somewhat offended. "The memory of Chani is not even remotely cold." He arose brusquely. "Why are we even discussing this?!"

"Sorry," said Kerra. "I sensed, maybe, such thoughts might bring comfort—"

"Have I not caused her family enough grief? Chani is dead, and it is because of me. Because of my 'success' as a warrior. Should I be the cause of death for *both* daughters? It could never be. It is impossible."

"I said I was sorry," Kerra repeated. "I shouldn't have stuck my nose where it didn't belong. I just wondered if, perhaps, in your life, you might have earned for yourself a modicum of happiness. Perhaps even a few miracles."

"As I said before," Gid said flatly. "God causes miracles. God withholds miracles. We cannot control it. We can only control the magnitude . . . the *intensity* . . . of our emotions."

Kerra cocked an eyebrow. "The 'intensity of our emotions'?"

"Our passion for vengeance," he clarified.

"Oh," said Kerra. "You must have a *lot* of that."

"Indeed," said Gid. "I do."

"Vengeance against whom?"

He stewed a little then replied, "Pek saw him. He saw the killer. The assassin. He saw the man clearly as he fled. His face. The patterns of the tattoos that covered his flesh. You see, Pek is Chani's brother."

"And now you're on a quest to find this man?"

Gid had grown weary of the subject. "Even *that* is in God's hands."

"You really think everything is so arbitrary?" asked Kerra. "We have no control at all?"

"None," Gid confirmed with a shrug of bitterness. "None at all."

"Then why pray?"

Gid perked up. "What?"

"Why go through the motions of praying if prayer doesn't really have any influence? Why pray to God if it really doesn't *change* anything?"

Gid turned away. His face became inscrutable. "I *don't* pray."

"You don't?"

"No."

"But you still believe in God?"

"Of course."

Kerra harrumphed. "That sounds weird—to believe in God but to not want to pray to Him?"

"Lately I've had nothing to say." Gid shrugged. "What about you? By your tone am I to conclude that you do *not* believe in God?"

"Never much thought about it. Never cared. Except for the past six months."

"What occurred six months ago?"

She sighed. "That's the last time I saw Kiddoni."

"Ah, so you've begun to pray in hopes that God might reunite you with him?"

"No," said Kerra. "I don't pray either."

"You *don't?*"

"I've never had a reason."

Gid's eyebrows shot up. "Never had a *reason?!* You have never had a conflict that required the aid of God?"

Kerra smiled crookedly, mocking Gid's traditional grin. "Look who's talking. Didn't you just say it made no difference?"

Gid frowned and turned away again. "Yes. That's what I said."

"Commander, you and I are a little different," said Kerra. "I don't pray because, well, I've never done it. Not even sure I know how. The reason *you* don't pray, if I understand correctly, is because you're mad. You're peeved at God."

Gid stuck out his jaw. "This is a pointless discussion." He arose and gazed toward the apex of the temple. "Where is your father? They should have reached the summit by now."

An instant later, Pek made an appearance, looking down at Kerra and Gid from the pyramid's top edge.

The setting made it unnecessary to raise his voice. He said simply, "We have climbed in vain. Mi´con is still unsure of our position."

Gid furrowed his brow. "Where *is* he?"

Kerra's father appeared. Lemech was close behind him.

"I'm sorry," said Dad, deeply frustrated. "I told your uncle—I *warned* him—that my knowledge of Hermounts was limited."

"But you said you recognized this land!" said Gid. "Do you remember no landmarks?"

Dad scratched his head and stared into the distance. "I can't be sure. This structure is not as high as I'd hoped."

Gid made a growl in his throat. He clenched and unclenched his fists, pacing back and forth. His eyes settled hard on Kerra. He stepped up close. "My uncle believes that you possess profound spiritual gifts. Only a few hours ago you assured me that this was true."

Kerra was taken aback. "Profound? I-I never said—I mean, I never meant to *imply*—"

He seized her shoulders and raised her to her feet. "You will exercise those gifts now."

Kerra swallowed painfully. "What do you suggest that I—?"

"PRAY!" said Gid harshly. He pointed toward the darkened chamber of the temple. "You will go in there. You will not return until you have received an answer. Do you understand?"

Kerra gaped at the commander. It was a direct order. Yet only a moment ago he'd bluntly proclaimed that prayer changed nothing. How was she supposed to get her head around this? Gid's eyes burned like firebrands. She felt sure if she hadn't ascended those stairs on her own, the commander would have carried her into the chamber and dumped her there. So ascend she did. As she reached the entryway, she turned back. Gid's expression remained the same. Kerra sighed and faced the dark interior. Reluctantly, she entered the chamber.

Safely inside the shadow, her tears overflowed. She dropped to her knees and sobbed quietly. How did she get into this mess? *Spiritual gifts*! What were they all talking about? This was Grandpa's fault! *He* was the one who'd told her she could hear things—*feel* things—that no one else could hear or feel. It wasn't just Grandpa. It was also

Captain Gidgiddoni. Why did they believe this nonsense? What did they *expect* from her?!

She fought to stifle her sobs, fearing Gid would hear her loud and clear. Her father and those on the temple roof could likely hear her as well. She wiped her eyes and gazed into the darkness. Her vision started to adjust. She distinguished shapes and shadows. The chamber had multiple compartments. At least six were built into the back wall, and more on either side. The satanic symbols that Gid had identified along the flange were also carved above every compartment. In here the elements hadn't diminished the colors. Murals were as vivid as the day they were painted. The scenes were morbid—priests in feathered headdresses proudly held aloft severed heads. Additional captives knelt in line. Another mural depicted grotesque behemoths with gaping jaws, body parts being flung into their throats. Blood and gore was a consistent theme. One illustration showed rivers of red streaming down a pyramid's steps—probably *this* pyramid. Another depicted priests engaged in self-mutilation. *Sure thing*, thought Kerra. This was a perfect place to utter a first prayer! Just *perfect*!

What was she supposed to pray for? Should she ask God for a flashing sign pointing "*THATAWAY*" to Akuhuun's lair? Should she request that God reveal another energy rift? Maybe Gidgiddonihah expected her to locate a secret doorway that would drop the assassins right at Akuhuun's feet. Afterward they could spring back into the rift before his henchmen could react.

Kerra drew a deep breath. She pulled herself together.

A prayer to God.

She tried to recall the formula as explained by Elder Leota and Elder Paisley: 1. Address Heavenly Father by name. 2. Express thanks. 3. Ask for blessings. 4. Close in the name of Jesus Christ.

It seemed unnecessarily complex. The only part she really wanted to do was number three. Was the other stuff really mandatory?

At last, she began: "Our dear, kind, gracious, beloved Heavenly Father . . ." She'd noted that Latter-day Saints often put multiple adjectives before Heavenly Father's name, perhaps as a way of buttering Him up before arriving at the main purpose of the prayer, which was invariably number three.

Thank you, she thought.

She was stuck. What did people generally thank Him for? It usually seemed like a long list of clichés: "Thank you for this day." "Thank you for my family." "Thank you for the weather." Kerra decided to skip all that. She didn't want her very first prayer to come off as insincere. To avoid pretension, she felt she should get right to the point.

Please God, she prayed. *We're lost. I mean* really *lost. Dad doesn't know which way to go. Help me. Help me find another way. Help me figure out what Grandpa Lee and Captain Gidgiddoni said about me. If it's all a bunch of hogwash, that's fine. I don't care. Just tell me some*thing. *Commander Gid wants an answer. He's counting on me. They're all counting on me. They believe in me. Even if I think it's nonsense, they don't. So . . . just a clue. A hint. Anything. Anything. Help him. Guide me. Tell me anything. But help him. Help Kiddoni. Save him.*

Her concentration was intense. She never got around to officially closing the prayer. An idea—vibrant and fully formed—flashed in her mind.

"*Whoa!*" she whispered, exhaling deeply.

She gazed straight ahead at the central compartment along the back wall. Bloody murals adorned either side. But the compartment itself was empty. No murals or etchings. Just three blank walls. Bare canvasses. She caught her breath. Her heart pulsated. Was it really this easy? *No way!* It *couldn't* be this simple.

She arose and approached the compartment, half expecting a shimmering vortex to appear, like the hazy, luminous "window" that had loomed under the archway of the fallen tree. No vortex materialized. Obviously it wasn't going to be *quite* so simple. She brought her feet together, body completely inside the four foot square compartment. Still nothing occurred.

Or did it?

Instinctively, senselessly, Kerra pressed her palm against the cold rear wall, sticky with cobwebs. She couldn't shake a certain feeling. Whatever it was, she felt something was *drawing* her forward. Something in front of her. Not inside the compartment—*beyond* the compartment. Perhaps quite some *distance* beyond. She glanced up. The ceiling was barren, like the walls. An image burned in her thoughts. A circle. A stone circle, floating above. It meant something. *What did it mean?*

Kerra turned and walked swiftly back toward the entryway. As she emerged from the chamber, Gid was watching her like a hawk. She hastily descended the steps. Dad, Lemech, and Pek happened to be approaching from the right, along a ledge that skirted the pyramid's base.

Gid unfolded his arms and followed her. Oblivious to him and everything else, Kerra walked past her father and the others on the ledge. She slipped around the corner and out of sight.

"What's going on?" Dad asked.

Gid shook his head. He decided there was no time for discussion. He drew his obsidian sword and picked up his pace. Dad, Lemech, and Pek followed.

Kerra hastened along the temple's northern face. A thunderclap resounded overhead as she hurried around to its western flank. She was now on exactly the opposite side of the entryway. She perpetually glanced toward the pyramid's summit, but whatever she was looking for, it did not come into view until she'd reached the middle part of the western edge. As a blue web of lightning crisscrossed the sky, she saw what she was looking for.

More than a hundred feet overhead, at the pyramid's apex, stood one of the only features of the temple not yet obscured by dirt and vines. It was a pinnacle of sorts, like a weathervane, but crafted of stone. It was a circle, like the circle on a plastic stick for blowing bubbles, three feet across and carved from a single chunk of limestone. Kerra shielded her eyes to see it clearly as the rain began to fall. The circle wasn't perfect. A portion on the left side had fallen away. It resembled a letter C, floating aloft like a lightning rod.

Rain pattered against the ground as Gid, Dad, Pek, and Lemech caught up to her.

She turned swiftly to Gidgiddonihah, "What *is* that?"

"What is what?"

She pointed desperately. "*That*! It relates to what you said earlier, right?"

Gid was perplexed, "What I said earlier . . . ?"

"The summer solstice!" Kerra cried, her body trembling. "The day of sacrifice! That thing up there! It has to do with *that*, right?"

Gid shielded his own eyes and studied the object. "Yes," he confirmed. "I've seen things like it. On other buildings. Atop other temples, like the ones built by the people of Zarahemla before King Mosiah's arrival. The shape is meant to capture the first light of day as the sun rises from behind the eastern mountains. A shadow is cast—a perfect circle—illuminating a sacred target, usually an altar of sacrifice. But the positioning is only correct one day—one *moment*—out of the entire year."

"I know all that," said Kerra impatiently. "The summer solstice. But the shadow cast by *that specific circle*—where would it have been cast?"

"Hard to say," said Gid. "It's the wrong time of day; wrong day of the year. Even if today *was* a festival day, the circle is broken on—"

"Over there!" Kerra interrupted. She pointed westward as straight as an arrow. "Wherever it was cast, it has to be *that* way! We have to find it—the exact place of ground that circle once lit on the day of sacrifice."

Everyone studied the terrain directly to the west. Numerous buried mounds were visible, but nothing stood out as a target to be outlined by a circular shadow at dawn. At a certain point about two hundred yards west lay a barrier of particularly dense jungle.

"If we find this place," asked Gid, wiping the rain from his face, "what exactly would it mean?"

"I don't know," said Kerra. "But that's where it's coming from—the sound. Don't you hear it?"

Gid, Dad, Lemech, and Pek listened intently. There was another rumble of thunder in the heavens, but no one apparently perceived the same sound as Kerra. She could hear a whistle—ever so slight—above the patter of the rain. It was the song of the Whistlers, but the tone was very different, almost like nails on a chalkboard.

She looked around at the blank faces. "*None* of you can hear that?"

One by one they shook their heads.

"But that's okay," Dad reassured. "We don't *have* to hear it, Kerra. As long as *you* can hear it."

She faced west again. "Follow me."

Dad glanced back at the broken circle atop the pyramid. He tried to match it against the mountain range in the east, not yet hidden by storm clouds. He faced forward again, trying to envision a direct line from the place where the sun would rise, shining perfectly through the broken circle and casting a distinctive shadow onto the western terrain. Since the high eastern mountains were quite some distance, the line would be fairly level. The place they sought could be as far as a mile westward. Also, the target may no longer exist. It might have already succumbed to centuries of decay and ruination. Would they even recognize the target point, even if they happened to be standing right on top of it?

Kerra McConnell marched forward. Her determination was irrepressible. Whatever obstacles appeared at her feet, she insisted on following a direct westward path, true as possible, eyes never straying. Suddenly Pek stuck out his arm and halted her. She sent him an irritated glare. Gid's second-in-command pointed toward a silky white web, undamaged by raindrops, festooned like a tent among the tall strands of grass. It stretched out into a four-pointed pattern waist high, directly in her path. Atop this web crouched a black-legged spider, four inches in diameter, prickly red hairs around its pincer mouth, and a fat purple abdomen. It was looking right at her with its beady little eyes, *daring* her to disturb its domain.

"Funnel-web spider," said Pek. "Deadly. Best go around."

Kerra's expression became apologetic. She nodded in gratitude and did as Pek had instructed.

The company of five, led by Kerra, marched across two more mounds of buried ruins. At the summit of the second mound, she paused and looked back toward the temple, then westward again, performing much the same analysis as her father. Thunder and lightning were increasing in frequency; the rain was coming down in sheets.

"We have to be close," she said. "It can't be much farther."

However, it seemed there was no way to advance. At their feet stretched a morass of foliage so thick that their eyes couldn't penetrate more than a few yards. In all directions, including overhead, the canopy of leaves, vines, and branches was so tightly knit that it practically blotted out the sunlight. There was no way around it. This jungle wall meandered to the north and south as far as the eye could see. Marking a trail would be next to impossible. Entering such a labyrinth, especially in this weather, one could easily lose his bearings after a few hundred feet. It was conceivable that anyone so foolish might never return.

"You expect us to walk into *that?*" asked Lemech.

"That's where it is," Kerra declared.

"Where *what* is?" asked Pek.

Dad tried to speak to her more patiently. "Another portal? A shortcut to Akuhuun's encampment?"

She shut her eyes and raised her hands defensively. "I don't know. I just know it's where we're supposed to go. *We have to hurry!*"

Lemech's confidence was waning. He turned to Gid. "Remind me again: Why are we following her?"

"Because," said Gidgiddonihah, "my uncle said that she would serve as an important guide at critical moments. I think *this* is one of those moments."

Pek interjected, "I thought your uncle said *Mi´con* was our guide. Now the *girl* is our guide?"

Gid grumbled in frustration. "Mi´con *is* our guide. But the girl is . . . she's . . . a *special* guide. For special challenges."

"I don't follow this reasoning," said Lemech.

Kerra was becoming soaked. She started shivering. Softly, she said, "Pleeease. We must hurry."

Gid turned to Lemech and Pek. "You both saw what happened this morning. We *all* saw what happened when we crossed over that . . . that—"

"We don't even know what to call it!" said Lemech. "*None* of us knows what it was!"

"*She* knows," Gid insisted, pointing. "She has a gift to understand places like the one we passed through this morning. And I believe she knows how to locate other places like it."

Kerra wasn't even certain if she agreed. She wasn't sure she understood *any* of this! She knew only that there was no time to argue.

"We have to go," she repeated. "We can't delay any longer."

"In my experience," said Lemech, "men who are feebleminded enough to wander into virgin jungle so thick and congested never again set their eyes on civilization. They become disoriented. They panic. The wilderness strips away their sanity. The jungle swallows them whole."

Dad put his hand on Kerra's shoulder. "How far into this mess do you think we'd have to travel?"

She shook her head. "I told you! I don't know. Not far. *We're wasting precious time!*"

"Why is the time so critical?" asked Pek.

"*I don't know! I don't know!*" cried Kerra.

Dad turned to the others. "I trust her. She *does* have a gift."

"*What* gift?" said Lemech. "She just admitted she has no idea how far we must go or even why we must hurry."

"*Please, please, please!*" said Kerra breathlessly, the rain now mingled with her tears.

Pek said to Gid, "You're my commander. You were nearly my brother-in-law. I'd follow you into the jaws of the Great Maw. But I must tell you, I have grave reservations."

"So do I," said Gid. "But I believe in my uncle. So follow me, Pek, into the throat of the monster!"

Gid started to strap his sword behind his shoulder. Pek and Lemech began to unstring their bows.

"*What is everyone doing?!*" asked Kerra with alarm.

Pek looked at his weapon, then curiously at Kerra. "It would soon be ruined."

Gid said, "In such congestion and weather our weapons would snag and tangle. The stone edges will break and wear—"

"*Arm yourselves!*" Kerra commanded. "Be ready to fight!"

The warriors looked at Gid. Deep concern creased every face. What did she think they'd encounter in this rain-drenched vegetation? As another thunderclap shook the air, the commander finally nodded in concurrence. The warriors filled each hand with a weapon. Lemech gave his obsidian-edged sword to Dad. Gidgiddonihah carried an obsidian-toothed sword with a three-inch tip and, of course, his trusty copper hatchet. There were also two knives on his belt— one of flint and one of volcanic glass. Lemech and Pek, despite the tangled morass, carried their bows, one arrow nocked and another under their thumbs. Jagged knives also waited on their hips.

"Keep tight!" ordered Gid. "Shoulder to shoulder. Ready? *Let's go!*"

Kerra continued shivering, blood rushing behind her temples, surging through every limb. The company heaved aside dripping leaves and vines, crushing the vegetation underfoot in an effort to forge a pathway. Kerra remained beside her father. She was the only soul in the company who did not carry a weapon, but she hardly thought of this. Her eyes surveyed the rain-drenched terrain even as it became exceedingly difficult to see.

Ten feet into the morass, the light changed dramatically. Faces were cast in heavy shadow, nearly as dark as the final hour of daylight. Kerra looked upward. Infrequent rays of sunlight cut through the rainclouds, dappling leaves and limbs high overhead, but failing to penetrate anywhere close to the earth. She drew a deep breath, attempting to dispel claustrophobia's icy hand. The trill of the Whistlers remained pervasive in her ears. Knowing that only she could hear it was painfully lonely. It was no longer possible to travel in a perfectly straight line. The obstacles were relentless. Lemech had already snagged his bow more than once, fighting to yank it free. Kerra received perpetual looks from the men of the company, as if they expected more guidance, more details. She was screaming inside. She had no clue what she was doing or what was ahead. There was only the pounding rain and the pulsating impression that they were, indeed, moving in the right direction.

After twenty more feet, Kerra looked back. The stone circle atop the pyramid was no longer visible through the vegetation. Even if they hadn't penetrated so deeply into the jungle, by now the summit of the pyramid may have been hidden by low, whirling storm clouds. What could that shadow of so many centuries ago have possibly encircled? Had this suffocating foliage ever been cleared by human hands? It appeared as if this wilderness was still as pristine and untouched as it had been since the inception of time. She clenched her jaw. It was the *right way*. She *felt* it. That centuries-old oracle had once directed the first morning ray of sunlight at something very close—so near she might have reached out and touched it.

She pushed aside a vine festooned with thick, heart-shaped leaves. A stone pillar appeared before her face. She gasped in surprise. What did they call these things? A *stela!*—an upright stone slab with carvings. The carvings were encrusted with oily black lichen and drizzling with rainwater. It tilted to the left, like the Leaning Tower of Pisa.

Almost simultaneously Pek announced, "I found something."

Kerra could barely distinguish Pek through the undergrowth. He appeared to be pressing against a similar stone slab. His stela appeared to have broken into two distinct chunks. The top chunk budged but did not topple. It *swung*, more or less, as if supported by wires. Jungle vines had enwrapped it so snugly that they managed to support its weight.

"Stop—everyone!" Kerra announced.

Shuffling foliage and snapping twigs abruptly ceased. Only the din of the rain and the song of the Whistlers remained, the latter ringing solely in Kerra's ears.

She looked in both directions. The only person to her left was Dad. Pek stood at the opposite end of the line, with the others in between. No one had yet crossed the barrier separating the two pillars. Yet it was this very line that possessed and sustained Kerra's attention. It was the right place. *This*, she felt sure, was the spot of ground once highlighted by the solstice sun shining through the stone circle. Gid stood just inches behind the invisible boundary, weapons firmly in hand. He sensed instinctively that something desperate was about to unfold.

Kerra said to her father, "Get behind me. Walk around, to the right of me—to the right of this stone."

"Why?" he asked.

"Just-do-it-there's-no-time!" she said in one breath.

She made eye contact with every warrior, their faces sopping with sweat and rain. No need for words. They all understood. Whatever happened after crossing—*together*—between these two stelae, it would be intense.

Dad was in position. He nodded at Kerra. Kerra nodded at Gidgiddonihah. The muscles went taut in Gid's face. It was universally recognized: when Gid moved, the rest would follow.

Kerra's stomach coiled like a ball of snakes. She sensed a horrible secret—something the others could *not* know. Something no one could ever prepare for. What they were about to face would not only be intense, it would be one of the most soul-wrenching scenes that any of them would ever scorch upon their minds.

"Go-*ooo*!" Gid stretched the word into two syllables, more emphasis on the second.

As the five bodies rushed forward between the stelae, there was a moment of confusion. No energy wall appeared, as they had all expected, but Dad finally heard the Whistlers, high-pitched and deafening, for only an instant. The rain stopped, replaced by a warm, rushing wind from all directions. The landscape changed—and *violently*. Gray shadows peeled away, leaving a red sheen that seemed to ignite the vegetation in a raging fireball—again, only for an instant. The leaves, vines, and other foliage fled like a cinema wipe, transformed into a wide, smoke-filled clearing. Kerra and her four companions emerged onto a scene of horrifying carnage. Before them stood a dozen masked men with bloody knives. The air shrilled with dreadful chanting, like hyenas feeding at a kill. There was fire—bodies—*screaming!*—*death!*

Gidgiddonihah alone kept his wits and did not hesitate. His weapons swung into action, attacking the nearest figure in a demonic mask. Pek and Lemech discharged their arrows. Dad reacted next, striking downward on a second masked figure. Kerra blinked her eyes, straining to comprehend the spectacle around her.

She stood inside a circle of crimson light—the first rays of a solstice sun. Sunlight encircled three stone pillars—three stelae—in a blazing halo. The seven-foot pillars were very different from the stelae they'd just passed between. These were perfectly vertical. They were blackened in fire and glistening in blood. Men stood against them, strapped in place. Two were dead: beheaded. What remained of their bodies was—only *seconds* before—drenched in something flammable and set ablaze. A pair of heads lay on the ground, inhuman in appearance, encased in masks—a tapir, an eagle. Both burning corpses were bedecked in feathers and fur. Human sacrifices dressed as animals. A third figure was tied to a stela on the far right, not yet beheaded. His body was doused and dripping in the same flammable liquid, but not yet set aflame. He was adorned like a jaguar: mask, fur, tail—the whole nine yards. Even the fingers of his bound hands were painted like narrowing white claws. His head hung limp. *Was he dead?*

Gid's company had materialized amid an unfolding ceremony— a rite of sacrifice and horror. They stood upon a mosaic of large flat stones, fifteen feet wide. The platform was surrounded by a frenzied throng: a hundred Gadianton worshippers, now dispersing in all directions. The company's dramatic appearance had disrupted the ongoing murders. Screams replaced chants as worshippers fled in fright, undoubtedly convinced that such a supernatural entrance was an augury of omnipotent disapproval.

The Gadianton priests, adorned in costumes of tanned human hides and masks—initially fought back against the invaders, wielding long, black sacrificial blades. Gid killed four of them. Dad also took out several. A handful of others had fallen to the arrows of Pek and Lemech. One in particular—a figure wearing a tall headdress of orange and white feathers along with a demonic mask featuring a protruding forked tongue—escaped with an arrow to the shoulder. He, along with the audience of worshippers, swiftly fled into the forest like roaches scattering from a beam of light. The undergrowth here was not as dense as where they'd been, but it was thick enough that the jungle soon concealed every fleeing soul.

Gid retrieved his hatchet from the chest of a dead priest. "They'll be back," he predicted. "Armed and ready."

Pek turned to Kerra's father. "Where are we?! Do you know this place?"

Dad nodded. "I know it all too well. The Reds call it the Place of Life. Obviously that's a misnomer—a name inspired by evil."

Kerra scanned the area. Her mind reeled with revulsion. Death was rampant in all directions. The odor was horrid—rotting flesh, smoke, and the acrid smell of whatever substance had been poured over those who were tied to the pillars. Fires burned at every corner of the platform. A swift, muddy river flowed a stone's throw to the north. All around them were heaped piles of human bones and scatterings of skulls. This smoky clearing, fifty yards wide, was more than just a place of sacrifice. It was a place of "preparation." They were preparing human meat for . . . Kerra cringed to ponder it. She *couldn't* ponder it—not without retching or blacking out.

"An encampment sits about a mile up this river," said Dad. "When I was here, it was the largest camp of Nephite and Lamanite prisoners of Akuhuun and his cohorts."

"Then we're close," said Pek.

"Akuhuun?" repeated Gid, stepping closer to Dad. He pointed toward the jungle with great intensity. "That priest with the orange headdress—the one with an arrow in his shoulder—*Who was he*?!"

Dad shook his head. "A leader. He would have to be a Gadianton high priest."

"Akuhuun *himself*!"

Dad nodded. "It's possible. He was usually the one who conducted—"

Gid didn't wait to hear more. He charged toward the jungle in hot pursuit. Pek followed.

Lemech, however, did not join them. His eyes were drawn to carnage on the mosaic platform. Suddenly he gasped and dropped to his knees. He began howling in anguish. Kerra realized that this particular corpse had meaning for Lemech. The face had partially fallen out of the eagle mask. Lemech gazed upon it in devastation. It was a face he knew.

Kerra's father stepped closer. Then he recognized it too. Dad's complexion darkened with grief. Kerra didn't need them to tell her who it was. She knew it was Lemech's son, his eldest, a young man named Menkom, and a man who'd been her father's fellow prisoner for two years. Lemech's only reason for joining this expedition was now lifeless before him.

Kerra's mind reeled with regret. They'd taken too much time. They'd wasted precious seconds. She'd *known* there was no time to spare! Lemech's doubts and complaints were a major cause of delay. They wouldn't listen to her! *Lemech* wouldn't listen!

Why, God? she cried inwardly. It was only her second prayer, and it was a prayer of confusion and condemnation. *WHY?!*

Something compelled her to turn her head. She gaped at the man in the jaguar costume, tied to the third stela. He was motionless, chin against his chest. A headache began to throb in Kerra's skull. She trembled like a leaf as she approached the bound figure, who was either unconscious or dead. Amid Lemech's wails of torment, Kerra reached out and grasped the hood—an ear of the jaguar mask. She tried to jerk it away. It wasn't easy to remove. She grabbed inside the costume's "snout," affixed top and bottom with what were certainly genuine jaguar teeth. She ripped some of the stitching then wrenched the entire hood off his head.

Her heart stopped. Her lungs froze. Every sound vanished—the crackling fires, Lemech's wails, her father's voice trying to comfort him—all of it fizzled out or floated away like wisps of smoke. She felt enclosed in a bubble of time and space. She concentrated on the face. The skin was filthy, crusted with dirt, mottled with bruises. The lips were swollen and bleeding from fresh cuts. The figure's eyes opened slightly, focused fleetingly on Kerra, then rolled back inside his head. The man was alive, breathing. Tears blurred Kerra's vision.

It was Kiddoni.

CHAPTER 17

THE HUNTING PARTY, CONSISTING OF Brock and Chemnon, set out immediately. Grandpa Lee remained behind to look after Manazzeh and hopefully catch up on some sleep. Chemnon, of course, was armed with all his weaponry, including a bow and a dozen arrows.

Brock carried Manazzeh's obsidian-edged sword. It was a heavy sucker—at least three feet long and crafted of the heaviest wood Brock had ever lugged. After a short distance it put quite a strain on his wrist. Chemnon noticed his various awkward efforts to carry it with two hands or balance it on his shoulder. The shoulder thing was particularly dangerous if he let that razor-sharp edge accidentally slide against his neck. It might cause a nasty "laceration."

"I thought you said you were experienced with a *macuahuitl,*" said Chemnon. "And yet you left behind the sling that Manazzeh wore upon his back."

"I didn't think we'd be walking so far," Brock said defensively.

Chemnon snorted. "Is it so hard to admit your mistakes and weaknesses? Out here if you keep any secrets, you get yourself killed—and often those who accompany you as well."

"Fine," said Brock. "I admit it. I don't know your stupid weapons. Where I'm from we have a little thing called a .38 Special. Fires a bullet. Moves faster than any arrow. The target dies of lead poisoning, so to speak."

"Why didn't you bring one of these weapons?"

"Good question," said Brock. "A mistake I won't make again. Trust me."

"A real warrior would not make such a mistake in the *first* place," said Chemnon.

Brock shrugged. "I guess hunting deer or shooting Gadianton robbers wasn't in the brochure."

Chemnon halted and faced Brock. "You have no formal training as a warrior whatsoever. Do you?"

Brock gritted his teeth but confessed. "Not a whole lot. No."

"And you also have no experience as a hunter."

"Well, I . . . No."

"Why are you here?"

Brock pulled in his chin. "What do you mean? I'm here to help you."

"By serving what purpose?"

Brock thought a second then said stiffly, "By helping to carry whatever piece of meat you kill."

Chemnon made a dismissive grunt. He removed a strip of hide from a pouch on his belt and reached toward Brock's neck. Brock flinched and moved away.

"I'm going to tie it around your neck," he said. "Then you can rest the sword on your shoulder without nicking your jugular."

Brock seemed to ponder this, frowning. Chemnon finally eased in and tied the strip of hide in place.

He turned away and started walking again. "Beyond everything else," he added, "I hope that you know how to keep silent and stay out of my way."

Brock followed two steps behind, inwardly cursing the youngest son of Gidgiddoni. Despite the uninvited kindness of providing protection for his neck, Brock had a mind to use his Nephite sword to split Chemnon in two like a hunk of wood. However, after traipsing another hundred yards into the forest, his temper started to mellow a little. He even felt ashamed. Here he was putting on airs of being this tough-as-nails, Conan-style warrior, yet he couldn't fool the likes of Chemnon even for a minute. If these were the streets of L.A., it'd be different. Or would it? The truth was, he'd never even fired a gun. Holy halibut! What was he even *doing* here? He contemplated making his way back to the cave and waterfall, but honestly, he wasn't one-hundred percent certain of his ability to find it. So he was stuck here serving as Chemnon's lackey.

Brock estimated that they'd ventured another quarter mile into the wilderness when Chemnon quickly raised an arm and motioned for Brock to stop. The Nephite heard something. Or *sensed* it. Brock followed his lead and crouched down in the brush. Just ahead was a dark copse of trees with dense ground cover. Chemnon drew an arrow and placed it on the bowstring. They waited. They watched.

After a full minute Brock finally whispered, "What are we doing?"

Chemnon turned his neck, eyes flaming. Brock realized that he'd also failed in his efforts to keep silent.

After waiting another infuriating half minute, Brock failed again. "Listen, Chemnon. Maybe you'd be better off if I—"

Chemnon twisted around again, raised his fist and clenched it—a clear threat that if Brock didn't shut his trap, the consequences would be severe.

Brock sucked it up. He waited another full minute. He began to suspect that whatever had caused Chemnon to halt, it wasn't necessarily game. It might've been something else. Something dangerous. Brock wondered if whatever they listened for might *also* be listening for *them.*

Brock finally heard something—the crack of a twig, maybe a rustle of leaves. It had definitely come from the jungle. All at once two creatures darted from behind a pair of leaves the size of full-page newspapers. What *were* they? Brock had seen pictures of them before, like oversized guinea pigs—the size of little barking dogs. *Agouti!* *That's* what they were called. So these forests were *not* entirely devoid of game. Chemnon arose and fired his arrow. The squeal confirmed that his aim was true—an incredible shot considering how fast the critter was moving.

Brock had an uneasy feeling. *Something's not right.* The dead agouti had been scuttling like the proverbial "bat out of Hades." *Both* critters had been running *away* from something—and not Chemnon or Brock. Something *else* had spooked—

At that instant a creature burst from the undergrowth like an exploding canon. *A jaguar!* A Demon Balám! Brock recognized it from that first day—the same four-hundred pound, orange-and-black-mottled monster that had emerged from the rift. It lunged toward Chemnon. He'd turned his body, even directed his bow. But there was no projectile. His arrow was spent, as if . . . as if the creature had *planned* it! As if it had meant for Chemnon to shoot the agouti, wasting the arrow that might've saved his life. If so, it was a strategy beyond anything that Brock would have conceived an animal capable of devising!

He heard the earsplitting roar. He heard Chemnon cry out. He saw the creature impact his body and clasp its jaws around his skull. There was a crack—like an egg. Brock's heart flew into his throat. Chemnon's body went still. He was a dead man! He was *dead*!

Only as this fact fully snagged in his mind were his muscles set free. He began to run, his thoughts in a cyclone, his legs seemingly spinning like pinwheels. He dropped the heavy obsidian sword. Actually, it was yanked from his hand as it got tangled in some vines. He didn't go back. Just ran blindly. He had to keep fleeing. Chemnon was dead. The son of Gidgiddoni had been slain! Brock was next. How could he possibly outrun the apex predator of these jungles? Especially a predator possessed by demons?!

He tripped on a root. He caught himself hard, shredding the skin of his palms. Feeling no pain, he scrambled again to his feet, still running, still flying as fast as adrenaline allowed. He swore that he heard something crashing through the forest behind him. Once—only once—did he dare look back. This was a mistake.

His eyesight bounced wildly—he wasn't able to distinguish anything. For a split second he lost his bearings and collided with a tree. A *thick* tree. His mind blacked out. His next memory was fuzzy. His eyes opened to a blurry world. Brock was lying flat on his back. He spit something from his mouth. Something rubbery. A mushroom? After that, he tasted blood. It poured from his nose.

He heard breathing—not *his* breathing. After rolling his head, he tried to focus his gaze. Something was stalking toward him. Something black as coal, like a supernatural wraith. Not bounding. Not charging. Just closing in as he lay there, helpless. Moving in for the kill.

What was it? If this was a jaguar, it was *not* the same jaguar that had killed Chemnon. It was the *other* Demon Balám: the obsidian-black beast from the night before—the one that had killed Lemech's friend. Brock realized he was about to die. He threw his arms over his head. If he protected his cranium, its jaws couldn't crush his skull, right?

As Brock felt its heated breath on his face, he cried out, *"Stop! Please!!"*

His mind was dizzy, vision still blurry. The black mass *had* stopped. It was two feet away, maybe closer. And yet, inexplicably, its jaws did not clamp down for the kill. The creature just lingered there, watching its defenseless quarry with . . . *curiosity??*

Brock heard a snarl. A weird, broken snarl. There was emotion to it. Moreover, Brock *understood* it. He knew what the sound *meant.* Not just the inflection or intent—he divined *actual words* that the jaguar was trying to say! Was this possible?? Clearly, that tree had jarred his brain. He was seeing hallucinations. That is, *hearing* hallucinations. Brock swore that the creature had asked, *"Why should I?"*

Or maybe it *wasn't* the jaguar who addressed him. Maybe it was a human. Was there someone standing behind the predator? This made sense, because, well—*jaguars couldn't talk!*

Brock heard himself reply, "Because I wanna live! I don't want to die!"

Silence. The creature didn't move. It just gaped at him, the gems on its collar occasionally shooting shafts of sunlight in his already-blurred vision, its tail undulating like a cobra. Brock's eyes were starting to clear. He realized the beast wasn't entirely black. There were patterns on its back, just like any other jaguar, but much, much darker. And besides that, the tip of its tail was bright orange, like a dancing flame. It was also somewhat smaller than the other jaguar—the other demon monster. A difference of maybe fifty pounds.

He heard another snarl. Or rather, *several* snarls in succession. Incredibly, words resounded in his brain. How was this happening?? He literally understood what the cat was *saying.* It really *was* possessed! Brock was hearing the human voice of an actual demon!

He heard, *"If I don't kill you, Master will be angry."*

"Master? Who's your master?"

More snarls. *"A human. Like you. He speaks to me. Like you."*

"Speaks to you?" Brock repeated, sensing somehow that talking forestalled his own death. He had to keep prattling on. "What do you mean?"

A roar, and Brock heard, *"I understand his sounds."*

Brock clasped both sides of his head. He was conversing with a demon. But if it was evil, why hadn't it already crushed his skull? Was he dreaming? Perhaps this was his "Moses moment," like the burning bush. Was this an angel's voice? The voice of God? These ideas didn't make sense either. Brock continued addressing the voice as if it was an actual jaguar.

"You mean . . . you understand the meaning of his words when he speaks to you?" asked Brock.

"*Yes. You are only the second man I've encountered whose sounds I understand. Or who understands my own sounds.*"

"And this other guy is your *master?*"

"*Yes.*"

"What's his name?"

"*Akuhuun. And his command is that I must slay you.*"

"What for?"

"*Because that is his command.*"

"Why does he want to slay me?"

There was a pause. It repeated, "*Because that is his command.*"

Brock raised up his head and shrieked, "That doesn't make sense! You're a *freakin' jaguar*! You're the lord of the jungle! Why do you take commands from *anyone?!*"

The creature continued to stand there on its four paws, seemingly contemplating this question. It appeared to be searching all of its faculties for a reasonable answer.

The best it came up with was, "*Because . . . I understand him.*"

"Well, now we know *that's* not unique, don't we?!" Brock shot back. "You understand me too, right? So here are *my* orders: *Don't* kill me! You got it? DO NOT KILL ME!"

Its feet didn't budge, orange-tipped tail twitching like a firefly. The Demon Balám seemed genuinely, thoroughly puzzled.

How could he reinforce his argument? Brock decided to ask, "Do you enjoy killing?"

The question only seemed to mystify and antagonize the animal further. It replied, "*I have always killed.*"

"Yeah, but for *food*, right? Not for *fun*! Not because some lame-brained human jerk-face *asked* you to! Don't you have a conscience? Don't you know the difference between right and wrong?"

Brock couldn't believe he was saying this. Philosophizing with a *jaguar?!* He'd never argued like this with another human *being*, let alone a predator that stalked on all fours. Of course, he'd never had to engage in this kind of debate to save his life either. Still, he couldn't believe such words were coming from his mouth.

He heard another roar. Loud. Frightening. No particular meaning. Just confusion. Frustration. Fury. Brock curled into a ball, again shielding his face and head with both arms. This was it. His philosophizing had failed. The beast would carry out its master's orders. It was just simpler that way. Once more, Brock braced himself for death.

The foliage rustled. Silence reigned. Slowly, his arms parted. Cautiously, he opened his eyes and glanced about. The jaguar was gone. The rustling had been the Demon Balám making an exit. Brock sat on his haunches, carefully searching in all directions. He touched his nose with the back of his hand and studied the blood. The bleeding had mostly stopped, but his nose, especially the bridge, throbbed with pain. He saw blood on the ground where he'd lain. It had streamed down his chin. There was a tender bruise on his chest. Surprisingly, these were the only injuries he'd received from the tree trunk. It seemed miraculous. In reality, that tree had saved his life. Because he was addled and dazed, just lying there helpless, the jaguar had approached slowly. He'd been given enough time to *speak*.

Brock sat there, thoughts congealing like the blood in his nose. The wonder of what had occurred hadn't quite sunk in. *Would it ever?* His memory jolted back like a slingshot: Chemnon was dead, slain by the first, larger jaguar. Brock would have to tell Manazzeh. He'd have to find his way back to the waterfall. He'd have to find it *alone*. How could he find anything? He still felt disoriented. His thoughts were scrambled. Everything shuddered inside, like a private earthquake.

In the midst of these muddled thoughts, he heard another voice—this time *definitely* human. He heard it twice, five seconds apart.

"Huracan!" the voice cried. "Huracan!"

The individual was coming closer. Brock didn't know whether to run or hide amid the vegetation. So he sat there, frozen. Catatonic. At last a human shape emerged from the undergrowth. As he and Brock met eyes, the stranger halted.

In a subdued, bewildered voice, the man declared, "Brock?"

Brock didn't reply. Just gaped at him, eyes like saucers.

The man stepped closer, grinning. "Holy mother—it *is* you! Brock McConnell! *Ha*! I don't believe it!"

The man was draped in first-century leathers and hide. He wore a thick, dark beard and dark shocks of long hair hanging below his shoulders. In his right hand was an obsidian sword, much like the sword that Brock had lost in the vines, only this weapon was studded with gems and jade.

Brock was on the verge of apoplexy. A talking jaguar. And now this. The man's appearance was strange, but he was no "stranger." The beard and long hair did not disguise him. If nothing else, Brock would've recognized his tattoos. They were not the typical Gadianton style. In particular, Brock recognized the dragon tattoo plastered across his shoulder.

The man leaned in close and waved a hand before Brock's face, trying to validate whether or not the teenager could see. "You remember who I am? Do you recognize me?"

Brock nodded awkwardly.

The man stood back and opened his arms, presenting himself as an old, cherished friend. "Then say somethin', bro! Geez, what's it been? Three years? Four years? At least say hello!"

"Hello, Hitch," replied Brock.

"How ya doin', essé! It's great to see ya! The nose looks broke, by the way. Hold still." With just that much warning, Hitch seized the bridge of Brock's nose between two fingers and pinched it hard.

Brock shuddered in pain, but he didn't resist. Afterward, Hitch stood back and admired his work.

"Good as new. *Better* than new. Like a movie star! And you're a *man* now! Busted nose is like a rite of passage. Nobody wants a perfect noggin. Who were ya boxin' anyway?"

"A tree," said Brock tonelessly.

He looked over Brock's shoulder and pointed. "That tree?"

"Uh-huh."

Hitch stepped over and examined the trunk. A few of the pinkish, bracket mushrooms that shimmied up the bark had broken off; otherwise, it appeared unmolested. "Mm-hmm. Looks to me like you lost, dawg." He laughed exuberantly, sadistically.

Brock continued to watch him in disbelief.

Hitch put his hand on Brock's shoulder. "Listen, I'm sure you got a long, poetic tale explaining what yer doin' here. I'm anxious to hear it. Really. But first I gotta ask: You seen my black panther? You seen Huracan?"

Brock shook his head. He wasn't sure why he denied it, but he shook his head all the same. *Huracan.* Brock heard the name as Hitch pronounced it. He perceived a deeper meaning. Maybe this deeper understanding was part of the same gift that helped him understand these ancient people at all. The name meant "wind and fire." That is, "god of wind and fire." The jaguar was indeed named for a demon.

Hitch seemed thoroughly stymied. He gazed off into the jungle fore and aft. "I jes' don't understand that girl. She never acts like this."

He set two fingers in his lips and created a piercing whistle. He called out another name.

"Cociyo!" he shouted. "Com'ere, boy!" He whistled again.

Brock's internal earthquake ramped up to 9.0 as the first jaguar, the *original* Demon Balám with the orange-and-black pelt—the monster who'd only moments ago used its jaws to crush Chemnon's skull—slipped lithely out of the jungle, moving with a grace that was almost serpent-like. *Cociyo.* Again Brock heard it with hard C's, just as Hitch pronounced it, but additional meanings registered, unavoidable, like a tiny red light he couldn't snuff out. "Lightning." Or rather, "*demon* of thunder and lightning."

With its head erect, the beast stood nearly as tall as Hitch, but its eyes were not directed at Hitch Ventura. Its shiny black orbs were fixed on Brock McConnell. The creature's chin was matted with blood from Chemnon's veins. Gore was smeared on its jadestone collar. It made a low, ominous growl. Like the black jaguar, Huracan, Brock discerned its words. He understood the "meaning" of its growl.

The jaguar asked, "*Kill now?*"

"No, no," Hitch replied, scratching the fur behind its neck. "Not now. Not yet. I just wanted to introduce you. This is an old friend of mine. His name is Brock. You like him?"

Another low growl. "*Good smell.*"

"I knew you'd think so." Hitch chuckled. He turned to Brock. "He likes you. The truth is, Cociyo likes whomever I *tell* him to like.

If I change my mind, he changes his, too. He's very . . . obedient that way."

Brock realized that Hitch didn't know that Brock perceived the jaguar's words. Hitch thought he was the only one who understood. *Weird*, thought Brock. Why would he think he was the only one? It seemed to Brock the ability to comprehend the various hisses, chirps, grunts, and snarls of the animal kingdom—the ability to translate such noises into actual thoughts—might come with the territory. It was part of the whole "time travel" gig. Brock wanted to say something—*anything*. He wanted to verify that the male cat could understand *him*, like the female. Unfortunately, his tongue was tied. Cociyo was not staring in a way that suggested it "liked" Brock at all. It merely looked hungry. It had apparently acquired a preference for the flavor of human flesh.

Hitch stroked its head. "Don't worry. I'll grant your wish. I'm your 'tooth fairy,' Cociyo, remember? Right now, I need you to find your mate. Find Huracan. She's AWOL again. Find her and meet us at the lava beach. *Comprende?* Our black-sand paradise. Remember the passageway?"

Cociyo snarled aggressively, clearly saying, *"Of course I remember!"*

Then, in one mighty leap, it hurled itself into the jungle, instantly and soundlessly slipping into the undergrowth. Brock gaped in awe at the disappearing monster then gaped back at Hitch.

"You promised it . . . a wish?"

Brock already knew what Hitch had meant. He knew the murderous nature of the wish. Still, he pretended ignorance. Or maybe he really *hadn't* understood. Maybe it was a joke. What if Hitch was only *pretending* that he would feed Brock to the jaguar? Either way, Brock wasn't about to confess that he'd plainly followed both sides of their conversation. Not yet. Maybe not ever.

"Up and at 'em, amigo!" said Hitch, helping Brock to his feet. "How's your head? Okay? Nose? Better, eh?"

Brock nodded affirmatively to every question.

Hitch ruffled his hair. "Yeah, that's what I thought. You's one tough kid. Was a time, essé, I had big plans for you. You were in line to be my right-hand man. That is, before the whole mess with the gym bag and all that trash. You recall all that?"

Brock swallowed and nodded again. He remembered perfectly. The last time he'd seen Hitch Ventura was not a particularly happy occasion. He'd tossed a quarter-million dollars' worth of drugs down a dark well near the hollow's old horse corral. Hitch was pretty steamed about it. So steamed he nearly emptied every slug of his pistol into Brock's chest. That's when Kiddoni's arrow flew out of nowhere. It impaled Hitch's shooting hand. Brock glanced at Hitch's palm and swore he could still see a scar.

"Not me," said Hitch, answering his own question about the gym bag. "I don't recall a thing. Clean slate. That's what you and me got now. I always liked you, Brock-O. And I know you respected me. Am I right or am I right?"

"Right, Hitch."

"*'Course* I'm right. So follow me, bro. You and me are goin' into the 'wild blue.' I know you know what I'm talkin' about. You wouldn't *be* here if you didn't know. I'm talkin' about those special places. Those funny little ripples in space and time."

With his hand firmly set on Brock's shoulder, Hitch led the teenager into the jungle—straight into what seemed to be the thickest nest of leaves, vines, and ferns.

"Thing is," Hitch continued, "I worked out a whole road map. You hear what I'm saying?"

"Not really," said Brock. "What are you saying, Hitch?"

"Exits and entrances. *That's* what I'm saying. I got a nose for it. Might even call it a talent. Limitless, countless exits and entrances. They're *everywhere!*—that is, if you know where to look. I been using 'em now for four straight years. I got me a secret doorway to more than two dozen 'anchor points' in this tropical armpit. Some anchor points—that's what I call 'em—are in slightly variant periods of time. But here's the ugly catch: I can't seem to find a way home to my sweet domicile in Los Angeles. I miss my satin sheets. A nice, hot shower. So I guess the little 'ripples' ain't *exactly* limitless. There are boundaries. I can move back and forth a couple of years. Two years 'fore I arrived, and 'bout two years after. Yeah, I know. It don't make much sense. Didn't make sense to me for a looong time. But after I figured it out—hoh, *baby!* It's *cool!* So let's go on a safari, Brock-O, my bud. I'll tell you the whole sordid tale of my Tarzan-esque adventure. You'll be the first to hear it. But before all that, maybe we oughta visit that fat grandpa of yours, eh?"

Brock froze in place. "What?"

"Don't get cutesy. Your *grandpa*! And that other slimy son-of-a-Nephite swine. The ones back in that crevasse by the waterfall."

Brock's heartbeat zipped into overdrive. His breathing became erratic. Hitch enjoyed the show, especially the kid's chameleon-like alterations in facial color.

"Sure," he admitted. He put two fingers up to his eyes then pointed the same fingers at Brock. "I been *watching* you, bro. Cociyo smelled the whole lot of you the day you dropped in. Still, I was surprised when I saw your faces. That would've been about the time you kissed your Walmart rags good-bye and started wearing these native gunny sacks. Hey, remember this?"

Hitch reached into a pocket and produced Brock's MP3 player, complete with tangled earbuds. Brock's brows shot up like rockets. No need to say, *Where'd you get that?* Brock's expression said it without having to utter a word.

"Never *mind* where," Hitch answered. "Just know you can't keep secrets from me."

Instinctively, forgetting that such actions might incite retribution, Brock snatched the MP3 player back. Hitch laughed.

"No problem," he said. "It's yours, after all. Ain't much good. Left ear cuts out. What about this?"

Hitch produced the cell phone that had belonged to Brock's father. So he'd stolen that too. But when? Exactly when did he have a chance to rustle through their personal property and walk away with the only items they'd kept from the modern world? It was as if . . . as if he really *was* magic. Or as if he could make himself invisible.

"Shiny," said Hitch. "No battery power anymore. But the natives, see, they *like* shiny things. Especially things like this. You'd be shocked how many brownie points I can earn just by flashin' one of these things around. Ah, but what *you* wanna know is, how did this get from *your* pocket into *mine*, eh? Don't worry about that just now. The point is, I'm like this 'all-seeing maharajah.' You can't surprise me, Brock-O. There's nothin' you can do that I won't eventually find out about. *Capisce?*"

As if to challenge this proclamation right out of the gate, Brock reached inside his collar and produced Hitch's necklace. He dangled it under the gangster's nose.

"Hey!" Hitch exclaimed. "My Che bling! Where'd you find it?"

"Right where your jaguar first sniffed us," Brock replied. "I thought you said you saw everything."

Hitch took the necklace, throwing back his head and scrutinizing Brock carefully. "Don't be cocky, kid. Maybe we *won't* go see your grandpa and Gidgiddoni Junior. At least not yet. First, I wanna show you another mutual friend. You'll enjoy this a lot. Come on, Brock-o-Matic. We ain't got much time. Step into my parlor . . ."

They entered a dark corridor of overhanging limbs, further obscured by vines and other vegetation. It was like a tunnel. Brock perceived only a vague hint that there was any kind of energy wall ahead. This was just seconds before they breached the barrier.

An instant later, the corridor was empty. Brock and his unlikely new "best bud," Hitch Ventura, had vanished.

CHAPTER 18

KERRA AND DAD HAD SEVERED the cords that bound Kiddoni to the stela. They were prepared to carry his unconscious body to a safer place. Kerra's nerves were frayed; her face was etched with tears. Kiddoni appeared to be dying. He might soon be dead. Nothing was certain.

The company was scattered. Gidgiddonihah and Pek had raced after the priest whose shoulder had been pierced by an arrow, hoping this man might be Akuhuun, son of Giddianhi. Bounding after a mysterious, masked, and wounded priest seemed terribly foolhardy. Maybe it was, for anyone besides Gidgiddonihah. Nevertheless, according to Dad, Gid and Pek were charging headlong into a massive nest of Gadianton warriors.

As for Lemech, Dad's Lamanite brother-in-law, he sat motionless upon the sacrificial platform. His son had been among the immolated dead. He held what was left of his son's body, still encased in the eagle mask and regalia he'd been wearing when the execution occurred. Lemech's actions may have seemed morbid, but Kerra knew these were different times, different customs. Blood and gore were daily sights among these people—whether hunting or preparing food, etc. The father held all he had left of his son.

Dad's voice was fierce and urgent. "Lemech, we have to move downriver. There's a place I know. A place of warm mineral springs. We need to get Kiddoni there. You can't stay here. As Gidgiddonihah warned us, the Gadiantons will return, armed and ready."

"Go," said Lemech, his voice barely audible. "I will . . . come soon."

Dad looked at Kerra. Every ounce of her being was focused on saving Kiddoni's life and moving him away from this landscape of murder and blood. She shook her head. They could not wait.

Dad said to Lemech, "We'll be downriver. Not far. This side of the bank."

Lemech nodded listlessly.

They did not want to leave him by himself, defenseless and in mourning. Lemech left them no choice. Dad hoisted Kiddoni over his shoulder and carried him along the riverbank. Kerra sometimes tried to hold the Nephite's hand, but it was difficult along the rocky, uneven bank. She sensed that, at times, his fingers were gripping back. She took it as a hopeful sign.

The river was swollen from rain. Even in the best of times the river's edge was a rough and tangled pathway. They were often forced to travel inland. Dad's back and legs soon felt the strain of Kiddoni's weight. Still, he kept moving. For nearly half an hour he and Kerra trekked along the river's winding course until Dad spotted an obscure trail, nestled by tall trees, leafy undergrowth, and fern-softened stones. With some effort, they lifted Kiddoni over numerous obstacles and lugged him toward the river.

A whiff of sulfur and other chemicals soon overwhelmed Kerra's nose. Shortly the trail opened wide. They traversed an ivory-colored surface of smooth sediment, like hardened chalk. Water trickled along many grooves in the surface, each rivulet burgeoning with green, blue, and copper-colored algae. The turbulent river flowed twenty yards further on. Between them and the rapids, the smooth surface was pocked with numerous pools and cauldrons of bright turquoise or xanthous-colored waters. Some of these cauldrons were so hot they steamed incessantly and noisily, like a boiling pot. Others steamed less, mingling with the cool rivulets that flowed from the forest.

"It's like a Roman spa," said Dad. "Some pools might be considered caldariums, others tepidariums, and others frigidariums. I know the perfect warm-water basin where we can wash his body, perhaps revive him."

They made their way across the chalky floor. Kerra paused above a particular cauldron that emitted steam like a generator at a power plant. It smelled awful, like an Easter egg found in August. The pit had an elliptical shape, about seven feet. She could hear violent rumbling below. Because of the steam, it was impossible to see the pool's boiling surface. She estimated that it was about fifteen feet below where she was standing. There was something odd about it—about this particular cauldron. The feeling . . . was inexplicable.

Her father called her attention to another crystalline pool with stratified bluish green edges and a purplish bottom. It was about a dozen feet wide, emitting the merest mist of listless steam. Kerra felt it perfectly resembled a modern Jacuzzi, with bubbles oozing up from crags in the shallow floor. Its depth was about four feet, but the eastern edge was even shallower, only six to twelve inches.

Kerra's hopes were revitalized as she helped her father lay Kiddoni in the shallowest part of the basin. The warmth had an immediate effect, causing the Nephite commander to flinch but also to sigh with relief. The rejuvenating warmth was initially combined with twinges of pain as the healing mineral water caressed his bruises and seeped into his various cuts and scrapes. Paint from his hands, applied to make his fingers resemble jaguar claws, melted into a colorful cloud. He still wore pelts from the jaguar "costume" that had been intended as his funeral robe. The fur reeked of whatever flammable liquid it had been doused with. Kerra shuddered, knowing that if they had shown up just a few seconds later, Kiddoni would have been set aflame. He would have died almost instantly. Just as with the body paint, the flammable chemicals dissipated into an oily, rainbow-hued residue that dissolved into a steamy froth. Dad helped to strip much of the upper part of his jaguar costume so that minor injuries on his back and chest could be better soothed.

"Kiddoni," Kerra said softly, holding the Nephite's hand while also supporting his shoulder to prevent his face from slipping underwater.

The Nephite's eyes fluttered open. They did not focus on Kerra, but on the rays of sunshine sparkling through the mahogany branches overhead that shaded the springs. Dad used his leather canteen to drizzle a bit of water onto Kiddoni's parched, bleeding lips.

"Kiddoni, it's me," she repeated. "Sakerra. Do you recognize me?"

With seemingly great effort, he transferred his focus onto Kerra's face. His lips moved a little.

"What's that?" Kerra placed her ear directly over his mouth.

"Angel," he whispered. "Angel."

Fresh tears filled Kerra's eyes. She pulled back and shook her head. "No. Not yet. Just me. It's just me."

His eyes pinched tightly again, minutely shaking his head. His lips moved again. This time Kerra easily heard his words.

"Heaven," he said. "This is . . . heaven."

"Wrong again," said Kerra. "You're alive. *I'm* alive. I'm with you. My father is here too."

Kiddoni altered focus. He spotted Kerra's dad—Chris McConnell. Mi´con continued tossing small handfuls of water across Kiddoni's shoulders and chest to rinse away dirt and blood.

"Encourage him to look at *you*," said Dad. "I promise, you're a much more healing sight. Without my beard, I doubt that he even knows who I am."

Kerra suddenly felt self-conscious. What could she possibly look like after all these days of roughing it? A "*healing*" *sight*? Surely she better resembled Bellatrix Lestrange!

Kiddoni shook his head at Kerra's father. "I know you," he insisted.

His eyes closed again. He seemed to faint. Kerra looked up at her father gravely.

"I think he'll be all right," Dad reassured. "He just needs time now. Time to recover. They beat him pretty badly. His back is covered in welts. They apparently knocked his head a few times too. I don't see any major swelling. I doubt if there are any broken bones. He's very lucky. And these springs, I swear, have antiseptic qualities."

Her father's words brought color and confidence to Kerra's cheeks. She sobbed with relief. Her eyes shut as she laid her face on Kiddoni's chest, her body soaking in the same waters of the rejuvenating pool. Her exhaustion, and the hurricane of emotions, had finally caught up to her. She told herself it was finally *okay* to sleep. She'd accomplished her objective. For now, she just wanted to forget everything else: Lemech's grief, Gidgiddonihah, Pek, and all the mortal dangers still swarming around them. Kiddoni was alive. She'd found him. For the moment, it was enough. It was quite enough.

She did manage some restful slumber, though she wasn't sure for how long. A stir of voices awakened her. Men were coming. They approached along the same jungle trail that she and her father had used to bring Kiddoni to the springs. She sat up, warm water dripping off her upper body. Kiddoni remained unconscious. Her dad had decided to stand, weapon in hand, awaiting whoever was about to penetrate the vegetation.

It was Gidgiddonihah, Pek, and Lemech. However, they weren't alone. A fourth man—a stranger—was being frog-marched in front of them. His wrists were bound. Gidgiddonihah used one hand to grip the man's hair while his other seized the arrow shaft imbedded in the stranger's shoulder, almost as if it was a gear shift used to drive the prisoner forward. The man they'd apprehended was obviously the priest who'd run away from the Place of Life. Pek glanced back into the jungle several times, an arrow balanced on his bowstring, as if expecting the enemy to arrive at any second. Lemech directed his obsidian-edged club at the priest. Every ounce of Lemech's grief and vengeance was directed at this single wounded Gadianton. But who was he? As Gid approached her father, Kerra presumed that learning the answer to this question was precisely his objective.

"What happened?" Dad inquired.

"Unfortunately for him, he couldn't scuttle as fast as his cohorts," said Pek. "We killed six of his presumed bodyguards. We know he must be an important leader. But at the moment, he's not talking."

Gid wasted no time. He yanked on the man's hair, raising his face for Mi´con's inspection. "Do you know this man?"

Dad took several steps forward. One of the priest's eyes was nearly swollen shut. He'd been struck several times while being subdued. Lemech didn't seem to particularly care about the man's identity. He apparently wanted the personal privilege of chopping off this man's head. For all Lemech knew, this was the very person who'd done the same thing to his son or set his body aflame. It didn't matter. He was a Gadianton priest. Judging by the pretty headdress he was wearing when they'd appeared out of the rift, this man was likely the ranking priest at that specific sacrifice. Somewhere along the trail his fancy headdress was lost or discarded. Other accoutrements remained: feathered leggings and greaves, as well as strange, scaled shoes with three sharp eagle talons, apparently meant to represent a bird of prey. The shoes were mostly in tatters. They weren't designed for all the running or for being marched to the springs.

Dad studied his face closely. All eyes were upon Mi´con, especially those of Gid and Lemech, awaiting a single word of confirmation.

"So is it him?" asked Gid sternly. "Is it Akuhuun?"

Dad shook his head. "No. But it's a big haul. You've captured Zemnarihah, Giddianhi's right-hand man."

Lemech and Pek grinned widely. Pek couldn't withhold a whoop of victory. Lemech was ready to plunge his sword into the notorious Red leader's belly. Curiously, Gidgiddonihah did not hear this news with any particular sense of rejoicing. His expression was difficult to discern.

"You're sure of this?" he asked Mi´con.

Dad nodded. "Zemnarihah was in charge of the captives. He was always Giddianhi's acting high priest. While I was languishing in their prison, he personally oversaw many torture sessions and most of the executions."

Lemech punched Zemnarihah in the face. "You killed my son, you piece of excrement!"

Gidgiddonihah surprisingly came to Zemnarihah's defense—at least temporarily—and placed himself between the Gadianton and his abusers. "Lemech, stop!" Gid commanded. "We must sort this out."

"Sort *what* out?" said Lemech. "He's the leader of all the robbers!"

"Bind your hatred!" Gid raged. "I promise you, Lemech, you'll have your revenge. But *not yet!*"

Lemech lowered his sword, teeth gritted and eyes burning.

Gid turned to Pek. "Take Lemech and go back by the trees. Give us a moment to interrogate him."

Pek's eyes flashed disapproval. He didn't understand. They'd *all* risked their lives to capture this man. Why shouldn't they *all* relish any words that came out of his mouth during an interrogation?

Gid put his hand on Pek's shoulder. "You have always been loyal to me. Trust me now, Pek. Take Lemech. Withdraw. It is only for a moment."

Pek's loyalty appeared on the brink of disintegrating. He sent Gid a disdainful scowl then finally motioned to Lemech. "Let's go."

Lemech was wound up more tightly than the spring of a catapult, conceivably ready to erupt with an instant surge of violence. Gid watched him until a mere fraction of tension left his shoulders. Pek placed a hand on Lemech's back, and the pair reluctantly withdrew fifteen yards to the place where the trail exited the jungle. Kerra was tempted to join them. She wasn't certain why Gid had let her stay. Allowing a woman to remain at a time like this would only exacerbate Lemech's and Pek's resentment. The river's roar cloaked the interrogation in relative privacy.

Gid asked the captive, "Is it true? Are you Zemnarihah, lord of the Gadiantons?"

Zemnarihah's eyes were fixed on Chris McConnell. Clearly he recognized Kerra's father. He appeared genuinely distressed to see him. Kerra assumed this was because it meant the jig was up. He could no longer pretend anonymity. He couldn't lie about anything that might help his circumstances. However, a large portion of his animosity also seemed directed at Gidgiddonihah.

He replied with a scathing look and then snarled, "You will not live to see the setting of the sun. *None of you!* My blood warriors are on your trail. They know of this place. They will arrive soon enough. And they—"

Gid slapped him hard—so hard it knocked him down. He tried to keep from rolling onto the arrow in his right shoulder blade but failed. He clenched his teeth and tried to contain a wail of agony. Again, he failed. It was curious behavior for Gid, considering his defense of Zemnarihah a moment earlier. Kerra glanced at Pek and Lemech. They watched the scene with intense interest.

"Just answer the question," said Gid, glowering.

Zemnarihah looked at Gidgiddonihah. "I know you. You're the nephew of that Nephite coyote, Gidgiddoni. Curse you!" He spat upon Gid's shin. "You murdered my brother, Gamnor!"

"That's right," Gid confessed. "A favor that shortly I may also perform for you."

The Gadianton then looked at Kerra's father. "And curse you!" he sneered. "Curse Lord Kush that he did not slay you in the forest two years ago."

"He was a little busy being slain himself," said Dad acidly. "Killed by *that* man!" He pointed at Kiddoni. "The same man you tried to execute an hour ago."

Kiddoni remained unconscious. Kerra stayed beside him in the warm pool.

Gidgiddonihah reached toward the arrow in Zemnarihah's shoulder, prepared to twist it again if the Gadianton leader again refused to provide a direct answer.

"Yes!" Zemnarihah admitted. "I am lord of the Gadianton peoples. But slaying me will gain you no advantage. Chaac and the other fire gods will simply ordain another to take my place. Lachoneus and the vermin of Zarahemla cannot escape destruction."

"*Who* will be ordained?" asked Dad. "You mean Akuhuun?"

Zemnarihah made the sourest face he could manage. He spat into the same pool where Kiddoni was lying. "Akuhuun is *no one!*" Zemnarihah declared. "Where did you hear that name?"

"I knew him when I was your prisoner," said Dad. "He was the son of Giddianhi."

Zemnarihah laughed bitterly. "The son of Giddianhi?! *Bah!* It is a vile lie! A lie perpetuated by a deceiver and a fraud!"

Gidgiddonihah said, "You hate him because he is Giddianhi's heir—a threat to your power."

Zemnarihah roared, "I hate him because the son of Giddianhi *does not exist*!! I knew Master Giddianhi for twenty years! Don't you think I would know if he had a son? There *is* no son of Giddianhi! He had no heir!—only an imposter whom the gods will strike down as a tarantula in the flames! He seeds this lie among all the children of light! Akuhuun is not a name! There *is* no Akuhuun!"

Kerra's father stared blankly at Zemnarihah. So did Kerra and Gid. They glanced at one another. This information was confusing. Even disturbing. Akuhuun had been the object of their mission of assassination. He was the whole focus of *everything* they had done. Now to hear that he was . . . a kind of phantom . . . was terribly disconcerting. Kerra concentrated on the name. It suddenly clicked. Her natural "gift"—that is, her gift of understanding the ancient languages—made it perfectly plain. Zemnarihah was telling the truth. Akuhuun was *not* a name. It was a *title*. It merely meant "witch doctor." Or "priest." Or, more accurately, "shaman."

"It's true," said a voice.

Everyone turned. The voice belonged to Kiddoni. His eyes were halfway open. He was looking up at Zemnarihah and the others.

"*What's* true?" asked Gid.

Kiddoni answered weakly. "Giddianhi. He had . . . no son. No heir. Akuhuun is an imposter. He claims to be the former king's son. But only to stir up dissension."

"But I've *met* him," Dad insisted. "I've heard him speak." He pointed at Zemnarihah. "I've seen him standing by your side with his two jaguars—the Demon Balám!"

"I know of Akuhuun and his bedeviled jaguars," said Zemnarihah. "I, *too*, was deceived. I was starting to become his puppet and pet. But no longer. This Akuhuun practices a very dark magic. But it is a *false* sorcery. Not the power of Chaac."

This is too weird, thought Kerra. Zemnarihah believed there was a *darker* sorcery than the sorcery he practiced with his other Gadianton zombies? Kerra reassessed a concept she'd learned in the last six months among the Latter-day Saints—the idea that the devil never supports his followers. The Evil One happily lets them bicker and fight and self-destruct. He'll watch them slaughter each other with infinite delight. It was important to remember that every follower of Satan was still—at the very heart and core—a son or daughter of the omnipotent God of heaven and earth. The adversary's twisted creeds were designed, first and foremost, to destroy the individual who practiced them. If such creeds destroyed others in the process? Well . . . that was just frosting on the cake.

"I know him," said Kiddoni.

"You know *who*?" asked Gidgiddonihah.

"Akuhuun. I know him." He said to Kerra, "You know him, too."

Her eyebrows shot up like a window blind. "I do?"

"Yes. The man I shot . . . with an arrow . . . in the hand. The man with the monster . . . the monster tattoo . . . on his shoulder. The serpent . . . on his arm. Hitch. Akuhuun . . . is Hitch."

Kerra's mouth hung open in consternation. Amazingly, her surprise was dwarfed by the intensity of emotion on Gidgiddonihah's face.

He leaned very close to Kiddoni to be sure he heard correctly. "What did you say was on his shoulder and arm?"

"The tattoo . . . of a monster. A dragon. And on his left forearm . . . a serpent."

Every muscle was stiff, motionless, as Gid gawked, stupefied, at Kiddoni. All at once he cried out the name of his lieutenant.

"*Pek!!*"

Pek and Lemech returned from the edge of the jungle.

As Pek arrived, Gid seized his second-in-command by the shoulders. "Tell me again," he said. "The man who killed Chani—who killed my fiancée: *What was tattooed on his shoulder and forearm??*"

"On his shoulder, a dragon," Pek declared. "And on his arm, a snake."

Gid returned to Kiddoni. "What else can you describe about this person?"

"He looked different." Kiddoni again looked at Kerra. "I mean, different from when I first saw him in the forest. When I first pulled him away from you. His beard and hair . . . have lengthened. Thick and dark. But he is the same man. The one I shot in the hand."

Gid turned again to Pek.

Pek nodded. "Yes. Long hair and beard. Moreover, he was not a Nephite. Nor did he have the features of a Mulekite. In truth, he looked more like one of *them*." Pek nudged toward Kerra and her father.

Kiddoni added, "He was there. He was at the Place of Life. He was there until just before the ceremony began. And then, he walked into the forest. He disappeared."

Kerra was beside herself. It made no sense. Her father had *known* this man—had seen him with his demon-possessed jaguars. And yet these events had occurred *before* her father had ever returned to the modern world! If Hitch was the same person everyone now called Akuhuun, why didn't her father recognize him? Why didn't he—?

Then it occurred to Kerra. Hitch and her father had never met—at least not that day in the hollow, when the Gadiantons marched through her aunt and uncle's property. Dad and Hitch had never directly crossed paths.

Still, this left many unanswered questions. Kerra still couldn't fathom what it all meant—how it fit together. "It *can't* be the same man," she insisted. She said to her father, "Hitch Ventura and his thugs followed us to Utah. How could you have known him while you were a prisoner? During those years he was just a petty drug dealer. A nothing. A wannabe who wanted to rule the L.A. drug scene."

Dad shook his head, eyes piercing. "Adjust your thinking, Kerra. It's *linear*. If we've learned anything from what we've witnessed, it's that time is only linear for the individual who experiences it. Different people may move along different tracks. Look at what's happening right now! Today is the summer solstice. But that's *not* what it was this morning when we left your brother and grandfather. The date had *altered!* It changed when we crossed between those pillars in the jungle. Only by a few months. But it changed. It jumped forward."

Kerra remained mystified. She knew there was one sure way to verify this. She turned to Kiddoni. "How long have you been a Gadianton prisoner? How long ago was your battalion attacked?"

Kiddoni pondered the question. He looked on the verge of fainting again. Finally, he replied, "Eight months."

"Then it's true," Gid confirmed. "The days *have* altered."

Kiddoni tried to focus on the conversation. "What does . . . that mean?"

Kerra took his hand. "For Gid and Captain Gidgiddoni and the other Nephites, not as much time has elapsed. Two days ago the Chief Captain told us that you'd only been missing for *four* months."

Kiddoni blinked his eyes. He seemed to wonder if he was fully conscious, or if this was just part of another dream or hallucination.

Gidgiddonihah said to Kerra's father, "Then . . . it is your belief that these doorways—these "rifts"—make it possible for time—for the days and months of a given year—to jump forward as well as backward?"

Mi´con looked uncertain then replied, "Yes. *Obviously*, yes. Or Kiddoni wouldn't be here. He visited *our* day. Then he returned. So yes, it's possible that the man called Akuhuun . . ."

Kerra finished his thought. ". . . is really Hitch, the leader of . . . the *Shamans!*"

As the name of Hitch's L.A. gang crossed her mind, she realized that the word "akuhuun" meant the same thing. *Akuhuun* and *shaman* had practically the same meaning. Hitch hadn't really changed the title he'd gone by as a gangster in Los Angeles. He'd merely changed the spelling and pronunciation.

"He is also," said Gid coldly, bitterly, "the assassin who killed my mother and father, my two sisters, my only brother, Coriantor, and my fiancée, Chani."

Kerra reeled with revulsion. Was Hitch Ventura really capable of such overwhelming violence and mayhem? Could he really have slain so many members of Gidgiddonihah's family? Could he have orchestrated the mass slaughter of three Nephite battalions, including the warriors who were butchered in last night's raid? Could Hitch—the arrogant creep that she knew from California—be the same man who'd started the routine practice of cannibalism among the starving Gadiantons?

Kerra had only known him as a bully, a thief, and a petty drug dealer. Of course, there were *other* rumors—rumors of despicable things that he'd done, crimes he'd committed. But these stories didn't seem real. They'd happened to people Kerra had never met. No one wanted to believe such vile and gut-wrenching things about someone they'd spoken with face-to-face. Kerra remembered Brock's friend, Spree, and the fate that had befallen him. In fact, Hitch had *bragged* of Spree's murder. Suddenly it struck Kerra . . . who would *better* fit the description of the sorcerer called Akuhuun than Hitch Ventura?

Yes, Kerra realized. It was more than possible. Hitch and Akuhuun were surely the same man. It was undeniable!—especially if Hitch possessed a "power" similar to hers. That is, the ability to locate or pinpoint critical junctures where time and space intertwined like coils on a helix. Places where centuries and landscapes became like fluid elements—water, wind, or even fire. In the hands of someone like Hitch Ventura, such power could conceivably transform a petty gangster into a megalomaniac. It could transform such a person into a mass murderer of infinite proportions, a villain with ultimate delusions of grandeur.

Gidgiddonihah suddenly focused all of his energy back onto Kerra. "How can we find him?" he implored. "This man named Hitch! How can I find him and kill him?!"

Kerra was breathless. How in the world did he think she could solve this puzzle? It was true—she'd demonstrated certain gifts. But beyond what she'd already done . . . What he was asking was insane!

"I-I don't know," Kerra stuttered.

"Yes, you do." The confident voice belonged to her father. He was glaring at her with the same intensity as Gidgiddonihah. "You can do it, Kerra. You can find him. You can bring this nightmare to an end!

You have an incredible gift. You can also find my wife and son. You've had the ability all along. Just concentrate, sweetheart. Utilize your—"

The whoosh of an arrow interrupted Dad's speech. Lemech's eyes widened and his back stiffened. Pek caught him as he collapsed. Just like that, as fast as a lightning strike, Dad's brother-in-law was limp and lifeless.

More arrows zipped out of the jungle. They were under attack! Just as Zemnarihah had predicted, the Gadiantons had found them. Red warriors—their faces and limbs smeared in fresh blood—were taking up positions in the vegetation around the hot springs. Pek released Lemech's silent body. He and Gidgiddonihah loaded their bows and returned fire. Zemnarihah, his hands still tied behind his back, an arrow protruding from his shoulder, started squirming across the limestone toward the safety of the foliage.

Dad's focus had not veered from Kerra. His question was the same. Only now it wasn't Hitch or his family that he wanted. Once again, their lives were in Kerra's hands. It was up to her to save them.

Then Kerra remembered: the cauldron! She looked toward the steaming, churning pit just a few feet away from the pool where Kiddoni convalesced. She recalled the sensation that she'd felt just moments ago, as she'd stood near its edge. It was a feeling that, somehow, this boiling pit was drawing her in.

"We need to jump!" Kerra cried. An arrow whisked over her head.

"Jump where?!" asked Gid.

She pointed. "In *there*!"

The men glanced at each other, as if to confirm: did she just say what I thought she said?

"It's suicide!" shouted Pek, firing another arrow into the vegetation.

"It's our only escape!" Kerra insisted.

Dad peered over the edge. "We'd be boiled like lobsters!"

"It has no bottom!" shouted Gid.

Kerra gritted her teeth and raged, "You both said I have a gift! An ability! So trust me now! *Jump*! The window will only remain open a few more—" Kerra shrieked as an arrowpoint grazed her arm, just centimeters from imbedding deep in her flesh. Kiddoni had seen it—had watched the bloody scratch appear.

"Sakerra!" he cried, pushing himself up on one knee. This only made him a better target for Gadianton archers. Arrows were flying at them from multiple directions.

Kerra gritted her teeth and steeled her resolve. She'd have to go first—set the example—or no one would follow. She stumbled toward the cauldron's edge, paused one instant in the roiling steam, and leaped.

She heard several voices call her name as she seemed to drift into the noxious white cloud. The cloud quickly darkened. Her flesh felt the sting of blistering heat.

And then she felt nothing at all.

CHAPTER 19

BROCK CONTINUED TO PUSH ASIDE a seemingly endless assortment of vines and leaves. Hitch remained on his heels, close enough that if Brock had attempted to run, Hitch would have grabbed him again in a heartbeat. Heck, where could be run? He already had no idea where he was. Or where Hitch was leading him.

"You can go on and ask," Hitch invited. "I know yer curious. So be my guest. *Ask* me."

"Ask you what, Hitch?"

"Cociyo and Huracan! Ah, come on, essé! You must be a little curious as to where I found such fast feline companions. It's kind of a funny story. A little like Androcles and the Lion. You know that story?"

"No," said Brock.

"Are you serious? Your first grade teacher never—? A guy pulls a thorn from—*never mind*! Here's *my* story: I find Cociyo in a cage, see? Yeah, this was soon after the Nephites released me from prison. Oops. Lemme back up. See, the Nephites, they had my keister in prison. I was there with a bunch of other Gadianton POWs. The Nephites, see, they start this 'spiritual reclamation program.' Funniest thing I ever saw. So I lets 'em preach to me. Yeah, they preach. And they pray. And they sing. For a couple months I jes' gotta stand there and renounce Satan and praise Jesus. '*Ooooh, holy, holy Mr. Jesus! How I looove you and wanna follow you!*' Yeah, I did that song and dance awhile. Then, *bam*! They let me go. Just like that. Lickety split! Some of the other prisoners, they didn't like that so much. They wanted to hang me up by my oysters, if you know what I mean. Lemme tell

you, some of them *guerreros* are certified *psychos*! Real hardcore die-
for-the-cause *militaristas*. Get my drift? Anyway, one of them curses
me, see? Real, genuine voodoo-style curse. Says I will 'die as meat
in the jaws of a balám.' Get it? Of a *jaguar*! So's when I come across
this cage in the village, well, that struck me as kinda profound, right?
Like fate. These hunters, they'd trapped poor Cociyo, injured his leg,
and penned him up like a sorry ol' soul. Ah, but he was *beautiful*!
And then the magic, eh? I discover somethin' inside me. Somethin' I
didn't formerly know I had. I guess I was born with it. See, we *speak*
to each other, the jags and me. We *comprende* one another, like some
kinda Rosetta Stone thingamajig. That's right! So we become friends!
Man and beasts! I spring Cociyo from his cage. I nurse his wound.
Then I follow him into the jungle. He rounds up his mate, Huracan.
And we become a team. Voilà! The three of us! An inseparable posse!
Ever heard of anything so cool in your life? First thing I did was find
that mangy Red who cursed me. Then I invites Cociyo to tear him
limb from limb. Sort of a 'boomerang' curse, wouldn't you say? Right
as he's dyin', I croons to him, '*I'm rubber, you're glue. What you say
bounces off me and sticks to you*!' Oh, it was classic! One of my best
moments. Don' worry, amigo. I'll let you meet my kittens again—
closer up, this time. I give you my solemn oath. But right now, let's
see what we might find behind Door Number *Three*!"

With all the flare of a game show host, Hitch pulled aside a "curtain"
of vines and leaves. What he revealed was a shocking scene of gore and
devastation. Never during their jaunt through the thick jungle did Brock
ever notice a "rift" or "doorway" of any kind. No shimmering lights or
plasma-like vortex. Yet somewhere, somehow, they'd breached a passage
to a different location. Brock felt sure of it as soon as he stepped through
the leafy curtain. It was further confirmed as he turned back to see where
he'd been. The landscape was different. Still dense forest, but of a different character than where he and Hitch had just passed through. Even the
air smelled different. The pressure in his ears had altered. The altitude felt
higher. They were up in the mountains now. The gruesome scene before
him, however, remained exactly the same.

It was a stone platform with three black and bloody pillars. The
landscape was littered with death: neat piles of human bones—skulls,
ribcages, etc. The hairs inside his nose curled at the putrid scents of

death and smoke. There were bodies tied to two of the pillars—bodies burned beyond recognition. In fact, they were headless.

A lone, living figure sat in the center of the platform. It took Brock a moment to recognize him. It was Lemech! There was something in his lap. Brock swallowed heavily. What was left of a human. Lemech clutched at the feathered mask that still adorned its head. He looked despondent, a figure of profound devastation. Brock realized he was weeping. But why was he alone? Where was his father? Where were Kerra, Gid, and Pek?

Hitch was *also* strangely disturbed by the scene before them, but for a different reason.

"What happened?" he said. He wasn't addressing anyone in particular, just speaking to himself. He took one long stride toward the platform and yelled at the man who sat in the center looking inconsolable. "Hey!" Hitch yelled. "Where is the man who was tied to the third pillar? What did you do with his body?"

Brock was flummoxed. What was going on? What had Hitch expected to find here?

Lemech did not respond. He didn't even bat an eye. Brock might've sworn that Lemech hadn't heard Hitch at all. How could he *not*? Hitch was only thirty feet away, shouting at the top of his lungs.

"Did you hear me?" Hitch shouted, adding profanity. "What happened to the body of Commander Kiddoni?!"

Again, Lemech did not react. Hitch uttered another foul curse. He started to march forward. He stopped abruptly, realizing he'd left young Brock behind. As an irritated afterthought, he grabbed Brock by the collar, yanking him forward, still shouting at Lemech. "Answer me, you moron! Or I'll make your head roll like the one in your lap! *Are you listening to me?!*"

Hitch halted in his tracks. The scene in front of Brock and Hitch "shimmered." It took on a strange, watery appearance and shifted subtly in and out of focus. They found themselves standing before an energy wall. It seemed to shoot up from a crag in the earth, three feet in front of their faces. It wasn't even a crag. It was just a place in the ground with a crooked shelf running north and south, perfectly flush, although the foreground was two or three inches higher.

Hitch was furious. He studied the massive rift up and down. Then he let out a frustrated growl and plunged forward. He crossed the uneven ground and breached the "membrane" of the wall, dragging Brock in his wake. Brock flinched and blinked. Somewhere in the middle of that that blink, Lemech disappeared. In fact, numerous things about the landscape transformed. For one thing, the odor improved markedly. Death still lingered in the air, but only as a faint hint of what it had been. There were no fires or smoke. Bones lay scattered around the stone platform, but the piles were nowhere near as substantial. Most profoundly, there were no burned corpses tied to the pillars, and no sign of any other human beings in the area.

Hitch cursed again. "I *hate* it when it does that!"

"Where are we?" asked Brock. "*When* are we?"

"It appears we went back a bit," Hitch declared. "Maybe . . . back to a little while after we attacked the first Nephite battalion . . . but *before* we surprised the second. In any case, it's a bit before we really started to kick this place into high gear."

"What are you talking about? What is this place?"

"Ah, c'mon, bro. Don't look so squeamish. Ever been to a slaughterhouse? Where do you think you get those juicy barbecued ribs and Whopper Jrs.?"

"Those aren't animal bones," said Brock. "They're *people*!"

"Good eye, Brock! *Ka-ching*! See, when I came along, the Gadiantons had themselves a bit of a conundrum. They'd plum run outta Whoppers and chicken nuggets, know what I mean? I talked 'em into an imaginative alternative. You like Charlton Heston?"

"Who?"

"*Planet of the Apes*! *Earthquake*! C'mon! Charlton Heston! Don't you ever watch any movies?"

"I watch movies all the time," said Brock with a hint of defensiveness.

"Well, you mighta missed this late-night classic: *Soylent Green*. See, the world gets way overpopulated, and to feed the masses they have to invent this special little cracker. *Yum, yum*! Only at the end, Supercop Chuck Heston—he discovers the secret. And the last line of the movie, right before they drag off ol' Chuck to be exterminated for the public good, is an all-time gem." Hitch cleared his throat and attempted a ragged, albeit high-squealed, Heston impression. "'*Soylent*

Green is PEEE-OPLE!!!' Get it? Instead of burying corpses, they was bakin' crackers! Yeah, what a flick! *Mucho primo!*"

Brock was mortified. It clicked in his mind what Hitch meant—what this former L.A. gangster was saying that he'd done. In a typical sideways fashion, he was claiming that he'd solved the food problem among the Gadiantons—solved it with the flesh of Nephite soldiers!

Hitch continued. "I guess I got the timing wrong on that last anchor point. Timing is everything. If you mess up the timing, you mess up the whole soufflé. I don't usually make a mistake. It's kind of a sixth sense of mine. Like talking to animals. Hey, maybe it's a *seventh* sense!"

"Like your ability to find a way back home?" Brock deadpanned.

Hitch frowned. "You are a cheeky little cuss, aren't you, Brock McConnell? Maybe I don't *need* to find a way home. Maybe I *like* it here. Anyway, it's too bad I barely missed the window, 'cause I wanted to show you the fate of your old benefactor, that pretty-boy Nephite who put this teensy little scar in the middle of my palm."

Brock gritted his teeth. "What did you do to Kiddoni?"

"That's the cool part! *I* didn't have to do a *thing*," Hitch replied, lacing his sentence with expletives. "I left it to that bonehead, Zemnarihah. But by the look of things, he might've screwed that up too."

He released Brock and started pacing back and forth, gripping the obsidian sword so tightly his hand trembled. It seemed to Brock that he almost drifted into a trance, rambling the whole time.

"Jes' hold on," he mumbled. "Gimme a minute. Jes' one New York minute to figure this thing out . . . Lemme think. Let. Me. Think . . ." All at once he stopped pacing. His eyes seemed to illuminate. "I got it! Let's go!"

He seized Brock's arm.

"Where are we going?" Brock demanded.

"My kittens," Hitch replied. "I needs my kittens."

CHAPTER 20

GRANDPA LEE STOOD JUST UNDER the lip of the overhang, eying the menacing sky with irritation.

The day had turned into a veritable cloudburst. Rain had been pouring for hours. The storm began shortly after Brock and Chemnon left on their hunting expedition. Since that time, the waterfall had expanded in size, rumbling like a perpetual thunderclap, making it impossible for him and Manazzeh to carry on any conversation without shouting.

At the moment, it appeared the weather was finally starting to let up. But daylight was fading. The sun was slipping fast into a horizon of fractured gray clouds. Grandpa's anxiety had long since reached a boiling point. It wasn't just nervousness for Brock and Chemnon. He also had to worry about what might have become of his son, his granddaughter, and the rest of their company. Who could possibly travel in weather like this? Hunting for food also seemed impossible. Had Brock and Chemnon located a shelter and simply decided to wait out the storm? Grandpa had his doubts about this. How far away would they have wandered in search of game? They'd been away for far too long. Something was amiss. Grandpa Lee could feel it in his bones. His grandson *needed* him. With each passing moment this instinct ballooned until it was about to pop.

He knew Manazzeh was watching him carefully. The Nephite, of course, felt the same anxiety about his younger brother. Now that the downpour was subsiding, Manazzeh was surely wondering what the old man was going to do.

Grandpa turned around and loudly announced, "I'm going to look for them before it gets too dark!"

Manazzeh grimaced with disapproval. "It's *already* too dark!" he shouted back, competing with the roar of the falls. "You must wait until morning!"

Grandpa pulled a Ronald Reagan, holding a hand to his ear, pretending not to hear. Then he yelled, "I won't be gone long! I just wanna get far enough away from this dad-gummed waterfall that I can hear my own voice as I shout their names!"

Manazzeh shook his head. He honestly hadn't heard the second part of what Grandpa said. Grandpa didn't bother repeating himself. Shucks, he'd practically be back by the time he said it again. All he wanted to do was cross the stream, climb to the top of the ravine, and call out Brock's name. If nobody responded, he'd return and wait till sunup before mounting a serious search.

Grandpa stepped to the place where stones had been laid out to safely cross the stream. They were harder to see than before. Not only because of the fading daylight, but because the water level was higher and the rains had mucked up visibility. The first stone was discernible enough, so he took a step. The second stone was also visible just below the surface. Wisely, he poised both feet onto the first stone before stepping to the second. No need to be overanxious. It wasn't worth slipping in and being dragged over the next waterfall.

Despite all of his patience and prudence, the next step did not go well. That stone was further beneath the surface than he'd guessed—by four or five inches. One instant he was perfectly balanced, carefully placing his foot onto the adjacent stone, and the next his legs were whipped out from under him. His arms wheeled in a desperate effort to regain stability, but it was hopeless. There was a mighty splash, a cold shock to his body, and an angry self-abasement as he blustered curse words under water that he hadn't uttered in decades. Manazzeh had surely watched him fall in. The Nephite must have thought ol' Lee′con was the stupidest old klutz on two continents.

His initial emotions were replaced by pure, unadulterated dread. Grandpa's face poked above the surface. He drew a quick breath. How in blazes had this happened?! *Gracious!* He was only two steps from shore! Why was the current so doggone strong? Again, it was that lousy downpour! How could he have allowed himself to be so unprepared? He really *was* as old and senile as he often joked.

So, he thought, as the current again pulled him under, *I 'spose this is the end. You deserve it, you old coot!* Drowning. He'd heard somewhere that it was not such a horrible way to die. Sorta peaceful. Then again, death by drowning was a wishful thought. As his vision again briefly surfaced and he glimpsed the fast-approaching falls, he realized he'd most likely be pulverized against the jagged stones at the base. *That* kind of death didn't sound pleasant at *all!*

Oh well. Too late to worry about any of that. He actually felt the stony edge of the cliff and made a feeble effort to find a grip, but the mossy rocks slipped easily through his fingers. The effort twisted his body, causing him to plunge over the falls headfirst. Grandpa Lee shut his eyes and awaited oblivion.

Even through his eyelids he perceived multiple arcs of lightning bursting and popping like a Van de Graff generator, with a million purple and golden tentacles. The smell of ozone penetrated deep into his lungs. His skin tingled with rapid waves of a tickling electrical current. But as he opened his eyes, there was only blackness. *Uggh!*— and a bruising impact on his shoulders! However, not quite as bone-shattering as he'd anticipated.

Holy smokes! Grandpa remembered something Kerra had said just before she departed. She'd warned him to be careful crossing the stream 'cause—How did she put it?—*"There's something . . . weird . . . over there."* It was such a peculiar remark that he'd let it flop right out of his memory. He now realized she'd meant a *passageway!* A rift! At some juncture while he was careening over the falls, he'd passed through an energy barrier much like the one on the surface of that jade boulder atop the ravine, or beneath the fallen tree trunk.

To his dismay, he realized he was upside down, stuck in some kind of subterranean shaft. Near-freezing water poured around his body. Bending his neck to look down, he perceived a light. It was faint—not so much because it was far away as because the shaft had a curvature, like plumbing under the kitchen sink. This curvature subdued any daylight.

Where in creation am *I?* Grandpa pondered. Wedged upside down in a fissure flowing with icy springwater? Good thing he didn't have claustrophobia—or rather, not a full-blown case. He knew he should've been shouting praises of gratitude to have even survived.

But had he really survived? All those extra helpings of cream-cheese mashed potatoes at Corinne's Sunday dinners had finally caught up with him. It was like Winnie the Pooh in Rabbit's hole. But unlike Pooh, he couldn't wait a week to lose the necessary poundage. If he didn't figure out something fast, he'd soon expire from hypothermia.

Grandpa twisted to the right, but this awkward effort only painfully ground his shoulder against the rough stone. Water kept filling his nostrils. He pinched them to improve his breathing and tried twisting to the left. A shoulder worked loose. He dropped several feet, fighting to catch himself with outstretched arms while simultaneously trying to avoid shattering his spine. As his body wedged itself in a new position, this time slightly sideways, he thought of that pesky Grinch squeezing down those Whoville chimneys. Amazing how animated cartoons captured this predicament so well.

Springwater ceaselessly splashed in his face. He continually coughed liquid from his throat. But as he assessed his new position, the daylight below seemed a tad brighter. He perceived a certain "greenness" about it. A reflection? That could only mean there was a living world down there. Again he maneuvered his arms, twisted his legs, and wriggled his buttocks. Something tumbled past his chin. It was his pocket-sized Book of Mormon, thoroughly drenched. *Ah, crud!* Somehow losing that book—a thing practically attached to his person for sixty years—was more disheartening than any other affliction he'd endured.

He could see the opening now. It was directly below him. However, the incessant spray of water prevented him from ascertaining how the opening actually *worked.* As best as he could figure, he'd be upside down till the very moment he got free. Frankly, it was a miracle that he'd managed to squeeze any distance at all. He recalled Manazzeh's injury, along with things his son had mentioned about how a time-traveler's molecules could mingle with the molecules of stationary things—with fatal results. Gratefully, this hadn't happened. What good deed had he performed to have earned such a propitious blessing?

As he pulled himself a little farther down, he felt water pressure building behind him. His midsection had veritably plugged the tunnel. If he waited long enough, he might cannonball out of the opening like Augustus Gloop in Willy Wonka's chocolate pipe. Ah, but too many leaks trickled up his face. He was shivering like a tuning fork. He yanked and he yanked—striving to progress just a few more blessed inches.

At last he gripped something like an edge and pulled with all his remaining strength. Perhaps some of the pressure behind his gluteus maximus was just enough to expel him into the daylight. He received a new bump to his noggin and additional bruises to his arms and shoulders, but somehow he managed to escape the vertical tunnel, popping out much like a babe from the womb. He lay there in a muddy puddle and glanced back at the place where he'd emerged. It was indeed a vertical cave, a local source of glistening springwater. After rubbing the bump on his crown, he rolled onto his back to worship the heat of the sun. However, those much-desired rays were soon blocked by a pint-sized silhouette.

It was a child. A boy. He stood before Grandpa Lee with his feet nestled in a patch of ferns, eyes crater-wide with fascination. Grandpa shielded his eyes; the boy fell into better focus. He couldn't have been more than four or five years old, just standing there alone, no fear, fighting a grin that might've split his face in two. The kid's expression made it seem like he thought Grandpa was Santa Claus— some kind of *Nephite* Santa Claus. One of his hands clasped a clay pitcher, a vessel for transporting water. Surely this particular trip to the spring wasn't like other trips. It wasn't every day that the cave in the cliff vomited a fat old man! Yet the boy didn't act a bit surprised. Just entranced, as if . . . as if his arrival was right on schedule. As if Grandpa's emergence was fully *expected!* In the boy's opposite hand was Grandpa's pocket-sized Book of Mormon, dripping but intact.

He and the child locked eyes. Grandpa's heart skipped a beat. It immediately struck him: this was no run-of-the-mill boy. His features were certainly Nephite or Lamanite—no doubt about *that*. But there was something else about him—something about the radiance in his eyes and cheeks. Was it just more wishful thinking? He was four years old. A four-year-old *boy*. *Nah*, the coincidence was too extraordinary. Yet it was only natural for his mind to drift in that particular direction. How could it *not*? It was that face. Something about that cherubic face. Something . . . European. Something . . . *McConnell!*

No. Too easy. Too convenient. Too *miraculous*!

Grandpa struggled to think of some words to say. His chattering teeth didn't help as he spluttered, "H-h-h-hello there."

The boy took off like a jackrabbit. Now, why did he do that? Grandpa couldn't say for sure. Was it excitement? Was he off to sound the alarm? In any case, he'd scurried down a dark brown path into a vibrant green jungle and disappeared.

Grandpa blew the air from his lungs. He was disappointed. He felt ridiculous. Such a hasty conclusion. No doubt *any* four-year-old boy he met ran the risk of being mistaken for his grandson. Such were the impetuous conclusions of an exhausted, old man. He crawled out of the muddy water and onto the carpet of ferns. His shivering stabilized. He soaked in the warmth of the sun. He felt it draw blood to the surface of the skin, refilling the empty capillaries, restoring sensation to his benumbed face and arms. *Time for that prayer*, he thought. Grandson or no, he owed his Father in Heaven some sincere words of thanks.

No sooner had he started his prayer than he heard voices in the forest. Folks were coming, approaching *fast*. More than a few. The kid had tattled on him—that seemed sure. Grandpa braced himself for the arrival of soldiers—most likely those Gadianton cusses—or maybe just farmers with axes, pitchforks, and a raucous chant of "kill the beast!"

The voices, however, were not particularly angry or vicious. Heck, they weren't even *male*. A whisker later a woman emerged from the jungle. The four-year-old boy held her hand while his other hand still gripped the ceramic vessel. He tugged the woman forward so eagerly that Grandpa felt very important. In the woman's other hand was the waterlogged Book of Mormon. More women appeared behind them—*dozens* of 'em. And children, most younger than twelve.

The four-year-old boy said to the woman, "I *told* you, Mom. I *told* you he was coming."

He said more, but the rising chorus of rambunctious females drowned out his words. Most women expressed statements of shock and surprise. Unlike the little boy, the rest of the crowd was gripped by suspicion and fear.

"Who is he?" was an oft-repeated phrase. "What is he doing here? What does he want?"

The four-year-old brought his mother to within inches of Grandpa's reach. Grandpa studied her face. She was pretty, or so he thought. Hard to tell under all the rags she wore, and with such an underfed, skinny figure, or with that dirty, leathery cast over her skin. *All* of the women and children looked like this: overworked, malnourished, and burdened with something Grandpa interpreted as a dearth of hope. After all, there were no men in this gathering. The days of usefulness for male slaves among this band of robbers appeared to have expired—perhaps only recently. As a result, the women's faces were overcast with a dreadful grief and distress, as well as the full weight of a cruel world.

Still, the little boy's exuberance could not be contained. He persisted excitedly, "See, I *said* he was coming! And now he's here! He's here to *save* us! To take us *home!*"

That last word reverberated forcefully in Grandpa's eardrums. It shook him to the core. *What did that kid say?* Grandpa felt inclined to joggle his skull to be sure freezing water hadn't perforated his eardrums. Here to *"save"* them? Were those his words? What the devil was he talking about? Who did these people think he was?

The woman studied him, her intense concentration a tad intimidating. Her expression was, perhaps, like any other mother who'd repeatedly shrugged off the idle fantasies of a child only to one day discover that his prattling words had come to pass!

"What is your name?" the woman inquired, her voice barely audible.

"Lee," Grandpa replied, also quietly. He raised the volume a bit and added, "Lee´con."

Everyone who filled the area around that spring had their eyes riveted on him. They seemed stricken with . . . apprehension? Anticipation? It wasn't quite clear.

"I am Paísha," said the woman. "This is my son, Mi´conhah." She returned Grandpa's soggy Book of Mormon, then she straightened her shabby skirt and worked up a final shred of courage and asked, "Is it true? Are you . . . my son's grandfather?"

Grandpa Lee felt a swelling in his chest like Mount St. Helens on the brink of eruption. *Thanks be to God!* he exclaimed inwardly. All of his initial instincts—his silly, impetuous conclusions! Great balls of fire! They'd proven *right*! He'd found them! He'd found his son's bride! He'd found his grandson!

"Yes," Grandpa declared. "YES!" He looked at the boy. "I *am* your grandpa!"

Suddenly another voice boomed behind the gathering. Like a bullet fired into the canvas of the *Hindenburg,* every particle of joy vanished in a fleeting, fiery instant. "What's going on?!" the thunderous voice demanded. "What is everyone looking at?!"

The ragtag gathering of women and children parted as a warrior decorated in tattoos from the tip of his bald head to the tops of his feet drew a bead on Grandpa Lee and swiftly approached him in three overextended steps. He brandished a spear and a long obsidian sword, brushing past Paísha and little Mi´conhah as if they were insects.

"On your feet, intruder! Get on your feet, or I'll split you open like an armadillo!"

Well! thought Grandpa. Nothing like an enthusiastic invitation to get one's muscles moving. He palmed the Book of Mormon and hoisted himself to his feet.

The robber moved somewhat to the right, and then to the left, looking him thoroughly up and down. "Who are you? Where did you come from?"

Little Mi´conhah answered. "He came from inside the spring!"

The warrior crinkled his forehead. He glanced at the vertical cave then back at the child, grunting in disbelief. He raised the obsidian sword a little higher to encourage a more convincing reply. "I asked where you're from, old man. I will not ask again. How did you enter this valley? How did you get past our patrols?"

Grandpa opened and closed his mouth. "I-I—uh—Well, that's an interesting—"

"How did you get wet?!"

Grandpa shrugged. "Uh, as the boy said . . ." His eyes flashed toward the dripping spring.

Grandpa took it as another miracle that the angry Red did not immediately carry out his threat. He glanced once more at the dark hole then turned toward the servile gathering. "I will only ask one—more—time! Who saw where this old man came from?"

The guard had turned his back. Grandpa could hardly believe his luck. To the robber's eternal misfortune, he did not view Grandpa Lee as a threat. Just a wet, feeble old geezer.

Grandpa snatched the ceramic vase from his little grandson's hands. Not quite certain where he mustered the audacity or spine, he aggressively smashed the vessel onto the Gadianton's head. It was a tough container, no doubt designed to withstand the antics of a four-year-old child. It cracked, but did not shatter. The hollow, musical note that echoed from inside it caused everyone in the gathering to cringe with vicarious pain.

The sentry staggered. The captives swiftly moved out of the way. It seemed to Grandpa that he even made a token effort to spin around and swing his sword. Finally, he collapsed onto the solid earth, out like a light.

The women in the crowd became agitated. Several wept with hysteria.

One old woman shook her fist at Grandpa. "Do you know what you've *done*? You've gotten us all *killed*! Us and our children! Attacking a guard is a capital offense!"

"Calm down!" said Grandpa. "Lower your voices! Where are the other guards?"

Paísha answered. "At the encampment. Beyond these trees. There are not many. Most have been sent into battle."

"And even more were called away this morning," said another woman. "A disturbance downriver, at the Place of Life."

Mi´conhah tugged on his grandfather's mantle, those innocent blue eyes as big as robin's eggs. "It will be all right. Tell them, Grandfather. You're here to save us."

"Well, uh, I—" As Grandpa hemmed and hawed, he realized that Paísha clung to the same belief as her son. Or perhaps she just *wanted* to believe. *Many* of them wanted to believe. Indeed, it seemed he wasn't the only one who'd figured out that Mi´conhah was no ordinary little boy.

Several other children pushed their way to the front. They stared into Grandpa's eyes. "Is it true? Have you come here to save us? Have you come here to take us home?"

Grandpa's heart thumped like a mackinaw trout in a canvas bag. He felt overwrought. Overwhelmed. They were gazing at him like a savior—a miracle worker. They believed in him with every beat of their hearts. How could he burst their bubble? How could he tell them anything besides what they truly believed? If they had this kind of faith in him, how could he deny such faith in himself?

"Yes," said Grandpa Lee. "I'm here to take you home. I promise. I'm just not quite sure . . . I mean . . ."

"Don't be silly," said little Mi´conhah. "Just tell them." The child took several steps toward the ice-cold spring that led upward into the dark recesses of the cliff. "Tell them that we'll go home the same way that you got here. They'll believe *you*, Grandfather. They'll believe anything you say—if you tell them."

Grandpa swallowed heavily, like swallowing a bowling ball. "Uh . . . yeah," he replied. "We'll climb into the spring."

Even as the words fell from his lips, a conviction burned in his breast. A conviction that what he'd said—what his little grandson had declared—was perfectly true. It was the solution. The answer. It was their escape route. He knew it with every fiber of his being.

Some of the women were shaking their heads in disbelief, convinced it was all nonsense—convinced the world had gone mad.

So with greater confidence, greater authority, and a conviction as great as any other in Grandpa Lee's heart, he repeated, "That's right! We'll climb into the spring! Do you hear? *Listen carefully*! Everyone within earshot of my voice! The boy is right. My grandson has spoken the truth. I'm here to rescue you. I'm here to take you home. *We'll climb into the spring*!"

CHAPTER 21

KERRA MCCONNELL WAS LYING FLAT on her stomach, facedown in a bed of warm, dark sand. She raised her face and spit particles from her lips. She focused upward and saw a canopy of palm fronds. She turned right and perceived irregular columns of palm *trunks* extending several hundred yards into the distance until arriving at a wall of dense tropical greenery dishearteningly similar to another dense tropical morass they'd recently traversed. This meant that the place where the "rift" had deposited her was not jungle—not exactly.

She smelled the salty air and heard the breaking surf even before she rolled her head to the left. There it was!—a turquoise-colored ocean. It kissed a sandy shoreline about a hundred yards in the distance. The dizzying abundance of "blue" beyond the beach made it difficult to distinguish where the horizon ended and cloudless sky began. Between her and the waves stretched a coastline of the blackest sand she'd ever seen, as if she'd been laid out upon a bed of fine charcoal. However, it left no stain on her skin, and the texture confirmed that it was, indeed, sand.

Kerra felt the sting where the Gadianton arrow had cut a short stripe across her upper arm. She pressed it with her palm and shuddered as she wondered if the arrowhead had been dipped in poison. However, she quickly dismissed this fear. If she felt no ill effects by now, it was a very weak poison or it'd been neutralized by the steam of the cauldron.

She glanced again at the palm fronds overhead, rustling gently in an ocean breeze. As reality settled in, a tremor began in her head and echoed outward through every limb. How in the world did she get *here?* Did she fall from the sky like a meteorite? She pondered if, perhaps, some kind of energy "window" loomed above her. In this case it might have been described as a horizontal energy "plane," ten or twenty feet overhead, hovering just below the fluttering fronds. If so, this plane was invisible. No shimmering molecules or iridescent waves jostled things in and out of focus.

Ironically, a sudden disturbance overhead created exactly the image she'd just imagined. There was a flash of light. An object breached some kind of membrane twelve feet overhead and dropped to the earth several yards in front of her. A shimmering wave traveled outward from the place where the object had disturbed the vortex. She gasped as she realized the object was *Kiddoni*! He fell onto the sand with a dull thud, buffeting her with a spray of black granules. The Nephite came to his feet, a bit unsteady. However, thought Kerra, he looked considerably stronger than she might have expected.

She went to him and slipped her arm behind his back for support. "Are you all right?"

He turned to see her. Kerra's face loomed unexpectedly close. He glanced once or twice from her lips to her eyes, then replied, "Better. Happy that I am not presently boiling alive."

"Why did it take so long for you to follow me?" she scolded. "Where are the others?"

"So *long?*" said Kiddoni defensively. "I jumped in only seconds after you—"

"I've been alone here for at least a minute," said Kerra.

Kiddoni continued. "—and Mi´con and Gidgiddonihah were ready to jump in behind me."

Interesting, thought Kerra. "If that's true, then they should fall through the rift at any—"

The translucent "ceiling" flashed again. Her father hit the ground about fifteen yards in back of them. Another flash struck as Gidgiddonihah fell twenty feet closer to the ocean. He landed on his feet, dropping to one knee to cushion the impact. Every piece of weaponry remained firmly in his fists. The last to breach the rift was Pek, landing in the soft sand near the ocean's surf, nearly a hundred yards away. He looked around a moment, finally spotted the others, and jogged toward them. Dad brushed himself off. Gid also joined Kerra, Kiddoni, and Mi′con.

She concluded that their leap into the boiling cauldron had not only expanded time, but *space*. Each person was deposited randomly across a radius of at least a hundred yards. In any event, this beach was surely hundreds of miles from any hot springs in the wilderness of Hermounts.

As everyone gathered, Kerra said, "Thank you following me—for trusting me."

"A leap of faith," said Dad.

Kerra added, "We jumped in the nick of time. That window was shutting down. I don't think it would have remained open too much longer. Five minutes—tops."

"Meaning," said Pek, "that if we'd tried to hold our ground against the Reds much longer—"

Dad finished his basic thought, "—we'd have faced the same fate as a Maine lobster in a cooking pot."

Gid had no interest in science or semantics. "Where are we?" he asked stiffly.

Kerra shook her head. "I'm not sure."

Dad faced the ocean. "Is that the Atlantic or the Pacific?"

"Uhh." She studied the sky to see if the sun's position might give her a clue. But this was silly. *Anybody* could've done that, except that it usually took half an hour. Gid and the others wanted specific info—the kind they believed only Kerra could provide.

"I don't know this coastline," said Pek. "The sand here is like granules of obsidian. I don't think it's part of Zarahemla. Nor Bountiful."

"We can't remain here," said Gidgiddonihah impatiently. "We have ventured further from our goal than ever before!"

Dad simultaneously mentioned his wife and son.

Kerra's mind felt engulfed in a storm. She covered her ears in frustration. "I *know* all this! I *know*. I need to think. I need time to sort out—"

Multiple flashes illuminated the vortex overhead. The "ceiling" radiated with iridescent waves from multiple points, like tossing a handful of pebbles into a pond. Kerra heard something hit the sand behind her. She turned to face a Gadianton warrior. Like Gid, he had not crumpled to the sand, but landed squarely on his feet. To her left she saw another blood-swathed warrior. Then a third!—impacting the ground very close to the place where Gidgiddonihah had landed.

"The sky is raining Reds!" Pek declared, yanking an arrow from his quiver.

Gid swung his hatchet and took out the warrior who'd landed behind Kerra before he'd managed to get his bearings.

Kerra was nonplussed all the more by this development. There was only one explanation. The Gadiantons of Hermounts—those Reds who had surrounded them at the mineral pools—had actually *followed* them into the steaming cauldron. Why would they do such a thing? A jump like that should have unnerved even the most stout-hearted villains. It would have seemed like certain death! The solution to this mystery shook Kerra to the core. It was Akuhuun. These men had taken this risk *only* because of assurances provided by Hitch Ventura. Somehow, somewhere, he must have been present, hidden in the forest about the hot pools. His visit may have only lasted a moment, as if he was performing the role of a great warrior spirit—Gandalf or Obi-Wan Kenobi—spouting wisdom at his witless followers: "*Leap into the cauldron, you fools! The enemy is getting away!*" Yes, it could only have been Hitch. He'd spent all his breath educating the Gadiantons about the energy portals. It meant that no one was fooled when Kerra and the others leapt into the cauldron. They understood precisely what had happened. And so, on Hitch's orders, they'd pursued their quarry directly into the blistering steam.

Another jarring proposition gripped Kerra. If Hitch Ventura was *there*, at the springs, he might also be *here*.

"A weapon!" demanded Kiddoni.

She looked at him and shook her head. She almost forbade it. Kiddoni couldn't possibly fight in his present condition. However, Gidgiddonihah judged differently. He promptly tossed him his personal obsidian sword with the three-inch tip. The commander felt secure enough with just a copper hatchet and a white flint blade.

As Kiddoni balanced the volcanic sword in his grip, a Gadianton robber dropped down directly in front of him. He made a perfect landing, like several of his comrades. But unlike Gidgiddonihah's first victim, this warrior was ready to fight. The first target of his wrath was not Kiddoni, but *Kerra.*

A smart *Gadianton,* thought Kiddoni. He *knew* that Kerra was the more important target. Without her, Gidgiddonihah's company was helpless—immobilized in one single, solitary dimension.

As the blood-slathered warrior swung his sword toward Kerra's neck, Kiddoni grabbed the only thing he *could* grab—Kerra's hair. He jerked her backward, tossing her onto the sand and out of range of the weapon's swipe. Kiddoni thrust the three-inch obsidian tip directly into the Gadianton's heart. The fragile tip broke as the Red crumpled. The tip still left was shorter, but equally sharp and dangerous.

Gidgiddonihah was taking on a second opponent. Pek had fired two arrows and now faced a third attacker. Even Dad was caught up in the mayhem. Kerra was amazed to watch him dodge and parry numerous strikes, finally delivering his own lethal blow. She got quickly to her feet and made a 360-degree assessment of the terrain. She counted fifteen more Gadianton combatants rushing into the fray.

Dad yelled at Kiddoni, "Get her out of here!"

Kiddoni grabbed Kerra's arm and dragged her in the only safe-looking direction—straight toward the jungle. An arrow zipped in front of them, barely missing Kerra's waist and driving into the bark of a palm tree. Another charging attacker shifted directions to pursue them. Dad dove toward him, stretching his obsidian sword far out front and as high as the man's shins. The assailant collided with the razor-sharp blades and wailed in agony as he tripped and fell onto his face.

Kerra and Kiddoni continued running toward the jungle. They drew to a sudden halt as a horrific sight appeared before them—the dead body of a Gadianton. The Red had obviously fallen from the sky like his comrades, but his flesh was bubbled, blistered, and hanging from his bones like a chicken in a broiler. Kerra concluded that this was the last of them—the last Gadianton who'd leaped into the cauldron and passed through the vortex. But he was too late; his efforts had a gruesome side effect. By the looks of it, his body had taken a good half minute to slip through the rift. Kerra paled at the grisly scene. Kiddoni altered their course to avoid the obstacle.

As they arrived at the edge of the dense rainforest, Kiddoni turned back to see if anyone was pursuing. Kerra faced ahead, peering into the foliage. She dug her fingernails into Kiddoni's arm.

"What's wrong?" he asked.

Her mouth was agape, eyes frantically searching the undergrowth. Kiddoni asked, "Did you see something?"

She nodded.

"What?"

At that instant they both heard a low snarl, reverberating somewhere in the leafy shadows. Kiddoni seemed quite familiar with this sound.

"Jaguar," he said.

He acted as if he was well aware of the habits of these predators, believing they generally did not attack unless provoked. Thus, he focused his attention on the Reds and turned again to make sure none had followed

Kerra, however, had a very different opinion of these beasts. The orange-and-black apparition that had passed before her eyes was so quick, so fleeting, that her mind was still trying to decide if she'd seen anything at all. What she couldn't dismiss was the impression of a jeweled collar around its neck.

"Not just any jaguar," Kerra informed. "*Akuhuun's* jaguar."

Suddenly Kiddoni seemed to understand.

* * *

"Shout her name," Hitch whispered sternly in Brock's ear.

"No," Brock whimpered. "You'll hurt her."

"I won't. I promise."

He shook his head. "I won't do it."

Hitch placed a steel dagger against Brock's ear. "Shout it or I'll cut it off. Then your *left* ear. Then your nostrils. Then each finger—one by one. Don't test me, Brock-O. I'll give you a three-count. One . . . two . . . *THREE!*"

* * *

"KEEEERRRA!"

She looked to the east. It was Brock's voice. But how? Why? What was going on?

"Is that your brother?" asked Kiddoni.

"Yes!" She veered left and headed toward the voice. Kiddoni caught her arm.

"How would he have gotten here?" he inquired.

"I don't have the foggiest idea," she admitted. "I have to go to him."

"It's a trap," said Kiddoni.

"He's my brother!"

Kerra pulled away and hastened toward the sound of the voice. Kiddoni had no choice but to follow. They sprinted along the edge of the rainforest, dodging palms and other foliage and debris. Kerra passed through a narrow space between two palm trees. She spotted him. He stood about twenty yards away, pressed against a palm's thick, ragged trunk. Or rather, he was *tied* there. His arms were stretched behind him. Kerra swore she could see rope entwining both wrists. Her brother was staring at her, open-mouthed, terrified. The space between Kerra and Brock was littered with palm fronds and dappled by harsh shadows and bright sunlight.

"Brock!" She continued toward him with no break in her stride.

Kiddoni remained on her heel. Brock began vigorously shaking his head.

"Kerra, stop!" yelled Kiddoni, skidding to a halt.

It was too late. The fronds under Kerra's feet began to cave in. Kiddoni had been right. It was a trap—an artificial pit, overlaid with thin branches. Fresh fronds had completed the camouflage. As Kerra fell through, she dragged foliage and fronds after her. Kiddoni soon discovered it was also too late for *him*! He'd stopped precisely at the pit's edge. As foliage yielded under Kerra's feet, it pulled out from under Kiddoni, causing him to slip. He tried to spin around and seize the edge, but his efforts failed. The trap's entire roof collapsed, plunging Kerra and Kiddoni to the base of a pit, about twelve feet below the sandy surface.

The pair fought to clear leaves and branches away from their faces. The pit had a circumference of twenty feet. The bottom was soggy with mud. Much deeper and it would have been a well instead of a pit. Kerra heard twisted laughter above her. She raised her eyes. Her focus first fell upon Brock, wrists still tied, arms stretched back halfway around the width of the tree. Tears streaked his face. He felt so ashamed and heartsick that he couldn't return his sister's gaze.

He knew he'd shouted to save his own hide. Like a coward. An absolute, spineless coward. He wished Hitch had simply killed him. Now he'd be forced to watch as Hitch murdered his sister and Kiddoni.

Kerra finally met the eyes of Hitch Ventura. He'd stepped forward from behind the tree where Brock was tied.

"*Ya'at'eeh!*" he crooned in affected Navajo. "Well, well. Kerra McConnell. One of my favorite females. And my old friend, the One, the Only, Donny the Kid."

Kerra cringed. She wasn't sure where he'd ever heard that childhood nickname. It freaked her out, but this seemed to be exactly Hitch's psychological intent.

He continued to Kiddoni. "You must be startin' to think you got nine lives, Commander. Sorry to disappoint. I thought for sure yer hide would be stretched out and drying in the sun by now, waiting to be sautéed, smoked, and marinated into some down-home, country-style jerky. Valuable stuff. You probably know, Reds place a high premium on what meat they eat, and your flesh, I assure ya, would rank as grade-A prime. Somethin' about—I dunno—the 'power' inherent in a warrior of high rank. No accountin' for taste, eh?" He cackled at his own morbid joke.

Kerra and Kiddoni said nothing. They stood still, watching the gangster gloat.

He studied them a moment longer then blew out another laugh. "You should see the look on your faces. Wish I had a camera. Too bad. Wrong century." He raised his chin and looked toward the area where Kerra and everybody else—including the robbers—had fallen through the rift. He seemed to be listening. "Hmm. I don't hear no more fightin'. I presume my warriors took care of everyone else in your little clique. If not, Cociyo and Huracan will happily take care of any remainders." He pulled in his chin and put a hand to his ear, milking the drama. "What's that you say? You never met Cociyo and Huracan? Well, lemme introduce ya!"

Hitch put two fingers in his mouth and whistled. He smiled and again watched the faces of his captives, eager to relish their reaction. Kerra heard rustling in the brush behind Hitch. A moment later a black jaguar came slinking out of the undergrowth. It was the same dark-pelted creature that Kerra had seen on the night that Gidgiddonihah's battalion was attacked. The balám approached the pit's edge rather slowly, almost reluctantly. Hitch became impatient.

"Get over here, girl! Let my friends have a look at 'cha."

The piercing yellow eyes of the beast with an orange-tipped tail homed in on Kerra and Kiddoni. Menacing, hypnotizing.

"I rather like the way this pit-thing has worked out," said Hitch. "Just high enough so's a man can't escape, but no challenge whatsoever for my pets. Now don' go thinkin' you two're the first guests we've ever had in here. This little arena has brought us *hours* of entertainment."

"Let my brother go," Kerra blurted out. "He's thirteen years old."

"Thirteen?!" Hitch balked. "Is that all he is? Well, I guess that's old enough to toss a quarter million dollars' worth of honey-powder down a well. No, ma'am. I don't forget a thing like that. But just outta curiosity, where would you presume that I should let him go?"

"Anywhere," said Kerra. "He'll find a way home."

Hitch snorted at that. "Darlin', I been trying to find a gateway that leads back to the good ole' U-S-of-A for better'n three years. What makes you think *he* can find what *I* can't find, eh?"

"Because I taught him how to find it," said Kerra. Her expression was unflinching, despite the fact that she'd just told an outright lie. Still, her delivery was as smooth as molasses.

Hitch jacked up his eyebrows. "*You?* You know how to find yer way around all these goofy little doorways and windows?"

Brock picked up on the lie and played along. "I don't remember what you said, Kerra. I can't find it by myself." He turned to Hitch. "You need her. She can take us all home."

Hitch barked an expletive. He challenged Kerra with, "You think you know these time rifts better than me?" He bit off another expletive. "*Amiga*, I been here for *four years*. I know every anchor point there is—where it leads and *when* it leads. How long you been here?—a couple of *days*??"

"I only need to know *one* passageway that leads home," said Kerra.

Hitch began to stew. He seriously pondered her words. The jaguar called Huracan released a low, guttural growl, closely watching its "master," waiting to hear what he would do. Kiddoni maintained his silence, studying every inch of the pit, searching for a possible escape. He noticed some bones that looked like a human rib cage sticking up through the collapsed palm fronds. Not a particularly confidence-building sight.

"Okay," said Hitch. "I'll bite. Where is this fabled gateway? Tell me and I might—I repeat: *might*—spare your life."

"Spare *all* of our lives," said Kerra. "That's the only deal I'll take."

Even as she said it, Kerra realized that she'd pushed him too far.

He made a click in his cheek. "Sorry. No deal. But I'll give you one last chance to change your mind." He looked at Huracan. "Just kill the male—the one draped in the furs of one of your slain cousins. Spare the girl for now."

The jaguar fixed Kiddoni in its gaze and released another low snarl. Kerra kneaded her eyebrows. Something strange was happening here. How could a jaguar possibly understand such a specific command? Of course, that begged a much *bigger* question: how had Hitch Ventura managed to train killer jaguars in the first place? It made no sense. It was as if . . . as if the massive predator understood precisely what he was saying. But that was ridiculous. For crying out loud, it was a *jaguar*!

Huracan seemed to be vacillating. Once more, Hitch lost his patience. He actually threatened the feline with his obsidian sword. "What are you waitin' for?" he snapped, adding a derogatory curse word. "*Do as I said*!!"

The jaguar released a hellish roar and leaped from the edge of the pit. Kiddoni sucked a deep gasp and pressed his back against the rear of the pit. The beast landed five feet in front of its victim. One more lunge and it could easily seize Kiddoni by the skull, cracking it like a walnut.

But just before the jaguar made its final lunge, Brock shouted, "Huracan, no!"

The beast paused. It held Kiddoni in its dreadful gaze, but it did not lunge.

Brock continued. "It understands you, Kerra! Talk to it! *Talk to it!*"

Hitch was dumfounded. A whole string of profanities spluttered from his lips. "Huracan! What are you doing?! Kill him. *Kill him!*"

Huracan roared again. But to Kerra the sound was *more* than a roar. There were intricacies, subtleties. Something clicked in her head. *Holy cow!* She understood! She comprehended what the beast had said. It was a single word.

"*Why?*"

It was immediately apparent that Hitch *also* understood. "*Why??*" he repeated in aggravation. "Because I *commanded* you to! THAT'S why!"

Huracan growled again. Kerra couldn't believe what was happening. Her ears, her mind, again registered the meaning of the growl.

"*Is he a bad man?*" the jaguar inquired.

The expletives were spouting from Hitch's mouth like lava from a volcano. "What are you *talking* about? *Yes!* He's *bad!* He's *bad!*"

Kiddoni stood perfectly still, his mind spinning in consternation, his breath snagged in his windpipe. Kerra realized he wasn't following *any* of this. She strained desperately to comprehend this phenomenon. For some reason—perhaps because Kiddoni and Huracan were denizens of the same century—the Nephite possessed no gift to understand the beast's snarls and growls. She wasn't sure how Brock had figured it out, but she was intensely grateful that he had. Where did this ability even come from? Was it part of the same gift that allowed her to understand the language of Nephites? Or that allowed the Nephites to understand her? But if *that* was true, it meant Huracan might also comprehend *her* words!

"That's wrong!" Kerra shouted at the jaguar. "He's *not* bad! You *know* it. You're a smart girl. A very smart girl."

Hitch was beside himself. He began rambling mindlessly. "I can't believe this. Debating morality with a stupid cat! What is this? High school ethics? Aristotle, Plato, and Jiminy Cricket?" His face reddened with rage. "*Just kill him,* Huracan! Kill him like you've already killed for me a dozen times! Kill him because it's *in your nature!* In your blood! What's *wrong* with you?! KILL HIM!!!"

Kerra watched Huracan closely. The animal's expression seemed to change right before her eyes, the fires of hatred softening, much like a candle as it reaches the end of its wick. Finally, the creature sat back on its haunches. It was clearly not going to attack.

At such a peculiar moment, something the LDS missionaries had taught her back in St. George sprang to mind. She felt as though she could hear Elder Leota's voice as he sat on her couch and declared, "The light of Christ is given to every man. Every man knows by nature the difference between good and evil."

He was paraphrasing a scripture. Something from the Book of Mormon. However, its meaning was restricted to *people*, right? Not animals! Not the lower creatures of the earth. *People* had the light of Christ! *Men and women* knew the difference between right and wrong! No lesson or sermon had ever adequately prepared her mind for what was going on here. Inexplicably, the jaguar's spirit had been *quickened*. There was no doctrine to explain it. And frankly who *cared*?! Huracan had become as docile as a kitten. No, that wasn't quite true. Kerra sensed a deep, visceral sadness in the jaguar's features. Sadness and pain.

The cat growled again. Again, Kerra understood.

"*I do not believe he is a bad man. I will not kill him.*"

Hitch was so enraged that Kerra thought he might combust. His limbs were quaking, but not out of fear—out of fury. The same fury was apparent in his trembling weapon. He gripped his obsidian sword so tightly she wouldn't have been surprised to see the handle disintegrate into sawdust.

"Get out of the pit, Huracan," Hitch said through clenched teeth, his voice low and rumbling, like a receding wave before a devastating tsunami. Next he shouted at the top of his voice, "*Cociyo*! COCIYO!!"

Kerra's tension ratcheted up further. He was summoning the *other* jaguar—the orange-and-black monster that had emerged from the rift when they first arrived in this century. Even that day Kerra had sensed a dark, almost degenerate spirit about this particular beast. She already believed that it would likely not respond in any way similar to Huracan. Kerra was virtually certain that it would eagerly obey Hitch's every command. She had no evidence of this, just a feeling, an instinct. This instinct told her that the jaguar named Cociyo *enjoyed* following such orders. It had adopted a singular fondness for killing humans and a fondness for the rewards it received after the deed was done.

Again Kerra watched Huracan's eyes. She sensed that the animal was confused, even ashamed. Its head hung like a whipped hound as it turned and made the mighty leap out of the pit. There, it waited at its master's feet for whatever punishment he might mete out. Perhaps it merely expected a swat. Perhaps it expected a strike with the blunt side of Hitch's sword. In any case, the magnificent cat appeared resigned to its fate.

To Kerra's astonishment—and revulsion—Hitch's punishment was far more severe. He raised his weapon, the razor-sharp edge poised vertically over the target. Kerra, Brock, and Kiddoni watched in horror as Hitch struck downward, embedding the blades deeply into the flesh behind the animal's shoulder.

Huracan bellowed in pain. Brock could see the gaping wound.

"Get away from me, you miserable beast!" Hitch yelled. "You flea-bitten piece of filth!"

Huracan did as Hitch commanded. It limped, practically crawled, into the undergrowth of the forest and slipped out of sight. Kerra saw blood dripping from its wound. Was it wandering off to die? It seemed almost certain. What beast in the wild could possibly survive such a barbaric injury?

"*You're* the beast, Hitch Ventura," Kerra seethed. "You're the only piece of filth here."

"Shut up!" snapped Hitch. He called out again, "Cociyo!"

Kerra realized now that it was Cociyo's shadow that she had seen in the rainforest's vegetation. Hitch had implied that Cociyo had been ordered to follow up and complete whatever job the Gadianton warriors had failed to finish. He'd sent it to kill Gidgiddonihah, Pek, and her father—presuming the Reds had bungled the job. Kerra's heart skipped a beat as she again heard rustling in the brush. This time the rustling and crunching came from *behind* them. Cociyo was approaching from the same direction as Kerra and Kiddoni before they were caught in the trap. This was not good. It meant that the jaguar had come from roughly the same vicinity as Dad and the others.

Kiddoni flinched as a massive, orange-mottled head appeared directly over the place where he'd been pressed against the dirt wall.

He moved swiftly back into the center of the "arena." Kerra moved too, grabbing his arm, determined that whatever fate Kiddoni faced, she would face it with him. The 400-pound feline named Cociyo watched Kerra and Kiddoni closely, a glint of playfulness in its eyes. It appeared to like what it saw: two trapped and helpless human beings in a tightly enclosed area—no escape. Kerra shuddered as she noticed that its jowls were already stained and dripping with blood.

"What took you so long?" Hitch asked angrily. His patience for the animal kingdom clearly running very thin.

The beast growled, and as with Huracan, Kerra also understood Cociyo.

"*Feeding,*" it declared.

Hitch offered up his first simpering, melodramatic grin in several minutes. "So glad to hear it. Feeding on what?"

"*Man flesh,*" Cociyo proudly confirmed.

"Excellent. I hope you're still hungry."

Another growl escaped its throat, curiously self-indulgent.

"*Always,*" the creature replied.

Hitch focused again on Kerra and Kiddoni. "I apologize for the behavior of Cociyo's mate. Fortunately—for me—that no longer matters. As they say, the show must go on. Oh, and Kerra, I've carefully meditated upon your claims of finding a passageway home, and I regret to say, I think it's a bluff. I just don't believe you know squat about any portals leading home. If there was such a portal, I'd have already found it. The fact is, Cociyo has an insatiable appetite. He just never seems quite satisfied. Might say he has something of a hollow leg. Or a hollow tail."

"You're making a terrible mistake," Kerra announced, doing her best to sound coy, although her voice quivered. "I can get you home. I can lead you back to Los Angeles."

In the middle of her plea, Cociyo uttered an unexpected growl. The meaning was clear enough.

"*Where is Huracan?*"

"Don't worry about it," said Hitch.

Brock wasn't going to let him get away with that. "He killed her, Cociyo! He sliced her with his blade! Come smell the blood! Your master killed your mate! She limped off into—"

Hitch propelled his fist directly into Brock's face.

"Hitch, stop!" Kerra cried.

The boy was out cold. His chin sat against his chest while the ropes that were secured to his wrists behind the palm tree kept him from falling forward.

"Huracan is fine!" Hitch declared. "Honestly, I'm a bit taken aback by all of this. Apparently, my good friends here possess an ability somewhat similar to mine. They are able to communicate with you and Huracan. But believe me, Cociyo, the boy lied. Do you understand me? He did not tell you the truth. Sure, I may have tapped her with my club—but that was for her own good. If I inflicted a scratch, it was minor. She's off right now licking it clean and contemplating her mistake."

"*I want to smell her,*" said Cociyo. "*I want to see her.*"

"Fine!" snapped Hitch. "Do you as you like. Just remember, I've never lied to you, Cociyo—not in three years! Am I right? Have I ever lied to you?"

A low growl. "*No.*"

"You'll have all night long to help lick her wound if that's what you want," said Hitch. "Right now I need your claws. I need your powerful jaws. The same lethal weapons you used to kill those *other* useless Nephites."

Cociyo raised his neck. "*What other Nephites?*"

"The ones back at the beach," said Hitch impatiently.

"*I saw no Nephites,*" snarled Cociyo. "*Only Mighty Ones.*"

Kerra presumed that the phrase meant Gadianton warriors.

"Then what's all that on yer chin? Where'd the blood come from?"

"*I found a Mighty One. Already dead. Burned in hot water. Good smell.*"

Kerra bristled with hope. The jaguar had *not* killed her father, Gid, or Pek. It had found the body that she and Kiddoni had passed among the palms—the one that had boiled to death in the cauldron while slipping through the rift. Something about the partially cooked flesh had attracted the beast's curiosity.

Once again Hitch's face turned beet red with indignation. "Just kill them!" he repeated, pointing into the pit. "Feed to your heart's content!"

Cociyo's paralyzing gaze again fixed on Kerra and Kiddoni. Kerra perceived the same wicked glint in those black and yellow eyes that she sensed the very first day she saw them. The monster released an earth-shaking roar—no particular meaning. Just a roar of dominance—a confirmation of its murderous intentions.

As it drew back on its haunches, preparing to pounce, an arrow whistled through the air. Cociyo was struck in the abdomen. It howled in pain and fell over onto its side. It batted at the arrow's shaft with its paw, likely just embedding the arrowhead deeper into its flesh. Another arrow whisked toward the jaguar. This one missed, shattering as it deflected off a palm trunk. Cociyo scrambled to its feet and dashed awkwardly into the underbrush, fleeing in much the same direction as its mate. Its wound was serious, but whether or not it was fatal was impossible to confirm.

Pek emerged from behind a palm tree, drawing another arrow from his quiver. Hitch hesitated a mere instant, smoke practically spouting from his ears in unquenchable frustration. He quickly read the writing on the wall and hightailed it into the jungle.

Dad came to the edge of the pit and looked down at Kerra and Kiddoni. "Is everyone all right?"

Kerra nodded. "We're fine."

He went to Brock, who was still groggy, nose bleeding from Hitch's punch. Dad chopped at the cord with his obsidian-edged blade to cut him loose.

Gid also appeared at the pit's edge. Kerra might have expected him to pursue Hitch, but his immediate concern was her.

Pek said to Gid, "That was Akuhuun! He's getting away!"

The commander pointed at Kerra. "We need *her*—or we'll never find *him*."

Kerra felt faint. She felt as if her emotions had been abused, beaten, and dragged through the mud. She just wanted her part in this nightmare to be over. Gidgiddonihah set his weapons at the edge and leaped down into the pit. Pek knelt near the edge to assist as Gid made a stirrup of his hands to raise up Kiddoni. He did the same to lift Kerra. With Pek's help, both of them climbed to safety with relative ease.

Kerra turned back, obviously wondering how Gid intended to escape the pit.

The commander was already walking backward, studying the wall's dimensions. After he reached the opposite side, he took four giant strides across the muddy, frond-littered pit and leaped for freedom. With stunning athletic grace, he grasped the top edge and hoisted himself out. Kerra had once compared Gid to a jaguar. Her comparison, she realized, was more accurate than she'd first presumed.

Gid turned to Kiddoni. "Stay with Mi´con and the boy. More Reds may well drop from the sky. Kerra must come with us."

Kiddoni looked at Kerra. "I don't want to leave her," he said urgently, desperately.

Gid responded harshly. "You think you're fully recovered, Commander? You think you can fight at full strength? Don't be a fool! You'd put her life—and *mine*—at greater risk. *Stay here!*"

Kerra took both of Kiddoni's hands, a gesture of reassurance—a promise that all would be well—despite the fact that she possessed no authority or knowledge whatsoever to make such a promise.

"We cannot delay!" Gid barked.

Kerra reluctantly slipped away from Kiddoni's grip. The Nephite watched in dismay as she, Gid, and Pek disappeared into the labyrinth of the jungle.

CHAPTER 22

GID AND PEK KEPT KERRA pressed in the middle—acting as body-guards fore and aft while they pursued the same basic route into the forest that Hitch had used to flee. With each step the foliage became increasingly more suffocating. A thin, muddy pathway—likely a trail for small game—led them deeper into the vegetation. In single file Hitch's pursuers forged ahead, tossing aside an infinite array of leaves and vines. Kerra's mind felt muddled, blurry, intoxicated with near emotional overload. For the first time in her life, Kerra began to realize her own fragility. She truly had limitations. She was not an all-powerful warrioress—not by any stretch of the imagination. She firmly believed that a breakdown, a complete collapse of her mental faculties, was only moments—or seconds—away. She tried to pray as she ran. Her prayer felt more like a mantra: *I can do this*, she intoned in her head. *I can survive this. I can hold it together. Help me, God. Please help me hold it together!*

All at once the trail opened up. A freshwater sinkhole, or cenoté, came into view. It was forty feet long, shaped almost like a figure-eight, but more curved on its closest edge, like two water sacks hang-ing over someone's shoulder. The water was lime-green, reflecting sunlight so brightly that it projected prism-like patterns upon the surrounding ceiba trees and other underbrush. The cenoté's edge con-sisted of layers of limestone in various shades of black and gray, rising approximately four feet above the surface of the water. The cenoté's shape made for an elevated promontory in the center, where the figure-eight divided. This promontory projected out over the water like a diving platform. Below this platform the otherwise lime-colored water was stygian dark, meaning it was probably very deep, perhaps leading to a submerged cavern— the very place that Mayan myths would have defined as the impenetrable "Underworld."

Kerra, Gid, and Pek entered the clearing at the far right end of the cenoté. The instant that Kerra's focus fell upon the dark green water, her fractured thoughts suddenly cleared. She felt impressed to raise her finger and point.

"There," she told Gidgiddonihah as he came up beside her. Pek also arrived, standing close on her right side. "Hitch—Akuhuun— would have gone in there."

"What is it?" asked Gid.

"A tunnel," said Kerra. "But it's also a rift."

"How do you *know* this?" asked Pek. "Do you see it?"

She shook her head. "No. At least not with my eyes. More like . . . with my *spirit*." Even to Gid and Pek she sounded brittle and exhausted. "That's the best I can describe it."

"Where does it lead?" asked Pek.

"Does it matter?" said Gid. "As long as it leads to Lord Akuhuun." He looked at his second-in-command. "Ready for a swim?"

Pek opened and closed his mouth, clearly not looking forward to such an expedition. Then, in a flash, the expedition no longer mattered.

Just to the right of where Pek had positioned himself was the trunk of a massive ceiba. Its roots tapered outward from the tree's base in a starfish pattern. The tapering roots were as tall as a man and offered natural hiding places. Hitch Ventura had cunningly selected one of those niches.

He erupted from his place of concealment, yipping like a stereotypical Indian brave and swinging his bejeweled obsidian sword. The weapon struck Pek directly in the stomach, cutting deeply. Kerra and Gid leaped backward. As a reflex, or perhaps to utilize his last ounce of strength, Pek gripped Hitch's sword in both palms, forcing him to let it go. Gid's lieutenant dropped to his knees then crumpled forward. Hitch pulled a knife from a sheath behind his back—not an ancient weapon. It was of modern steel, and it was the same knife that Kerra remembered from her confrontation with Hitch six months ago in the hollow—the switchblade that Kiddoni had easily deflected with the butt end of his spear. Hitch drew back his arm to throw it. His target was Gidgiddonihah.

Gid twisted evasively, but somehow Hitch anticipated this move. Gid did not twist quickly enough. The knife struck the commander's leather vest over his right shoulder. By the look on Gid's face, Kerra knew it had penetrated his flesh. Gidgiddonihah dropped his white flint blade, staggering backward until he collided with another ceiba trunk.

"You lose again, old friend!" Hitch shouted exuberantly. "I'd kill you now, but hey, I'd miss you too much! You're still my favorite adversary!"

Kerra knew this wasn't the reason he didn't finish off Gidgiddonihah. The gangster was unexpectedly unarmed—and he lacked his precious Demon Balám as backup. Most of all, Hitch saw that Gid still gripped his lethal hatchet in his left hand. Hitch seemed fully aware of Gid's talent with that hatchet. He seized Kerra around the waist, using her as a shield. She punched and struggled, but Hitch only tightened his hold, making it difficult for her to breathe. He dragged her toward the promontory above the deepest part of the cenoté, taunting Gidgiddonihah the whole way.

"Haven't I polished off enough of your friends and relatives, Commander? Do I gotta start knockin' off neighbors and second cousins? Don't worry—your *uncle* is still on my to-do list. You can count on that. Bring me a new battalion, essé! The Reds are always hungry for fresh meat!"

He was about to leap into the water. Kerra realized Hitch was not only using her as a shield. He was taking her *with* him! He obviously felt it was the only way to ensure the enemy's "blindness." He had to make it impossible for her to help them.

With strenuous effort, Gid maneuvered himself so his left arm had free range. Hitch was only a few steps from the promontory's edge. Kerra's struggling had forced Hitch to hold her slightly sideways. This was Gid's only advantage—his one chance. With all his might he flung his copper hatchet. The aim was low. Any higher and he risked hitting Kerra. That risk could hardly be avoided anyway. However, Gidgiddonihah's skills exceeded his own expectations.

The hatchet hit its mark—the target's shin, right above the ankle. Hitch released a shrill, almost feminine-sounding yell and dropped to the ground at the lip of the promontory, inches from rolling over the edge into the cenoté's green darkness. He released Kerra, who scrambled frantically toward Gidgiddonihah.

The commander adjusted his head, anxious for Kerra to get out of the way so he could assess the damage. As he witnessed its extent, he was exceedingly pleased. Kerra also saw the wound. It appeared that the hatchet had sliced cleanly through the bone. *Gracious!* He'd practically severed Hitch's right foot! It seemed to hang by a single thin tendon, bleeding profusely.

The leader of the Shamans howled in agony, writhing atop the limestone, cursing as loudly as his lungs permitted. At that moment, something orange and black with a blood-crusted chin emerged from the rainforest. It paused just a few scant yards above the body of Hitch Ventura.

Cociyo, the Demon Balám, didn't seem to notice Kerra or Gid or even the dormant figure of Pek—the very human being who was responsible for firing the arrow that now protruded from its ribs. All its attention was focused on the agonized figure atop the promontory. Kerra watched it stalk closer to Hitch. The jaguar's movements were no longer fluid or graceful. It stumbled forward. The beast seemed to be on its last legs. Yet its will remained powerful enough to close in on the object of its wrath.

"Cociyo!" Hitch screeched. "Get help! Fetch Zemnarihah! Hurry! *Hurry!*"

The jaguar paused again, only twelve inches shy of Hitch's face, glaring at him with malevolent eyes. Kerra could feel Cociyo's hatred radiating like a corrosive beam of energy. It released a penetrating growl, like the rumble of a Harley Davidson.

"*I found her,*" it snarled. "*You cut her badly.*"

"Cociyo, listen to me. We've been together—worked together, played together—for more than three years. She changed. She was erratic. You know it. She wasn't acting the same."

"*She was my* mate!" Cociyo roared.

"She'll be fine," said Hitch. "Look at *me!* At my foot!"

"*She's dying,*" rumbled the beast. "*So am I.*"

"Then take your revenge!" Hitch pointed at Kerra and Gid. "Look! It's them! It's *her*! It was her fault all along! Because of her you were shot with an arrow! She confused Huracan's thinking! It's *them*! Don't you see? RIP THEM APART!!"

The jaguar growled a final time. The meaning was clear in Kerra's ears. "*I* will *take my revenge. On* you!"

The monster lunged. Kerra wanted to avert her eyes but couldn't. She witnessed the full horror as Cociyo attacked, encasing Hitch's skull in its jaws—what she now realized was a jaguar's modus operandi. It drove its claws into Hitch's face and slashed downward as he helplessly clutched the fur on its neck. Then came the awful crack. The pitiable sound issuing from Hitch's lungs ended abruptly. His body fell limp.

Just killing him didn't seem to satisfy Cociyo. It wanted to feed. Gidgiddonihah no longer had any desire to stick around. He grasped Kerra's hand and pulled it toward his shoulder. He wrapped her fingers around the handle of the metal blade.

"Yank it out," he said softly.

Kerra did as instructed. The knife retracted soundlessly from his flesh. Gid hardly winced. He never closed his eyes. Hastily, he recovered his white flint blade and staggered toward Pek. As he and Kerra reached Pek's body, they heard a raspy breath. He was alive. Gid pried Pek's fingers away from the obsidian sword that still cut into his lieutenant's stomach and tossed it aside.

"Help me carry him," he commanded Kerra.

Gid glanced a final time at Cociyo feasting upon its former master. Kerra realized the commander wanted to get as far away from Hitch and the dying balám as possible. Even with his wounded shoulder, Gid and Kerra managed to carry Pek some distance down the narrow trail leading back toward the beach. Pek opened his eyes several times. Kerra expected him to groan or cry out, but he showed hardly any reaction. The wound was so large, so gaping, that pain no longer seemed to factor into the equation.

Finally, Pek told his commander, "Set me down. Please."

Gid and Kerra respected his request.

Gid took his hand and leaned in close. "Please, old friend. Endure the pain. We must get you to a physician." He looked at Kerra. "Can you find another way? Another passageway back to Zarahemla?"

Kerra stumbled out a weak reply. "I'm not sure. There might be something near the beach, where we fell through. But it may not be accessible. The window might've closed. The timing may be all wrong."

"We have to try," Gid insisted.

Pek feebly shook his head. "No, Commander. No further. Here. I will die here."

"Why do you want to give up?" said Gid bitterly.

Pek tightly gripped Gidgiddonihah's leather cuirass. "Listen to me, my friend. My brother. I feel no pain. It's my time. I want . . . your word. Give me your word."

"My word for what?"

"Marry her," Pek said.

"Marry who?"

Pek laughed quietly. "You *know* who. Rebha. My sister."

Gid shook his head. "I've caused your family too much sorrow. And now *you*—"

Pek gritted his teeth and again yanked Gid's cuirass. "She loves you. It would honor Chani's memory."

"Your father would never have it," said Gid.

"You *idiot!*" Pek snapped. Afterward his energy seemed to fizzle away. He continued in a much softer tone. "My father loves you as much as Rebha. As much as Chani. Maybe more. If Rebha refuses you, marry *him*."

Gid laughed, tears pricking at his eyes. He gripped Pek's hand more tightly. "All right, my brother. You have it—my promise."

Pek shut his eyes. He whispered, "Good. Now leave me . . . for the balám. It's what . . . I wish. It's honorable. *Ho . . . nor . . . able.*"

Pek's mouth fell open slightly. His eyes glazed over and his fingers went limp. Gid placed Pek's hand gently upon the warrior's chest. He shut Pek's eyes. Afterward, he and Kerra paused a moment more, searching for any further signs of life. Finally, Kerra looked up pleadingly at Gid. It was time to find her father and brother, time to find Kiddoni.

Gid nodded. He arose and drew a deep breath. He clasped one hand to his wounded shoulder and stared down the pathway that led back toward the beach.

The brush behind them erupted.

Cociyo, the 400-pound monster, crashed through the foliage, its blazing eyes fixed upon Kerra McConnell. It clearly desired one final victim. She screamed and tried to leap out of its way. Gid was knocked backward into a tall nest of leaves, seeming to vanish from sight. Kerra felt the creature land upon her back, smashing her flat against the ground, forcing the air from her lungs. Its claws protracted, pinning her in place. Kerra felt its hot breath and smelled the stench of the contents of its stomach as Cociyo released a heart-stopping growl.

"*Master is dead. But he was right.* You *are to blame.*"

She couldn't suck any air. It was crushing her ribs! She sensed that it was about to engulf her head inside its jaws, piercing each temple with its fangs.

Kerra heard something else crash through the underbrush. She heard Kiddoni shout her name! The beast gathered its strength for a last lunge against one final attacker. Kerra felt the additional weight against her stomach as the jaguar used *her* as a springboard. But the monster's efforts were short-lived. Kerra raised her eyes. Leaves obscured her vision, but she discerned enough to see that Kiddoni had been armed with a spear—undoubtedly the weapon of a fallen Gadianton. As Cociyo had lunged, the beast ensured its own demise. Kiddoni had jammed the spear's butt into the earth. He used the creature's inertia against it, much as he had once done against a Gadianton opponent named Bakaan in the woods of the hollow. Cociyo had leaped against the spear point, embedding the tip deeply into its own breast. Death was almost instantaneous. Kerra caught a glimpse of its final death throe. She turned away and closed her eyes.

It was over. The nightmare, she prayed, was finally over.

CHAPTER 23

KERRA, KIDDONI, AND GIDGIDDONIHAH HAD nearly reached the end of the narrow game trail. They were ready to emerge from the dense vegetation when Kiddoni drew their attention to something off to the right. Something was over there that he obviously wanted them to see. Kerra heard a voice—her brother's.

She glanced at Kiddoni. "Why would he have gone into the jungle?"

"He's with her," he said. "The female."

Kerra understood. He meant Huracan, Cociyo's mate.

Kiddoni followed her. Gid followed warily, still putting pressure on the wound in his shoulder. After a few yards she also heard her father's voice.

"Dad!" she cried. "Brock!"

"Over here!" Dad replied.

As she came upon the scene, Brock and her father were gathered around the great black panther with a fire-tipped tail. Huracan was lying on her stomach, breathing erratically. The wound that Hitch had inflicted behind her shoulder was easily two inches deep, the tissue pink and swollen, but no longer bleeding very much. The balám allowed Brock to touch its head in a gesture of comfort. It seemed a surprising act of tolerance for such a dangerous animal—particularly one that had served so long as one of Hitch's personal executioners.

Dad met Kerra, Kiddoni, and Gid as they entered the private cubby hole in the thicket.

"What happened?" Dad inquired.

"Akuhuun is dead," Gid said. "Slain by the other Demon Balám— the male."

"And Pek?" he asked.

Gid looked down. Kerra shook her head solemnly.

Dad released a dreary sigh. "Ishlom, Lemech . . . now Pek."

Brock overheard. Reluctantly, he added, "And Chemnon."

The news took the others by surprise. Brock's heart was heavy as he offered up the details. It seemed strange. He thought he'd hated Chemnon. But now that he was gone . . . Brock blamed himself. He regretted acting like such a jerk. The fact was, Chemnon was only fifteen years old, a warrior, and the son of a prophet.

"We were hunting," Brock explained. "He was . . . killed by Cociyo. It happened so fast. And it happened just before Hitch found me in the forest. Hitch was spying on us—*all* of us—all along."

The news was particularly devastating to Gidgiddonihah. "I will have to tell Chemnon's father."

Dad continued to mourn. "I'm sorry. So sorry for all of it. All these tragedies—the Gadianton conflict dragging on so long . . . The blame rests with us—*our* people. People I led here. People who came from my time."

"The blame rests with *one* man," Gid corrected. "One wicked man from your . . . *time*. And it's over. The news of Akuhuun's downfall will be celebrated by Lachoneus and by my uncle. Gidgiddoni's sons were warriors. He will be proud. Proud of what we all accomplished. If it is the will of God, this war with the Reds will end much more swiftly than otherwise. Our citizens can soon return home."

"What about Manazzeh?" asked Kerra.

"I'm not sure," said Brock. "Hitch threatened to hurt him—and hurt Grandpa—but I don't think he got around to it. As far as I know, Manazzeh and Grandpa are safe."

"No one is safe until we get them out of the wilderness of Hermounts," said Gid.

Dad noticed the commander favoring his shoulder. "What happened to you?"

"Nothing," said Gid. "A flesh wound."

Kerra smiled. She thought of the Black Knight in *Monty Python and the Holy Grail*. Gid and that ludicrous knight had a common stubborn streak. Even if Gid's arms and legs had been chopped off, he might have still called it "only a flesh wound."

The commander homed in on a nearby jungle plant with spikes like a porcupine—similar, thought Kerra, to aloe vera, but with somewhat longer shafts. The tips were as sharp and stiff as needles. Gid snapped off one of these tips. As he tore it away, a fibrous string naturally stripped away along with the point, all the way to the stem's base. Gid raised the fiber and tugged it twice with both hands. It didn't break. Durable stuff. What Gid now held in his hands uncannily resembled a needle and thread, and that's exactly how he used it. He exposed the wound in his shoulder to the open air and began the process of self-suturing, with a little help from Dad.

Kiddoni said to Kerra, "Your brother found the balám here. He continues to speak to it. He understands its words. I cannot understand a single sound."

She knelt beside Brock and Huracan. "What have you told it?"

"*Her,*" Brock corrected. "I've told her that she's going to be okay."

"A weighty promise," said Kiddoni, "considering the seriousness of that wound."

"Without help, yes, her situation would be much worse," said Brock. "But you don't understand. She'll *let* us help her. I know it." Brock turned to Gid, still closing off his inch-deep knife wound. He asked, "If Huracan were a soldier, what would you do?"

He took another moment to finish suturing his wound. Afterward, he approached Brock and the jaguar somewhat gingerly, still wary in the presence of a lethal predator. He inspected the wound and said, "I'd clean it and bind it, much like my shoulder. But the wound is much more serious."

"Would you clean it . . . with alcohol?" asked Brock.

"Possibly," said Gid. "Or some other physician's concoction."

Brock eyed the leather canteen on Gid's belt—the one that did *not* hold water. "Do we have any other 'physician's concoction'?"

Gid shook his head, understanding the boy's insinuation. "We don't."

Brock persisted. "She could've killed us. She spared our lives. She *saved* us. Now we can save *her. You* could save her."

Gid grunted cynically. "You think you can pour corn grog on the open wound of an animal like that without setting off a reaction like a firestorm? The balám would tear your head off."

Brock turned to Huracan. He tried to speak soothingly. "I promised that we could help you. But in order to do that, I have to pour something on your wound. It's medicine. Do you understand medicine?"

Huracan made a small growl. "*No.*"

Brock sighed and tried again. "Something to keep it from getting infected. Er . . . something that will help it heal and get better. Stronger. Do you understand?"

"*No.*"

"That's okay," said Brock. "You don't need to totally understand. You just have to trust me. It will hurt a little. But it's a *good* hurt."

Huracan snarled more dramatically. "*What hurt could be good? No man has ever hurt me. I kill any man that hurts me, just as Cociyo has gone to kill our master.*"

Brock shuddered inwardly. "That's where the *trust* comes in. Will you trust me? I just . . . I want to save your life. That's all—and this will help. I promise."

The creature lowered her head and closed her eyes, issuing another low growl. "*Do what you will do, small man. I will attempt not to kill you.*"

Brock swallowed and looked back at Gidgiddonihah. He smiled nervously. "She says go ahead and do it."

Gidgiddonihah grinned crookedly. He removed the leather canteen from his belt and pulled out the wooden stopper with his teeth. "The last of my stash. Took six months to brew. The rest went up in flames."

"Means there will be nothing left to wash away the bad memories," said Brock. "I'm sorry."

"Eh," Gid grunted. "It never really worked anyway."

"Are you sure about this?" asked Brock.

Gid nodded, handing him the canteen. "But don't dawdle. Just pour it—*all* of it—on the wound."

Brock again studied Huracan. She still lay with her eyes closed. Gid stepped well out of the way. He began snapping off additional "needles and threads"—for the jaguar, and possibly for the boy if Huracan reacted badly to having that wound doused with alcohol.

Brock thought about voicing a final warning. He decided there wasn't much point. She was either going to slash him to pieces or she would endure the pain. Kerra noticed that Kiddoni had armed himself with an obsidian blade, prepared to defend Brock if the beast responded badly.

Brock took a breath for courage. Then he poured—quickly. No sense dragging it out. Huracan roared ferociously and came to her feet. She spun around on her muscular legs, eyes full of venom and fury. Instead of showing fear, Brock said merely, "I'm not finished. Lie back down. You're making it worse. Remember: *trust.*"

The jaguar panted raggedly through its teeth, making foam like an overworked horse. As Brock had said, her quick motion had only further inflamed what the alcohol was trying to cleanse. Eventually, Huracan's fury dissipated. Could a jaguar weep? Hard to tell, but Brock swore that he perceived tears. Incredibly, she lay back down and submitted to Brock's will. He finished pouring the alcohol onto the wound. Huracan trembled, but she did not release another growl. Her eyes again closed and her breathing remained erratic. Perhaps, thought Kerra, she tried to concentrate on some faraway thought—whatever constituted a positive memory in a jaguar's brain.

Gid stood nearby and watched the last drops of his grog drain from his canteen. "And there goes the last of it," he said nostalgically. He looked at Brock. "Boy, you may have saved me."

"You saved *her,*" he corrected.

Gid's fingers pinched several needles and threads. "Tell her what I'm going to do. I don't want my skull crushed."

Brock explained to Huracan, "The man, Gidgiddonihah, is going to stitch up the wound. He'll close it so that it no longer bleeds."

"Who?" Huracan growled, only half-opening her eyes.

"Our leader," said Brock. "I guess you could say he's your new master."

The jaguar released a long staccato growl, almost a purr. "*No new master. I will never have another master.*"

"Well," said Brock, "if you did, he'd be a good one. Not like your last master. You'd like him. He's a lot like you, in spirit. And when he's done, your injury will get better. The pain will go away. After a few weeks you'll feel good as new."

The cat made a whining sound, like a human patient. "*I cannot wait a few weeks. I must run and hunt.*"

"Not for a while," said Brock. "That's not how it works. You'll tear the stitches. You will have to accept help from human beings. You'll have to let us feed you."

She growled again, but it had no particular meaning. Just a snarl of futility. Perhaps encouragement for Gid to "just get it over with."

As Gid stitched the open wound, the jaguar made no reaction at all. Her breathing even seemed to steady. It almost appeared that she'd fallen asleep.

Dad said to Kerra, "We've accomplished almost everything. Every goal but one."

Kerra understood immediately. The only goal that remained unresolved was the very reason her father had returned to the first century. She looked in his eyes. They were weary and full of despair. Kerra felt so overwhelmed that her own mind and her muscles literally ached. Her father spoke to her as if she had all the answers. As if any hope of success rested solely with her.

"What can we do?" Dad asked. "Can we still find Paísha? Can we still find my four-year-old son?"

"Why are you asking me this?" said Kerra wearily. "Nearly everything I've learned about faith over the past few months I've learned from you."

"No," said Dad. "I could never teach what I've learned from you in the past few days. So . . . can you find a way back to Hermounts? Can you take us away from this ocean? After all, we still need to find your grandpa Lee and Manazzeh."

"If we do this," said Kerra, "we need more than just *my* faith. More than my prayers. We need everyone's combined."

"You have it," Dad assured. "You already have it—from all of us. We'll finish up here. Don't worry. Seek some solace. Take Kiddoni with you. Please Kerra. Listen to your spirit. And to the *Holy* Spirit. Find another portal."

She studied his face. It seemed just that simple to him. Maybe it was. Maybe faith was already in play. Already her ally. It seemed astonishing. Somehow she'd gained an entirely new perspective of herself and the world around her.

She looked at Kiddoni. The Nephite warrior took her hand. He waited for her to decide which way to go. Finally, she pushed aside some vines. They headed toward the sound of the crashing surf.

As they emerged from the underbrush and crossed through the palm trees, Kerra seemed to falter.

"What's wrong?" asked Kiddoni.

"I-I'm not sure," said Kerra.

"Are we going the right direction?"

"It's not that." She looked at him squarely. "What will happen, Kiddoni? What will happen to *us*? Will we just . . . separate again? Return to our own worlds?"

He sighed. "I don't know. But I've learned this much: fate seems to draw us together at the most critical and opportune times—even as I am about to be executed by Gadianton priests."

She said, "If we added up all the moments that we've spent together since we were children, all those moments might amount to less than a day."

Kiddoni nodded thoughtfully, then he said, "But it's those moments that have ruled my thoughts—ruled my dreams—most of the days of my life."

"What if you get to know me and find that you don't really like me?" she asked. "What if we really have nothing in common?"

He sent her a peculiar look. "Nothing in common?" The phrase itself seemed to strike him as odd and foreign. "Are these the thoughts that trouble the women of your century? We are both human beings. We are young. We *build* our commonalities together. We are drawn to each other. And to God. What more is required?"

Kerra looked down and nodded uncertainly. "What will you do? You're a warrior. A commander. You can't leave."

The corners of Kiddoni's mouth sagged. "It's true. I cannot abandon my duty." He took her hand. "Why must you return home? Is your century so much better?"

Kerra shrugged. "I understand it. I don't understand your world at all."

"I'll teach you," he said determinedly. "My *family* will teach you. My mother knows all about you. If she ever thought you were a hummingbird spirit—a ghost of my dreams—by now all of my descriptions of you have made you as real to her as any person she has ever known. My father is gone. My mother yearns for a daughter, as much as I yearn for . . ."

"For what?" Kerra persisted.

"A friend. A companion. The last time I saw you, in the woods near your uncle's home, I promised that we would not be separated long. Not as long as before. Now see? I was right. *You* have brought us back together. So . . ." His voice became unsteady. ". . . I do not think . . . I could endure it . . . if you were to leave me again so soon."

She smiled. "I'm not going anywhere. At least not away from you. But . . ." She focused again on the problem at hand. ". . . There must be a way back. Back to the fortifications. And back to where we left my grandfather."

She began walking again through the palm trees, straight toward the ocean, across the charcoal-colored sand. Kiddoni followed closely. As they arrived at the place where the surf met the sand, Kerra drew to a halt. She concentrated. She closed her eyes. She uttered a few words of prayer.

When it seemed she'd stopped speaking under her breath, Kiddoni inquired, "What do you sense?"

She opened her eyes and looked up at the sky. "This is an extraordinary place. It's like . . . a gigantic bubble. A greenhouse. We fell through a rift that functions as a ceiling—a portal that hovers just beneath the canopy of the palm forest." She turned back toward the ocean. "Here, at this place, the rift curves downward and comes to an end." She pointed. "I mean, out there, where the waves are breaking."

"What does that mean?" asked Kiddoni.

At that moment they heard Brock's voice. Brock, Dad, Gidgiddonihah, and the jaguar named Huracan were coming toward them through the palms. The foursome moved slowly on account of Huracan. Brock kept one hand on her back, either to steady her as she limped or just to show support. Kerra and Kiddoni waited for the group to arrive. No one asked Kerra any further questions. They just looked at her, knowing that when the time was right, she'd tell them everything they needed to know.

At last Kerra declared, "We need to walk forward, together, into the water, just as a wave is breaking. And at just the right time."

"I presume," said Dad, "you'll let us know when that time is?"

She nodded, looking nervous and unsettled. "It's a little tricky."

"Why?" asked Gidgiddonihah.

"I'm not sure . . . if there's room," said Kerra.

Brock furrowed his brow. "Room? What's *that* supposed to mean?"

"Space," she said. "I mean . . . I'm not quite sure."

Dad tried to clarify. "You mean, if we all walk into the same wave, there may not be enough 'space' for us all to cross the rift together? We may not all emerge at the same location?"

"Or the same *century*," Kerra added disconcertingly.

Brock thought about this and said, "What if we scrunched together really tightly?"

Kerra curled her lip and shook her head. "Even if we were programmed like robots, we could never walk uniformly enough. The breaking wave would mess it up anyway. Nature just isn't that absolute. It doesn't have to do so much with formation as . . . volume, weight, even the impact and speed of the wave—"

Gid grew weary of the lecture. "Fine. As with all things, our fate is ultimately in the hands of God. Just tell us when to walk forward."

"Don't walk," said Kerra. "*Run*. Try to meet the wave at its same speed. At least . . . that will help."

"When?" asked Kiddoni.

She concentrated. She studied the forming waves, a little like a surfer seeking the perfect curl. Her dad studied her eyes. To him it didn't seem that she focused on the waves. Her eyes weren't particularly zeroed in on anything. They looked beyond the waves, the ocean, and the horizon.

Huracan made a rumble in her throat. Brock understood.

"*I cannot run.*"

He leaned down beside her ear. "Just stay near me. We'll move together."

The surf crashed. Water washed up around their feet. Another wave was steadily rolling toward them. Kerra raised one of her hands.

"Ready," she said softly.

The wave started to curl. It was preparing to break.

"*Now!*" she announced.

Kerra, Kiddoni, Dad, Gid, Brock, and Huracan marched forward into the surf, some more swiftly than others. Brock realized he'd passed the jaguar. He paused to wait.

"Huracan!" he cried.

As Brock turned back to see the wave, he watched it barrel over the top of Kerra, Kiddoni, Gid, and his father. One instant their bodies appeared tangled in the foaming surf, the next they were gone! Brock was terrified. Had he waited too long? The same wave finally struck him. He never registered whether Huracan had caught up to him or not. Still, he felt comforted to think that even if he was separated from his family, he'd have the jaguar's company. He wouldn't be alone. After that, Kerra would find a solution. She'd find a way to bring them all back together. He was sure of it.

Brock let the wave crash over the top of him, spin him around, wash him off his feet, and seemingly carry him back toward shore. He closed his eyes to protect them from salt water. He left them closed as the wave dissipated and receded, leaving him crouched on all fours in the moistened sand. He raised his arm to wipe his eyes before opening them.

As he lifted his eyelids, it was dark. It was *night*! The sound of the ocean transformed into something like a blast of wind, complete with a screaming choir of what sounded like voices. All of the noises soon became something hollow and deep, as if Brock were holding seashells to both ears. He saw no flashing lights, but his skin experienced bizarre sensations. A tingle, followed by a shock, followed by a wave of nausea. One of his arms collapsed. He caught himself before his face smacked the sand. Brock started to vomit. He coughed and spit the acidy taste from his mouth. He still couldn't see a thing.

"Dad!" Brock shouted, his voice sounding strained and gravelly. "Kerra!"

The sound reverberated. He heard his own voice reply as an echo. He was in a cavern! A pungent smell suddenly invaded his nostrils. Oh, it was *sickening*! Sour and rancid, like vinegar and other substances he refused to name. The feeling under his fingers had altered slightly. It was still moist. It had a sandy *quality*, but it was also sticky and slick.

"Huracan!" he cried.

He strained his ears to hear the snarl of the balám. There was no reply.

All at once the air around his body seemed to burst into life. A terrible screeching drowned out the echo of his shouts. He threw his arms over his head as hundreds—perhaps thousands—of bats flapped around his shoulders, between his legs, ramming into his back, scraping the corners of their wings against his arms, and becoming tangled in his hair. Brock shuddered to the depths of his soul. *Soooo grooooossss!* He spit more vomit. Was this sensation any different from being cast into a pit of slimy snakes or spiders?

The onslaught buffeted him for about a minute, though it seemed to last forever. The density of the flying rodents steadily decreased until he heard only random screeches as the last stragglers fluttered past his head.

Brock finally dared to stand. He staggered forward in the dark. His skin, his clothes—absolutely *everything*—was coated in something sticky. Something creamy. Guano. He was convinced it was bat droppings. Again he tried to retch, but there was nothing left in his stomach. The darkness was pervasive. Was there a way out? If so, the bats knew. He tried to follow the course of the bats.

Brock hit his forehead and cursed. The ceiling was very low. He scrunched down and held one hand out front for protection. He trudged forward carelessly. He might have stumbled over a cliff, plunging to his death. He didn't care. He had to get out. He staggered on.

All at once he began to perceive walls. The light was increasing. An exit! He could see it just ahead! The light was dim. It might have been sunset. That made sense. Bats didn't leave their cave unless it was sunset. Or maybe that rule didn't apply here. Maybe his voice had frightened them. For all he knew, the sun was rising, not setting.

At last he stumbled out into the daylight. For the first time in minutes he allowed himself to draw a deep breath of air. He feared the stench of bat urine and guano had left his lungs permanently poisoned and damaged. He looked at his arms and clothes. They were caked in guano. He felt like modern art—a target for Picasso as he dipped his huge flat brush in black, white, and green oil paint, flinging it freely at his clothing and face.

Where in tarnation was he? The terrain was still tropical, but it wasn't the same. Not as dense. Different plants and trees. His heart was hammering out thunderbolts.

He filled his lung cavity with air and called out again as loudly as possible, "*Dad! Kerra! Huracan!*"

No reply.

He was alone. Truly alone.

"Aww, suck!" he said.

CHAPTER 24

KERRA STEPPED THROUGH THE WALL of water and wiped her eyes. *Strange transition*, she thought. After the ocean wave slapped her face, she tasted ocean salt. An instant later, before she opened her eyes, the temperature of the water had adjusted. Cooler. *Colder.* And it crashed down instead of smashing her backward. The saltiness on her tongue . . . disappeared.

She took two steps forward and emerged from the water, although she could still hear it crashing behind her. There was no longer a foaming blue ocean or piercing blue sky filling her vision. Just a river. Not *even* a river. A wide but shallow stream. And a little ways off loomed the edge of another waterfall.

I know this place, thought Kerra. *I've been here.*

Suddenly it wasn't the terrain that drew her attention. It was the figure of a little boy. A soft-haired cherub with eyes so big he reminded her of one of those monkeys—lemurs—from Madagascar. He stood to the left, on the bank of the stream. Kerra turned her head to the right and saw her father. His focus was *also* fixed upon the little boy. She turned a hard left and saw Kiddoni and Gidgiddonihah. They had stepped out from behind the waterfall. Beyond the Nephite warriors, the waterfall was not as heavy or thick. The cascade tapered off until it was only a few streaming lines. But a crevasse or overhang of stone *behind* the falls continued some distance beyond the dripping water. It stretched beneath the cliff for another twenty yards, until a cliff veering northward alongside the current of the stream brought it to an abrupt end.

It was the place where they'd left Brock, Grandpa Lee, Chemnon, and Manazzeh. Dad was still gawking at the little boy. Kerra's eyes searched for Brock and the jaguar. Neither one had stepped through the sheet of water.

There were other people—mostly women and children—gathered under the overhang of the cliff. They'd all arisen to greet the strangers who magically walked out of the waterfall. That is, all but this small boy, no more than four. He appeared to have been standing there *waiting* for them—as if he'd been anticipating their arrival all along. And then, from the midst of the gathering, appeared the ruddy cheeks and cheerful smile of Grandpa Lee.

Kiddoni spoke with increasing excitement. "It's the captives. The women and children! *From Zemnarihah's encampment!*"

Kerra felt a fresh rush of emotions. A woman stepped forth from the gathering. There were tears in her eyes. She fixed her gaze on Kerra's father, who stood there soaked and chilled. She rushed forward to embrace him. It was Paísha. Kerra knew it. And the boy. The boy . . . was Kerra's brother. Her little *half*-brother. No one needed to say it. But where was Brock? Where was her *other* brother?

She heard herself call his name. Panic pervaded her tone. The panic seemed completely out of character with the joyous reunion underway all around her.

"Brock!" she cried again.

She heard Gidgiddonihah shout, "Huracan!"

She was still trying to wrap her mind around all that was happening as Gid leaned in close to her, one hand still putting pressure on his shoulder wound. "What happened to your brother and the balám?"

"I-I told you," Kerra mumbled. "The timing was . . . was critical."

She heard her father call her name. "Kerra! Come! They're here! They're *here*!"

Suddenly Grandpa Lee was standing in front of her. He offered a quick embrace, then asked, "Have you seen Brock? Do you know anything about your brother?"

"He's f-fine," she responded.

The statement sounded peculiar even in her own ears. *Fine?* How did she know this? And yet she sensed that it was true.

She continued. "He's not with us . . . but he's fine. That is, he's alive."

"And the balám?" asked Gid.

She started rambling. "The balám . . . Huracan . . . is n-not with him. She's with others. They're in the same time. Or *almost* the same. But not . . . not together. Not yet. But soon they . . . soon they may find . . ."

Kiddoni watched as Kerra's eyes became glazed and hazy. She was teetering back and forth, on the verge of fainting. He caught her in his arms. He said to those pressing around her, "Watch out! Give us some air. Let me lay her down."

After that, she did faint. Or rather, she drifted away. Drifted into a kind of dream. Not an unhappy dream. Not a nightmare. It was a warm and pleasant place where her eyes could rest and her frazzled mind could sort everything out. A place where she could kiss Kiddoni's lips and embrace her stepmother and press cheek-to-cheek with her precious new little brother. Or maybe those things really happened and she was merely half asleep. It wasn't entirely clear. And that was okay. She was smiling. Somewhere beyond the roar of the waterfalls, the voices of adulation, and the tears of joy, there was a voice in her mind. A voice of indescribable comfort, incomparable peace.

All is well, Kerra McConnell. You have gained the victory. You have defeated the darkness, for now. All is well.

* * *

Brock hid among the pines at the very edge of the vast plain at the base of the hill. There was another hill to the east—higher than the hill with the cave where he'd emerged the evening before. His attention was focused upon the plain. Never had Brock witnessed such an overwhelming spectacle.

There were thousands of men—perhaps *hundreds* of thousands—encamped and entrenched on the plains, many assembled into ranks, as if awaiting orders to invade or attack. Hundreds of campfires burned as far as the eye could see, covering the plains with an oppressive smog that obscured the air. This pollution even continued for some distance up the slopes of the eastern hill.

This smog partially obscured the ranks of soldiers assembled at various heights along these slopes. He presumed they were *opposing* soldiers. Brock swore he could perceive figures positioned all the way to the summit, although many were smaller than ants. This made it difficult to figure out who was here to fight whom. He might have guessed there were five or six contending armies stretching all the way to the eastern, southern, and northern horizons. Some clusters of soldiers were arrayed in such divergent uniforms and dispositions that it seemed to Brock that a massive free-for-all was about to erupt—a bloodbath of apocalyptic proportions.

He noted that some warriors were arrayed in styles and costumes similar to the Gadianton robbers from Kiddoni's neighborhood. Or rather, from his *time* period. Like their counterparts in the humid rainforest, they were smeared in blood and wore as accessories the dismembered body parts of their enemies. Or maybe all those feet, fingers, and skulls did *not* belong to their enemies. *Heck*, thought Brock, *considering the depravity of Gadiantons, such dismembered parts might've belonged to their own mothers!*

In any case, it was the largest assemblage of human beings that Brock had ever laid eyes on. Even the Staples Center in L.A. filled to capacity did not compare. The feeling of impending destruction and doom shook him to the core. This forest of pine trees and leafy undergrowth where he took refuge was not particularly vast. Brock estimated that it only occupied a couple square miles around the base of this smaller nub of a hill. If and when those battle trumpets finally blared, it seemed entirely unlikely that any square inch of this forest could avoid being overrun.

Where in the world *was* this place? Was it anywhere near Zarahemla or the wilderness of Hermounts or even St. George, Utah? Suddenly he wished he'd never marched into the ocean surf. He'd only been following his sister's directions. Huracan the jaguar had been at his side. Well, *sort* of. Because of the jaguar's wound, she was moving a little slower. Anyway, Huracan was gone now. So were Kerra, her father, and all his other companions. It made no *sense*! No other rift had ever separated everybody like this. Maybe his father and sister were *also* separated, along with Gid and Kiddoni. Maybe the rift had deposited each person in lands and centuries all across the spectrum. Everybody had become so dependent upon Kerra's supposed "gift." Well, gift or not, she'd majorly screwed up this time.

Brock thought about the cave where he'd emerged the night before. *I should go back there*, he thought. Clearly there was some kind of "portal" inside that tunnel. If his sister was going to find him, that was the first place she'd look. Yes, she'd start searching at the same cavern that had spewed forth all those hideous bats. Returning to that hole in the earth was not an especially appetizing prospect. Bat guano was as thick on the ground in certain places as meringue on a lemon pie. The first thing Brock did yesterday after stumbling out of that cave was to find a miserable little creek a hundred yards below the opening and take a full half hour repeatedly immersing himself and his Nephite clothes. He then spent a very cold and uncomfortable night nestled in the ant-infested cavity of a rock. However, despite the chill and the pests, he'd actually slept like a log. His experiences with Hitch Ventura had sucked a lot out of him. He slept long past sunup, finally rousing only as his brain began to register the beat of drums. He swore that incessant drumbeat had been pummeling his mind for hours before it finally awakened him. By the time he reached the edge of the forest, the drumming had stopped, but the armies were still firmly in position.

It was looking like he'd have no choice but to return to that disgusting cave. Maybe he wouldn't have to actually wait *inside* the tunnel. Maybe Kerra would locate him just outside the entrance. And if Gadiantons or some other soldiers wandered too close, there were several places for him to hide. The trees weren't particularly thick. But there were numerous crags among the rocks. Hey, maybe he could wait out this whole bloodbath of a million-plus soldiers without anybody even noticing that he was there!

Right, he thought. That didn't seem very likely.

His stomach rumbled like the engine of his cousin Skyler's Mustang. He desperately needed to find something to eat. Maybe when it got dark he could sneak out among the various encampments and steal some food. In any case, there was no point worrying about it now. Despite the overcast of clouds and the pollution of the campfires, it was still too light. Any one of a million scrutinizing eyes might spot him if he hung out here much longer. He needed to crawl back into the brush and find that cave.

Something stirred in a thicket to the north. Brock held his breath and waited. The noise ceased. Brock finally drew a breath, but he feared the noise was too loud. He began scrambling on his hands and knees back into the relative secrecy of the forest. Finally, he worked up the courage to stand and run. After bolting over a small ridge, he leapt into a gully and pressed his back against the far side of a sizable boulder. He shut his eyes and listened, fighting hard to control his panting.

After a moment he swore that he heard more movement. Someone was walking along the top edge of the short ridge, drawing nearer to the boulder. He searched the ground for a weapon. A heavy stick lay a short distance in front of his legs, but if he reached for it now, he'd surely be exposed to whoever was on the ridge.

All shuffling had ceased. Everything fell quiet. Brock felt sure that whoever was up there already knew that Brock was hiding down here. If this was true, grabbing any kind of weapon had become critical.

He lunged for the stick just as a shadow pounced from the top of the boulder. As he tried to raise the stick, a massive dark shape landed on top of him, pinning his arm to the ground. Brock abandoned his plans to swing the stick. He blinked his eyes and found himself face-to-face with a snarling black jaguar. It looked so much like Huracan that he was almost fooled. Black panthers with fire-tipped tails apparently weren't so rare in these parts, because this creature was definitely bigger. Bulkier. No jeweled collar. No wound on its shoulder, and . . .

Wait a second.

The creature just stood there, gaping at him. If he didn't know any better, he'd have sworn the animal was *smiling*. At last it made a very unusual growl. Brock's gift of interpreting the snarls and rumbles of beasts did not fail him.

"*I knew that I knew that smell,*" growled the jaguar.

Brock narrowed his eyes, scrutinizing the animal more closely. He found himself drawn to the animal's yellow and black orbs. No, it wasn't Huracan. But those eyes—those *eyes* definitely *were* Huracan!

Could it be, he wondered? "Is it really you?" he said.

"*It's really me,*" she purred.

Brock blurted out a single spontaneous laugh—an exclamation of utter delight. He threw his arms around the beast's neck. Then he withdrew one hand, knowing that he was pressing right against the spot where Gidgiddonihah had stitched her up.

"Sorry!" said Brock.

"*That wound healed long ago.*"

"Wha—? That's impossible! I just . . . Where have you been?"

"*Many places,*" Huracan growled. "*More places than you. You have not grown or aged the way a little human should grow and age.*"

"Well, you haven't exactly aged the way a *jaguar* should age either! What *happened* to you? Listen, right now I don't even care!" He again wrapped his arms around her neck. "I'm just so glad you're here. So, so, so, so, glad!"

Huracan interrupted with a contorted snarl/growl combination. "*You cannot remain here, Brock. If you do, you may die.*"

"Where do you suggest I go? I don't even know how I got here. I'm sort of stranded. I'm alone."

"*You are not alone. You will travel with me. We shall find other human friends.*"

"Sounds good," Brock replied. "Sounds *great*! You don't happen to know the location of the nearest Carl's Jr., do you? I'm *starving*."

"*Follow me,*" said Huracan, bounding toward the north. She glanced back, her fire-orange tail dancing, to make sure Brock was rising to his feet. She snarled once more: "*Follow me.*"

* * *

It was about midnight as Kerra directed the refugees—all the women and children who'd been discovered and liberated by Grandpa Lee—to enter, one by one, into the semitransparent jadestone portal at the top of the ridge. Kerra was assisted by Kiddoni, now dressed in a much more suitable Nephite tunic rather than those silly jaguar pelts. At last, the longtime captives were going home. Some of these children didn't even remember what it was like not to be slaves, including Kerra's half-brother, Mi'conhah.

Kerra had waited for two entire days to see if Brock or Huracan might step through the waterfall. At last she decided that everyone had waited long enough. The third waterfall, where Kerra had first parted ways with Grandpa Lee, Brock, and the sons of Gidgiddoni, was an odd sort of rift—an entry, but not an exit. The exit was downstream, accessed by plunging over the fourth and highest falls. And this exit was not particularly practical. At least that's what Kerra's instincts seemed to be telling her. That's what she *sensed*. However, as time wore on she began to wonder if her gifts were somehow fading. Her brother had not arrived. The portal behind the falls seemed to have closed—permanently. She didn't know what to think of this. However, she still felt strangely drawn to the jadestone wall atop the ridge. She perceived that this particular rift was very much alive and active. It also struck her as the most efficient way of helping the refugees return home. She realized she was sending them back to the battleground where Giddianhi had been slain and where Gidgiddonihah's Rattlesnake Battalion was attacked and destroyed, but she could only hope that the Gadianton warriors had long since vacated the immediate area. From there, she urged the refugees to make the half-day trek out of the valley to reach the fortifications of Lachoneus.

Again, Kerra felt it was a matter of timing, and she'd discerned that the safest, surest time would be the evening of the second day, at around midnight.

Her heart was tender with emotion as she instructed the various time travelers. "Enter the rift quickly. Don't linger. You can all see that there is daylight beyond the jade wall. When you get on the other side, travel northward. Don't delay. There may still be Gadiantons in the area. Keep your children close at your sides and march toward the fortifications as quickly as possible. Commander Gidgiddonihah will lead the way."

Indeed, Gidgiddonihah had been the first to enter the jadestone rift. His blurry image was visible even now, guiding each refugee in turn as he or she passed through the vortex. Grandpa Lee aided Manazzeh. The oldest son of Captain Gidgiddoni was still limping, even with his foot protected inside Grandpa's shoe. Kerra watched sadly as the young Nephite and her grandfather approached the doorway. Manazzeh's heart was heavy. He'd lost his younger brother in this terrible conflict. The news would hit his father, the Chief Captain, very hard. But the tragedy of war had been felt all across Zarahemla. Only with the death of Akuhuun, or the "Shaman" named Hitch Ventura, was it hopeful that this conflict might reach a swift conclusion under the feckless leadership of the Gadianton named Zemnarihah.

Before he entered the rift, Grandpa Lee said to Kerra, "I'll be helping Manazzeh till I get him back to the fortifications." He almost whispered as he added, "If, for some reason, you and I are separated for a bit . . . Don't worry about me, sweetheart. I've felt more alive these last few days than I have since your grandmother's passing. I think I'll be just fine among the Nephites for a while."

"What about your medications?" asked Kerra.

Grandpa pursed his lips. "Oh, I lost those pert'inear the first day we got here."

Kerra looked back at him in surprise.

Grandpa shrugged. "Haven't needed 'em." He made a crooked grin. "I kinda think these rifts have a rejuvenating quality about 'em. Maybe a little like the fountain that Ponce de León was lookin' for."

Kerra shook her head, mystified. Finally, she smiled, kissed him on the cheek, then watched the two men cross the rift. She could perceive Gid giving them assistance on the opposite side.

The last to approach the rift ahead of Kerra and Kiddoni was Kerra's father, as well as her stepmother and her new little brother, Mi´conhah. Kerra embraced Paísha. In just the last two days she'd enjoyed her company enormously, as if Kerra had finally been given the kind of mother that she'd always wished for. And as for little Mi´conhah, Kerra couldn't have been more delighted and impressed. This child's gifts, Kerra sensed, made hers seem like those of a novice. There were great adventures ahead for this little boy. There seemed little doubt.

It was Mi´conhah who announced, "It's getting weaker, Mother. We have to go through."

Kerra said to her father, "He's right. You better hurry. Or the rift will close and someone might be injured. When you get to the other side, Dad, wait a few hours. Then peer back through the rift, as if you're looking back at me. But it won't be me that you see. If I'm not mistaken, right at sunrise, that portal will transport you back to the hollow near Aunt Corinne and Uncle Drew's home. The window will only open for a moment. You have to pay very close attention. Afterward, you can take Paísha and Mi´conhah to the twenty-first century."

"What about you and Kiddoni?" asked Dad with concern. "Aren't you coming back with us?"

Her eyes welled up with tears. She glanced at Kiddoni then back at her father.

Dad pursed his lips and nodded. He understood.

He embraced his daughter tightly. "I love you, Kerra. Thank you." He leaned back and looked at her, wiping away one of her tears with his finger. He added, "I know you're worried about Brock. Sometimes a dad has a gift that a daughter may not. Just know this: He'll be okay. When the time is right, he'll be shown the proper pathway home. I'm sure of it."

Kerra fought to maintain a smile. Her father may have possessed certain gifts that she lacked, but she wasn't sure at all if this was one of them. And she felt no internal confirmation that what her father said was true. Sentimental words. These were just sentimental words to comfort her. Brock was *not* all right. But whenever she prayed or tried to concentrate on the particulars of his predicament—his whereabouts or how she might find him—she was afflicted by a peculiar stupor of thought, like an impenetrable wall. It was as if she was being deliberately kept in dark. Maybe it was just part of another lesson she needed to learn. Another lesson about faith.

Once she'd heard a Church instructor describe an event wherein Christ's disciples were unable to cast out a particularly nasty demon. After Christ had performed the miracle and finally cured the child, He told His disciples, "This kind can come forth by nothing, but by prayer and fasting." She wasn't quite sure how this related to her situation, but she felt it did. She greatly feared that in order to aid her brother, it might require more faith than she'd previously had to muster. The trouble was, she felt she didn't yet have all the tools. She needed the Holy Ghost. That is, she needed its gift. She wasn't a Church member. However, this was a problem she planned to rectify at the first opportunity.

Kerra kissed her father and said, "I love you too, Dad."

Kiddoni also embraced him. "I'll take care of her. I promise. And when it's right, I'll bring her home."

"I know you will," he replied, then with greater emphasis: "I *know* it."

"Dad, we have to go!" Mi´conhah urged again.

"All right, all right," he responded.

Dad sent Kerra and Kiddoni a last farewell glance then he and his wife and young son entered the rift. Kerra and Kiddoni continued to watch as the surface of the vortex slowly stirred, like bright colors in a dark can of paint, eerily clouding over as a chorus of "Whistlers" filled the air, until all that remained was the smooth, greenish surface of the jadestone. And shortly, not even that. The surface became featureless. The blackness of the midnight world had returned.

Kiddoni took Kerra's hands. "So when will it open again?"

She laid her cheek against his chest. "Soon. *Too* soon. A few minutes actually. It might seem a bit like an echo. And it won't remain for long. About a minute. Then . . . this particular rift may go dormant for quite a long span of time."

"You know all that?" said Kiddoni. "I'm impressed."

She shut her eyes, drinking in the way he felt. "I wish we could stay alone longer. We haven't really been alone since the moment we found you."

"Then I hope this is the first of many such moments. I have no plans, Sakerra, except to never again let you out of my sight."

"Right," said Kerra playfully. "Until the Chief Captain sends you off on another mission as the leader of a new battalion."

Kiddoni sighed gloomily. "I suppose the work of God . . . the fight against evil . . . must go on."

"Speaking of God's work," said Kerra, "I think I'd like to join your church. If the Church will have me."

Kiddoni chuckled. "If the Church will—? What makes you think it would not?"

She smiled. "I want you to baptize me, Kiddoni. Will you do it?"

"Of course I will." He grinned. "The Spirit has finally worn you down, eh?"

"If that's the corny way you want to put it," she replied.

"You've come a long distance, Sakerra McConnell. Do you remember what you said to me the first time that I asked you about faith? You told me that you believed in nothing. You said 'Nothing lasts, especially the things you love.' And you said that I could 'count on it.'"

"I remember," said Kerra. "I also said you weren't real. That you could disappear at any moment, and that I might never see you again."

"Do you still believe those things? That nothing lasts, especially the things you love?"

"Partly," said Kerra.

Kiddoni wrinkled his forehead. "*Partly?* Which part do you still believe?"

"That nothing lasts," she replied. "That is, nothing lasts *except* the things we love. It's those things, and *only* those things, that last forever."

He smiled warmly. He leaned forward and began to kiss her. Then, as so often occurred, the moment was interrupted—this time by the rift. It reopened, a bit like the living aperture of an electric eye. A dizzying swirl of colors loomed before them, dimly revealing the light of the place beyond.

Kiddoni squeezed Kerra's hand. She nodded in response. Together, they stepped hastily into the rift, soon blurring and blending with all the shimmering shades of daylight. As Kerra had warned, the passageway was only open for a moment. Soon it faded and wrapped in on itself, leaving only the starlight of the Milky Way to illuminate the wilderness world that they'd left behind.

EPILOGUE

BROCK PAUSED AS HURACAN CAME to an unexpected halt. The jaguar peered through a thicket of brush toward what appeared to be a trail. The pathway meandered along the slope of the hill, perhaps running all the way from the top to the bottom. Voices were approaching—voices that Brock didn't recognize. Huracan raised her ears in an uncommon way, as if these voices struck her as familiar. Brock watched as more than a dozen figures marched into view, descending the trail.

"You will both stand before the Council," a man declared loudly. "They will decide your fate." He was an elderly warrior, but his voice carried unmistakable authority.

Brock heard the screech of a bird, high overhead. He searched the sky until he found it. The bird—a falcon or hawk—swooped down toward a man in his early twenties. This man held out a leather-clad arm. The falcon flapped its wings and made what looked like a textbook landing for a falconer. Then the bird squawked to high heavens, upset about something. Brock grinned as he realized some of those squawks made sense—much like Huracan's snarls. The falcon was asking the young man if he was hurt or injured.

"I'm fine," the man replied, a bit impatiently.

Weird, thought Brock. This guy seemed to possess his same ability—an ability that he'd come to believe only a time traveler possessed. In fact, it occurred to Brock that this falconer's features really didn't look Nephite or Lamanite at all. He looked, well, like a white guy. That is, a Caucasian—er, somebody from his own race.

Another man—an older, seasoned warrior—stood beside the falconer. There was an expression of longing on his face, as if caught up in some faraway memory.

Huracan stirred, as if she might dash forward, eyes fixed on this older warrior.

"Don't be stupid," Brock whispered. "Let's go back. *Now!*"

Even as he said this, the jaguar was off like a shot. It crashed through the thicket and bounded down the hillside. The men on the trail halted in surprise and watched.

The seasoned warrior called out in disbelief. "Huracan?!"

He opened his arms. The jaguar bowled him over as he reached out to catch her. Brock was mystified. Just how many people did this jaguar know? It obviously got around a lot more than he might have supposed. The warrior laughed like a kid as he wrestled with Huracan in the grass.

"No licking!" the warrior insisted.

Brock scrunched his eyebrows. He knew that voice. Nah, he was imagining things. It wasn't possible. The voice could not belong to the person he thought. And yet Brock's feet, almost involuntarily, took several steps forward, making him immediately visible to the soldiers on the trail.

Huracan playfully tackled several other men. All of them received her affections with rejoicing. That is, all but the bird, who squawked in protest in an effort to discourage the jaguar from leaping upon the young man who carried it. Instead, Huracan circled around the falconer's legs like a house cat.

That's when they spotted him. Or at least, that's when the man holding the bird spotted him. Everybody's attention swiftly transferred from Huracan and the falconer toward Brock.

Their laughter quickly faded. They gawked at him as if he was an alien. Stupid, *stupid!* Why did he step out of the brush? Any second one of them would launch an arrow right between his eyes.

Another man, also in his twenties, stepped forward. Something about him reminded Brock of the older man with the authoritative voice. He presumed they were related.

"Child," the man said firmly but kindly. "Who are you? What are you doing here?"

Brock swallowed and uttered the first thing that popped into his head. "I-I was, uh, traveling with the jaguar."

The seasoned warrior whom Huracan had first tackled returned to his feet. He stared at Brock with more intensity than everybody else combined. All at once his eyes widened in consternation.

"I *know* this boy!" he proclaimed.

Brock studied the warrior's face. Could it be? He was older. More lines creased his battle-weary brow. Certainly more scars. Yet it was him! Every word he spoke filled Brock with greater assurance.

"You *know* him?" asked the man with the falcon.

"Yes," Gidgiddonihah proclaimed. "I know him. He saved me in a way you cannot imagine. I know him very, very well."

Unbelievable, thought Brock. It was really Commander Gid—the very Nephite he'd stood beside on that black sandy beach two days earlier. Only he'd *changed*. He was at least twenty years older. Maybe more. Despite the years, Gid had not forgotten him. Nor had he forgotten his name.

"Brock McConnell!" Gid exclaimed. "Bro´con! One of the bravest Gadianton hunters I ever had the privilege of knowing! If I didn't see him here with my own eyes, I'd swear he was a mirage. Welcome to Cumorah, Brock! Welcome back to the ranks of the warriors of Zarahemla!"

Author's Notes

As should already be apparent to most readers, this book is a continuation of the story that began with the novel and motion picture *Passage to Zarahemla*. Attentive readers (and/or viewers) of *Passage to Zarahemla* and The Tennis Shoes Adventure Series," Vols. 1–11 will have noted that characters from *both* series are included in *Escape from Zarahemla*. Also, readers will notice that certain events coincide with the final chapters of *The Tennis Shoes Adventure Series Vol. 11: Seers and Sorcerers*. Therefore, subsequent novels in The Tennis Shoes Adventure Series *after* volume 11 are destined to be sequels to both *Seers and Sorcerers* and *Escape from Zarahemla*. These novels, which began as independent adventures, are now to be united in one single epic. Readers who enjoyed *Escape from Zarahemla* should also read The Tennis Shoes Adventure Series—especially volumes 8–11—to be immersed in the setting and familiarize themselves with the various characters and events.

Passage to Zarahemla and *Escape from Zarahemla* are both associated with the Book of Mormon time period during the reign of Judge Lachoneus and Captain Gidgiddoni. This period is discussed in 3 Nephi 3–4 and comprises the years from AD 15 to approximately AD 22. At this time, Chief Judge Lachoneus, in an effort to protect all Nephites and Lamanites who refused to align themselves with the Gadianton cult, sent out a proclamation for all loyal citizens to gather their families, belongings, and livestock to a central location in the land of Zarahemla. This was done out of necessity to preserve their culture and religion against an infestation of the Gadianton robbers among the general populace. This gathering place is defined as "the land of Zarahemla, and the land which was between the land Zarahemla and the land Bountiful, yea, to the line which was between the land Bountiful and the land Desolation" (3 Ne. 3:23). From this we assume that the capital city of Zarahemla of the *land* also called Zarahemla was *not* part of this gathering place and may have been overrun by those supporting secret combinations. The scriptures imply that a number of closely associated locations may have been fortified by Gidgiddoni and his armies.

In 3 Nephi 3:18, Gidgiddoni is described as the "chiefest among all the chief captains" and that he had a reputation as a man possessing "the spirit of revelation and also prophecy." He and Lachoneus are both described as "great prophet[s]" in this verse. Some LDS writers, such as novelist and essayist Orson Scott Card, have suggested that Gidgiddoni may have been the most talented military strategist in Nephite history and that details of his campaigns may have been overlooked by Mormon during his abridgement, possibly because of his personal preference for Captain Moroni, whose story is preserved in considerably more detail and passion, and after whom Mormon named his son (Orson Scott Card, "The Book of Mormon—Artifact or Artifice." BYU Symposium: Life, the Universe, and Everything, February 1993). Whether or not this is true, Gidgiddoni defended the Nephites with great faith and skill, especially in his construction of fortifications or places of safety. In AD 19 he successfully repulsed a major Gadianton offensive. Mormon described this battle as so great and terrible that "never was known so great a slaughter among all the people of Lehi since he left Jerusalem" (3 Ne. 4:11). It is this battle that was dramatized at the climax of *Passage to Zarahemla* and is often referred to in *Escape from Zarahemla* as the "Great Battle."

Passage to Zarahemla, utilizing fictional characters and devices, recounts this military offensive and encompasses the defeat and death of Giddianhi. *Escape from Zarahemla* places its characters in the same setting approximately two years later. The novel speculates that a power vacuum may have existed among the Gadiantons after Giddianhi's death, preventing the robbers from mounting an effective counterassault, despite the fact that they still possessed a formidable army. It's clear that some dynamic allowed for a stalemate that lasted several years, preventing either side from making serious progress.

The Nephites, under Lachoneus and Gidgiddoni, did not make substantial headway toward ending the conflict until after the robbers exhausted nearly all of their provisions and made the wilderness virtually barren of edible food and game (3 Ne. 4:19–20).

Escape from Zarahemla, using the same fictional devices as its prequel, dramatizes Zarahemla's circumstances during this "stalemate" period. Such circumstances certainly included a growing anxiety and restlessness among the loyal populace, who had coexisted for more than three years in a limited geographical domain. During this time many families had abandoned lands and homes to looters and vandals, letting their fields go fallow and uprooting their lives. These realities were likely the cause of increasing daily tensions. Aside from religion, some of these citizens may have had little in common, historically or ethnically. At least three ethnicities were represented: Nephites, Lamanites, and Mulekites (or as they are called in the scriptures, the people of Zarahemla). Among them may have also been the ancestors of certain factions of the Jaredites. (This is evidenced by the commonality of Jaredite names during this period of the Book of Mormon, like Teancum and Morianton.) The fact that all these divergent peoples remained loyal subjects of Lachoneus and Gidgiddoni during these critical years, until about AD 22, when the Gadianton leader Zemnarihah was finally defeated and hanged, stands as a remarkable testament to the faithfulness of these ancient Americans during the first decades after the birth of Christ.

ABOUT THE AUTHOR

Chris Heimerdinger has become a bit of a "renaissance man" in LDS entertainment. After successfully publishing eighteen novels since 1989—including eleven in the popular and ground-breaking time-travel epic, the Tennis Shoes Adventure Series—he also produced, wrote, and directed a feature film released in 2007 entitled *Passage to Zarahemla* based upon a novel of the same name. For his entire writing career, Chris has also served as the principal reader for his audio books.

He also took on a small acting role in his motion picture. In 2008, Chris produced and wrote a song album entitled *Whispered Visions* in association with the movie *Passage to Zarahemla,* also performing many of the songs. In the future, Chris plans to tackle myriad creative projects, including additional motion pictures, board games, and music productions. However, at this time he is most committed to completing the twelfth novel in the Tennis Shoes Adventure Series (current working title: *Thorns of Glory*). For further information, updates, and articles from Chris, readers are invited to participate in, and become a member of, his online blog at www.frostcave.blogspot.com.

Chris currently resides in Salt Lake County. His family includes eleven children, ranging from twenty-two years old down to two months old, including Steven, Zachary, Christopher Ammon, Alex, Sariah, Haleigh, Hannah, Michael, Liahona, Angelina Cumorah, and Hunter Helaman. His biggest fan and best friend is his eternal companion, Emily.